Natasha Bache is a former editor
folklore and gripping murder-n
based novels include her conter
Winter Crone, Sister of the Moon a.. ... ., ..
well as her darkly funny murder mystery *12 Ways to Kill Your
Family at Christmas.*

When she's not plotting murders (of the fictional variety …
maybe) or immersing herself in fantasy realms, she's probably
out exploring the Shropshire countryside with her husband
and two children.

If you're interested in hearing more about new and upcoming
releases, subscribe here:
https://www.natashabache.com

instagram.com/natashabache_author
facebook.com/NatashaBache
tiktok.com/@natashabacheauthor

12 WAYS TO KILL YOUR FAMILY AT CHRISTMAS

NATASHA BACHE

ONE MORE CHAPTER

One More Chapter
a division of HarperCollins*Publishers* Ltd
1 London Bridge Street
London SE1 9GF
www.harpercollins.co.uk
HarperCollins*Publishers*
Macken House, 39/40 Mayor Street Upper,
Dublin 1, D01 C9W8, Ireland

This paperback edition 2025

First published in Great Britain in ebook format
by HarperCollins*Publishers* 2025
Copyright © Natasha Bache 2025
Natasha Bache asserts the moral right to
be identified as the author of this work

A catalogue record of this book is available from the British Library
ISBN: 978-0-00-878510-9

For Stuart, Aeryn and Magnus

PROLOGUE

AFFIRMATIONS AND ACCUSATIONS

Breathing to calm my nerves, I went over my affirmations: *you are safe, you are loved, you have nothing to hide.* Well, safe except for the fact I was being accused of committing the brutal murders of ten of my family members in cold blood. Sure, there may have been times I'd daydreamed about sticking Tristan's netherrod in a chappy chopper or flailing the twins alive while they cried for mercy, but how anyone could think *I* might actually have gone through with those things I'll never know.

Detective Chief Inspector Randolf clicked the button to begin the formal interview. I cleared my throat and attempted to swallow, my tongue unwieldy and coarse inside my mouth. Reaching for the glass of water, I failed miserably at keeping my hands from shaking. I kept my eyes fixed on the detective, determined to prove my innocence.

'This interview is being tape-recorded and may be given in evidence if your case is brought to trial. We are in an interview room at Shrewsbury Police Station. The date is the second of January, 2026. The time by my watch is two thirty-four p.m. I am Detective Chief Inspector Lakeith Randolf and with me is Detective Sergeant Helen Birch. We will now continue with the interview.'

I nodded, smiling enthusiastically so that Randolf and Birch could see how helpful and how very *clearly* innocent I was. But the mask was threatening to slip. Six hours into this interview and I was seriously beginning to flag. My mothy-smelling solicitor shifted in the seat next to me, readjusting his crotch. I wrung my fingers in my lap, desperate not to let my irritation show.

'Go through with us again, if you will, your movements the morning of the fifteenth December, 2025. Describe for me where you and the members of the family were and what you were doing the morning that George Weiss fell from the roof.'

I shifted in my seat. 'As I've said before, Detective Inspector, it was around ten or eleven in the morning, I can't exactly remember. I had gotten up early that day, I like to get in a swim in before seven, you see... Anyway, after I'd finished showering, I headed to the kitchen and had granola and a banana. Everyone else was still in bed—' I racked my brains. Everything was such a muddle. So much had happened ... so many deaths. I could hardly keep track of one day to the next. Which murder was he asking about again?

'What about the time of the murder? Where were you?'

'I don't know, we were all in the house, all of us, and then I heard shouting. So, I suppose I was in the kitchen, yes, that's right, the kitchen. He had fallen. It just looked like an accident,' I protested.

'You were in the kitchen of Weiss Manor?'

'Yes ... no.' I rubbed my fingers into my temples. This was impossible. I must be in deep shock or denial because I couldn't remember.

'You were alone?'

'Yes. No one was around. I don't know where they were. But then I heard a funny sort of buzzing. Then, the lights went bright for a moment and they all shorted – everything just cut off suddenly. Then I heard ... I heard a commotion outside.'

Randolf leaned forward, his tired dark eyes surveying me intently. 'And what exactly did you hear?'

'Yelling. Someone yelling to come quick. At first, I thought perhaps a car had hit something in the street.'

'And then?'

'I rushed out of the kitchen and into the foyer. Half the house was already there when I opened the front door.' There was no hiding my trembling hand this time as I reached for my glass and drained the lot.

'The sun had fully risen by then.' I heard my voice saying the words, but I sounded very far away. 'I remember that because steam was rising... It was cold, you see. It took me a moment to realise who was lying there. His hair was standing up,' I raised my hands over my head to demonstrate. 'Smoke rising off him, and a – a ... sizzling sound. Then I noticed his leg at a very funny angle, and the smell of burning...' My voice cracked with emotion. 'Sorry.'

'Is going over this again really necessary?' the moth-man chimed in. 'My client is fatigued.'

Randolf sighed and gave Birch a pointed look. Without a word, she rose to her feet and left the room. 'Let the tape show that Detective Sergeant Birch has left the interview room,'

Randolf continued. 'As I'm sure you are aware, you have been unable to provide us with one solid alibi. Not one person who can corroborate your whereabouts at the time of death of not one, not two, not three, but ten of your family members.'

'Yes, I'm aware of that,' I replied a tad snippily as I rubbed the grit from my eyes. As if I wasn't aware of the things that had happened merely a week ago. There was no need for him to lay it on so thick.

The door opened and Birch scurried back in, clutching what looked like some sort of transparent, zip-locked sandwich bag.

'Let the record show that Detective Sergeant Birch has reentered the room, and has submitted evidence lot 279, collected on the first oft January. The evidence bag contains a small black notebook.' Randolph nodded to Birch in thanks as she sat down. He held up the sandwich bag. 'Do you recognise this?'

I squinted hard. I'd seen many little black books in my life, so it was hard to say.

'No – I mean yes, I've seen notebooks like that, but I don't currently own one myself.'

He let out a frustrated sigh at my non-committal answers. He produced a thin brown folder and slid out of it two pieces of paper, which he held up for me to see.

'For the benefit of the tape, I am now holding up photo-copies taken of the contents of the notebook, of what appear to be diary entries dated between the twelfth of December 2025 and the twenty-fourth of December 2025.' He tapped the greyish photocopies with a long finger. 'Do you recognise this handwriting?'

'Umm,' I said, my composure threatening to break.

'Not at all?' He procured my witness statement and put the papers side by side. The handwriting was uncannily similar, blocky capitals scrawled with blue pen. The tail on the *y* was different on some of the lettering in the diary – a slight curve to it when mine always pointed straight down.

'This is outrageous!' I looked at my solicitor, who was picking at his nails. 'I'm telling you, I didn't have anything to do with it. Someone is trying to set me up! What possible motive would I have for killing my entire family?' I almost laughed, it sounded so preposterous.

'That's exactly what I'm trying to find out,' said Rudolf gravely.

'Is this a joke?' I retorted. 'Do you think I'm such an imbecile that I'd leave evidence like that lying around?'

Randolf didn't answer, his expression steely and unfaltering. The photocopies lying between us vibrated slightly from my shaking legs beneath the table. My eyes furtively darted over the scrawled entries.

12th December 2025

... pink, blue, red, yellow ... He held onto the string lights ... sparks flying ... But it wasn't that that killed him – no...

I skimmed over another entry.

14th December 2025

I had meant to cut the tree down, I swear. It had been a long time coming for that lying, cheating son of a bitch.

'No – no that's not my writing,' I protested, 'I didn't write that.'

The lawyer cleared his throat, pushing up his glasses with one nail-bitten finger. He leaned close to me and whispered into my ear, his coffee breath hot and cloying.

'If you can't provide an alibi,' he said, addressing me but looking at Randolf, 'perhaps we should consider the advantages of cooperation. There'll be much more leniency with that route.'

'I swear to you,' I hissed at the inept lump of a man, 'I didn't do it!'

DRIVING HOME TO CATASTROPHE

I sat watching the Shropshire countryside fly by as Miles cranked up the volume button on Chris Rea's 'Driving Home for Christmas'. I craned my head back to see the kids' reactions; Callum predictably had his headphones in, and Martha looked out the window with an irked scowl. No one in the car, not even Miles, subscribed to Rea's sentiment, '*I can't wait to see those faces*', but it was undeniably a great song.

Miles caught my eye and I squeezed his leg reassuringly. It was going to be fine. If we all kept our heads down and didn't rise to the bait that would undoubtably be set for us, we would get through the next two weeks, and would not have to see the Weisses for the foreseeable. Once we moved to Australia in January ... the excitement at not having to have Miles's family in our lives caused a grin to creep across my face.

'You look strangely happy for someone who's about to endure my family for two whole weeks,' Miles said, glancing from me back to the road.

'I'm just thinking about Australia,' I beamed. 'Sun, surf and sushi.'

Miles huffed a laugh and made the right-hand turn off the road and through the immense wrought-iron gates.

Martha's face dropped further into abject self-pity. Miles and I didn't want to talk about Australia too much around her; she had just started seeing someone and had absolutely made her feelings clear that she did not want to move.

The gravel crunched under the tyres as we rolled up the long driveway, the imposing Georgian mansion looming larger with each passing second. A gap in the clouds let through a ray of sunshine, illuminating the golden stone of the house, causing the glass in the windowpanes to glitter momentarily, before the clouds won out once more. I felt my stomach tighten, the brief moment of Australian-induced joy evaporating as quickly as it had come.

'Here we go,' Miles muttered, his knuckles whitening on the steering wheel. 'Seriously, I don't know many women who could survive eighteen years with my insane family. I can't believe you ever agreed to marry me.'

'Well, when we first met I thought you were hot and rich. And then you trapped me by knocking me up with these two,' I teased. 'Perhaps we're your consolation prize for dealing with them your whole life?'

Miles glanced back at the kids and smiled. 'Is it too late to get a refund on these two?'

'Oi!' Martha whipped her hand across the back of his head and Miles chuckled.

Callum finally joined the land of the living and ripped his headphones off.

'Do you think we'll get anything good for Christmas from Gran?' He eyed Weiss Manor looming ever closer.

'What do you mean by good?' I asked.

'Well, like … you know how I've been asking for money for my new set-up?'

'Grandma won't give you any money, Cal,' Miles cut him off. We'd had this conversation one too many times. 'You know she doesn't believe in giving money instead of presents.'

Callum grumbled inaudibly, but I caught the sentiment, *what the hell's the point in all this then?* And honestly, I couldn't argue with that. They were richer than God, and yet here we were driving up to their mansion in a decade-old car with a crack in the windscreen that could spread at any minute.

The car pulled up in front of the house and I saw one of the curtains twitch in the front parlour. No doubt Aunt Clementine in her favourite spot, peering out at us and relaying her critiques to Miles's uncle Fergus; our arrival time, our choice of vehicle, our very existence…

'I'm going to tell them about my girlfriend,' Martha said with defiance.

'No, *please* don't, darling,' I begged, 'we just want to get through this visit as smoothly as possible.'

Martha's brows rose, her mouth pinched and ready to argue. 'Are you ashamed of me? Are you embarrassed that I have a girlfriend?' Her voice began to rise.

'No, no, it's not that at all!' I placated her. 'You know we love Sarah. It's just…' I looked to Miles for back-up.

'You know what they are like, sweetheart,' he said softly. 'We just don't want the headache. Besides, do you really want them knowing about your private life?'

Martha stared at us with defiance. 'I'm not ashamed, and I won't pretend to be something I'm not just to please them,' she said crossing her arms.

'And we don't want you to,' I agreed. 'We are so proud of you. We're just trying to avoid any friction—'

Martha rolled her eyes.

We'd barely pulled up when the massive oak door swung open, revealing Miles's mother, Jeannie, resplendent in a fine cashmere Christmas jumper and an impressively thick gold necklace with matching earrings that probably cost more than our monthly mortgage. Jeannie's short silver hair was always meticulously styled, as if she'd had a professional blow-dry every morning.

'Ready?' Miles said ominously.

'Absolutely not,' I said, taking a deep breath before setting my face into a pleasant smile and swinging open the car door.

'Miles!' Jeannie trilled, her voice carrying across the driveway. 'Lunch is on the table. We thought you were arriving at one?'

'Bad traffic,' he called, rounding the car and trotting up the stone steps to greet her. She aimed a kiss right for the lips, and he artfully evaded it with a swift kiss to her cheek.

From behind Jeannie, a flash of beige fur. Gloria bounded out of the doors, her golden tail wagging, tongue hanging out and brown eyes shining as she excitedly greeted us. Miles bent down and put his forehead to the golden retriever's face and scratched her lovingly behind both ears.

I ascended the steps, Callum and Martha trailing behind with the reluctance of prisoners being led to the gallows. Jeannie's eyes swept over me, her smile never wavering but a flicker of disapproval passing through her gaze. She had been avoiding me ever since Miles had told her of our move to Australia – even though we were technically going for his work, she made it clear she thought it was my fault.

'Olivia, darling,' she said, air-kissing both my cheeks.

'So good to see you, Jeannie.' I went in for an awkward hug. 'You look lovely as always.'

'Have you changed your hair?' she asked, her gaze already drifting away from me to survey Callum and Martha.

'No ... no, I haven't,' I replied, trying to think whether I had in fact changed my hair since the last time she saw me. I had always kept my natural blonde hair mid-length. I realised a little too late that what she really meant to say was, *still sporting the same old hairstyle, then?*

'Something smells great,' I managed, stepping over the threshold and into the grand foyer.

The scent of roast meat hit me immediately, along with the underlying mustiness of old money and antiquated furniture. Voices drifted from the dining room. The hive where the hornets liked to gather.

Jeannie was fussing over the kids while Miles went to collect our bags.

'Don't do that, dear,' Jeannie waved her hand, 'Mrs Harlow will see to it later.'

Poor long-suffering Mrs Harlow the housekeeper; at least we would have the pleasure of one friendly face. *Two weeks, two weeks, two weeks,* I muttered under my breath as my feet took me over the black-and-white tiles and closer to the dining room of doom. But – two weeks was a horribly long time. Three hundred and thirty-six hours to be exact.

A lot could happen in three hundred and thirty-six hours.

As I stepped through the double doors, Uncle Fergus's booming laugh, Aunt Clem's shrill tones, and Grandma Toots's wispy voice stopped suddenly as they all turned to look at me. Miles's father, George, hardly ever spoke, and today was no different. He merely raised his glass in greeting and gave us a curt nod.

The enormous oak table was laden with a spread that could feed a small army – roast beef, Yorkshire puddings, mountains of roasted vegetables, and a steaming gravy boat.

'There she is!' Uncle Fergus bellowed, cheeks flushed beetroot-red. 'Looking lovely as ever, Olivia.' He got up from his seat and was upon me, grabbing me into a bear hug and planting a big wet kiss on my cheek that reeked of booze.

'That's enough, Fergus. Put the poor girl down, will you?' my father-in-law said from the head of the table.

'Hello, everyone.' I smiled and blushed, putting on my best *I'm a nice girl* act. 'Good to see you.'

'All ready for Christmas?' asked Aunt Clem, giving me a quick once-over.

'I don't think we need to be ready, do we?' I said, sliding into a vacant chair. 'Jeannie always has everything planned with military precision.' I had meant it as a joke, but it came out much more clipped than I had intended. So much for the *nice girl* act.

Luckily, the family were distracted enough by Miles and the kids entering, Martha pulling on the sleeve of her sweatshirt and looking more miffed than I'd ever seen her, and Callum with his nose in his games console. They found their seats in between Fergus and Clementine, who loathed each other's company so thoroughly that they never sat together.

Grandma Toots sat surveying them over her glasses as they sat at the table. Not one for small talk, she cut right to it.

'I hear you're abandoning us for the land down under?'

'Yes, Grandma,' said Miles, 'and we're all very excited. It's a great opportunity.'

'Well, what about your writing, Olivia?' Her fierce blue eyes were upon me. 'Don't you write those porn novels? Won't your publisher mind?'

Martha choked on the water she'd been sipping.

I reached for a Yorkshire pudding. 'I can write my novels in Australia. Really, it's the perfect place for writing,' I said sweetly. 'I can just talk to my editor over Zoom. It won't be much different to now really, except I think getting outside more and being more active will give me a better quality of life.' Was this conversation heading south already? Probably.

'It's not porn, Grandma,' said Miles gently, 'it's Romantasy.'

'I'm just going on what our Jeannie told me.' Her lips quivered with mischief as she cut into her beef.

I felt Miles squeeze my hand under the table in solidarity.

'What's Romantasy?' asked Clem. 'I've never heard of it.'

'It's Fantasy with Romance,' Martha offered.

Toots huffed a sharp laugh. 'What, like ... silly made-up creatures falling in love?'

'Yes!' boomed Fergus, 'but it's much better than that! It's big muscly men with pointy ears absolutely smashing the brains out of gorgeous young women with huge breasticles and tiny waists.' He guffawed, throwing his head back and letting us see everything he'd just chewed. Martha looked profoundly disturbed whilst Callum gave him a withering look. Fergus just looked straight at me and winked. 'The latest book was my favourite yet.' I glanced at Aunt Clem just in time to see the death stare she was levelling at her husband.

Jeannie entered, her back ramrod-straight and her lips pursed at hearing our topic of conversation.

'Talking of muscly men and gorgeous young women,' Fergus said, turning to Callum, 'bet you'll be going to those nude beaches in Oz, won't you, lad? Getting a right eyeful! I know I would.' He nudged Callum so hard with his elbow that his console fell out of his hands and clattered onto the floor.

'That's quite enough, Fergus,' said George with a warning glance.

My knife scraped loudly as I cut into the meat Miles had served me.

'Where's Mimi, Tristan and the twins?' I asked, saving Callum from any prolonged embarrassment as he scooped up his Switch and glared at Miles and me like it was our fault he'd dropped it.

'They'll be here this evening,' Jeannie chirped. 'Tristan's just bought the most sublime car, hasn't he, George?'

'Mm-hmm,' George mumbled.

'What's it called again?'

'Top-of-the-range Audi, isn't it, George?' Fergus asked.

I felt Miles growing tense at my side. Now it was my turn to give him a reassuring squeeze under the table.

'He's doing ever so well at his company,' Jeannie said, turning to Clem. 'He just got another promotion and an upgrade on his company car. Now George, you will remember to talk to Tristan before Artie gets here, won't you?'

'Yes, yes,' sighed George, looking utterly defeated by life – or, more accurately, his wife – as he smoothed down his wiry moustache and waved his hand dismissively.

'And I've asked you several times to put the lights up outside,' she griped. 'I really wanted them to be up by the times Miles and the children arrived.'

'I *know*,' he said through gritted teeth, 'I said I'd do them in the morning.'

Jeannie turned to us with a grin. 'I've got something very special planned for our first evening, you won't believe it.'

Martha cocked her head to one side, her shoulder-length brown hair swaying. 'Is it a murder-mystery evening?'

Jeannie's expression dropped slightly. 'Um, yes, actually, it is. How on earth did you know that?'

Martha and I exchanged a glance and I tried not to laugh as Martha fought to control herself. Jeannie organised a murder-mystery night every Christmas.

'Well … anyway,' Jeannie persevered, 'I want everyone to dress in their best. It will be such fun!'

'*No*, it really won't,' Callum mumbled under his breath.

'Hear that, Martha?' Toots piped up, eyes sharp and glinting. 'No jeans with holes in them!' Her mouth perked up at the edge.

'Hmm, yes,' Jeannie said thoughtfully. 'And is that purple streak in your hair … permanent?'

'Yep,' said Martha, extremely satisfied with herself. I could already tell she was one hundred per cent planning on wearing ripped jeans to Jeannie's murder-mystery party.

'Callum was saying how much he loves your cooking, Mother,' Miles redirected with a quick grin.

'Pah!' Fergus leaned into Callum before thumping him on the back and sending his fork flying. 'After some pocket money, are you, lad?'

Callum didn't dislike many people, on account of being so laid-back he was practically horizontal, but I could feel his displeasure at his uncle seeping from every pore.

Clem leaned forward, sniffing out drama like a bloodhound. 'I can't believe you'll be missing all the Christmases with us. Won't you miss it?'

Jeannie sighed theatrically. 'A summer Christmas doesn't feel right at all.'

'I'm sure we'll manage,' I said, pasting on my smile again. 'We thought we'd have a BBQ on the beach.' These conversations were going to get old pretty quickly.

'But you'll be coming back for Easter, won't you? For the big charity egg-hunt Jeannie's putting on?' Clem persisted.

'We'll have to see, it's quite soon to be coming back,' I said, stabbing at my peas.

Jeannie looked at Miles, eyes glistening.

'Maybe I could come back?' Martha said, her eyes lighting up.

God, give me strength. I would need it for when the others arrived tomorrow … this was only the beginning. The real fraying of the nerves would start when they arrived.

2

BAUBLES, BOWS AND BURIED GRUDGES

Dressed in a flowing emerald-green dress and Swarovski earrings that skimmed my collarbone, I'd hoped to make an entrance that evening. I'd even attempted to tease my hair into Hollywood waves and applied red lipstick. It was a lesson I'd learned the hard way from my first ever Christmas with the Weisses – when I had assumed all I would need would be kitted jumpers and leggings.

That first year, I'd had to go to dinner in my socks and a hideous dress Jeannie had lent me because she said it was sacrilege to wear trainers, and my 'hooves', as she so charmingly called them, didn't fit into any of her old-lady shoes. The embarrassment I endured when she held up a patterned 1970s velour dress for me to wear had not left me. Miles still liked to tease me about it.

We entered the wood-panelled dining room, candlelight dancing over the oil paintings and silverware. Miles looked gorgeous, as usual, his dark hair effortlessly tousled.

He'd opted for a crisp white shirt, the top two buttons undone, and a pair of black trousers. The kids had worn what they always did – I don't think they even owned smart clothes, and hell would be frozen over before they'd set foot in anything uncomfortable.

A large portrait loomed over us all, the light casting shadows on Eugene Weiss's severe expression. Candles adorned the mahogany chest directly beneath his portrait – a shrine to the man we had lost four years earlier. Eugene, Miles's grandfather, had inherited his fortune from his father's Welsh goldmine, and had trebled profits by becoming the sole maker and distributor of rare jewellery to some of the richest clientele in the world.

Mrs Margaret Harlow, the head, and now only, house-keeper, made her way towards us with a silver tray of bubbling champagne. Mrs Harlow had lost her husband two years prior, and as she had no children, Jeannie had insisted that she come and live with them full-time. For reasons I couldn't comprehend, Mrs Harlow had agreed and moved out of her small apartment. Each to their own, I suppose, but I couldn't think of anything worse.

Mrs Harlow gave Miles and me a warm smile as she prof-fered the tray.

'So lovely to see you both,' she said. 'Gosh, the children are growing so quickly, although they're not children anymore, I suppose.' She gave them an adoring look.

'Madge,' Miles said, kissing her on both cheeks. 'It's good to see you. Mother hasn't got you working too hard, I hope?'

She tssked at him. 'I always want to make myself useful, you know that.'

Mrs Harlow had worked for the Weisses since Miles and Tristan were boys, and they looked upon her as family. I took a flute of champagne, grateful for the liquid courage.

The room was already filling with Weiss family members, their voices a low murmur punctuated by occasional laughter. Jeannie appeared, resplendent in a crimson dress that hugged her still enviable figure. Her cropped silver hair was swept up in an elegant quiff, and diamonds dripped from her ears and throat.

'You all look wonderful,' she announced, though pursing her lips at Martha and Callum's choice of attire.

Her eyes swept over me almost approvingly as she said, 'Golly gosh, Olivia, I see you've learned a thing or two since that first Christmas.'

I smiled, feeling as awkward as my two teenage children. Part of me lit up within – it was so uncommon for me to receive a compliment from her that a traitorous part of me felt a little pleased by it. Before I could respond, a commotion out in the foyer caught everyone's attention.

By the sounds of it, Tristan had arrived, fashionably late as always. Mimi glided in first, her glossy dark hair matching perfectly with her effortlessly chic black dress, a mink stole draped around her bare shoulders. Every bit the Coco Chanel to my River Island.

'Sorry we're late,' Tristan announced, 'the roads were a total piss-take!' He brushed back a lock of blond hair and flashed a shockingly white and suspiciously uniform set of teeth. I scanned the room for Miles and we caught each other's eye. I gave him a look that I hoped said, *Did you see his teeth?* He nodded excitedly. We would enjoy picking that apart later.

As the room turned to greet Tristan and Mimi, I noticed Gloria was sitting like a sentinel at the door, her large brown eyes watching us rather forlornly. I headed over to her, bent down and stroked her luxuriously soft head and ears, her expression conveying exactly how I felt. I noticed Jeannie had tied an absurdly large red bow to the back of her collar that flopped about awkwardly. The retriever gave a little shake, then craned her head back in order to see what the hell was going on. I unwound the wire on the bow and chucked it into a nearby plant pot before whispering, 'Go on, Glors, go and have a nice lie down in front of the fire.' She seemed to like that idea, and trotted off past the new arrivals with nary a glance in the newcomers' direction.

Jeannie threw her arms open wide for Mimi, who flashed her a sparkly dentured grin. *Holy hell, they were some white gnashers.* I saw that Miles had spotted them, too.

'*Turkey teeth?!*' I mouthed to him, and he nodded conspiratorially.

Jeannie turned her attention to Tristan. 'My poor darlings! I'm sorry to hear that the roads were bad. I hear there's a storm coming.'

Of course Tristan would arrive late with his outlandish teeth and say things like 'piss-take' and be fawned over. If he'd strangled a carol singer on the driveway, Jeannie would probably congratulate him on his decisive leadership skills. They made their *mwah-mwah* sounds as I peered up at the portrait of Eugene, whose eerily lifelike eyes looked down over us, a faint smirk twisted upon his lips.

As I greeted Miles's family and drifted around the room making small talk, I couldn't shake the feeling that Eugene's eyes followed me. The champagne flowed freely, and soon the room was filled with the buzz of conversation and laughter.

Jeannie worked the room like a pro, flitting from one person to the next, very much in her natural habitat. She chatted in earnest about her work owning a PR firm, as if she still worked there and hadn't retired twenty years earlier. Miles once confided in me that it was how his mother and father met. Apparently, George had become embroiled in a scandal for cooking the books at the gold-mine, and Jeannie had been called in to minimise the damage to the family name and image. That sounded infinitely more romantic to me than the generic tale they put out – that they had met in The Ivy members club. A story as dreary as today's weather.

Outside, the sky had darkened ominously. Through the window I could see the first fat raindrops beginning to fall. A flash of lightning illuminated the manicured gardens, followed by a low rumble of thunder.

'What's on the menu tonight then, Mother?' Tristan boomed.

'You'll see!' she teased.

I found myself drifting towards the large bay window, seeking a moment of quiet amidst the growing noise.

'Penny for your thoughts?' Miles's voice startled me out of my reverie. He handed me a fresh glass of champagne, his fingers reassuringly brushing mine.

'Just admiring the view,' I said, forcing a smile. I didn't want to tell him what I was really thinking – that I loved him dearly but I wished he'd left me at home so I could finish my damn novel before Christmas.

'Well, how are you both?' Tristan said as he sauntered over, a Scotch in hand. 'Good to see you, brother.' He gave Miles a swift slap on the back.

'Tristan,' Miles said coolly. 'How are you?'

'Ah, you know, same old, same old. Very busy with work, it's been an absolutely crazy year.' He turned his sights towards me, 'Well, well, if it isn't my favourite sister-in-law,' he said, giving me an approving once-over, his eyes skimming across my chest. 'How are you, Livvy?'

Miles rested his hand protectively on my lower back. Protectively, territorially, both? I couldn't quite tell.

'I'm well, thanks, Tristan,' I said with a smile. 'You're looking dapper as always.'

Tristan smirked, running a hand through his perfectly coiffed blond hair. Strange that two brothers could be such opposite sides of the coin in every way, Tristan being fair and slightly heavy-set, the epitome of what he liked to think of as an alpha male, Miles being dark-haired and academic, but totally drop-dead gorgeous. That extra attention his brother had received from girls when they were growing up had stuck in Tristan's craw so badly, he'd made it his life's ambition to best Miles in every way.

'So, all ready for the big move?' Tristan asked, idly sipping his drink and looking away as if the answer didn't interest him in the slightest.

'Ready as we'll ever be,' I said dismissively, wanting at all costs to steer clear of restarting the topic of moving. 'So, you said work has been crazy?'

'Bloody nightmare. Getting rid of all these DEI hires has taken the best part of the year. Think we're through the bulk of it now, though, and we can get on with some actual work.'

Out of the corner of my eye, I saw Miles's jaw twitching.

'Where are the twins?' I asked quickly.

Tristan didn't have time to answer before Jeannie was tapping her glass with a spoon.

The room fell silent as all eyes turned to her. She stood at the head of the long dining table, her crimson dress shimmering in the candlelight.

'Everyone, if I could have your attention, please,' Jeannie announced, her voice carrying across the room as the chatter died down. 'Thank you, family, for all coming to our Christmas murder-mystery dinner. Before we sit down to eat, I have a few things I want to say.'

A public announcement – this wasn't the norm. My stomach clenched. What could this be about? I glanced at Miles, but his face betrayed nothing.

Jeannie continued, 'As you all know, it's been four years since we lost our beloved Eugene. And while his presence is sorely missed, I know he is here, looking down upon us all.'

Miles's father looked up at the portrait and raised his glass. As awful as Miles's family were to be around at this time of year, it was nothing compared to how Christmas had been when Eugene was alive. His death had seemed to ease something in Jeannie and George – to the detriment of the rest of us, because now they seemed to want us around even more. Or rather, they wanted to meddle in our lives more.

Jeannie paused for effect, her eyes sweeping the room.

'And this might very well be our last Weiss Christmas,' she said, emotion making her voice crack.

Oh God, was she ill? Cancer? I wouldn't put it past her to announce it in the most dramatic way possible.

'My Miles,' she said, holding her hand out towards him. 'He and his family are leaving us.' Miles shifted from one foot to the other as all eyes turned to him.

'Just going to Australia, Mum. Not Mars,' he joked. 'And you're all welcome to visit anytime.'

But please don't.

'Yes … well,' Jeannie said flatly, 'next Christmas will look very different, I'm sure.' Her expression was that of someone who'd just sucked on a lemon. 'I wanted to ensure we were all together, this one last time.'

Tristan glanced at Mimi and rolled his eyes.

'I did want us *all* here, to celebrate,' she said for emphasis, 'but I wasn't quite able to pull off my grand plan.'

'We're all here now, aren't we?' Fergus interrupted, impatient for her to propose the toast so he could resume drinking.

'Not all,' she remarked with a twinkle in her eye. We all looked around the room, counting heads to see who had not arrived yet. She watched with mirth, letting us stew. The twins weren't here yet, so I could only assume that's who she meant.

'I know it will be difficult, but Eugene Weiss, the head of our family, gave me a charge. To uphold the illustrious Weiss name. I take that job very seriously. I am the glue, the cog…'

Martha appeared at my side. 'She can't be the glue *and* a cog,' she muttered in my ear.

'And so, I have extra special news,' Jeannie continued.

'After Christmas, all being well, it looks as though Quentin will be getting out early,' she announced proudly.

We stood in dumb silence, mouths agape, watching her as she raised her glass into the air.

'I'm just sorry that it couldn't be sooner. However, I hope that we can make this the most special Christmas yet. To family!' She took a dainty sip of her champagne.

No one joined her, not sure if this was some cruel joke.

Instead of taking a long-awaited sip, Fergus's eyes darted from George to Jeannie.

'I beg your pardon?' he said, his jowls quivering.

'My boy?' Aunt Clem cried. 'You mean my boy is getting out?'

'He's not a boy,' Tristan spat, 'he's a goddamn criminal. And if he does get out, I don't want him around my girls!'

Clem cut her eyes in fury, before the expression vanished.

'It's what Eugene wanted,' Jeannie said, switching to her cold, corporate tone that didn't invite discussion.

Fergus looked at George, as if to appeal to his brother's better nature. George looked beyond angry, shaking his head and turning away. I realised that even he hadn't been informed of Jeannie's news. Fergus's shoulders slumped, and he took the opportunity to down the rest of his drink and get another.

Miles headed straight for his mother and spoke in a low voice. 'Did you have anything to do with Quentin getting out early? How on earth has he got off so lightly with what he did?'

Jeannie raised a brow and said curtly, 'It was an unfortunate accident, Miles. As I said, it's what Grandpa would have wanted.'

'You think he would want a hardened criminal going back to work in the family mine?'

Jeannie shrugged dismissively. 'It's impossible to say what Eugene would have made of Quentin now. You knew Grandpa as well as I did; perhaps he would favour him all the more. Regardless, this was Eugene's wish.'

As if on cue, a low rumble of thunder echoed in the distance, and a flash of lightning illuminated the room for a moment. I shivered, despite the warmth from the roaring fire in the hearth.

'Anyway … as I said, he won't be getting out before Christmas, so you won't have to worry about seeing him, will you?' Jeannie added pointedly. 'Artie and I really did try to do our best, but honestly, it's bureaucracy gone wild. But enough of my yammering, let's eat!' she trilled.

Miles stood frozen to the spot until I gently took his arm and led him to his seat. Everyone found their places around the table and sat down to eat.

'So,' Martha said brightly from across the table, 'who do we think is gonna die first?'

Jeannie hooted. 'I've written down everyone's names this year and put them in a bowl. That way, it will be completely at random who gets the murderer card.'

'We all know I'll win, though,' said Tristan grinning, 'I always do. No one beats me at bullshitting.'

'No one's going to argue with that,' Mimi quipped. I snorted at her quick retort, but when I looked at her expression, she didn't seem to be joking. Conversation managed to flow, despite the almighty nuclear bomb Jeannie had dropped regarding Quentin. I was *dying* to bring it up, though.

I had little knowledge of the details, but I had gleaned enough from Miles to know that what happened at the mine was no accident. Quentin Weiss, the only son of Fergus and Clementine, had been appointed manager of the goldmine several years prior to Eugene's death. Quentin was undoubtedly Eugene's favourite, his two sons, George and Fergus, proving to him time and time again that they were as useless and lazy as he deemed them to be. Eugene's eldest grandson, however, displayed many of the attributes he cherished; hard-working, no-nonsense – and completely and unashamedly ruthless to the point of violence.

Eighteen months before Eugene's death, Quentin's temper came to a head. Miles strongly believed that he had murdered one of his workers in a fit of rage. Mercifully, I was spared the arduous court hearing, but due to a lack of evidence, Quentin was sentenced to six years for corporate manslaughter and for breaching the Health and Safety at Work act. I was not privy to how Jeannie managed it, but Miles was so angry he refused to speak to her for over a year.

We were finishing up our desserts when the true stars of the show arrived: Mimi and Tristan's twins, Beebee and Ceecee. Dressed in vintage finds that would make most people look a hundred years old, the sisters sauntered in looking effortlessly cool.

They greeted us all with confident smiles, making a beeline for George and Jeannie at the head of the table, for proper hellos. As they then trotted to their seats, Callum and Martha eyed them with wary distrust, the twins mirroring their expressions right back at them. Despite their being cousins, there was no love lost.

'How is Oxbridge, girls?' Jeannie said, beaming, just in case any of us needed reminding that Beebee studied at Oxford, and Ceecee at Cambridge.

'Very busy, Grandmama,' they parroted sweetly. My fingers involuntarily gripped my knife so hard it scraped against the china. The insufferable bastards – you couldn't make them up.

'As it should be!' boomed Fergus.

Thankfully, they sat away from our end of the table, while Mrs Harlow busied around them getting their meal and drinks served.

Mimi chided the girls. 'Where have you been? Why are you so late? I've been trying to get in touch with you all day.'

Ceecee – at least, I think it was Ceecee – beheld her mother with acute boredom. 'Did you call me?' she asked with irritation.

'Yes, several times,' said Mimi.

'I don't answer phone calls,' Ceecee said bluntly.

'What?' said Tristan tartly. 'What do you mean, you don't answer calls?'

Ceecee looked down at what Mrs Harlow had put onto her plate with quietly concealed mirth. 'Well, you know how to type, don't you?' she said, her smile asinine.

'Yes—' started Mimi.

'And I know how to read, sooo … yeah. Send me a text next time,' Ceecee said, flicking her hair off her shoulder.

Tristan went scarlet and began to say something to the girls, which to my annoyance I missed because Jeannie began talking.

'George, have you spoken with Tristan about the papers?' she said quietly.

'He's just bloody got here,' George hissed. 'Does it look like I've had the chance?'

'You've been talking to him all evening!' she countered. 'Well, do it first thing, will you? And then I need you to put the lights up.'

'Blast it, woman,' George growled. 'Will you give me five minutes' *peace*?'

'What's this?' Miles asked.

'I've been on at your father to put the lights up out front for a week. But you know what he's like.'

George pointed his knife at Jeannie. 'Mention those bloody lights again. I dare you.'

Jeannie leaned forward. '*Lights*,' she taunted.

'Didn't you have a handyman?' I interjected, trying to defuse the tension. 'Tim, I thought his name was?'

'Oh, Tim retired last year,' she said, delicately popping a slither of panna cotta into her mouth.

'I wasn't referring to the lights,' Miles said. 'You mentioned something about papers? Is it something I can help with?'

'Oh, that! No. It's just a little admin we've got to work out with our lawyer. Tristan just needs to dot a few I's and cross a few T's.'

'Okay…' said Miles. I could see his brain working, contemplating whether he wanted to do this now or whether he could bear to wait and ask about it later. 'Is there anything you'd like me to sign?'

'No, no, it's all getting sorted this weekend. I wanted it all worked out so you won't have to worry about a thing before your move, I know how stressful it must be. I just didn't want to have any loose ends if anything should happen – *God forbid* – to me or your father, and when you're so far away in Australia that's the last thing you'll want to be dealing with. Tristan will look after everything.'

Miles stared at his mother, his face a mask of cold stone.

'Right,' he said simply.

Mrs Harlow began clearing away our bowls and plates. Jeannie loudly clapped her hands together.

'Right! Time for our murder-mystery game! I'm playing moderator this year.'

Aunt Clem scoffed. 'You're always the moderator, Jeannie!'

The table was awash with grimace-like smiles. The first year we'd played it, it had been a fun novelty, now the game was wearing decidedly thin.

'You are a bunch of stick-in-the-muds, aren't you!' Jeannie tutted, getting up from her seat and fetching the glass bowl from the sideboard, 'Come on, this could be our last time.'

She dropped a folded piece of paper on the table in front of each of us.

'Now, no cheating! No looking at each other's paper to try and speed things up. I will know.'

Rain hissed on the windowpane, punctuated by the popping of the crackling logs in the grate. She sat back down and placed a pair of pince-nez on the end of her nose, 'Right, you can all look now!'

I unfolded my paper.

MURDERER was scrawled in spidery blue handwriting. Thunder rumbled and the lights flickered.

'Honestly, Mother,' Tristan guffawed from the end of the table, 'do you invoice the weather, too?'

Jeannie gave a little smile, reached for the wine decanter and held it aloft.

'Before we begin, fruity Beaujolais, anyone?'

As I lay in bed with my nose in the laptop, Miles's electric toothbrush had been whirring away in the en suite for much longer than usual. I had artfully lied through my teeth and won the game of Murderer, to the shock and delicious irritation of Tristan and Mimi, who had to win everything.

'Are you okay in there?' I called.

The buzzing ceased and I heard him spit into the sink.

'What do you think she meant, "Tristan will look after everything"? Do you think she plans to cut us out of the will?'

I looked over the top of my screen as Miles walked in from the bathroom wearing only his boxers, and I gave him a sly grin, making it no secret that I was checking him out.

'Don't worry about it until you know more,' I said uselessly. 'It's probably nothing. I'm sure it's just the usual game-playing.' I tapped his side of the bed for him to come and join me. He walked over and sat down on my side instead, his beautifully toned back facing me. He sighed in exasperation, and I shut the laptop and put it down on the bedside table. Sitting up, I began to knead my thumbs into tense shoulders.

'I know this doesn't make it any easier,' I began, 'but it's always like this when we come here. Your mother always plays the same games; she pits the brothers against each other, you and Tristan, your father and Fergus. She even gets a kick out of putting the cat amongst the pigeons with me and Mimi.'

He laughed. 'Are you sure it's my mother doing that? Or is it just the fact that you absolutely can't stand the sight of each other?'

'Your mother doesn't help.' I smirked. 'But you don't really think she's going to cut you out of the will, do you?'

'Do I think she's going to, or do I think she's capable of it?' He thought for a moment. 'Yes, and yes. I do think that.'

'Surely not? Just because we are going to Australia?'

'Absolutely because we're moving to Australia.' Miles turned to face me, his brows furrowed. 'You don't understand, Liv. This isn't just about the move. It's about everything. The way she's always favoured Tristan, the constant disapproval of my choices, the snide comments about our relationship. She looks down on me because I don't earn a six-figure salary … and you because—'

'Because I write smutty novels and come from a working-class family? Because I don't wear expensive clothes or look like I'm always about to head into a board meeting like Mimi does?' I reached out and took his hand, giving it a gentle squeeze. 'I know it's hard, but your mother's always been like this. Remember when I first met the whole family in the cabin in Aspen, and Jeannie kept hinting that Tristan would get it one day?'

Miles was silent. Letting out a deep breath he said, 'He did get the cabin.'

'What!' I pulled him to turn towards me. 'You didn't tell me that? Christ, Miles, you loved that place. Why did he get it? Tristan doesn't even like skiing.'

He couldn't meet my gaze. His silence a heavy stone between us. I thought back to that first trip, the pained look on Jeannie's face as the week had gone on and I'd proved to her repeatedly that I wasn't up to scratch. Especially the night I got a little bit too merry on Irish cream liqueur and threw up in the snow outside. And a little bit inside. Okay, I threw up in the bed. So sue me.

'Was it because she didn't want you to go out with me?' I asked finally.

He looked at me now, a hardness in his eyes. 'It's not you, Liv. She was like this with all of my girlfriends...'

That was a yes, then.

'I know it's hard,' he continued, 'but try not to take it personally. It's always been this way; she tries to take every-thing I love away until I follow her commands. It's the only way she knows how to maintain control. Until you came along, that is ... and I fell madly in love with you. Now she's realised she's lost her grip, and she doesn't like it.' He leaned over, cupped my face in his hand and stroked my cheek with his thumb.

His touch and the notion that I'd gotten so thoroughly under his mother's skin gave me a shameful thrill.

I reached out and held his face in my hands. 'She's always been the master manipulator, and we've played nice, until now. We're leaving for the other side of the world in just over two weeks. It will be a brand new chapter, and it sends a pretty clear message to all of them that we've chosen to be as far away from her and the rest of the family as humanly possible. If Tristan wants to spend his whole life pandering to Mummy just so he can live in this house … then good luck to him.' I ran my fingers through Miles's silky dark hair.

He leaned into my touch, closing his eyes. 'How are we going to survive two weeks of this hell?' He shook his head bitterly. 'More to the point, how will we survive knowing Quentin is about to be set loose on society again?' Miles said his name like it was a bad taste in his mouth.

I threw back the covers and got out of bed. Walking over to the bedroom door, I let the strap of my negligée drop off one shoulder, then the other. The silk slipped off my body into a pool at my feet.

'Fancy a swim?'

A devilish smile broke out across Miles's face.

3

DENIAL AND DOM PÉRIGNON

Miles and I nursed mammoth hangovers from the champagne we had pilfered from the pool-bar fridge. We were an hour late for the breakfast Jeannie and Mrs Harlow had laid out on the huge kitchen island. The chatter coming from within the kitchen made my head pound, the wafting scent of bacon grease and fried egg not promising to be the antidote I was hoping for.

'Big brother! Livvy!' Tristan bellowed as we appeared in the doorway, 'you're finally awake.'

'We had no idea everyone was already up,' Miles offered sheepishly, 'otherwise we'd have come down sooner.'

'Well, y'know, some of us have real jobs,' Tristan bantered. 'We don't keep university hours. No, I had some business to attend to with Father.' He turned to me and gave me a wink, his heavy cologne mingling with the smell of sausages and assaulting my somewhat delicate constitution. It appeared that that my in-laws, true to their word, had met with the lawyer already. A small part of me had hoped it had all been a bluff.

My father-in-law acknowledged us with his signature cursory glance.

'Morning,' George said, before going back to chewing on a piece of bacon whilst reading *The Telegraph* on his iPad.

Mimi glanced up from her phone long enough to see that we had entered the room.

'Hi, you're looking lovely,' she said getting up from her bar stool and giving us both perfumy air kisses that couldn't have been further away if she tried.

'Where are the twins?' I asked. I couldn't utter the three women's names in succession without sniggering. Mimi, Beebee and Ceecee. What I wouldn't give to have been a fly on the wall the day Jeannie heard their names for the first time.

'Probably on their phones.' She shrugged. 'You know what kids are like.'

I nodded, trying to mask my relief. At least we'd be spared the twins' vapid chatter and cutting remarks for a few more hours.

'I guess they aren't really kids anymore,' I said sadly. 'In the next two years it will be Callum's and Martha's turn to go off to uni.'

Mimi raised an incredulous brow. 'You think that's a possibility, then? I mean—' she caught herself. 'In Australia?'

'Yes, they have universities in Australia,' I said drily, opting for a croissant, the only thing on the countertop dry enough not to make me nauseous.

'Coffee?' Tristan offered, proffering two cups and pouring the coffee in without waiting for our response.

'Please,' Miles said, accepting the steaming mug. I declined with a small shake of my head, my stomach roiling. I was blaming it on the champagne, but maybe it was churning from anxiety about the family drama I could feel brewing.

Jeannie breezed in, always the whirlwind. She could never seem to sit down and chill the hell out. Gloria trailed on her heals, sniffing the air to locate the bacon.

'Finally with us, I see?' She gave me a barbed look. Oh, she wasn't happy about something – although strictly that wasn't unusual.

'George?' Jeannie said, raising her brows expectantly, 'I think now's a good time, don't you?'

George finally looked up from his iPad, his bushy eyebrows furrowing as he regarded us. 'Ah, yes. Well, now that you're here, we might as well get down to business.'

I felt my stomach drop further. This was it. The moment we'd been debating and mulling over since last night. I glanced at Miles, whose face was unreadable to those who didn't know him like I did. George set his iPad down with a decisive click.

'There have been some changes regarding the future of this family and our estate,' he announced.

Jeannie perched on the edge of a bar stool, her perfectly manicured nails drumming against the marble countertop.

'Your father and I are getting on, and we need someone who can look after the assets, maintain the estate, keep on top of the staff. There are finances to track.' Her eyes danced over us, lingering on Miles and me as she dangled the hammer over us.

'We feel that Tristan is best placed to manage all of that,

what with being nearby.' She turned to address Miles directly. 'We wanted to be as transparent as possible. Now, when you leave for Australia, you won't have to worry at all if anything should happen. Tristan will be executor of the will and make sure everything is properly taken care of.'

I felt my heart racing. This was moving faster than I'd anticipated. I'd hoped we'd at least have a day or two of false pleasantries before the facade fell. Tristan leaned against the fridge clutching a glass of freshly squeezed orange juice, a smug smile playing at the corners of his mouth. I resisted the urge to shove my croissant down his throat.

'So that means what exactly, for my family and me?' Miles fixed Jeannie with a stony stare that would put Medusa's to shame.

'Well, he can't be expected to do all of that work for nothing,' George said flatly. 'Tristan will inherit the lion's share.'

'I see,' said Miles. 'And my children? Will they get anything?'

'All of the finer details still need to be ironed out and discussed,' Jeannie said, 'but it will be up to Tristan to distribute what's left amongst the family, as he sees fit.'

Mimi was nodding away as if this was the fairest thing she'd ever heard.

I felt a surge of anger rising within me, my hands clenched into fists at my sides, and I fought to keep my composure. My in-laws had done nothing over the years to ease the tensions between our family and Tristan and Mimi's, in fact, they promoted savage competition at every opportunity.

Miles had confided in me that ever since the boys had been young, their parents had been big believers in weaponising that competition between the brothers, to spur them on. But now that their machinations involved our children … well, that was a whole different ballgame.

I could see the storm brewing behind Miles's eyes, but he kept his voice steady.

'I see,' he said, his voice dangerously quiet. 'So, you've decided to essentially disinherit me, my wife and my children because of what? Because we are moving?'

Jeannie waved her hand airily. 'Oh, don't be so dramatic, darling. This makes the most financial sense. Tristan will see to it that you get something. But you can't expect handouts, dear. You're a grown man.'

I would have blown a gasket then and there if I had not noticed the blood rising to the surface of Miles's neck and cheeks. I'd rarely, if ever, seen him this angry.

'We don't want handouts,' Miles said through gritted teeth. 'I don't want anything from you. In fact, I've *never* asked for anything. I just didn't think you would resort to playing games out of spite because I decided to move away for a few years with my family. But as you say, it's your money. Do with it as you see fit.'

'Oh, don't be like that, Miles,' Jeannie chided. 'If you're going to behave this way, it will ruin Christmas for everyone.'

I gently took the mug out of Miles's hand before he managed to crush it in his tightening grip.

'Any time you want to read over it, you're more than welcome,' George said. 'It's in my office.'

'Oh, sounds tremendous fun, thank you,' Miles said coldly.

Mimi was scrolling on her phone, looking at her work

emails like they were the most interesting thing she'd ever read.

'George,' Jeannie picked up the pitcher of orange juice and poured herself a glass, 'Mrs Harlow has left the lights in the foyer. Would you *please* put them up like I asked?'

I looked away from them, my brain pulsing inside my skull like a second heart. I took a few deep breaths before I said something I'd sorely regret. As I looked away, I noticed Gloria was sitting by her empty bowl, still waiting to be fed.

George growled something under his moustache and snatched his iPad back up.

Wordlessly, fists still clamped into balls at my sides, I made to leave the room.

'Oh, Olivia dear?' Jeannie said, 'would you mind getting the children out of bed? Toots will be arriving later, and she likes pâté with crusty bread. I thought the children could go into the village and get it; the fresh air might put a bit of colour back into their cheeks.'

'Feed Gloria, Jeannie, she's hungry,' I said coldly. I didn't even turn around to acknowledge her request.

'There'll be no good trees left at the farm by the time we get there,' I heard Jeannie tutting to Mimi.

The car almost left the ground as I floored the accelerator over the small stone bridge as we drove back through the iron gates in the direction of the village to buy Toots her sodding pâté and crusty bread for lunch. No one had uttered a word for over twenty minutes; Callum and Martha had taken one look at our faces and decided it would be wise to keep a low profile.

'Christ, Olivia.' Miles clutched onto the door. 'Take it easy,' he warned.

'Sorry,' I mumbled. I hadn't even noticed I was going so fast. Every fibre of my being was screaming at me to put my foot down and drive away from that house as quickly as possible.

'Maybe we should just completely cut ties with them once and for all and be done with it,' said Miles.

I considered it for a moment. 'Well … why not? We'll be far enough away that it would be easy enough.' We should have done it sooner, like we'd said a million times before. 'Why not today? Why not right now?' I looked in the rearview and saw Martha's eyes darting between us. We never discussed our issues with Miles's side of the family in front of the children. But Martha and Callum were sixteen and seventeen now; we couldn't shield them forever. Besides, learning about the true nature of their family would be beneficial in protecting themselves.

We never had to have these discussions about my family. By and large they were fairly unproblematic people with simple lives, who, more importantly, stayed the eff out of our business. In fact, they showed *zero* interest, which had been the case my whole life. Which had made Miles's family even more of a shock to the system.

'Because, well…' Miles sighed, 'I guess it's been harder than I thought to say goodbye to fifty million.'

I almost choked. I knew Miles had been set to inherit a lot of money, but he'd never told me the exact figure.

'So, Tristan, Mimi and the twins will get one hundred million?'

'Give or take, if they sold the assets and the land. No doubt they'll be tied up to keep it running somehow. It's not including the mine though... You don't want to know how much the mine is worth. That's assuming there's any gold left. Let's hope there isn't,' he said drily.

Martha reached over and tapped Callum on the arm, pointing to us, signalling for him to take his earphones out and start listening.

'What's happened?' Martha asked, 'Why are Grandpa and Grandma leaving everything to them?'

Callum perked up. 'What's this?'

I glanced at Miles. 'It's better that they hear it from us, otherwise I'm sure the twins will find a way to bring it up.'

Miles considered it for a moment before nodding reluctantly.

'Grandma and Grandpa told us this morning that Uncle Tristan will be taking over the running of the estate. When anything happens to Grandma and Grandpa, their family will get everything. And if there are any scraps, maybe Uncle Tristan will throw us a bone. But I wouldn't hold your breath.'

'And ... will they really get a hundred million?' asked Martha.

'Yup,' Miles said bitterly.

'What!' Callum exclaimed. 'Those absolute tools will get a hundred million?'

'Yup,' I parroted.

'Well ... do we really need the money?' asked Martha innocently.

'No,' I said, 'we don't *need* it. But your father and I don't make that much money, and we wanted it as security for you both. Not for anything other than to give you freedom. Freedoms that we never had. That's part of the reason we wanted to go to Australia. We have never felt free to do as we pleased.'

'And now, because I decided to do one thing for myself and for *my* family, you're all being punished for it,' Miles added.

'Money isn't everything...' offered Martha.

'No, it isn't,' I said, 'but it does open doors that would otherwise be closed. We just wanted that for you both.'

We settled into silence.

'Maybe the Christmas tree will set on fire and burn the whole house down,' Callum scoffed. 'Will we get something then?'

'Callum!' I laughed. 'I dunno ... maybe we would.'

'It's not the worst idea I've ever heard,' Martha said as she stared out of the window, lost in thought.

We spent a lovely few hours in the quaint village near to the house. The independent bookshop was one of my favourites, especially when it was decorated beautifully for Christmas. I purchased the kids two of my favourite novels to read while we were here; for Callum I chose Truman Capote's *In Cold Blood,* and for Martha, Agatha Christie's *And Then There Were None.*

We sat down for coffee and cake at the teashop where I whipped the books out and presented them to the kids. They both looked beyond reluctant, but when I gave them a quick synopsis of each, I felt quietly confident that they would give them a go.

We had almost forgotten about the tension awaiting us back at the house. Winding our way back up towards the stone bridge, tiny splatters of rain peppered the windscreen. Pulling up to the drive, we saw George perched on a ladder, battling with string lights that were flapping wildly about his legs.

'Need any help?' offered Miles as he got out of the car. Whatever twisted trials and games Jeannie had subjected her boys to, she had unfailingly drilled manners into both of her sons.

With a row of steel nails perched in his mouth, George moved his lips to the side to speak. 'Your mother will never let me hear the end of it if I don't do the one thing she's been asking me to do for weeks.' He plucked a nail out of his mouth, retrieved the hammer sticking out of his back pocket and started hammering the front of the timber canopy. 'Great Grandma Toots is in the front room, you should go and say hello,' he said to Martha and Callum.

The kids exchanged a grimace. No one wanted to be in the firing line of that cantankerous old bat. 'We will,' they said in unison, scuttling inside.

'You know, Dad,' Miles said looking towards the horizon, 'it's threatening to rain…'

George squinted up towards the grey clouds we'd just driven through and set to hammering with renewed vigour.

We entered the house, the sound of George's hammer blows fading behind us, replaced by the muffled voices of Jeannie and Aunt Clementine coming from the kitchen. Mrs Harlow had left boxes upon boxes of decorations in the foyer. Miles and I swept our gaze over the pile, then at each other. We hesitated, knowing that we too would be put to work.

'I should probably get some work done before we get roped into putting all of this stuff up,' Miles began, gesturing towards the boxes.

I nodded fervently, 'I might try and get some writing in before she sees we're back.'

'Martha, would you take these to Grandma, please, darling?' Miles said, handing her the bag containing the bread and pâté.

She was about to open her mouth to object.

'Thanks!' he said, before darting off towards the study.

Martha turned to Callum. 'I have to call my girlfriend,' she said. She rammed the bag into his chest and fled upstairs before he could say anything.

He stood gaping up after her, then slowly turned towards me.

'Mum?' he said, opening his eyes wider and gingerly holding the bag out to me. '*Please* don't make me go in there.'

I pursed my lips. 'Oh, give it here,' I said, snatching it from his hand. He knew damn well I couldn't refuse that doe-eyed look.

'Thank you! I owe you. Love you, Mum!' He darted off, leaving me standing alone.

I stared at the boxes and then back towards the entrance where George was still hammering away. After steeling myself, I took a deep breath, and made my way towards the kitchen.

I found Jeannie and Aunt Clem seated at the kitchen island, two teacups and a large teapot before them.

'*If you breathe one word of this to anyone,*' Jeannie was threatening under her breath, 'if you so much as *sniff* in Toots's direction with this, you'll both find yourselves in line at the job centre, do I make myself clear?'

'I'm only telling you what I heard!' Clem admonished. 'I just thought you should know, what with the changes… What if they divorce—?'

Their conversation halted abruptly when Jeannie saw me standing there. Her eyes darted between Clem and me, before she swiftly fixed a brittle smile onto her face.

'You're back,' she said, her voice overly bright. 'Did you have a nice time in the village?'

'It was lovely,' I replied, my tone equally sunny, as if I hadn't heard a thing. 'Here you are, pâté and crusty bread as requested.' I dumped the bag on the island. 'I'm off to do some writing in the pool room if you need me. I'm on a strict deadline.'

I saw Jeannie straighten, about to object. It was unheard of that each of us didn't do something to help out around the house, making lunch, putting up the Christmas decorations, a spot of cleaning. One year I did my back in pulling up all the brambles in some forgotten corner of the vast estate because Jeannie had got it into her head to create a sunken seating area with a pizza oven.

Well, if we were getting cut out of the inheritance, there was no way I was going to slave away on a 'working holiday' as Jeannie liked to call it. She could do it all her damned self.

'Olivia, wait a moment,' Jeannie said, lips pursed as she drew the teacup to her lips and blew the surface.

I turned, hand on hip. *I will not let you boss me around.* 'Yes?'

She fixed her piercing blue eyes onto mine. 'If you're going to the pool room, put this back in the fridge, will you?' From under the counter, she pulled out a bottle of champagne. 'I hope you enjoyed my 2015 Dom Pérignon last night,' she said icily.

I froze. How did she know?

'We have cameras,' she said, answering the question for me.

Oh. God… His mother had *seen* us … that meant she saw what we did in the pool. She had seen us … *going at it*. That's why she'd given me that look at breakfast. She was staring intently, waiting for my apology, and by the look on her face she was taking sinister pleasure in my embarrassment.

I looked at Clem, who was finding a speck on the marble countertop extremely interesting.

I smiled and walked forward to take the bottle, 'Of course,' I said, heading once more for the exit. I waited until I was almost out the door when I turned and said, 'Jeannie?'

'Yes?' she said icily.

'I hope you enjoyed the show.' I winked. The satisfaction I felt at turning on my heel as her jaw hit the floor felt like all my Christmases had come at once.

Making my way to the pool room, I selected one of the loungers that sat behind a faux palm-tree divider to get a little privacy. The heat from the swimming pool steamed up my glasses and was making me sweat in my knitwear and leggings. I'm sure it was nothing to do with the embarrassment I'd just endured. Huffing, I ripped my jumper off over my head and discarded it on the lounger next to me.

The elongated windows looked out towards the iron gates. To my relief, I saw Tristan and Mimi's Audi snaking down the side entrance of the grounds, disappearing as it turned the corner of the lower gates. I checked the time: noon. Hopefully they wouldn't come back for a while, and I'd be left in peace to get a solid hour of writing in before lunch was served. I went back to my laptop, willing my brain to forget about what had just transpired. I *had* to finish this goddamn book before my editor clocked off for Christmas.

Ten minutes into typing, I heard giggling echoes emanating from down the hallway, growing louder as footsteps approached. Those laughs could only belong to Beebee and Ceecee. I scowled, unsure whether I could leave now without seeming rude. Instead, I froze, hidden behind the partition. I heard them enter, chatting and tittering, before the sound of items being dropped onto one of the beds was followed by one loud splash after another.

They whooped and hollered, competing with one another as to who had the best diving technique. I should have got up and gone when I had the chance. Now if I emerged from behind my peeping-tom screen, I would just look weird. The sounds of splashing stopped, and their voices neared as they swam closer to the deep end. *Shit*, I realised with dread, they must be close to my side of the pool. I was stuck... I couldn't even resume typing in case they heard me and thought me even *more* weird for not making myself known when they entered.

'So... Aunt Clem just told me something really disturbing,' Ceecee sneered. I could tell it was her because almost everything she said came out in a sneer.

'Ew. Do I want to know?' replied Beebee. 'Aunt Clem and

Uncle Fergus are rank. Have they ever heard of an exfoliation brush? They're practically shedding everywhere they go.'

Ceecee sniggered. 'You're gonna want to hear this. Grandmama caught Uncle Miles and Aunt Olivia absolutely *going* at it last night.'

'Oh my God, *noooooo*,' Beebee gasped. 'That is disgusting! They're like fucking fifty!'

Ceecee chortled with glee. 'And that's not the best bit! Guess where she saw them?'

'Where?'

'Right *here*,' Ceecee cackled.

Beebee let out a shriek. Water splashed as she presumably jumped up and out of the pool. 'You could have told me that before we got in! Ew-ew-ew-ew, we've been swimming in their juices?' She cried.

'Relax…' laughed Ceecee. 'The chlorine kills all of that stuff. Funny, though, right?'

'It's effing gross,' Beebee insisted. 'She is so, so *weird*. Is she a sex maniac or something? What's with the porno books and doing it in the in-laws' pool? I think she needs therapy.'

'You're not wrong about that. Although, she does look quite good for her age… But I have to agree with Mum, Uncle Miles is *way* out of her league.'

'Totally. If he wasn't my uncle…' Beebee dropped her voice provocatively.

'Eurgh!' I heard a slap of skin and a yelp. 'Don't even joke about that, Bee.'

Beebee laughed uncontrollably. When she'd finished she said, 'Hey … guess what? I think Callum has some weed.

I smelled it through my window last night. We should totally go into his room and steal it.'

'Oh my God, stop. What if he says something?'

'He's not going to admit he has weed, is he? You know Gran would shit a brick.'

Ceecee giggled. 'That's true. Okay, let's do it.'

'Cool, let's shower and go back, I've got a video I need to film.'

I heard more splashing followed by wet feet padding away.

My palms were sweating. God I *hated* those girls and their stuck-up, fugly parents with their stupid teeth. I looked *great* for my age? Thanks very much. And I was nowhere near fucking fifty. I'd been working hard to keep myself in shape this past year, and here we were: the fake teeth, tits, ab implants and botox queen telling her two brats that Miles is too good-looking for me. Mimi probably said that because Tristan was always drooling over me.

Every year I marvelled that Miles and Tristan were born to the same household. I wasn't thrilled that Callum was smoking weed, although I'd had an inkling. I made a mental note to warn him about the girls' plan, and to drill into him not to get caught smoking by Jeannie.

I stared at my screen, mulling over everything they had said about me being weird and not good enough for Miles. It was blatantly clear that's how the whole family had felt from early on, but to hear it said out loud by the poisonous twins was something else entirely.

Through my whirling rumination, I heard a muffled cry.

'What now?' I rolled my eyes, my voice echoing over the still water. I slammed the laptop closed and set it down next to my jumper. I strolled leisurely out of the room, not in a rush to have my solitude interrupted again.

The hallway leading from the pool extension was long and winding, paved with tiles in case any wet swimmers should go trailing through to the main house. Old paintings of glossy-brown show horses, long since dead, lined the walls. The wooden panelling did nothing to dampen the sound of my encroaching footsteps and the closer I neared the doorway, the louder the commotion beyond the door became. But it didn't sound like arguing – it sounded like panic.

I quickened my pace and burst through the door to the foyer. I was met with a group of pale, drawn faces. A cold breeze blew through from my left, and I turned to see that the front door was wide open, the rain beyond pattering heavily.

'What's the matter?' I asked Martha, whose face was taut. 'What's happened?'

'It's Grandpa,' she said, her voice flat, her eyes slightly wide with shock. She gestured towards the open door.

I walked towards the entrance to see what she was pointing to. I stood in the doorway, my brain struggling to keep up with what my eyes were relaying.

George lay outside on the gravel, a ladder toppled over and lying at his side. One of his legs was hoisted upwards, tangled in a mass of Christmas lights that still partially dangled from the canopy above. He was staring at the sky, rain falling onto his face. Miles was poised over him with his arms straight, his hands over his heart as he administered chest compressions.

I clamped my hand over my mouth as I wordlessly watched the Christmas lights flickering in their merry dance, chasing one after the other around his leg.

I could hear Uncle Fergus on the phone asking how long the ambulance would take.

A hand gripped my shoulder and pulled me. I looked around to find Callum with a glazed, far-off look in his eyes as led me back inside. I glanced back over my shoulder to see Miles giving George mouth-to-mouth.

'We think he fell,' Callum managed. 'Or – or maybe he had a heart attack.' He squeezed my arm tightly and we held on to each other, Martha joining us as we huddled together, unsure of where to go and what to do with ourselves.

'I can't believe it,' I said shakily. 'This is just awful!' I pressed the kids into me, burying my face in their hair and holding on for dear life, hoping for their and Miles's sake that this wasn't going to be as bad as it looked. Perhaps George would miraculously pull through…

That's when I noticed Jeannie, sitting ramrod straight in a carved wooden chair next to the grandfather clock. Her eyes locked onto the open doorway.

'You're letting all the warm air out,' she snapped. 'Shut the door please, Martha.'

I blinked, my mind lagging. Was the old shrew more concerned about the open door than her husband lying lifeless in the rain? Perhaps what she meant was *You're letting all the warm air out … and George back in.*

'Um, o-okay,' Martha said as she released herself from my arms. She crossed to the entrance, and before she closed the door, I saw that Fergus was now crouched next to Miles. He stared down at George and fisted his hands into the eight grey hairs he had left.

'Do you think he'll be okay, Mum?' Callum asked quietly.

'I hope so, darling,' I said, his brown hair ruffling under my breath. I could hear a siren in the distance, and I breathed deeply to try to steady the hammering of my heart against my ribcage.

A moment later, the door flew open again and slammed into the wall behind it, causing me and the kids to jump out of our skin. Fergus stood there breathlessly.

'Is the ambulance here, Fergus?' Jeannie asked, as if he hadn't nearly ripped the front door off its hinges.

'It's here,' Fergus replied dourly, 'but this is why we hire help, Jeannie!' he shouted, red in the face.

But Jeannie just sat with her hands folded in her lap, waiting.

4

SECRETS, SAUSAGES AND STIFF UPPER LIPS

12th December 2025

On the first day of Christmas my true love gave to me... George Weiss trussed up like a Christmas tree. He'd moaned about those lights for days. Perhaps subconsciously he knew they'd be the death of him.

He had no idea I'd stripped back the wire.

As I watched him decking the halls, he called down to me and put his thumb up to signal I should turn them on. I whacked the plug into the outlet. The lights burned brightly – too bright – pink, blue, red, yellow. Then the sparks flew. He held onto them for dear life, almost as if he was incapable of letting go. But it wasn't that that killed him – no, what finally put an end to his miserable life was when I gave the ladder a good kick from under him and he went crashing down onto the patio.

'**M**rs Harlow is an absolute gem, really she is.' Jeannie's voice sounded raw. It was the first time she had spoken in the three hours since men in smart suits had come to take George's body away. Blots of mascara clustered in the corners of her eyes, the only visible sign that she'd had any sort of reaction.

The family sat in silence, the rain beating an incessant drum upon the windowpane outside. No one had the ability to respond; a shell-shocked silence permeated the sitting room.

She continued, voice wobbling, 'Not only has she said she would see to the – the arrangements, but she's also offered to help me with the tropical Christmas party.'

Fergus let his let his hand drop from his face as he studied her with his mouth open.

'What's this?' he exclaimed. 'Tropical Christmas party? You've got to be bloody joking, Jeannie!'

'No, I'm not joking, Fergus!' she said, wide-eyed. 'And don't you swear at me. It's our turn to host our friends this year, the invites have been out for months, and I've already spent a fortune on it.'

'Mum,' Miles began, 'do you really think that's appropriate—'

She was completely still, an asp ready to strike as her lips held a taut line.

'Appropriate?' she bellowed. 'Don't you talk to me about what *is* and *isn't* appropriate!' She gave us both a pointed look. 'It seems to me that I am the only *appropriate* one around here.'

Everyone shrank back in their seats, wishing the earth

would swallow them up. I chewed on my cheek, watching Fergus's face turn from puce to purple.

'My brother has just died,' he ground out, lips twitching.

Jeannie eyeballed him. 'Don't pretend you suddenly care for him now, Fergus. If anyone has the right to be upset, it's me. The only thing you're upset about is the possibility of the gravy train ending.'

Aunt Clem, who hadn't uttered a word all evening, let out a shocked little gasp.

'Mum,' Miles protested, 'I know you're in shock but … please. This isn't the time or the place.'

Jeannie seemed to catch herself. She looked around at our faces and took a moment to regain composure before continuing.

'At a time like this we need family. We need friends. What won't do any of us any good is shutting ourselves away, crying in the dark.' She looked up at the ceiling just in case any of us needed a reminder of who she was talking about. Tristan, Mimi and the girls hadn't come down since George had been taken away, and I couldn't say I blamed them.

'A time such as this is all the more reason to be with our friends.' Her tone put an end to any rebuttal. Clearly no one was to mention to Jeannie what had happened to George. We would be expected to carry on as if he had gone on a business trip, which was fine by me.

'Fergus and I were talking—' started Aunt Clem.

'Not now, Clem,' Fergus cut in.

Clem persisted, 'We were just saying, that if we can help in any way … if you don't want to be alone when the children leave after Christmas, then we could always come and live—'

Jeannie let out a curt, dismissive huff. 'I'll be perfectly fine, thank you. Besides, who knows what the living arrangements will be now that George—' She wouldn't allow herself to finish the sentence. Changing the subject she said, 'Mrs Harlow also found some more of the boxes from the attic, and now they're cluttering up the entrance. We need to get the decorations up. So, tomorrow, we are going to the Christmas-tree farm to buy a tree—'

Fergus made a move to protest, but she halted him with a look. 'Then the children can dress the tree. I don't want a bare house. All of this is depressing enough as it is.'

Miles winced. The kids nodded, clearly counting down the seconds until they'd be allowed to leave and go to their rooms, and I just sat there wondering whether our car had been totalled on the drive over here and I'd in fact died and gone to hell. Although I couldn't quite say George's death could be considered all bad ... perhaps now Jeannie might even renegotiate the will? Hey, a girl can dream.

Jeannie's face was a mask of practised composure, the kind that wealthy women perfect through years of private disappointments and public smiles. I couldn't help but wonder if she'd already called Artie Peverill to shuffle some funds around and line up the next chess piece.

'I think a tree is a wonderful idea,' Clem offered, her voice too bright.

Miles cleared his throat. 'About tomorrow ... I've got some work calls that—'

'Cancel them,' Jeannie said, not looking at him. Her fingers traced the rim of her wine glass. 'Family comes first, especially now.'

The irony wasn't lost on me. George had spent forty years putting everything but family first, and now his absence was being used to enforce togetherness. Classic.

Mrs Harlow brought out some cold cuts, and we grazed mostly in silence, save for a few barbed exchanges between Fergus and Clementine, followed by furtive glances between myself and Miles. I was just thankful Toots had already been driven back to the home, and therefore wasn't here to rile Jeannie even further.

As soon as we were excused, we skittered off sharpish, but not before I grabbed Callum's arm and whispered the twins' plans to steal his stash of weed, adding that on no account was he to be caught smoking. He seemed surprised that I knew, but the relief he felt that I wasn't about to confiscate his weed was palpable.

Understandably, Miles had barely uttered a word since George's body had been taken away. I put my arm around him and ordered him to lie down on the bed, telling him I'd be up in a moment, after I'd helped to clear up.

I couldn't put my finger on why I felt so uneasy… Yes, Miles's dad had just dropped down dead unexpectedly, but the unease I felt wasn't due to that. Then, I had a horrible, fleeting thought that made my stomach lurch and I felt as if a weight had been taken away. I felt … strangely relieved. I was sad for Miles, of course; losing a parent is never easy. But when Miles had once told me his grandfather Eugene used to discipline him and Tristan with a belt when they were young, while their father merely averted his gaze, it made me see red. Presumably George had endured the same abuse when he was a boy and thought it was par for the course. But in my opinion, that was all the more reason for George to step up and protect his son from the same fate. When Miles had revealed that information to me a few years ago, I'd wanted to burn out Eugene, George and Jeannie's eyes with red-hot pokers.

Yes. Maybe it was okay for me to admit to myself that it felt damn good that the impotent old bastard was dead.

Making my way to the kitchen, I was surprised to find Fergus already in there, staring at the dirty dishes in the sink. In my nineteen years of knowing him, I'd never seen him lift a finger to help out. Silently, I slotted in next to him, inserted the plug, squeezed some washing up liquid into the basin and turned on the hot tap. The sound of running water seemed to jolt him out of his reverie. He picked up the cleaning brush and began scrubbing.

I waited patiently in silence for him to hand me an item. Eventually, he passed me a suds-covered plate that he hadn't rinsed properly, and I soaked it up with a tea towel as best I could. I could feel the tension radiating from him as he scrubbed away at the plates and glasses and I dried them.

'She's always been a bit mad, but now I think she's truly lost her mind,' Fergus muttered finally under his breath, 'completely off her rocker.'

I nodded sympathetically, not daring to voice my agreement out loud in case she suddenly appeared behind me.

'All this pressure she puts on herself and the rest of us. I always told George it would kill him one day.'

'I'm so very sorry, Fergus … about George.'

He thought for a moment, his mouth downcast. 'George wasn't a particularly nice man. Even when we were young boys, he was always rotten to me. But … he was my brother.'

I thought I heard Fergus's voice crack, but he quickly wound back in any emotion that was unspooling.

'He was always working away, so he didn't have much to do with Miles and Tristan growing up. I should like to be there for them now, but I fear it's far too late. I regret that … I regret I wasn't a better uncle to them. Hell, how could I be a good uncle when I wasn't even a good father? I regret a lot of things.'

I was at a loss for words. Fergus had never spoken more than a handful of words to me, other than to be a lecherous old bastard. Now here he was, voicing his darkest thoughts and his deepest regrets. I almost didn't want to move a muscle in case I scared him away.

'It's never too late—'

'Oh, but we both know it is. The damage has been done. I think Clem thought that by mollycoddling Quentin and sending him to the same boarding school George and I went to we were doing what was best for his future. But somewhere along the way, he turned out to be as cruel and nasty as my father … and I just let it happen. I didn't break the cycle. And now … now he's getting out. What the *hell* does Jeannie think she's playing at—?'

A hand appeared on Fergus's and he jumped out of his skin.

'Oh, Mrs Harlow! You scared me to death!'

'Don't blame yourself, Fergus,' she said sadly. 'We all should have spoken up when we had the chance. Quentin is your son, it's understandable that you want to protect him.'

I was always afraid to ask anything about Quentin. It was one of those taboo subjects that was never raised. But if I didn't ask now, then I might not get the chance again. 'What ... what happened with Quentin?'

Fergus shook his head sadly.

'Miles didn't know,' Mrs Harlow said tersely. 'Please do not mention any of this to him. He is the only good one in this family, and he does not deserve to be tainted—'

'Fergus?' came a sharp voice from the doorway. I turned to see Aunt Clem looking furious. Had she heard our conversation? 'Come on, what are you doing all of that for?' She snapped. 'We need to get going. Just leave them there and Mrs Harlow will see to them in the morning.'

Fergus shook the suds from his hands and wiped them straight down his cardigan, abandoning the cutlery and the scourer in the sink.

Mrs Harlow and I bade him goodnight and I decided to stay and help her finish up. I tried to bring up the subject of Quentin again, but Mrs Harlow shot me a warning look that almost seemed fearful, changing the subject and inquiring about the kids.

By the time we'd finished, the house was quiet. Everyone had gone to bed, and the only light came from the crackling fire in the living room. As we made our way upstairs to our rooms, I saw Jeannie standing at the foot of the stairs, watching us go. I bade Mrs Harlow goodnight, hurrying along the gallery and down the hallway towards my room.

As I passed outside Tristan and Mimi's room, I heard his voice, dampened by the thick mahogany door, but unmistakably angry. I paused, hovering, paralysed with whether I should listen in case he was about to get violent.

'This wasn't supposed to happen!' Tristan barked.

'Keep your voice down,' Mimi hissed.

I felt a chill ripple up my spine. What wasn't supposed to happen? Did they mean George dying, or something else? I gingerly pressed my ear against the door, holding my breath.

'What are you so worried about?' Mimi said. 'You're getting a huge payout.'

'We're not talking about the money!'

'Ha! That'd be a first. It's all you've been talking about since we got here.'

There was a silence, and I wished I could see what was happening.

'Mimi, if—' Tristan stopped abruptly, and I realised the door was starting to open. I bolted down the hallway and didn't stop until I reached our room.

5

TRIGGERED

Despite my best efforts clucking around Miles, Callum and Martha – offering them hot beverages, snuggles on the sofa and even coaxing them to come out on a walk with me – they had shooed me away. I wanted to be there for them after George's death, but in true Weiss style they much preferred dealing with things in private and on their own terms. Miles had buried himself in work, Callum had reached a critical moment in his *Fortnite* tournament, and Martha was spending every available moment on FaceTime with her girlfriend. I'd *even* asked Jeannie if she needed any help with the funeral arrangements, but luckily for me she said that Mrs Harlow was dealing with it all.

Miles suggested I seize the moment and spend it working on my book, which was his polite way of telling me to stop pestering. So, once again, I found myself alone and sitting in the pool room at my laptop, staring at a blank document. I was trying to think up a steamy scene between my female protagonist and her arch-nemesis-turned-lover, but all I could think about was George all tangled up.

I scrubbed at my face and willed away the image of his glassy lifeless eyes that seemed to have burned themselves into my retinas. Was anyone in this household not slightly scarred by seeing him on the floor like that? I had to get my head back in the game. *Okay Olivia, think... Sexy, fated lovers.* I glanced over to where Miles had taken me against the side of the pool just two nights ago. Perhaps I could use that as inspiration.

I began to type out the scene: my female orc-warrior with her human orc-hunter, finally succumbing to each other in the deep lagoon under the Tendairian waterfalls. I forced my brain and fingers to work in tandem and not think about that *other thing* anymore. Or Tristan and Mimi's argument and what the hell that had been about. Did it have anything to do with what Clem and Jeannie were talking about in the kitchen the other day?

No, stop thinking about that! I resumed typing.

As if my brain delighted in working against me, it rifled through some other pile of dirty laundry and triumphantly held up another but entirely different topic, the forum. That seedy little chat room where my most ardent haters converged to slander me and my writing. I had visited it so many times I could recite the posts off by heart.

BlackP!ll25
Shameless slut...

StaceeBabe
Can you imagine what she says to people when they ask her what she writes about?

NotaChad

Wonder if her parents are proud when they read her filth.

OpinionatedOgre1

It says in her bio she's married with 2 children. Imagine what her in-laws must think.

FantasyWh0re

Have you seen her socials? Her husband is fiiiit. I'm tempted to DM him and offer him a proper ride.

The comments were emblazoned in my mind. I even recognised the usernames who contributed regularly. My eyes wandered down the laptop screen to the tool bar, where the multicoloured Google widget seemed to call to me.

I hadn't checked the site in weeks – I'd promised my therapist I wouldn't go on that website ever again. Miles had made me block it on my phone because at one point I checked it several times a day. I wondered what new things the chat room had been saying since the last time I looked.

My fingers hovered over the touchpad, the temptation gnawing at me. *Just one quick look*, I told myself. What harm could it do? I'd been doing so well by staying away for months, surely I was strong enough now to handle whatever I might see.

Before I could stop myself, I was on the browser and typing in the forum into the search bar. The familiar site loaded, its garish red and black colour scheme an assault to the eyes. I searched for my pen name.

There it was. A whole thread dedicated to tearing apart my

latest novel. I read with morbid fascination as strangers dissected every flaw, every awkward phrase, every cliché. Their words cut deep, confirming my worst fears about my writing.

NotaChad
Jesus H. Talk about amateur hour.

OpinionatedOgre1
How did this drivel ever get past a publisher?

BlackP!ll25
I've read better fan fiction written by 12-year-olds.

My pulse quickening, I could feel the blood rushing to my head, my ears roaring with adrenaline and my heart racing as I scrolled, eyes devouring one cruel message after the next.

SickShadowDaddy
Did you see her latest reviews? #shesscrewed

OpinionatedOgre1
Can't believe she has the audacity to call herself a writer.

ProudKaren08
Someone should tell her to give up already.

FantasyWh0re
I've already told my reading group not to even bother. Worst fantasy novel I've ever read. And that's saying something.

Each word was a dagger, reopening old wounds I thought had healed. I knew I shouldn't be reading this, knew how it would affect me, but I couldn't look away. It was like watching a train wreck in slow motion. I clicked on 'show more' – I had to read on until I'd seen every new post.

The old self-loathing, the self-doubt, began to percolate. I couldn't do it. I wasn't good enough... I had embarrassed myself. Perhaps I could email that ghost writer... I opened Gmail and tentatively began typing out an email.

Suddenly, I felt a hand on my shoulder.

I jumped out of my skin and slammed the laptop shut. I whirled around to see Mimi peering down at me.

'Christ, Mimi,' I said breathlessly, 'you scared me to death.'

'Sorry...' She'd taken her shoes off, and was standing there in black stockinged feet, a woollen skirt and a silk blouse. Her eyes were rimmed with dark circles as if she hadn't slept a wink. Sitting down heavily on the lounger next to me, she swung her feet up and sat back.

Sighing, she looked up, fixing her gaze upon the rippling reflections of the water playing across the ceiling. 'How's the writing going?' she asked without interest.

'Not well,' I admitted.

'I'm sure you'll be fine. It always gets written in the end.'

She was right, of course, except this time felt very different. I had already asked my editor to push my deadline back twice, and with dwindling sales I could tell she was itching for an excuse not to re-contract me.

I glanced at Mimi. 'No offence, but you look like hell. Was everything okay last night with Tristan? We were worried when you didn't come down.'

'His father's just died,' she said flatly, 'of course he's not all right.'

'Yes, I know…' I bit my tongue. I so wanted to ask her what the argument was about, but I knew if I did, she'd close up and completely deny it. 'I'm asking about you, though. Is everything okay with you?'

I also desperately wanted to know what Jeannie and Aunt Clem had been discussing in the kitchen before George died, but the chances of Mimi opening up to me on that front were also slim to none.

'You know what it's like,' she said tersely. 'All this stuff about the will, they've got Tristan and I all tangled up in legalities. It's a goddamn mess, to be quite honest.'

Her choice of words conjured the image of a trussed-up George again, and I wondered if it would ever be appropriate to use his death for one of my characters. My guess was no…

Instead, I simply said, 'Oh?'

Outside, sleet began lashing at the windows. She breathed deeply before continuing. 'Did you know that there are stipulations to the inheritance? Did Miles ever tell you that?'

'Like what?'

She considered for a moment, clearly unsure of how much she should say.

'About having to stay married … basically forever. About … extra-marital affairs. Remarrying if they die before us, that type of thing. If those stipulations are broken, you and I … we get nothing.'

Tristan was playing away, then. To be honest, he seemed the type.

'I remember reading something like that.' I shrugged.

Mimi looked at me in surprise.

I continued, 'What's more surprising to me is that you didn't read the fine print of the prenup they made us sign. Did you not get your lawyer to look over it?'

'Lawyer?' She laughed. 'I was twenty-five. I didn't have a lawyer.'

'But … you didn't even read it?' I tried to say it delicately, but beating around the bush was never my forte.

'I glanced over it…' she said doubtfully.

'Well, it was all in there,' I said matter-of-factly. *God, Olivia. She's never going to confide in you if you act like such a smug know-it-all,* I chastised myself.

'So, you knew about these ridiculous rules? Did you ask to have them changed?'

'Nope. There wasn't any point, George and Jeannie made it clear that there were to be no changes. "Like it or lump it", I believe, were George's exact words. And at the time I didn't care about any of that. I still don't. Which is a good job, seeing as how whatever we do, we will probably end up with nothing anyway.' I felt my jaw clench then, remembering that Miles and I were set to get nothing anyway. *Poor, stupid Mimi,* I wanted to say. Just finding out now that it wasn't going to be wrapped up neatly in a bow for her and she was going to have to jump through Jeannie's hoops until the day one or both of them died.

'It doesn't bother you that if Miles left you for another woman, you'd get nothing?'

'Well…' I considered, 'yes, that would bother me. But I know he would never do that.' Mimi scoffed, but I continued. 'I just care about the kids—'

I suddenly remembered my children were already being done out of their inheritance, and I felt my anger rising anew that she was even griping about this to me.

'You trust Miles implicitly?' she asked suddenly.

I frowned. 'Of course I do. Do you trust Tristan?'

She looked me square in the eye. 'Of course I bloody don't. To trust anyone is the most foolish thing you can do. I don't even trust myself. I just think it's ridiculous that after years of marriage, after giving these men children, sacrificing our bodies and our careers, we could be left with nothing if *they* decide to walk away. How is that *fair?*'

I imagined FantasyWh0re sliding into Miles's DMs. Offering him a strings-free good time. Then a horrible thought occurred; what if Clem and Jeannie hadn't been talking about Mimi and Tristan's marriage? What if they were talking about my marriage? I felt my stomach turn over. This is exactly why my therapist warned me to stay off those sites – the spiralling.

I reassured myself that if any one of those people had ever had an affair with Miles, you could bet they wouldn't be able to resist posting about it. Whatever was going on was about Mimi and Tristan's marriage, not ours. And, as usual, Mimi was adept at trying to bring me down with her.

'Hang on in there, Mimi,' I said airily, 'just stick it out a bit longer and I'm sure all the pain will be worth the one hundred mill.' I reasoned that she wasn't going to tell me anything, so I might as well get a jab or two in. I'd only regret it later if I didn't seize the opportunity to say how I really felt.

Her head snapped towards me, mouth agape. 'What is your problem, Olivia?'

'*My* problem?' I laughed. '*I* don't have a problem.'

'Yes, you do. You don't exactly hide your contempt for us. Do you think the rest of us don't notice when you write about us in your books?'

'What the hell are you talking about, Mimi?'

She put her tongue in her cheek and raised her eyebrows. 'We're not as oblivious as you think. We read your books. We know you use us as characters.'

I made no reaction, only a blink to give myself away. 'Pffft, no, I don't,' I said, shaking my head unconvincingly.

'Yes, you do. You think I wouldn't notice that the spoiled, covetous orc happened to look suspiciously like me? Even her one-liners are mine. And then you killed her off in the most horrific way you could think of.'

'No,' I protested. 'Jesminda is nothing like you. Nothing whatsoever.'

Mimi arched an eyebrow at me. 'Sure. Whatever you say. And the evil queen isn't based on Jeannie, either, I suppose?'

A smile threatened to play on my lips as I said, 'I have no idea what you're talking about.'

'I'm just saying, you think you're the innocent in all of this, but we all know what you think of us.'

I didn't know what to say. After a moment, she got up to leave.

'Mimi?' I called after her.

She turned, cutting her eyes at me.

'If you've read my latest book, would you consider leaving a review?'

She turned back without saying a word and carried on walking.

'A *good* one?' I shouted after her.

Later that afternoon, a rotund man wearing a flat cap and Barbour jacket knocked at the front door. He whipped the hat off as I opened the door and said, 'Hullo, I'm Jim, George's friend. I'm so sorry for your loss. Is Jeannie in?'

I ushered him in. After a brief conversation with Jeannie, it turned out he was offering us all over to his farm to take part in what George loved to do best – clay-pigeon shooting. A few moments later we were all being frogmarched to put on our coats and hats to go off to Jim's place. There was nothing, *nothing* I wanted to do less than stand in the freezing cold aiming a goddamn rifle at a flying orange disc. But I'd already spent most of the day 'writing', so there was no way Jeannie would let me off the hook. Even the children seemed eager to get out of the house for a moment's distraction from the sombre atmosphere.

Jeannie sat in the front of Jim's weathered Land Rover. The scent of mud and wet dog filled my nostrils as I squeezed into the back between Martha and Beebee. I wasn't sure who'd drawn the short straw, Martha and I in the back of this filthy, stinking car that made my eyes water, or Miles and Callum in the pristine Audi with Tristan, Mimi and Ceecee and an atmosphere you could cut with a spoon.

As I sat in the back watching the countryside roll by in a blur of muted greens and browns, I noticed with excitement the dusting of snow up on the hills. I listened to Jeannie and Jim's easy conversation and wondered if she would ever consider remarrying after George. Of course, it was only three days since his death, but I liked to entertain the idea. Jim seemed like a lovely man, but I knew there was no way Jeannie would ever countenance marriage to someone as nice as him.

After a short drive we reached our destination. The farm was sprawling and picturesque, complete with sagging barns and fields that stretched into the distance under a powder-blue sky. The wind cut through us as we piled out of the vehicles. I stamped my feet on the earth to bring some feeling back to them while Jim handed out equipment – ear protectors, shooting vests and shotguns – with practised ease, his ruddy face creased in a sympathetic smile. 'George was always in his element here. This was his favourite way to spend a winter's afternoon,' he said sadly, then distributed boxes of cartridges like it was Christmas morning. 'He'd have wanted you all to enjoy it.'

'I very much doubt that,' said Callum wryly as he came up behind me. I wracked my brains to think of an occasion when George had spent any time with his grandchildren. Once he'd handed Callum a wad of notes to order 'any takeaway he and Martha wanted', and they'd ordered a Dominos. When George sat down and beheld the circle of baked dough with assorted toppings, he'd acted like he'd never seen something so bizarrely alien in his life. Honestly, a chicken doing the can-can on a bed of rice would have surprised him less than this crazy thing the kids called 'pizza'. That was the extent of their relationship as far as I could tell, and he certainly never showed an interest in taking them shooting.

I smiled at my son in solidarity as, despite the outdoor

chill, the cold metal of the gun began to make my palms sweat. I really ought to have brought some gloves, I lamented. George's farm must have sat higher than Weiss Manor, as I noticed here the ground was peppered with snow, our boots leaving prints as we began to trudge over the terrain.

The wind whipped across the open field, stinging my cheeks and making my eyes water. Jim positioned us in a line, explaining the basics of stance, aim and a quick rundown of safety procedures, to those of us less versed in the sport.

'We'll try one at a time first time round. Right, ready?' he bellowed, and the clay-pigeon trap whirred to life, its mechanical arm poised to launch the first target.

'Pull!' Jeannie's voice rang out, surprising us all. The orange disc arced through the air and, with a resounding crack, she hit it dead centre. Fragments rained down, dusting the snow-speckled grass. A flicker of pride crossed her face. The ear-splitting noise of the first shot made me flinch, my fingers gripping the gun harder. Jeannie, her face set in grim determination, was already poised to shatter her next clay pigeon.

'Pull!' Tristan chimed in this time, taking aim at the second disc. He squinted down the barrel of the shotgun as it sailed through the air, took aim and fired. A moment later, the orange shards cracked, raining down, stark against the white-dusted field.

'Well done, son!' Jim called out; his voice warm with approval. 'George would've been proud.'

'No, he wouldn't,' Martha muttered under her breath to me, rolling her eyes.

'Ready?' Jim called. 'Pull!'

I watched as Martha took her turn, her small frame barely absorbing the shotgun's recoil. The clay disc sailed past, untouched. Jim sidled over and patted her shoulder consolingly, but I could see the disappointment etched on her face. Miles caught her eye and gave her a wink and an encouraging smile.

The fourth clay pigeon was airborne, 'This one's mine,' Miles said, seeing his mother and brother already taking aim when it wasn't their turn. I held my breath as I watched him fire, willing for him to hit it. The disc flew by intact.

'Too bad, big brother, all that city living has ruined your game!' Tristan mocked.

My turn next. I watched the machine whir and fling another clay pigeon.

It sailed through the air. Taking a deep breath, I tracked it with the barrel, imagined it was Tristan's head. I took aim and fired, the gun recoiling into me like a battering ram. My shoulder barked in protest, my back and neck already stiff from years of sitting at a desk. I searched the sky, waiting for what seemed like an eternity as fragments of shot collided with clay and came splintering down.

'I say, bravo, Livvy!' Tristan yelled in surprise.

I rubbed my shoulder and excused myself. I had taken part – that would be all they were getting from me for today. I clicked on the safety catch, walked back to the wooden hut with the gun in my hands, opened the action, and removed the rounds from the chamber, as Jim had shown us.

Placing the gun carefully back on a mount inside the hut, I sat on a little plastic chair and attempted to warm my hands next to a tiny electric heater. I watched out of the window as

Callum took his turn. He aimed and fired, managing to clip the side. Not a total loss.

Beebee and Ceecee were up next. I didn't bother to watch, knowing that they would strike with potent accuracy; shooting had been part of the curriculum at Swanhaven, their prestigious boarding school; the same school that George, Fergus, Quentin, Miles and Tristan had attended. Miles had wanted to provide Callum and Martha with the same education he had benefitted from. However, with our salaries and living in London, we couldn't make it happen. Not without moving nearer the family – *no bloody thank you* – and making some serious cutbacks that would have made for a pretty dry existence. Besides, there was no way I was going to send Callum and Martha away at nine years old.

Jeannie and George believed that it was up to their sons to provide for their own families, and as Tristan schmoozed, crept and cut throats on his way up the corporate ladder, he had been able to 'provide' for his children in a way that Miles had not, thus further cementing pole position as heir to the family fortune.

As the years went by, I couldn't help but see it as a lucky escape. If my children not attending that boarding school meant them avoiding turning out like the four crazy bastards of the family, then I was more than fine with that. It was clear that Beebee and Ceecee hadn't got away unscathed in the unwholesome personality department either. Still, no one was mentioning Quentin, perhaps in the hope that if we all ignored it, the issue would all go away and his appeal would be quashed at the last moment.

'Your turn, Mimi!' Jeannie called.

'Oh gawd, watch your heads, everybody!' Tristan mocked, 'Mimi might look thoroughbred, but beneath all that make-up and the designer clothes I put on her back, she's your standard half-breed. She's got as much chance of hitting the mark as Miles does winning a Nobel Prize!' His laughter reverberated off the hillside, each taunt making the vein in my head throb just that little bit extra.

I would have been shocked at his jibe if I hadn't heard Tristan and Mimi's little tête-à-tête through the bedroom door. His dig at Miles was standard Tristan 'banter'; we were never allowed to be offended because it was just a joke, and our offence proved that we were nothing but snowflakes. Funny how he could dish it out but never take it.

Miles rolled his eyes, 'Fuck off, Tristan.'

I watched as Mimi took a few steps back in preparation for her shot. I frowned as she raised the gun. Her aim was way off, practically pointing in Tristan's direction. Surely, she wasn't going to—

'Pull!' shouted Jim, his eyes already on the skies.

I leaped up from my chair as Mimi aimed.

A crack sounded. Then, a bellowing roar.

Tristan wailed, clutching his hands to his head. I sprinted from the hut over to the group amidst the sounds of Tristan yelling and cussing and turning the air blue.

'Miriam!' Jeannie exclaimed. 'What on *earth* did you do?'

'I-I-I...' Mimi stammered. She waved the gun around in confusion. The kids ducked out of the way and Miles strode over to her, plucking the gun out of her hands before she could do any more damage.

I got to the group, woefully out of breath. Tristan was on

his knees, blood pouring from his head, leaving splatters in the snow next to him.

'You stupid fucking *idiot!*' he raged.

I sidled up to him. 'Here, let me see.' I attempted to pull his hand away, but it was stuck there like a limpet. 'Just let me see it, Tristan,' I demanded.

He shakily took his hand away. The top of his ear looked to be missing, and pieces of shot had grazed the side of his head, but there didn't seem to be significant damage. *Shame*, the twisted little voice in my head sneered. I walked back to Mimi.

'You'll be fine,' I said over my shoulder to Tristan. 'Miles, you drive Tristan's car to the hospital. Jim, would you mind taking the five of us back to the house?'

Jim nodded, his face drawn, clearly mortified and worried that he was about to get slapped with a lawsuit.

'H-hospital?' Tristan asked, going deathly pale.

'You need your ear cleaned up and bandaged. They might need to give you antibiotics.' I put my arm around a shaking Mimi and led her back down the field towards Jim's Land Rover.

'You dumb fucking bitch!' Tristan yelled after her. 'You did that on purpose!'

Mimi upped her pace, trying to put as much distance between them as possible. Jeannie stormed after her. 'My God, Miriam, you could've killed him! What were you thinking?'

Mimi shook from head to toe. 'It was an accident,' she managed.

Was it? I had to wonder after our conversation this morning. Because it looked to me like she just decided to shoot her husband at point-blank range in front of all of us. And if she did, well then, that just made me love her a little bit.

'Do you know,' I said to her as the snow began to fall with more urgency, 'I had no idea that Mimi was short for Miriam?'

6

OH, CHRISTMAS TREE, OH, CHRISTMAS TREE!

13th December 2025

Lady Luck was truly on my side today. Snow! And then we were invited out to the shooting range by Jim who couldn't believe what rotten luck we were having. How sad for us all that poor old George – the miserly curmudgeon – had finally popped his clogs – and so close to Christmas, too.

Quite a nippy day to be standing out in an open field, though. The clay pigeons were launched and POP! That pompous ass was shot in the head, splatting the freshly fallen snow like a Jackson Pollock. Very festive.

I'll make sure I get him next time.

J eannie and the kids had long gone to bed by the time Tristan and Miles had finished up at the hospital. I'd waited up for them, and as the snow came down outside in flurries, I read by the fire with Gloria sleeping at my side.

'My God.' Miles ran his hands down his face as he fell back into the sofa.

'How's Tristan?' I leaned forward and put my book down on the coffee table so I could give Miles my full attention. 'Where is he?'

'He'll be fine. He's gone back to their house. He said he couldn't face coming back here to Mimi.'

I screwed my nose up. 'Really? But it was just an accident. She seems pretty cut up about it.'

He levelled his gaze at me. 'He doesn't seem to think so.'

'Really?' I laughed a little. 'Of course it was,' I insisted, even though I had wondered the same thing. 'Mimi didn't mean to shoot him, she's just an incredibly shit shot.'

'That's what I said. He's adamant she did it on purpose though, and he said he couldn't be in the same room as her, otherwise he "didn't know what he would do".' Tristan gestured air quotes and shook his head.

'What?' I said, flabbergasted. 'Did he elaborate?'

'Not exactly, he wouldn't tell me what's going on there… As you know, we're not exactly close. But whatever is going on with them, it isn't good. It sounds like they might be heading for divorce.'

'*Interesting*,' I said, more to myself than to Miles.

'Is it? Why?' he asked, although his tone suggested that he didn't care one jot about the state of his brother's marriage. 'Do you know something?'

'Not specifics. But I overheard your mum and Aunt Clem

talking in the kitchen. Jeannie was telling Aunt Clem to keep her mouth shut around Grandma Toots... Then Aunt Clem said, "But what if they get a divorce?".'

'Oh, right.' I watched Miles carefully, but he gave no other reaction.

'Juicy huh?'

'I guess...'

I barked a laugh. 'What do you mean, you guess? I'd say this trip has just livened up.'

Miles shrugged. 'I guess it's mildly entertaining, my brother being shot by his wife ... but I could have done without the seven hours in A&E. It would have been longer, but Tristan started throwing his weight around and said that he was in the same class as one of the consultants... Insufferable prick.'

Gloria got up and left the room, our conversation clearly disturbing her sleep.

Miles noticed my expression and sat up. 'Sorry, I don't mean to be a grumpy sod. It's just, there's always some drama or other with them... Do you remember when she caught him in the hot tub in Mexico?'

I grimaced. 'How could I forget? The hookers in the hot tub. It's all anyone could talk about for the next two Christmases.'

'*Exactly*. All anyone does around here is talk about them. It used to be a fun bit of gossip but now... I just can't wait to get away from all the bullshit. I just can't bring myself to care about *them* and their marriage. They're awful, Liv.'

'Can't argue with that,' I said smiling. 'And please, don't apologise. You're not grumpy. I'm the awful wife who's gossiping about your family when you've just suffered the loss of your father.'

Miles stared into the distance. I searched his face for some sign of what he was feeling, and I could practically see the wall of impenetrable iron sliding up and leaving me alone on the other side. 'Do you want to talk about anything? About what happened to your dad?'

He continued staring ahead of him, not seeming to hear me. I ran my hand through his hair, and his attention snapped to me. He slowly traced his hand up my thigh. He leaned in close, brushing his lips across my ear.

'I don't want to talk about my father. I won't say I'm glad he's dead. Of course I'm not *glad*. But right now, the only thing I feel towards him is resentment. I'm resentful that he never took the time to be a good father to me or Tristan. And as for my brother and his vacuous wife,' he whispered, '*fuck 'em.*'

I turned to face him, so close we shared a breath.

'Yeah. *Fuck 'em,*' I breathed into him.

He slid to the ground, kneeling before me, and began unbuttoning my jeans.

God, I sincerely hoped Jeannie had a camera installed in here too.

The next morning the entire Weiss clan was herded to the Christmas-tree farm. The atmosphere was fully charged by the time we arrived, and steam practically rose off Aunt Clementine; she'd had to drive Uncle Fergus because he was too inebriated to do so himself. We walked down long rows of fat pine trees, thin pine trees, barely-hanging-in-there pine trees, lying-atop-one-another-like-they'd-had-a-heavy-night pine trees. Forty minutes of pointing out 'perfect' trees to Jeannie, and as per every year, none of them was 'the one'.

'I *told* you all we should have come here days ago; all of the best ones are gone!' Jeannie cursed as she stormed along. 'We might as well just wedge a branch into a stand and call it a year,' she grumbled, kicking a pinecone out of her way like a petulant child.

Uncle Fergus lit up a cigar, smoke curling into the frosty air. 'Best part of Christmas, the holidays,' he drawled, swaying slightly. 'Getting a little mulled cider in the hut after tramping around in the cold!'

Aunt Clementine snorted and pulled her scarf tighter. 'Speak for yourself,' she muttered.

Jeannie stopped short in front of a pleasant-enough-looking fir and crossed her arms. 'This is hopeless.'

Fergus staggered in her wake, tossing his barely smoked cigar butt into the snow. 'Let's get a drink,' he said as he changed course in the direction of the wooden huts.

'I'll find you a tree, Mother!' Tristan yelled as he raced ahead, determined to be the victor. The poor thing was soldiering on with his bandaged ear – which he dutifully only mentioned every hour or so. Miles had told me that once the nurse had cleaned the blood away, only the tiniest slither of ear was missing – he said you could barely notice it. The doctor did say, however, that Tristan might have permanently lost his hearing on that side. Which unfortunately for the rest of us meant that his obnoxious voice was louder than ever before.

Tristan had already got his story lined up for the guys at work; a dud cartridge that went off that could've killed him. I couldn't help myself when I chipped in, 'To be honest, Tristan, no story is better than your wife shooting you at point-blank range – I'd have gone with that one.' It earned a few disgusted looks from the family, despite my protestations that it was just a joke.

Mimi had hitched a ride with us, and she and Tristan were avoiding each other like the plague. According to Aunt Clem, he was still adamant that she had intended to kill him. But if she *had* intended to kill him, would she just casually shoot him in front of his entire family? Perhaps she just wanted to hurt him a little? Perhaps she just lost it for a second, thinking of all that sweet cash fluttering away with his cheating conniving little antics? Either way, I couldn't entirely blame her; if Tristan was my husband I'd want to blow his head off, too. There was one thing I knew for certain; I would now forever be looking over my shoulder whenever Mimi was around.

I thought about how angry she had seemed when we spoke in the pool room, mentioning infidelity and how she would get nothing if he were to leave her. Perhaps she thought she had nothing to lose? Perhaps when he called her a 'standard half-breed' she lost it? Or maybe her arms were just super weak? But that's a crazy idea because I could have sworn she said she did Pilates. Perhaps it was a warning shot, like, 'call me a half-breed again and I'll blow your brains out'? Because, let's be honest, it's pretty hard to miss someone with a shotgun at that range. If she'd really intended to kill him it would have been easy, even for a novice. Just imagine if she'd shot him... We'd have been finding bits of his brain in crevices we didn't even know we had.

We walked two by two down the rows of firs. We had seen them all twice over and still none had made the cut.

'So, Martha,' said Fergus, dangerously swaying into her. 'Have you got a boyfriend?'

I did a sharp intake of breath. *Here we go.*

'I have a girlfriend, actually,' Martha, her voice carrying across the whole line. I saw Jeannie momentarily stop in her tracks, before giving her head a little shake. I gritted my teeth at her back. The problem wasn't Martha telling them about her sexuality. Miles and I were truly happy with whatever the children did; if they were happy, we were happy. No, the issue was my reaction to the family's reaction. That was the headache I was truly trying to avoid. I was always on high alert when it came to the kids, watching and waiting as the cortisol rushed through my veins at the notion of any of them disrespecting my children.

I looked just in time to see Tristan nudging Beebee as he said something that made her snicker conspiratorially.

Beebee made a joke that I didn't catch, causing Tristan to guffaw.

Ceecee followed behind them, her comment loud enough to float to my ears. 'No surprises there, have you seen her shoes?' The three of them laughed as my nails bit into my palms and I clenched my jaw so tightly, I thought I might crack a tooth.

Fergus gawped at her like she had a scorpion on her shoulder. '*Girlfriend?*' he spluttered.

'Yep, her name's Sarah. You'd love her, she's fit AF,' Martha answered, her grin stretching from ear to ear. She pulled her phone out to show him her screensaver. 'But no letching, Uncle Fergus, she's mine.' He spluttered in offence. Well, I consoled myself, at least their reactions made her smile. And at least Toots was in the tea room so couldn't say anything about it. Small mercies.

The twins broke away to scout for the perfect place to film a TikTok dance. Callum went off to the farmers' shop, while Martha went to look at the potted plants, her goofy smile still stuck firmly across her face. Miles headed off to see if he could find signal anywhere to send an email.

I heard Tristan asking a staff member where he could find the twelve-footers, and a young man explaining that none of the pre-cut ones were that tall. He'd have to walk further on to the planted trees and call someone over to cut it down for him.

Snow began falling steadily, to the sounds of 'ooohs' and 'ahhhhs' from other families. It was an almost picture-perfect scene – picking Christmas trees in the snow.

Already cold and muddy, the remainder of the group split; some going to the farm shop, others going for a toilet break, all deciding that we would meet back up in half an hour in the wooden barn where the outlandishly priced sandwiches, dry cakes and mulled wine were being served.

After a wander around the stalls that were selling fresh garlands and wreaths, I spotted some discounted spring bulbs. I perused the packets, wondering whether irises and daffodils would grow in Australia's climate, before I remembered there was no way I'd be allowed to take them. Such a shame, they would have been a lovely reminder of England... I shrugged and bought them anyway. Perhaps I could give them to Jeannie.

After moseying around, I headed inside the barn, where the warmth from the overhead heaters and the scent of cinnamon and pine needles mingling with the aroma of bitter coffee grounds made a welcome relief. With no tables large enough to accommodate our group, I decided to get a few drinks while I waited for the others.

Standing in line, I heard Aunt Clem's shrill voice somewhere in the crowd, admonishing Fergus to go to the bathroom and splash some cold water on his face. I saw her then make her way over to Jeannie.

I wondered if Fergus's increased consumption of alcohol was due to the news that Tristan was to become executor of the will. Tristan and Mimi wouldn't be parted with a dime of their inheritance – especially not to Fergus and Clementine, whom they deemed to be money-grabbing scroungers. The irony.

I paid for the eye-wateringly expensive drinks and reluctantly headed over to where Jeannie and Clem were standing, unable to spot anyone else in the family. I clutched the rims of four plastic cups between my hands while the heated fumes from the mulled wine singed my fingers, and stopped behind them, resting the cups on an upturned barrel. Neither of them noticed me: a running theme, it seemed. Again, they were too absorbed in whatever they were gossiping about.

I hung back for a moment, waving my hands to cool them, when I heard Jeannie's angry protestations.

'I've *told* you, it is a vile, vicious rumour, Clementine, and if I hear you breathe one word of it to *anyone*, I will be forced to tell Toots what you did with her money. Do you understand me?'

'I haven't breathed a word!' Clem's voice was shriller than ever. 'But it's hardly a secret, everyone's heard about it...'

'There has never been any infidelity, nor will there ever be. I raised my sons as gentlemen.'

Err, hello, Mexico?

I considered joining them and asking outright what they were talking about. But knowing Jeannie, that tactic was a complete nonstarter.

Jeannie leaned in closer to Clem. 'Now, keep your mouth shut, if you know what's good for you. Got it?'

My mind raced as they stood there in silence. I had never heard Jeannie speaking like that to anyone, and Clem looked visibly shaken. After a few moments, I picked up the cups and brought them over, schooling my face into a banal smile.

'Here we are,' I said. 'Be careful, they're quite hot.'

'Oh, thank you, dear,' she said, taking a cup. 'Clem, shouldn't you go and check on Fergus? He's been gone rather a long time.'

'Hmm? Oh – oh yes, of course.' Clem nodded, avoiding eye contact with me as she grabbed one of the mulled wines and left me alone with Jeannie. An uncomfortable silence settled over us as we sipped the steaming, sharp wine. My mind was reeling from what I'd overheard. Infidelity? It was Tristan and Mimi they were talking about ... right? And what was that about Clem spending Toots's money?

As if reading my mind, Jeannie said, 'Clem and Fergus are having a bit of trouble with money again. Nothing new there.'

'Ah, that's a shame,' I said, taking a sip of wine and burning my tongue.

'It's not a shame, they are both totally feckless.' She took a sip of wine and winced; this was not the sort of wine Jeannie was accustomed to. 'Miles said the house is sold now?'

'Yes,' I smiled.

'House sales fall through all the time though, don't they...' she said, glancing towards the barn doors.

I let out a breathy laugh. 'Well, let's hope not.'

Jeannie opened her mouth to say something when Miles burst through the barn doors, his cheeks flushed. 'Help!' he cried breathlessly. 'We need help! Someone with phone signal!'

All heads turned to Miles as I rushed towards him.

'Miles, what's wrong? Where are the kids?' I looked behind him but couldn't see them. Miles held my arms, eyes wide. 'Call an ambulance, quickly!'

I pulled out my phone from my pocket, but no signal. Miles swore ferociously, looking around for anyone who could help.

'Where's Fergus?' demanded Jeannie. 'Is he causing a scene?'

'No. No, it's not Fergus. Don't go out there,' he said to Jeannie. 'Promise me, Liv, that you won't go out there.' He ran to the till to ask the girl behind the counter to use the phone.

Jeannie and I looked at each other, deciding at the same time we weren't going to stand idly around. Heading out of the barn, there was no one to be seen. Through the windows to the shop, people chatted casually, but I couldn't see anyone in the family. Further over was a small orangery-cum-tearoom where we could see Toots sat sipping tea on her own, completely in her element.

We headed towards the maze of Christmas trees, zigzagging through the lines, until we reached the end that led out towards the field. More trees. And a hundred yards away, a group of people. We trotted over the spongy, wet pine needles, I broke into a run whilst Jeannie straggled behind.

With a pounding heart, I approached the group of people. They were all gathered around a perfectly shaped twelve-foot blue spruce, their faces pale and serious. Next to the tree sat a large piece of machinery. A man strode away from the vehicle, turned his back to us and subsequently hurled his guts up into the snow.

I slowed my pace. I could see someone lying in the snow – a pair of feet … legs. I walked closer, squinting to make sense of what I was looking at. Smart, brown outdoor boots, a pair of blue jeans. A red sticky substance. Chips of wood, sawdust. My feet took me closer.

'Don't look, love,' said a large woman, pulling me away. My stomach dropped. Those boots. They were Tristan's. I couldn't see more than that. I glanced over at the machine the farm used to cut down the trees, blood sprayed out around it.

I stumbled backwards and collided with Jeannie. I whirled around, trying to block her view. Her eyes went wide, skimming over my face and past my shoulder to the scene behind me.

'Is that—' she started, but her voice failed.

I nodded, dumbly. Jeannie let out a sharp gasp and pressed her hand to her mouth. The rest of the family was nowhere to be seen. I held her firmly and tried to lead her away.

'This can't be happening…' Jeannie managed.

I shook my head, trying to keep myself from shaking all over. This couldn't be real.

Clem appeared then, looking frantic and dishevelled. Her eyes darted between us and the growing crowd. 'What on earth is happening? I saw Fergus run past me like he'd seen a ghost!'

'My boy!' Jeannie croaked. 'My boy is dead!'

7

SNOW, LIES AND SURVEILLANCE

14th December 2025

Went to that pitiful Christmas-tree farm we go to every year where the Nordmann firs are already half dead by the beginning of December. Tristan had to select one still planted in the ground, the pre-cut ones were too shabby. Forever the gent with the can-do attitude, Tristan was straight in there taking over everything.

While everyone was distracted, I managed to sneak away and put on a face mask used by the farm workers, as well as finding a green overcoat and hard hat in one of the nearby sheds. I trailed him, and he soon called me over when he found the tree he liked, thinking I worked there. I kept my head down low, got into the nearby vehicle used to cut down the trees and started it up. He could barely hear me anyway, what with one eardrum out of action. He bent down low, examining the base of the tree and I put my foot down. He barely had time to turn before I accidentally rammed the saw straight into him. I had meant to cut the tree down, I swear.

It had been a long time coming for that lying, cheating son of a bitch.

I managed to wrestle Jeannie away from the scene before she could see the full extent of the gore.

Miles ran like a madman trying to locate Mimi and the girls. He found Mimi first, standing next to her car in the car park. He told me she didn't even speak to him as black tracks of mascara snaked down her cheeks, and she clutched her phone to her ear. He said whoever she was talking to, she was begging them to help her, asking if she could come and stay with them.

He found Beebee and Ceecee shortly after. When he informed them what had happened to their father, I was sure everyone in a five-mile radius could hear Beebee's chilling wails echoing throughout the countryside. She fought like a wildcat to see her father, unable to believe what she was being told. The outburst seemed to snap Jeannie out of her shell-shocked state. Suddenly, she was aware of the very public scene unfolding, and donning her PR hat with terrifying speed, she forced Mimi and the twins into a taxi and back to the house. Ceecee's eyes were wide as she was bundled into the backseat, there were no tears, and for once she seemed at a loss for words.

The police had inquired amongst the staff who had been responsible for cutting down the trees and operating the machinery. Only two members of staff operated the tree cutter, and both were taking their lunch break together at the time and had several other members of staff to corroborate.

Of course, most of the employees were quite young, and no one would want to admit they might have accidentally just mown down a customer instead of a Douglas fir.

Jeannie kept muttering like a woman possessed about how these children barely out of their mother's womb were probably looking at their phones or listening to their podcasts instead of keeping their wits about them, and that she and Artie Peverill were going to sue the farm owner so thoroughly that this would be the last Christmas he'd remember what it was like to have a pot to piss in. The kids and I stayed with her, watching her hands unfurling and clenching again as she ran through all the things she was going to do to whoever was responsible for the accident.

Once the police and an ambulance arrived to take Tristan away, I drove Toots, Jeannie and the kids back to the house, watching Miles recede in the rear-view mirror as he spoke to the officers. They had taken the names and numbers of everyone there and assured us they would be in touch to begin to conduct a full-scale investigation.

Jeannie kept referring to it as a terrible *bloody* accident. I wanted to ask her if she thought it was a terrible *bloody* murder, but I thought that might be a tad inappropriate at this early stage.

The ride home was eerily quiet. Jeannie stared blankly out of the passenger window, her face pale. In the backseat, the kids gave each other furtive glances; even Callum didn't have his earphones in, as if even that was too much, given the gravity of the situation. I didn't notice how hard I was clenching the wheel until my fingers began to tingle. Toots had said only one thing: *I knew this was going to happen*. I don't know what the hell she meant by that, but I couldn't help but think it would have been good of her to warn us if she thought her grandson was going to get run through with a saw blade.

Jeannie looked like she was going to throttle her, so I dropped Toots back at the residential home, which she seemed pretty content with. Toots got out and slammed the door of the car, trotting up the path to the home like we'd just dropped her back after a few hours at Sainsbury's.

Classic Weiss behaviour.

They were like something out of the early twentieth century, like the passengers on the *Titanic* who didn't want to don lifebelts because they would cover up their bejewelled ensembles, or the royal family turning away their Russian relatives because they didn't want to compromise their position. A time that, although Toots didn't live through most of it, was referred to by her as 'the good old days'. It had taken me the best part of eighteen years to get my head around this family, and they still continued to surprise me. Sometimes I even envied their stiff upper lip… Until I realised how it drove them all batshit insane bottling up their emotions like that.

I barely remembered arriving back at Weiss Manor. As we pulled into the driveway, I noticed Mrs Harlow was upstairs, peering out at us from the curtains. We clambered out of the car and once we were inside the house, we stood staring at each other in the foyer, dumbstruck for the second time in two days. Each of us entirely at a loss as to what to do or say.

'I'm going upstairs,' Jeannie said, her voice sounding very far away, 'I need to lie down.'

The kids' faces looked drawn. They hadn't seen *it*, thank God… Hadn't seen their uncle lying there… I wasn't even sure what I was looking at myself. I couldn't stop my mind from trying to piece together the puzzle of clothes, flaps of skin and blood. I felt the mulled wine making its way back up my oesophagus, so I tried to pretend I was my badass orc warrior general and thought about what she would do upon seeing one of her own slaughtered. She would hunt down the killer, execute an impressive shield-hook, turning into a forward flip before smashing their skull in with her mace and spitting on their corpse. Not something I was probably going to pull off in this scenario, but it was a fun way to prevent myself from going mad. I quickly compartmentalised whatever it was I had seen in the 'lock it up and throw away the key' storage area of my brain.

I hugged Callum and Martha tightly before telling them to go and watch TV, lie down, play on their consoles, do anything to take their minds off what had just happened. I promised I'd bring everyone tea and biscuits. Tea and biscuits would solve sweet FA, but it would at least give the illusion for a second or two that things weren't completely and utterly out of control.

I headed towards the kitchen like a ghost, unhearing and unseeing. I busied myself with the kettle, grateful for a mundane task to occupy my hands and mind. The clink of mugs and spoons seemed unnaturally loud within the oppressive silence of the house. As I waited for the water to boil, I caught sight of my reflection in the kitchen window. Someone was standing right behind me.

The china cup I was holding dropped from my hands, smashing on the floor. I whirled around to see Mrs Harlow standing there.

'Mrs Harlow,' I breathed, 'you scared me!'

Mrs Harlow stared at the cup. 'Oh dear, that was one of Jeannie's best sets,' she said, stooping to pick up the pieces.

'Let me do it,' I said as I bent down to help her.

'Is it true?' she said in a hushed tone, 'about Tristan? Is he … is he dead?'

I reached to pick up a particularly jagged piece of bone china.

'Who told you?'

'I just saw Martha looking white as a sheet,' Mrs Harlow whispered, eyes glittering. 'How?'

I looked around to make sure Jeannie hadn't appeared before whispering as quietly as I could, 'The machinery they use to cut the trees … there was a terrible accident.' It was all I could manage to say. It didn't feel real. Even saying it seemed ridiculous and like I had somehow got my wires crossed.

Mrs Harlow grimaced.

'It was so awful, Mrs Harlow.'

Her mouth hung open slightly, her eyes searching as she took in the news of the death of a man she had taken care of since he was a boy.

'Here.' She gathered the rest of the pieces and put them in the bin. 'If Mrs Weiss asks, I'll tell her I broke it. I don't want you getting the blame. I will stay up tonight, no doubt it will be a sleepless one for her. I will help with anything she might need … with anything any of you might need.'

I wasn't surprised by Mrs Harlow's kindness; she'd worked here for thirty-five years and the Weiss family must have felt like her own. I knew she'd always had a soft spot for Miles; he'd told me that she saw him as her own son.

I finished up making the tea and placed everything on a tray. Mrs Harlow took up a china teacup and a plate for Jeannie while I went and found the kids sat close together on the sofa, which was a rarer event than finding unicorn poo. I lit a fire and sat next to them, pulling them closer to me. We sat like that for I don't know how long.

I watched the window, the snow outside coming down thick and fast.

After a while, Jeannie floated in, perching herself on the edge of her seat, hands folded in her lap, her gaze fixed on some invisible point in the distance. I sat up, pouring out another tea from the pot, and gently placed a cup in her hands.

'I … um…' she began before shaking her head, either forgetting or unable to say what she was thinking.

We, too, found ourselves rendered speechless. The whole thing was unprecedented. Yesterday, Tristan had nearly had his head blown off, and today he was dead. It was hard to chalk those two occurrences up to coincidence. Mimi was currently at the police station, and apparently it had been completely against her will. Miles and an officer had had to convince her to go – she'd been planning on getting in the car and driving God knows where. Hell, I wanted to drive God knows where. Anywhere but here. I wasn't sure what I expected to happen, perhaps I assumed that we would all go home again. Or maybe that's what I'd hoped. I imagined what the officers would think when they found out about the events at Jim's farm…

'They'll want to go and see him, of course,' Jeannie said absent-mindedly.

'Who will, Jeannie?'

'The girls. When he's up for visitors.'

It was so hard not to make a face. Was she referring to the chapel of rest? I had seen enough of Tristan's injuries to assume that the twins wouldn't be too keen. But hey, what did I know.

'And when he's able, he can come home and rest in bed, and we will all be together for Christmas as planned.'

It took us a moment to realise what Jeannie had said. The kids and I shot alarmed looks at one another. I opened my mouth to say something, but no words came out.

'Grandma,' Martha said softly, coming to my rescue, 'Uncle Tristan ... he's not coming back.'

'Of course he's coming back,' said Jeannie, as if what Martha had said was truly absurd.

Callum said slowly but gently, 'Uncle Tristan ... he's – he's not coming back, Grandma. He's gone.'

What did I do to raise such brave kids, doing the job of an adult when even their own mother couldn't pluck up the courage to speak?

Jeannie blinked a few times.

'No ... we don't know that yet until the doctors have seen him. There must be something they can do.' She put her cup down on the coffee table, stood up and brushed herself down. 'So much to do. So so much to do. I must find Mrs Harlow...' And with that she was out of the room, leaving the kids and me gawking at each other.

The kids and I waited hours for Miles, Mimi and the girls to return. We were relieved when we saw headlights wending up the driveway, winking through the snow flurries. But it turned out to be Clem and Fergus, who had picked up Toots on their way. They held Toots by the arms to steady her as she ascended the steps, the snow coming down harder than ever. I pulled my phone out and tried to call Miles again. He must have had thirteen missed calls from me. My heart raced as one thought kept going around in my head: what if Miles had been bending down at the base of that tree? What if, in one moment, he'd been taken from me? I wanted to tear the walls down until I got back to him again.

Night had fallen and everyone had gone to bed by the time they arrived, wipers swiping frantically to keep the snow off. A moment later, I heard the crunching of tyres on snow, and Mimi and the twins pulled up behind him. Miles trudged up the steps, his face grim and exhausted. Snowflakes clung to his coat and hair.

'Oh, my God, Miles, are you okay?' I said as I ran to him and flung my arms around him. I held him tight to me, vowing that I would never let him out of my sight again. I kissed his face and felt the snowflakes melting underneath my lips. 'What happened?' I whispered urgently as he stepped inside.

Miles shook his head wearily. 'The police had a lot of questions. I told them everything I saw, which wasn't much. They say it was an accident. A terrible, dreadful accident. It just seems so... It's so hard to...'

'They're treating it as an accident?' I didn't know if I was shocked or relieved to hear that.

'For now,' he said gravely. 'Then when we got to the bridge, it was practically impassable. I had to shift mounds of snow off it in order for us to pass.' He looked ashen, suddenly older than his years.

'Come on,' I said, leading him to sit down next to the fire. I snatched a blanket from the back of the couch and draped it over his shoulders. Wordlessly, he sat, locks of his hair falling over his face, the snow melting and dripping onto his nose. I enclosed him in my arms, squeezing him tight like my body alone could protect him from the fact that his brother and his father had died within such a short space of time. I kept him close to me until I felt him stop shivering.

I left Miles briefly to make him a hot toddy. I boiled the kettle and searched the downstairs rooms for Mimi and the twins to see if I could get them anything, but they had wordlessly gone up to their rooms. Back in the sitting room, I poured a good measure of whisky into a crystal tumbler and handed it to Miles. He looked up gratefully and threw it back in two gulps. I took it from him and refilled it.

'How's Mother?' he asked eventually. 'And the kids?'

'The kids are understandably shaken. Your mum is … in shock.' I didn't want to alarm him unnecessarily; I was sure she'd realise soon that Tristan wasn't coming back. 'So, the police… They will be back soon to ask more questions?'

Miles nodded, his eyes deeply set in the shadows from the fire. 'For now. There's only CCTV of the car park, but they know everyone who went in and out. God knows how they'll get back to us with all this snow though. They did seem concerned'—he stopped, looking towards the door, and then lowered his voice—'about what happened yesterday.'

'You told them about Mimi shooting him?' I whispered.

'The girls told them, apparently. They were going to find out, anyway; they would have found out from his hospital records.'

'True,' I agreed. 'God, poor Mimi, her husband's dead, and now she's going to have to explain that one away.'

Miles fixed me with a stare, his voice low. 'Do you think it was an accident?'

'Well, it has to be, doesn't it?' I laughed nervously.

'Could it just be a coincidence that my father and brother die a few days apart from each other?' he said darkly as he drained his second whisky. 'That's the nature of coincidences, I suppose.'

I stood up and headed over to him. I placed my hands in his thick, wavy hair and kissed his forehead. 'I'm so, so sorry my darling. I really am.'

His eyes were heavy as he looked up at me.

'Come on,' I said. 'You head up, I'll close everything up for the night.'

Twenty minutes later, I entered the bedroom and found Miles passed out fully clothed on top of the bed. I crept over to him, the light casting my long shadow across the wall. I tiptoed across and dimmed the switch on the lamp. Carefully undoing the laces of his boots, I slid one off and then started on the other. The left foot was more difficult, and I paused for a moment as he began to stir. When I was sure I wasn't going to wake him, I started pulling again, successfully yanking it off after the third heave.

Neatly placing them near the door, I was about to start getting ready for bed when I noticed dried blood on the toe and rim of both boots. I stared at it for a moment, before carefully picking them up again, taking them into the bath-room and methodically washing them in the sink.

The water swirled pink as it circled the drain, and I scrubbed until the leather was saturated. When I returned, Miles hadn't moved a muscle, his breaths low and steady. I placed the boots back and slipped under the covers beside him.

But sleep didn't come easily. The wind howled outside, battering the house with thick sheets of snow, and my mind whirled with unanswered questions.

8

MURDER, SHE MIGHT HAVE WRITTEN

The next morning, the world felt eerily silent; muffled under layers of fresh snowfall that clung thickly to every surface, four foot high now. The fire had gone out in the hearth, leaving only the ashy smell of extinguished warmth.

Miles spent all morning outside shovelling, in a vain attempt to cut a path towards the gates. He barely made it a quarter of the way before the snow started again, filling in the progress he'd made. I ordered him inside after two hours as it was clear no one would be leaving any time soon.

As Miles stomped his boots clean in the mudroom, I could see the exhaustion etched on his face. His cheeks were red from the biting cold, his breath still coming out in visible puffs.

'The weather app says there's more snow to come,' he said shaking his head, 'at least two days of it.'

In the kitchen, I handed him a steaming mug of coffee, which he accepted gratefully. 'We're just going to have to wait it out,' I replied, trying to keep the worry from my voice. Through the frosted windows, all I could see was white – an endless expanse of snow that seemed to mock our attempts at escape.

We made our way to the living room, where the fireplace had been freshly stocked and was crackling merrily, a picture-perfect scene so at odds with the events of the last seventy-two hours.

Toots sat in the armchair, her thin frame wrapped in an enormous, expensive-looking tartan scarf, her thickly framed glasses making her eyes appear five times their actual size. She sat surveying Martha and Callum, who were decorating a Christmas tree. Callum looked over at me wearily.

'Mrs Harlow found an artificial tree in the attic… Grandma said we should decorate it.' The kids shared an awkward glance, slightly bewildered expressions on their faces.

'I won't have moping,' Jeannie said, coming into the room holding a huge wreath in her arms. She walked over to the mantelpiece and draped it over the top. 'There,' she said proudly. 'I'll do the banisters next.'

'Mother…' Miles started. 'Are you—' He was clearly at a loss what to say next… *Are you okay? Are you sure you should be doing that?* In the end he just said, 'Is there anything we can do for you?' If we didn't have an audience, I would have kicked him in the shin. She'd find something for us to do all right, and I already had a ton of stuff I needed to be getting on with.

'You can make a start on tonight's dinner while Mrs Harlow trims the verge. It's a beef casserole, just cut up the carrots, onions, mushrooms and potatoes – they should be in the pantry. I'll see to the rest.'

I watched as Miles nodded, resigned, and made his way to the kitchen. The normalcy of Jeannie's actions felt surreal, almost jarring, given the circumstances. But perhaps this was her way of coping, of maintaining some semblance of control in a situation that had seemingly spiralled into unforeseen tragedy.

Toots cleared her throat, drawing our attention. 'It's just like the Christmas of 1962,' she said, her voice creaking like old floorboards. 'Snowed in for days we were. Your grandfather insisted on decorating, said it would keep our spirits up. Here, Martha, there's a big empty patch in the middle.' A gnarled finger rose from under her layers and pointed towards the tree.

Martha paused in her tree decorating, a glittery bauble dangling from her fingers, before putting it where she'd been instructed.

'So, my dear, what's this I hear about you being a *lesbian?*' Toots pierced Martha with a look of disdain.

'Grandmother—' Miles started.

'It's okay, Dad,' said Martha breezily. 'Yes, Great-Grandma,' she added, her back straight as she smiled for the first time today. 'I am gay. I have a girlfriend; her name is Sarah.' She fixed Toots with an unflinching gaze and I marvelled at her. How the hell had I raised such a brilliant, confident young woman? I hadn't; the truth was, this was all completely her. I'd always been a bit of a wallflower, so to see the emergence of this fiery, fearless queen was astonishing. I had never been more in awe of my daughter than in this moment.

She plucked another bauble of out the box and filled another gap. Toots shook her head and mumbled her disapproval. Miles studied me, the way my eyes were blazing as I looked at Toots, readying myself to say something. Maybe I could sometimes be accused of being a wallflower, but not when it came to Callum and Martha.

He pulled at my arm. 'Martha's got this,' he said under his breath. 'Look at her.'

I looked. Martha was smiling darkly as she plumped out the branches to make them fuller. She was getting a kick out of seeing the family's reaction. She truly seemed to be enjoying ruffling their feathers.

Toots's instructions alongside the soft crackling of the fire were all that could be heard as we left to prepare the stew. The house felt paused in time, as if the bricks themselves and everything and everyone within bated their breath, for what had been and what was yet to come.

I helped Miles with the preparation, gathering the vegetables from the bracingly cold pantry and hauling them over to the sink to be washed. As I took out the carrots and potatoes from their hessian sacks, I contemplated how, despite my best efforts, the trip had indeed turned out to be a 'working holiday'. As I held the veggies under the running water, an unwelcome flashback of Miles's bloodied boots entered my mind. I shook my head, batting the image away. Of course his boots would have Tristan's blood on them; he was one of the first on the scene, he would have walked all over those scattered, contaminated pine needles. *How did the blood get on the toes of the boots, though?*

I began peeling the potatoes, feeling like we'd found

ourselves in the midst of some war that I didn't understand the rules of. I slashed at their skins as if the peeler was my weapon against these trumped-up crazies who couldn't even handle death in a healthy way … whatever 'healthy' meant. Crying? Screaming? Tearing at their clothes in the snow? I don't know what I expected of them. Maybe just a little more emotion would have made me feel less on edge. I handed the naked spuds to Miles, who was stationed at the chopping board, lost deep in thought. He didn't seem to notice I'd been murdering the Maris Pipers as he reached for the knife block. Then his hand paused, wavering.

'Have you seen the chopping knife?' he asked.

I looked over at the block. Indeed, the bread knife and the smaller ones were present, but a vacant slot sat where the long knife was usually held.

'Check the dishwasher?' I said, still distracted by yesterday's events.

After searching, Miles shrugged it off and used one of the smaller knives from the block instead.

'Do you think my mother's okay?' he asked, struggling to cut through the large potato with the small knife.

'Well, no. But that's to be expected. Her husband and son have died within days of each other,' I checked behind me to make sure she wasn't there. I dropped my voice low. 'And she's never learned how to deal with her emotions, so she's trying to "keep calm and carry on." And this isn't the tough part, the tough part is when we all leave, and she's alone in this huge house.'

Miles nodded, sadly. 'Despite our issues, I don't like the idea of her being alone.'

I nodded in understanding. 'And how are you feeling? I mean – obviously, it's awful but...'

'I feel strange, Detached, almost. I think the only thing I feel is regret. Regret that I didn't have a better relationship with my family. Regret that they are ... were ... incapable of such things.'

I nodded, understanding his mixed emotions. The kitchen fell silent again, save for the rhythmic chopping of vegetables. Outside, the snow continued to fall, muffling the world beyond our windows.

We'd spent most of the day keeping to ourselves, trying not to tread on anyone's else's toes whilst maintaining some level of usefulness. The house was looking characteristically beautiful, bedecked with red berry garlands and wreaths and warm gold fairy lights that gave the impression that the events of the past few days hadn't actually occurred.

Aunt Clem and Uncle Fergus emerged, seemingly utterly unembarrassed that the last time we had seen Fergus he was roaring drunk. As Clem set the table, a serene smile on her face, I had half a mind to ask her whether she had registered the fact that Tristan had been practically cut in half yesterday. I'd never really understood the upper classes and how they operated, so as usual, I kept schtum.

I called the kids down to dinner, and the four of us, plus Fergus and Clem, sat down at the table whilst we waited for the others. Mrs Harlow busied herself bringing in the bread and butter, followed by the huge steaming pot of casserole and accompaniments. The poor woman was trapped indoors with all of us, and I wondered if she was missing out on seeing her friends and family because of all this snow. I invited her to sit down next to me, with the idea of getting to know her a little better.

Jeannie and Toots were next to arrive, Jeannie leading Toots in and depositing her at the head of the table, while Jeannie took the other end. I poured water into everyone's glasses, and we sat making small talk whilst we waited for Mimi and the twins. After a few minutes, Toots began huffing, puffing, tutting and squirming at the indecency of their lateness, continuously pulling her sleeve up to peer at her wrist, to look at a watch that wasn't even there.

Just as Toots's agitation reached fever pitch, Mimi sauntered into the dining room, the twins trailing behind her. She wore a black peplum dress, and if she could have, I'm sure she'd have worn a big black hat complete with veil and sunglasses to top off the widow-in-mourning look. The girls, in contrast, wore baggy sweats and oversized crew necks, their sleek dark hair slightly mussed as if they'd just rolled out of bed.

'So sorry we're late,' Mimi mumbled. She sounded sad, but there was no trace of puffy eyes or blotchy face; in fact her make-up was dewy and practically pristine.

Toots harrumphed loudly, her magnified eyes narrowing behind her glasses. 'Well, you're here now,' she muttered. Toots had seen and heard it all in her ninety-eight years, and she seemed to have lost any pretence of compassion. I doubt she'd seen anything like the sight I saw yesterday, though.

Mimi ignored her, sliding gracefully into a chair.

The twins plopped down on either side of her, looking terribly bored.

As Mrs Harlow began ladling out the casserole, we all waited patiently for our turn, not sure of the correct thing to say in this scenario. Two empty chairs sat ominously, and the gravity of them seemed to pull at the room, rendering easy conversation difficult. Once we had all been served, I picked up my spoon.

Toots snapped her head towards me. 'Aren't we going to say grace?' she demanded.

I lowered my spoon, heat rising to my cheeks.

Fergus steepled his hands together and began. 'For what we are about to receive, may the Lord make us truly thankful,' he intoned solemnly, 'and may He watch over those who are no longer with us.'

A chorus of quiet 'amen's followed, though I noticed the twins remained silent, their eyes fixed on their plates. As we began to eat, the only sounds were the clink of cutlery against china and the occasional creaking of chairs. The near-silence felt oppressive, laden with unspoken grief and confusion.

I cleared my throat. 'The casserole is lovely, Jeannie, thank you.' Although we had prepared the meal, Jeannie had insisted that she would finish making it.

Toots cut in, 'Why didn't you follow my recipe, Jeannie?'

'I did,' she answered brightly, 'I know it was George's favourite.'

We all remained still with tight smiles.

'Well, you can't have, the beef is very tough,' lamented Toots, 'I can barely get my dentures through it.'

Jeannie stiffened in her seat, her smile faltering for a

moment before she regained her composure. 'I'm sorry you feel that way. Perhaps I did leave it in the oven a bit too long.'

Miles cleared his throat. 'I think it's delicious.'

Toots harrumphed but said nothing more. The silence descended upon us once again. I noticed that the twins were pushing their food around their plates and hadn't said a word since sitting down, while Mimi ate with mechanical precision, her face a mask of calm.

'So, girls,' I ventured, 'how's university?'

Beebee slid her large brown eyes over me. 'Yes, good, thank you,' she said primly.

'And you, Ceecee?' I ventured, withering in the face of the girls' bored, verging on loathing demeanour. 'How is Cambridge?'

'I'm at Oxford, Beebee is at Cambridge,' she said, nearly rolling her eyes.

'Oh – sorry…' I began.

'Ignore them,' Mimi interjected. 'You were right the first time. Ceecee is at Cambridge and Beebee is at Oxford. They do love to tease.'

The girls smirked at the pink rising in my cheeks. 'And do you have any plans for after you graduate?' I pressed on. I didn't really give a rat's arse what their plans were, but at least no one could accuse me of not making an effort.

'Maybe some travel, a ski season in Aspen. We just really need a break and to let loose.' Beebee put a tiny amount of potato into her mouth and chewed.

'Sounds great,' I said. There, my part was done. I'd learned not to expect anyone to ask my children about their plans or aspirations. They didn't expect much from us and wouldn't even feign interest; we existed to watch them and talk about them and their lives.

'Would you mind serving the wine, please, Mrs Harlow?' asked Jeannie, still visibly ruffled by Toots's remark about the beef.

'Oh – yes, sorry, Mrs Weiss.' Mrs Harlow scraped her chair back, but Miles shot up, taking the decanter before she could reach for it.

'I'll do it, Mrs Harlow,' he said. 'You're not expected to be on the clock all hours.'

Mrs Harlow shot Jeannie a worried look before she sat back down gingerly and Miles began pouring the Merlot into everyone's glasses.

Fergus's cheeks and nose were already beetroot red, and I could tell Miles was wondering whether he could get away with refilling his glass only halfway.

'So, how will you pay for this gap year?' Fergus boomed. 'Are you planning on working?'

The twins looked at Mimi, and Mimi looked at him, brows raised in question.

'I'm just wondering,' he soldiered on, 'now that things have changed—'

Aunt Clem gave him a kick under the table.

'Ow! God, blimey, woman!' He scowled at her. 'Well, what's wrong with that? I'm not wrong, am I?'

Mimi blinked at him. 'What do you mean?'

'Fergus, now is *not* the time,' hissed Jeannie.

Mimi turned to Jeannie slowly. 'What is he talking about?'

Jeannie darted a withering look towards Fergus, her lips curling in disdain.

'I said, not now,' she ground out. 'Can we all just get through one dinner with a modicum of decency?'

The wind howled against the windows, rattling them in their panes. The dunes of snow undulated against the house, barely lit by the outdoor lights against the darkness of the winter's night.

'I've been telling you and George for years.' Toots's creaking voice joined in with battering of the wind. 'If you will raise dependants, this is what you get.' Her saucer eyes fixed on Jeannie at the far end of the table.

The tension in the room was unbearable. Mimi's eyes darted between Jeannie and Fergus, her confusion slowly morphing into anger.

'What are you all talking about? Just spit it out, will you?' she demanded, her voice rising. 'What's changed?'

Jeannie shot Fergus another scathing look before turning to Mimi with a forced smile. 'Nothing's changed, dear. Fergus has had too much to drink, as usual. Let's just enjoy our meal.'

But Mimi wasn't having it. She slammed her fork down, causing everyone to jump. 'No. I want to know what's going on.'

The twins exchanged worried glances, boredom now replaced with genuine concern.

Miles cleared his throat. 'Perhaps we should discuss this later, when everyone's had a chance to—'

Toots pointed her knife straight at Jeannie. 'Don't blame me when it all comes crashing upon your head,' she warned.

Callum mumbled something underneath his breath, the first thing either of my children had uttered all evening.

'What was that, boy?' asked Fergus.

'I said, are we not bored of this yet?'

Jeannie tittered. 'Bored of what?'

Callum sighed. 'Playing stupid games and winning stupid prizes.'

Martha and I gaped at him.

'Callum…' said Miles in a low tone.

'I'm going upstairs,' Callum said, red-faced. 'If this is going where I think it's going – more money talk and bullshit – I'd rather eat my dinner upstairs and play *Baldur's Gate*.' He snatched his plate up as we looked on agog, then listened to his retreating footsteps and the whistling wind as we tried not to meet each other's eyes.

'Well, let me tell you something…' Toots leaned forward and pressed her bony hands into the table. 'Just know that … I'm on to you.' Her huge eyes roved around the table, stopping on each and every one of us. 'I *know* that my Eugene's death wasn't natural. I just *know* it.'

'Grandmama,' Beebee piped up, 'are you saying that Great-Grandpa Weiss was murdered?'

I shot a look at Beebee, but held back my protest as I noticed she had her phone in her hand, half obscured under the table. I was pretty sure the camera lens was pointed directly at Toots.

'That's exactly what I'm saying!' Toots weakly beat the table with her balled-up fists.

'Toots,' Jeannie admonished. 'Let's not get all worked up again.'

'You!' Toots pointed straight down the table at her daughter-in-law. 'You put me in that home for speaking the truth.

But people don't just drop down dead. He was healthy, fit as a fiddle!' She clutched at her pearls.

'Grandma,' Miles said softly, 'Grandpa was ninety years old—'

'And? And? Just because you reach ninety doesn't mean you just drop down dead!'

'He had a short illness,' Jeannie insisted.

'*Yes*,' she hissed ominously. 'A brief illness that no doctor could explain. And then no autopsy, because according to them he was old and therefore must have died from natural causes. Well, I am no fool. I have had my suspicions. And now my George, and Tristan...' Her breath rattled.

'You must be careful, Mother,' warned Fergus. 'Your heart...'

Beebee now brazenly turned her phone's camera around to scan each of our faces. As the little black eye fixed its gaze upon me, I shot the lens and her a scowl for being so obscene.

'You were all here.' Toots let her finger rove around us. 'I know it was one of you. And I will get to the bottom of this, you mark my words.'

9

RIBBONS, RED HERRINGS AND REVENGE

I flung back the heavy curtains in anticipation. *Great.* Still snowed in. A sea of powder-white glittered under the morning sun, the light stretched and pale through the bare trees. Miles propped himself up on his elbow, eyebrows raised in question. I shook my head.

'Still at least four foot deep.'

'Better get back in bed, then, where it's nice and warm.' He threw back the pristine white duvet and patted the empty space. I giggled, scurrying back into the gap he'd opened. He launched the covers back over me and wrapped me up as the warmth from his body heated mine.

I jumped out of my skin as the door burst open.

'Mum!' Martha exclaimed, barging in and letting the door slam behind her.

Miles and I untangled quickly and sat up.

'What's the matter?' I asked, pulse hammering in my throat.

'It's Beebee...' She came over to the bed and sat next to me, holding out her phone. A video was playing; it was Toots pointing an accusatory finger at all of us, then the camera panning around. There I was, cutting a stare straight down the lens.

'Beebee's video has gone viral on TikTok,' Martha said breathlessly.

Sure enough, the likes underneath the heart displayed 122.5k.

'It's on its way to a million views, and it was only posted twelve hours ago.'

'Well... What does it mean?' asked Miles.

'It doesn't mean anything, Dad. Other than the fact Beebee and Ceecee are currently trending, and a bunch of armchair detectives are creating conspiracy theories about our family and which one of us is a potential murderer.'

I felt my skin prickle. 'Murderer? What?'

Martha scrolled through the comments, her eyes widening. 'They're saying that there's no way that three deaths in the family at Christmas is a coincidence.'

Miles chuckled nervously. 'This is just online nonsense. People feed off conspiracies these days.'

'Look at this one,' Martha said, pointing to a comment. '"The woman in the green sweater looks guilty AF. Bet she did it for the inheritance."' The video super-zoomed into the death stare I was levelling at Beebee, and I had to admit, I did look pretty psychotic.

'It's just nonsense,' I said, trying to keep my voice steady. 'You know how the internet loves drama.' The world seemed to move underneath me. The forum... How long before this hit the chat room? How long before my publisher saw that I was tangled up in some scandal?

'Can we get it taken down?' I asked.

'I've already reported it but … I don't think so.'

'I'll speak to the girls,' said Miles. 'I'm sure they'll take it down.'

I swallowed hard, my throat bone-dry.

'I wouldn't be so sure about that,' Martha said, her eyes still glued to her phone. 'Beebee's loving the attention. Look, she's already posted three more reels.'

My stomach churned. This was spiralling out of control faster than I could have imagined. I needed to think, to plan, to get ahead of this somehow.

'Let me see those,' I said, reaching for Martha's phone. She handed it over reluctantly.

I scrolled through Beebee's profile, my heart sinking with each swipe. There were close-ups of framed family photos, zoomed-in-on faces, with ominous music playing in the background. Another video showed a timeline of the three deaths, complete with dramatic sound effects. The comments section was a cesspool of wild speculation and amateur sleuthing.

'This is ridiculous,' Miles said, peering over my shoulder. 'Let me sort this.' He threw back the duvet, crossing the room in just his boxers, and pulled his clothes off the chair.

The girls refused to take the videos down. By evening, they had made more, but this time it was of them doing choreographed dances in their oversized clothes to sound bites about serial killers. Miles, Martha and I decided there was only one thing we could do.

The three of us stood in the doorway of Callum's bedroom. Piles of clothes, empty glasses, and plates with half-eaten food lay discarded around the guest bedroom as he lay sprawled on the bed.

He quirked an eyebrow up at us. 'What?' he said, crossing his legs with his console held in front of his face.

'We need your help,' I said. 'We need you to fix something for us.'

Martha was scrunching up her face at the teenage-boy smell.

He sighed. 'Can I do it later? I'm busy.'

'No,' I said firmly, 'I need you to do it now, darling.'

We reluctantly entered the room and Miles closed the door behind us.

I perched on his bed next to him. 'Beebee and Ceecee have made a TikTok about the family, and it's going viral. Not only is it bad for our family, but it's also bad for your father and I. What if one of the university faculty sees it, and your father is asked to leave? What if my publisher sees it?'

Callum carried on staring at his screen, violently tapping at the buttons as something or other came into view that required dispatching immediately.

'Yeah, I saw it. What do you want me to do about it?' he said distractedly.

'You're good at this stuff,' said Martha. 'Come on, Callum. We hate them. It will be fun to wipe those smug smirks off their faces.'

Callum looked at her momentarily.

'It would be fun. But it's a lot of effort just for that. It's TikTok, no one is going to remember it by next week.'

'We don't know that,' cut in Miles. 'We can't risk that. And anyway, it's the principle.'

'What do I get out of it?' asked Callum, already bored by the conversation.

'What do you want?' I asked, earning an exasperated look from Miles.

'I want a gaming computer—'

'No,' said Miles. 'I've told you, they're too expensive.'

'Then I guess you'll be riding out the storm,' Callum said cockily, 'literally and … metaphorically.'

Miles's neck was turning red.

'We can't afford it, darling,' I jumped in, 'not with the move as well. There must be something else? Please…'

Whatever was happening in his game must have come to an end because the sounds of gunfire suddenly ceased. He tossed the console aside and huffed.

'Fine. How about, when we fly to Oz, I fly business class.'

'No way, that's not fair!' exclaimed Martha.

'Hey, I'm not the one in the firing line here. I wasn't even in their stupid video.'

'I've told you, we can't afford it with the move,' Miles reiterated.

'I know you've got the air miles.' Callum chuckled to himself. 'Ha, get it? Air Miles.'

I thought the vein in Miles's head might explode.

'Deal!' I said. 'But if your father's going to use all of his points, we want the full works. A thorough takedown.'

'Yeah-yeah.' He waved his hand dismissively.

'Today,' I said. It was an order, not a question.

'I need at least twenty-four hours, with the time differences and everything...' He didn't elaborate what he meant by that and I wasn't sure I wanted to know.

It was gone midnight by the time we got into bed, and as usual, Miles was asleep within sixty seconds. I picked up my book and reading light, trying to forget about the twins. I had almost started to get stuck into a chapter when I heard giggles out in the hallway.

I huffed and turned over, rereading the sentence I was on, but my concentration failed me as my ears homed in on the noise coming from out in the hallway. Each high-pitched shriek set every cell in my body on fire as I imagined them making another video about me. How long would it be until people started spamming the reviews for my book with one-star ratings believing I was a murderer and I needed to be brought down by the armchair sleuths?

I crept out of bed, pulling on my dressing gown and heading for the door. Heart in my mouth, I cracked it open and headed towards the direction of the chatter. Stopping at the corner, I peeked round, watching them illuminated in the darkness by mini ring-lights attached to the top of their phones.

I watched as they filmed a dance, which thankfully didn't appear to be about me at all. At least I hoped not. I was about to turn around and head back to bed when I heard a door click shut and a deep voice talking to the girls. I dared to take another peek, and to my surprise I saw Callum emerge into the halo of their white-blue light.

'Hey,' he said, lowering his huge headphones away from his ears to sit around his neck.

'If you're here to complain about the noise, don't bother,' said Beebee.

'We probably disturbed his little hand-job session,' Ceecee mocked.

'Nope,' Callum sighed. 'But I thought you might like some of this...' He held up a bag of weed and a pouch of tobacco. 'It's good stuff.'

They paused, eyeing the contents of the bag.

'Why?' Ceecee asked suspiciously. 'What do you want for it?'

'I will personally roll you four big fat blunts for the bargain price of twenty quid. But I want you to take those videos you made about my mum down.'

The pair looked at Callum, then turned to each other and laughed.

'Don't be ridiculous. We could end up making a lot of money from those videos. They're doing way too well for us to take them down.'

'Okay.' He shrugged and turned to leave.

'Come on, Cal, give us a joint. We'll give you the twenty.'

'Nah. I'm good,' he said, walking back towards his bedroom door.

'Okay, twenty-five?' Beebee hissed after him.

He came back into the light. 'I came out here to be nice. To give you guys the choice for the easy way out ... but you two bitches are too dumb to see where this is heading so ... peace out. I'm off to bed.'

They shot each other a confused look. 'Look, can we have the joints or not?'

He pretended to think for a moment. 'It just went up to two joints for forty quid. Take it or leave it.'

'That's ridiculous, no way!' said Ceecee.

'Nighty-night then.' Callum began to pull his headphones back up.

'Wait!' Said Beebee. 'Two for forty, then. And you'd better make them big ones.'

Callum snorted like he was about to make a seedy joke but then thought better of it. He held out his hand waiting for the money, watching Ceecee as she served him her best resting bitch face. She took out her phone and asked for his email address as she tapped her screen viciously. Callum's phone pinged and he checked to see that the transaction had gone through. He sat down cross-legged on the floor and, retrieving a packet of Rizlas from his pocket, began filling the paper.

Great. My son was dealing drugs to his cousins in his grandmother's house and they weren't even going to take the damn videos down. Brilliant job, Cal.

'So, I hear Martha's a rug-muncher, then?' Ceecee asked scornfully.

Callum didn't speak, but I saw him pause for a long moment. He ignored them and the rustling of the paper between his fingers resumed. He licked the edge of the paper and twisted it deftly at the end. He held it out towards Ceecee between his fingers. She reached for it but he snatched it back at the last minute.

'Actually, I've just decided you get one joint.'

'What?' Beebee spat. 'We paid for two!'

'Yeah, well, then you decided to call my sister a rug-muncher, so I decided to deduct it. Got anything else you'd like to say?'

Their faces were filled with spite.

'You little chav! Give us our money back!' Ceecee launched herself towards him, but he stood quickly and towered menacingly over her.

'I don't like the way you look at me and my family,' he said in an icy tone that made my skin prickle. 'You think you're so much better than us … but you're just pampered leeches whose mum and dad despise each other. And I'm pretty sure that when they look at you, all they see is a reflection of themselves. That's why they hate you, too. Or should I use the past tense, now that one of them is dead? I can't be sure, on account of being a dumb chav.' He flicked the joint over the banister.

Callum walked off into the darkness leaving Beebee and Ceecee cursing and scrambling around. I quickly headed back to my room, my blood rushing at witnessing a side of my son I'd never seen before. As satisfying as it was seeing him stick up for himself and our family, I wasn't entirely sure I was keen to see that side of Callum again anytime soon.

10

FROM TIKTOK TO TRAUMA

The whole family convened for another round of fresh hell as the fireplace roared, the candles flickered and the Christmas lights twinkled, bringing a warm, comforting glow to an atmosphere that was anything but. After a day of the family avoiding each other, Jeannie had insisted we play a game of charades in the sitting room to 'stretch the limbs of the mind', whatever that meant. Either she was now fully enrolled in the batshit insane club, or the stone-cold psychopath society. My bet was she was president of both.

I clutched my glass of steaming mulled cider, dutifully prepared by Mrs Harlow, who, after a day of funeral arrangements and filling out paperwork, had excused herself and gone to bed early. I needed to get me a Mrs Harlow.

I breathed in the aroma of spiced apple, cinnamon and orange, hoping it would calm the tension knotting tighter and tighter in my stomach. I hadn't heard a whisper from my editor, not a dickie bird... Which wasn't particularly unusual, but at a time like this felt agonisingly ominous. I had written a measly 632 words today. Unsurprisingly, the steamy scenes weren't writing themselves when all I could think about was Tristan chopped up like Wagyu, or George half dangling like a discarded piñata. It felt like my veins were filled with rocket fuel; either I was going to take off to the moon at any moment or explode on launch. I could just tell my editor what had happened, but it sounded so unbelievable I'd be better off going with 'Gloria ate my homework'.

'Your turn, Olivia!' Jeannie's voice cut through my racing thoughts.

Leaning over to the coffee table, I put down my cup and picked up a folded piece of paper.

Scrawled in spidery blue ink it read, '*The Mousetrap* by Agatha Christie'.

I stood, brushing down my skirt, willing my mind to focus on the task at hand rather than the looming deadline.

Uncle Fergus and Aunt Clem were on my team, the two players that no one else ever wanted to be paired with, Jeannie had definitely done it on purpose.

'Time starts, now!' trilled Jeannie, looking at her wristwatch.

I moved my hands up and down to signal a rope and held up two fingers.

'A play!' Fergus bellowed. 'Two words!'

'*Second word*', I mimed. '*Two syllables; first syllable…*' I put my index fingers either side of my head to indicate ears, scrunched up my nose to show my two front teeth and made a squeaking sound.

'No noises!' chided Jeannie.

'A rat!' shouted Clem.

I shook my head and ducked down lower, trying to show her it was smaller than a rat.

Out of the corner of my eye, I saw Ceecee elbow Beebee, who was frowning at her phone. They both looked up and me and sniggered.

Fergus was swaying slightly in his seat.

I pointed to my ear, then mimed small, scurrying movements with my hands.

'A mouse! Mouse! MOUSE,' Fergus drawled, slapping his thigh.

I nodded, relieved. For the second word, I held my hands open, one on top of the other, and clapped them shut.

'Clap?' said Clem, looking confused.

'My God, so *tragic*,' Ceecee muttered.

'Time!' Jeannie called, looking incredibly pleased because her team was winning.

I exhaled and threw the piece of paper back onto the table.

'It was *The Mousetrap*,' I sighed, flopping back into my seat.

Clem looked bemused. 'Never heard of that one.'

Everyone fell into their own conversations, and I sat back once more, cradling the warmth of the cup in my hands. My eyes darted over to the twins every now and again to see if there was anything that looked like concern on their faces. So far, nothing.

Mimi had barely said a word, which I supposed was understandable when she'd only just lost her husband. I thought back to how they had fought, and how he wouldn't even come back here with her. She didn't look particularly sad. She did however look extremely fidgety and on edge.

Sometimes it struck me that Mimi and I were not as different as I liked to maintain. One thing was for certain, neither of us wanted to be here. I did note that she and the girls barely ever spoke to one another, though. Which, despite the fact that I loathed them all with a passion, I had to admit was very sad.

Toots was whispering to Jeannie, and I strained my ears to try and pick out what she was saying. Martha shuffled forward in front of the fire to take her turn next. She bent down and picked up a torn piece of paper. Studying it, she wore a pained expression.

'This is a hard one, Callum, you've got to pay attention.' Martha clicked her fingers in the air at him and he let his Steam Deck slide off his lap.

'Go on, then,' he said sighing in resignation. He watched her signing, oozing boredom from every pore. 'A film,' he said. 'Five words. First word, one syllable.'

Martha pointed to the window.

'Snow!' he shouted.

She shook her head, and a lock of hair fell loose.

'Umm,' he studied the window as she pointed up towards the sky. 'Night?'

She nodded excitedly and indicated the fourth and fifth word. She held her arms out and staggered forward, her mouth hanging open.

Ceecee and Beebee were in fits of laughter now as they watched her. As though she was the butt of some joke between them. What the *fuck* were they saying about my daughter and what blunt object could I use to cave their heads in?

'*Night of the Living Dead!*' Callum shouted.

Martha whooped and gave him a high-five, while Jeannie noted down the score.

'No way did he get *Night of the Living Dead* from *that*,' protested Ceecee.

'Not everyone's as airheaded as you two,' I snapped. All eyes turned to me in horror. Whoops ... did I just say that out loud? I felt my face burning up.

Mimi and the twins were glaring at me, but neither were as disgusted as Jeannie and Toots.

'How rude!' exclaimed Toots.

'Well, now, that was very uncalled for, Olivia,' said Jeannie in the most matronly tone ever.

Even Miles and the kids were looking at me wondering why I couldn't keep my emotions in check. I swear if anyone else had said it, no one would bat an eyelid, but *moi*, the quiet outsider? Somehow that was shocking to them. I had two options: I could say sorry or I could own it.

'Was that rude? Oh, I'm sorry,' I said in a faux-sweet voice, 'I thought I heard you making snide jokes, but I must have been mistaken.' I didn't take my eyes off them. I had no idea what they had said about Martha, but the innate desire to lurch forward screaming like a banshee and rip them a new one was burning hot.

They tried to stare back, but the intensity of my gaze proved too awkward and they eventually looked away. I continued to study them as Beebee's frown deepened and she nudged her sister and pointed to something on her phone screen. Ceecee's eyes shot to hers in alarm and they abruptly stood up to leave and made their excuses to Jeannie.

'Are you sure, girls?' Jeannie said forlornly. 'It's not because Aunt Olivia was mean to you, is it?'

They looked back at me and said, 'It's just all so much to cope with, Grandmama, first Daddy, and now this...'

Assholes.

'Oh, I understand, my petals.' Jeannie cut me a look.

'If they're leaving, can I?' asked Callum.

'No, you may not!' Jeannie snapped.

As the girls were heading out, Ceecee stooped down in front of Uncle Fergus and held her phone screen to his face. The blue light illuminated every pore and pock mark of his skin as he looked at it bleary-eyed.

'See those numbers, Uncle Fergus? That's what will pay for our gap year.' Ceecee smirked.

Beebee chimed in, 'But who's going to pay for that?' She flicked at his whisky glass, causing it to tilt and splash onto his hand.

Fergus spluttered, too inebriated and flabbergasted to come up with an immediate retort. Clem sucked in a sharp breath. 'Well, I never!' she exclaimed, watching them go.

I watched their retreating backs. Had Callum completely abandoned his plan to get those videos taken down? He did say it would take a few hours... But why was nothing happening yet?

I caught Toots whispering loudly to Jeannie, 'Artie Peverill knows a private detective from his army days. He's looking into things for me.'

Jeannie nodded in earnest.

I glanced around to see if anyone else had heard, but they were all absorbed in their own conversations.

Miles stood, looking out of the window. 'Oh no,' he said, his voice barely audible.

'What?' I jumped up to see what he was looking at, 'What is it?'

He shook his head and pointed into the darkness beyond.

I looked out. The white grasslands were blanketed as far as the lights could illuminate. And now more snow, flurry upon flurry, falling heavier than before. We shared a concerned look before turning back to the people left sitting in the room.

Miles leaned closer to whisper in my ear, 'Will we *ever* get out of here?' We sat back to resume the game with a sinking feeling.

An hour later a text from Callum appeared on my phone. I nudged Miles and showed him the aeroplane, red heart and sun emoji, which we took to mean that the job had been done... Whatever the 'job' entailed. Callum sat across from us, grinning from ear to ear.

***

I woke up with a start. The moonlight streaming in through the gap in the curtains hit right where Miles was sleeping soundly. Squinting, I rolled over and checked the time – one a.m. With a sigh, I rolled onto my back and closed my eyes, willing myself to go back to sleep. I pleaded with my brain not to think about the damn book and the incessant deadline hanging over me like the blade of a guillotine.

Too late. I'd thought about it.

I got up as quietly as I could so as not to disturb Miles. Creeping to the door, I opened it and padded out and down the corridor to grab some water from the kitchen. Before I turned the corner, a light moved at the end, and I could hear whispering voices.

Silently, I tiptoed to the end of the corridor, heart beginning a steady canter in my ears. Faint music wafted down the darkened hallway. I dared to peek round.

In the gallery, Beebee and Ceecee were whispering together. Ceecee grappled the phone away from Beebee and held it at arm's reach as Beebee tried to grab it, the faint beat of music still going.

They fought, but then Ceecee overpowered her sister, setting the phone down against the wall, pointing straight at them. She pushed Beebee, and hissed, 'Do it *again*, like *this…*' she showed her an arm movement. Beebee sniffled and copied her.

'Okay, ready?' Ceecee whispered, bending down and pressing something on the screen.

They stood side by side at the top of the gallery, perfectly still as a countdown beeped. The music started and they began their dance.

'No, no, *no!*' Ceecee grabbed Beebee. 'People already hate us as it is! Do you want them to see that inane fucking smile on your face? Our father has just died, you need to look sad, you moron!'

Beebee turned and grabbed her sister, bunching her hoody up in her fists and shaking her. 'Talk to me like that again and I'll throw you over the banister.' She was pushing Ceecee until her back was against the wood. She loomed over her, snarling in her face. 'It's *your* fault we're getting hate, everyone has seen what a malicious, spoiled brat you really are.' Beebee let her hoody drop and turned her back to her.

Whatever Callum had done, it was working.

Silently, I crept back to the room, wishing those airheads would sod off back to bed so I could get a glass of water. I was almost back at the bedroom door, when something jogged my memory. The first Christmas I came to the Weisses, Miles had shown me the panel in the wall that had once been used as the servants' staircase. He had explained how, as a boy, he had always used it to hide things from his parents.

Quietly heading down the warren of hallways, I took a corridor to the left. I remembered the panel was near the glass case, which housed a stuffed fox. Absolutely disgusting and just plain weird. I hoped the fox was an heirloom from a hundred years ago that Jeannie couldn't bear to get rid of, and not some poor thing Tristan and his psycho mates had hunted down on horseback.

I felt along the walls, not quite remembering which panel it had been. There was no way it would still be open; as far as I knew no one in the house ever used it or even mentioned it. I tiptoed along, sweeping my hand across the smooth, worn wood. Nothing. The moonlight streamed in, amplified by the sheer whiteness of the snow blanketing everything outside. I headed back the way I'd come, thirsty as hell. I'd just have to risk waking Miles up by drinking from the tap in the en suite.

11

YULE BE SORRY

Day three of being snowed in and I was feeling distinctly like Jack Torrance in *The Shining*. We had just finished lunch and had retired for coffee to the sitting room. Miles and Callum had snuck off, and Martha and I gave each other a look that said, '*Why the hell didn't we think of that.*' I looked around the room, absentmindedly daydreaming about what I'd do if I had an axe at my disposal.

'Look! Traditional plum pottage, Mummy-kins!' slurred Uncle Fergus, presenting a bowl of slop to Toots. 'Clementine made it for you, didn't you, ol' girl?'

'I did,' Clem agreed, cheeks blazing – either from the heat of the fire, or from sheer embarrassment at how badly Fergus was swaying on his feet after his seventh brandy. 'I know you had it as a girl,' she said eagerly.

'That I did,' said Toots, peering into the bowl. 'And you made this for me? Why?'

Clem looked around, unsure of what to say. 'Well ... um,

because you had it as a child, and I thought it might be a nice memory for you. Would anyone else like to try some?' Clem plunged a ladle into the pot of gruel she balanced on her hip.

We murmured our polite refusals.

'Are you after something?' Toots said, eyeing her suspiciously. 'When have you ever done anything nice for me?'

'Whaddya mean?' Fergus hiccoughed. 'We do plenty of nice things for you, Mummy!'

Toots ignored them, turning away from the bowl. 'I'll just let my lunch go down first. So'—she fixed her beady eyes on Martha—'Jeannie … have you heard about Martha's sexual proclivities?'

Fergus made a little burping sound and Martha coolly returned Toots's gaze.

Jeannie stepped towards her, her mouth contorting, and giving Fergus and Clem a dirty look for stirring the pot about Martha. 'I'm aware. But don't worry, Toots. It's all the rage these days. I'm sure she'll grow out of it,' she said flatly.

'Well … you want to do something about it now!' Toots demanded. 'You want to nip that bloody nonsense in the bud. Next thing you know she'll have a nose piercing and be wearing bovver boots. We need to continue the prestigious line of the Weiss clan – not start adopting children from Ethiopia or whatever the next fad with young people is nowadays. Honestly, Jeannie, you're losing your grip on them and it's sad to see. It's not what Eugene would have expected at all.'

'She's sixteen, Toots.' Jeannie waved her hand. 'It's not something we need to worry about yet.'

'It's not something you need to worry about *ever*,'

I growled. I leaned forward to begin my admonishments, but Martha gave me a cutting look that said, '*I can fight my own battles.*'

'What is plum pottage, then?' Martha asked, completely unfazed. 'Why don't you try some, Great-Grandma?'

Toots looked her up and down, assessing her attire with a sneer. Finally, she said, 'It's figgy pudding,' She turned back towards it and took a sniff at what was inside.

'Figgy pudding?' Ceecee said, wrinkling her nose. 'It looks like something a cat would puke up.'

Both twins had sourer faces than usual. I sincerely hoped it was down to whatever Callum had done. Toots shot Ceecee a sharp look. 'Mind your tongue, young lady. This is a traditional Christmas dish.'

'It smells ... interesting,' Martha offered, trying to be polite.

Clem fidgeted, her cheeks growing even redder. 'I followed the recipe exactly. I hope it tastes all right. Will you try some?'

'Oh, for Pete's sake,' Toots said, snatching up the bowl as Clem handed her a spoon. With a shaking veiny hand, she tentatively dipped it into the thick, dark mixture. We all watched in anticipation as she raised it to her mouth and tentatively took a mouthful. Her eyes widened slightly, and she swallowed slowly, her expression unreadable.

'Well?' Fergus prompted, swaying dangerously close to the fireplace. 'How is it, Mummy dearest?'

Toots swallowed hard. 'It's certainly ... memorable. What did you put in it?'

Clem's face fell at the lack of praise. 'Just ... just what was in the recipe. Dried plums, breadcrumbs, almonds, spices—'

'And a dash of brandy!' Fergus chimed in, raising his glass and shaking it. 'For added flavour!'

'I'd say it was more than a dash,' Toots said, pushing the bowl away. 'It tastes like you dumped the whole bottle in.'

'*Fergus!*' Clem hissed. 'You didn't put brandy in there, did you? I spent all day on that!'

Toots looked at Fergus and Clementine and pressed her lips into a line. Gingerly, she picked up the spoon and ate another mouthful. 'It's really not too bad, once you get used to it. Thank you, dear, it's very thoughtful of you. Anyone else want to try?'

We each shook our heads and said *no* in unison.

Beebee crossed her arms and loudly whispered to Ceecee, 'Looks and smells like cat shit.'

'Now, now,' Toots chided, forcing down another spoonful. 'It's the thought that counts. And it's … growing on me.'

Fergus stumbled forward, nearly knocking over the Christmas tree.

Jeannie was surveying him with no attempt to hide her disgust. 'I think you've had quite enough, Fergus,' she said through gritted teeth. 'Why don't you sit down before you hurt yourself?'

Martha stepped in, strong-arming Fergus to an armchair. 'Here, Uncle Fergus. Sit in my chair. We wouldn't want you falling flat on your face,' she said sarcastically.

Clem wrung her hands, looking close to tears. 'Toots, the thing is, I've been wanting to talk to you…'

'I knew you were up to something,' Jeannie said in a warning tone.

'Oh, will you just shut up, Jeannie!' Aunt Clem snapped.

'The thing is, Toots,' she continued, voice shaking. 'We have found ourselves very unstuck. We – we need some money.'

Toots straightened, putting her hand to her chest. 'Money?' she said, grimacing. 'What do you mean? How much money?'

Clem looked to Fergus, whose cheek was bunched up as he rested his head on his fist. 'Enough to … to stop our cottage being repossessed.'

Toots stared. 'What on earth are you asking me for? I don't have any money.'

'Of course you do, Mummy-Wummy…' Fergus slurred.

Toots inhaled sharply. She looked up at us, then coughed, hitting herself on the chest as if trying to dislodge something.

'I don't,' she insisted, rasping a little, a pained expression lining her face. 'Are you deaf as well as stupid? You were at the will-reading with the rest of us, weren't you?' She was breathless, wheezing as if she was at the beginning of an asthma attack. I wondered whether I should jump in, but I was too captured by the turn of conversation.

'Yes, but—' Clem stalled, then, 'Y-you have assets, don't you? And jewellery? I hate to ask, and you know I wouldn't unless it was really dire straits! And, and she—' She was dithering now, gesturing towards Jeannie. 'She won't give us a penny! We are going to lose everything! And now Tristan's gone, and do you know that Mimi'—her eyes narrowed into slits, looking between us and the twins—'she's not even been a faithful wife! She doesn't deserve a damn dime!'

Jeannie gasped, one hand flying to her pearls. The girls' mouths dropped open. Toots just sat there motionless. Just staring and staring at Clem, mouth wide.

'Now look what you've done, you're upsetting her. I told you not to say anything!' admonished Jeannie.

We all watched Toots with bated breath. The twins looked on, confused and angry.

We watched in horror as Toots began to fall forwards with an almighty crash; like a tree that had just been felled, she face-planted straight into the bowl of plum pottage.

Beebee and Ceecee shrieked, while Martha rushed to Toots's side. Jeannie stood frozen, her face a mask of horror. Fergus, startled from his drunken stupor, attempted to stand but only managed to slide further down in his chair.

'Oh my God, Toots!' Clem cried, her hands flying to her mouth.

I leapt into action, arriving at Toots's side. I picked her head up out of the bowl. My God, she was light, what was she made out of, paper? I gently turned her head to the side. Her eyes were open, her face smeared with the dark, sticky pudding. I eased her back upright, the slop falling from her face and down her front.

'Toots?' I said clearly, as I held my fingers in front of her nose and mouth to check if she was breathing. Not a whisper could I feel, but the plum pottage or figgy pudding or whatever it was got onto my fingers and I almost gagged. I checked her pulse as her head lolled backwards, the whole room watching me as I manhandled her like a ragdoll.

Slowly, I turned to look at everyone.

'I think she's … she's gone,' I said, my voice feeling surreal and disconnected. I gently pushed away the bowl and rested her head back down on the table. 'Martha, please get your father. Tell him to call an ambulance … the police… just dial nine-nine-nine.'

Martha nodded numbly and rushed out of the room.

Jeannie was looking at me wild-eyed. 'Start CPR, Olivia!'

I backed away shaking my head. Like hell was I putting my mouth around *that*. The figgy pudding was bad enough, but what if it was poisoned?

'I think you should do it, Jeannie,' I said, voice shaking.

'Absolutely not!' she said outraged. 'Martha, you do it.'

'She's not doing it,' I said firmly. 'One of the twins should do it!'

'Someone should do something!' wailed Clem.

'You poisoned her, you should do it!' I shot back.

'*You*,' said Jeannie, aiming her finger at Aunt Clem. '*You did this*!'

'I didn't do anything!' screeched Clem.

'It wasn't Clem's fault, it was the brandy's fault,' Fergus slurred, attempting to point an accusing finger at the bowl of pudding. 'Bad figgy pudding!'

'Even if you didn't put something in that pudding, you certainly gave her a heart attack by revealing all of those awful things!' accused Jeannie.

'No, no!' cried Clem.

Miles and Callum burst into the room, eyes wide. They beheld Toots, lying with a face smeared with lumpy brown mush.

'What's going on here?' said Miles, rushing to Toots to examine her.

'Christ on a bike,' said Callum. 'Not another one?'

'Well, you must have done something!' continued Jeannie.

'You *did* put something in that pudding. It makes perfect sense.' She shook her head bitterly as she approached Clem, like a rattlesnake about to strike. 'You thought, if you got rid of Eugene, you'd get a payout.

And when that didn't happen, you came begging George and me for handouts. And when we refused and told you it was being signed over to Tristan, you started sowing seeds of doubt about their marriage.'

'What?' asked Beebee, unable to take her eyes off Toots. 'What seeds of doubt?'

Jeannie ignored her, pushing her face right up against Clem's now. 'And when I wouldn't listen, you went straight for the source. You killed my George! And now I'm next. Well, I'll tell you now, you conniving trout, you won't get a damned thing!'

Clementine recoiled, her face a mixture of shock and indignation. 'How dare you! I would never—'

'That's enough!' Miles shouted, silencing the room. He knelt beside Toots, checking her pulse again himself. 'This is not the time for accusations. I'll call the police now.'

'Police?' Fergus slurred, attempting to sit up straighter. 'Why, what's happened?'

'Toots was nearly a hundred years old!' Aunt Clem said wide-eyed, 'It could have been a sudden heart attack. Do we really need the police here?'

Jeannie whirled on them. 'Now why would you say that?' she snarled.

'Yo-you're the one always warning us to never get the police involved!' Clem protested.

'Just calm down, all of you,' I said, surprising even myself with the force of my voice. 'We don't know what happened. It could have been natural causes. Toots was ... well, as Clem said, she wasn't young, and she *did* have a bad heart. I'll call them. Just everyone please think of the children.' I almost laughed at the cliché that had just come out of my mouth, and at how mad this all was, but I didn't think it would do me any favours.

I bustled from the room to make the call, wondering whether Clem really did have it in her to put poison in that pudding.

I explained to Miles what the emergency switchboard operator had said, that no one could get to the house until someone could come with a digger to clear away the snow around the surrounding country lanes. He looked as horrified at that prospect as I felt. How long were we going to have to leave Toots's body in the house?

I knew one thing, I wasn't going to sit there staring at the old bag's filthy face while the others paced, pulling their hair out and yakking about what we were going to do. I instructed Miles and Callum to lift her up, and place her in the pantry, the coolest place I could think of in the house. Mrs Harlow fetched a crisp white sheet from the airing cupboard, and once they had carefully placed her on the floor, she gently covered her.

We stood in the pantry, staring at the sheeted form of Toots looking like she was waiting to be carved up for Christmas. A heavy silence fell over us. The reality of the situation was starting to sink in.

'What do we do now?' Martha whispered from behind me.

Miles ran a hand through his hair, looking more dishevelled than I'd ever seen him. 'We wait, I suppose. And try to keep everyone calm.'

'Fat chance of that,' Callum muttered, glancing back towards the living room, where we could hear raised voices.

Everyone retired early to their rooms that evening, leaving Mrs Harlow's dinner untouched.

12

SEASON OF MISGIVINGS

18th December 2025

> *Rule 101 of murder mysteries. Don't tell a room full of potential murderers you're on to them. When I saw the mixing bowl, I knew it was a missing a key ingredient. I just so happened to be taking a stroll that morning when I remembered the greenhouse contained some particularly useful things, most notably the castor-oil plant.*
>
> *Hope Toots enjoyed her figgy pudding with a dash of ricin. Silly old bitch.*

The next morning, I came downstairs to the smell of ginger and caramelised sugar filling the house. Entering the kitchen, I dared a glance over at the pantry. The door was firmly shut. Perhaps it had all been a dream.

Jeannie was wearing her apron and oven gloves, peering into

the double oven. A timer went off and she began opening the doors, one after the other. The blast from the heat and the whirring fans ruffled her silvery hair and I couldn't help but wonder whether I was Gretel entering the witch's kitchen, minus the breadcrumbs and with a healthy dose of passive aggression.

'Everything okay, Jeannie?' I asked.

She swapped around a couple of the trays and banged the doors closed.

'Oh yes. Keeping busy.'

'What are you doing?' I asked.

She turned to look at me, nose scrunched. 'Playing tennis. What does it look like I'm doing? I'm baking.'

'Yes, but...' I was going to ask *why* she would be baking gingerbread at a time like this, but I think I already knew the answer.

'We're decorating gingerbread houses for the in-house competition. Surely you haven't forgotten already?'

Yup. That's exactly what I feared she might say. 'I just – do you think that's such a good idea, after what happened yesterday? I'm not sure everyone is—'

Another timer went off somewhere, and Jeannie walked over to the AGA and pulled it open. Honestly, it was like King Henry VIII's kitchen in here with the number of ovens. She plucked out a tray of caramel-brown gingerbread and carried it over to the sideboard. Taking off her gloves she grabbed a skewer to test the middle.

'So, what, we are all supposed to lie down and die now, too?' she asked.

'No... I'm just not sure people will be in the mood to—'

'Argh!' Jeannie yelped as she touched the side of the tray. In the next moment it had crashed to the floor.

I rushed over to help her gather up the scalding and broken remnants around her feet. Jeannie's face crumpled as she stared at the shattered gingerbread pieces scattered across the tiles. Her hands shook as she tried to pick them up, and I gently took her wrist.

'Let me,' I said softly. 'You'll burn yourself.'

She looked up at me, her eyes glistening with unshed tears. 'I can't stop thinking about her,' she whispered. 'Every time I close my eyes, I see her face. And that awful pudding...'

I placed a hand on her arm, feeling the tremors running through her body. 'I know. It's terrible. It was terrible.'

'What do you think it all means?' she said, barely above a whisper.

I swept the broken gingerbread into a dustpan, the spicy scent rising with the heat.

Jeannie dabbed at her eyes with her apron.

'I don't know,' I said, 'Perhaps it doesn't mean anything. It's all just... It doesn't make sense.'

'No,' she said soberly. 'If I was religious, I would think we were being punished.' She said it almost to herself.

'Punished for what?'

She shook her head, not wanting to admit what she was thinking. But I wanted to say it for her. *Do you think it's karma for being such shitty people?* I relished the idea of sticking the knife in while I had the chance, just me and her with no one else to hear.

'But we have to keep going,' Jeannie continued, 'don't we?

That's what we Weisses do. That's what Toots would have wanted.'

I nodded, thinking of the old woman's fierce determination and lack of fucks to give.

'You're right,' she said, standing up. 'Maybe the gingerbread-house competition isn't the best idea right now. But I can't just sit around doing nothing. I need to keep busy, or I'll go mad thinking about...' Her voice trailed off, and she busied herself with cleaning up the remaining crumbs. I watched her in silence, both of us lost in thought. Then she whispered, 'Someone in this house is harming my family, Olivia, and I think I know exactly who.' She stared at me, her blue eyes burning into my soul.

'Who?' I asked, not daring to look away.

She looked towards the entry way. 'Aunt Clem.'

I looked at her, not masking my doubt well enough.

'Do you remember the will-reading with Artie Peverill, four years ago? Do you remember what he said?'

Do I remember it? How could anyone forget?

'Y-yes,' I replied. 'But what has that got to do with Clem?'

'It has everything to do with the two of them and the way they reacted. They are the losers in this whole business, they are trying to take the money for themselves.' She picked up an ubroken piece of gingerbread off the counter and waggled it in my face. 'And if we don't keep our wits about us, we'll be next.' Jeannie was behaving like a madwoman. 'Let me do the gingerbread competition. Let's see if anything seems off. I know you are perceptive, just like me. I know you like to watch people and you see things that others don't notice.'

The glow of the ovens cast an orange light in Jeannie's eyes. What if she had put something in the gingerbread?

'What if…' I ventured, 'what if Clem did put something in the figgy pudding? What if it's in the gingerbread, too?'

'Nonsense! No one has been in here today except for me. And I will happily try each and every one of these trays in front of you now to prove I haven't put anything in them.'

She was as good as her word; she did in fact start nibbling at the corners of a piece of gingerbread to demonstrate.

'Okay…' I agreed finally. 'I will keep an eye out for anything … untoward.'

I left Jeannie to her frantic baking and headed back to our empty bedroom, flopping down onto the bed. My laptop lay on the bedside table with all the gravitas of a black hole.

I snatched it towards me and swiped it open. There was no *way* I could write in these conditions, which should have been great fuel for a murder-mystery novel. But I wasn't writing a bloody murder-mystery. My stomach dropped at what I was about to do. But I couldn't put it off any longer. The ghost writer…

The man who could write my book for me. I imagined that for him to do it in a week would cost double what I paid the first time. I'd only ever done it once, when the children were young, and I was a new writer with a three-book deal for an eye-wateringly low advance. I'd had to take a permanent position as a personal assistant – and by the time I was due to submit the third book I just couldn't keep up. Writing never had and still didn't make ends meet. But now, Miles earned just enough to keep us both going, and he had convinced me to quit the PA job and pursue my dreams.

The first time I managed to scrape together three hundred pounds to pay the ghost writer, the guy wrote it in his spare time, over two months. Now I was going to ask him to write a book in a week and a half.

I dreaded to think what the cost was going to be.

I went into my drafts folder, looking for the email I'd started. I stared at the screen and the empty draft folder. I was sure I had already written it… With a sigh I rewrote the email to him, detailing my desperate situation and the tight deadline. The cursor blinked accusingly, reminding me of the ethical line I was about to cross. Again.

With my finger hovering over the send button, a soft knock at the door made me jump. I slammed the laptop shut as Miles poked his head in.

'Everything all right, darling?' he asked.

I forced a smile. 'Just trying to work on the book. It's … not going well.'

He came and sat beside me on the bed, placing a comforting hand on my knee. 'I know it's been difficult, with everything that's happened. But you shouldn't push yourself too hard. Your publisher will understand if you need an extension.'

I swallowed hard, guilt gnawing at my insides. He looked so tired. I knew he hadn't gotten much sleep last night after what had happened with Toots, and now here I was laying more worries at his door.

'I've already had an extension…' I began. 'More than one. I think – I think I might have to pay back the advance.'

His face dropped. 'How much?' he asked.

I gulped.

He tried to hide the look of dread and to his credit it was gone in a flash – but I had caught it. I couldn't tell him. Twenty grand to pay back the advance, or … I don't know how much the ghost writer was going to ask for, but it certainly wouldn't be as much as that.

'Look, don't worry,' I said brightly, 'I'm being silly. You know me. I'm almost there – if I really get my head down and shut myself away, I can get it done.'

He looked into my eyes. 'Okay… If you need me to help, to read over anything, I'm here. Okay, Liv? I can help.'

I smiled into his warm brown eyes. Even with everything going on, he never failed to be there for me and the kids. Guilt gnawed at me. I always remarked on how selfish Mimi and the twins could be, but sometimes, I really was no better.

'Thank you,' I said, leaning forward and giving him a kiss on the nose.

'I'm going to make a coffee,' he said standing up and planting a swift kiss on my forehead. 'Want one?'

'No, thank you. I'm just going to get on with this,' I pulled open the laptop once more.

I watched him as he left the room, his shoulders bunched with tension. I had to sort my shit out so that I could be there for him, not the other way round.

He closed the door just as I hit send.

13

CLAUS FOR CONCERN

Four Years Earlier...

28th December 2021

Misery Miser Eugene Weiss had celebrated his 90th birthday a month before, and my God, he was fitter than all of us. It would be another ten years or more until he croaked it – and I am not one for waiting.

Greedy guts loves his Scotch so much it's practically replaced the blood in his veins. God forbid anyone else should drink Eugene's whisky.

The best thing about antifreeze is that the side effects are so similar to having a few too many and developing a cold. No one thought twice when he took himself to bed feeling groggy and a bit nauseous. Twelve hours later, we woke up to find the old boy had met his maker.

The reading of the will was four weeks later and the vultures circled and sharpened their claws. I could already hear their

*whispers, the subtle jockeying for position. Who would get the beach
house? The classic-car collection? The stocks? The goldmine?*

*Little did any of them know, old Scrooge had left us all a pile of
rotting shit.*

Four years ago, I sat amongst the family as Arthur
Peverill, long-time lawyer to the Weiss family, delivered Eugene Weiss's last will and testament. Peverill,
also known as Artie, Art, or plain old *The Shark*, sat back in
Eugene's dark green armchair. The smooth leather creaked
beneath him as he surveyed us over steepled fingers. We were
waiting on Tristan and Mimi, as usual.

Aunt Clem and Uncle Fergus wore tweed suits and
polished brown shoes, obviously dressed for the roles of soon-
to-be multi-millionaires. Jeannie lounged in an armchair, an
irrepressible smirk twisting the side of her face. She looked
them up and down and tittered to herself.

Sitting on a straight-backed chair beside Jeannie, George
perched with his usual bored demeanour. Whenever he was
anywhere that wasn't his own turf, he had an itchy look about
him that screamed, *Leave me alone, dammit, I just want to read
my book.*

I glanced at Miles, sitting so still next to me, he was barely
breathing. I clutched the top of his hand, giving him a reassuring smile that I hoped conveyed *Whatever the outcome, we
will be fine.*

Toots was on the other side of Miles, hunched over in a
huge wing-back chair that made her look like the matriarch of
a Mafia movie. She pulled a tissue out of her sleeve and wiped

her nose. The rest of us sat in silence, the laboured ticking of the grandfather clock and Toots's sniffing being the only sounds.

Tristan sauntered in, Mimi trailing behind him like a perfumed cloud.

'Sorry, folks,' he drawled, 'traffic was murder.'

Aunt Clem sniffed disapprovingly, her nose wrinkling as if she'd caught a whiff of something unpleasant. Uncle Fergus merely grunted, his thick fingers drumming an impatient rhythm on the arm of the sofa.

'Now that we're all here,' Artie began, his voice as smooth as oil, 'let's get down to it, shall we?' He reached into his brief-case and pulled out a thick envelope, sealed with red wax bearing the unmistakable E.W. crest.

Miles and I held our breath, the air around us feeling thick and cloying.

As Artie broke the seal, the crackle of wax seemed to reverberate through the room. He cleared his throat, unfolded the document with deliberate slowness and began to read.

'I, Eugene Weiss, being of sound mind and body, do hereby declare this to be my last will and testament...'

I could sense everyone leaning forward, hanging on every syllable. Aunt Clem's nails dug into tweed as she gripped Fergus's arm. Jeannie's smirk had faded, replaced by an intense, almost predatory glare. Tristan exuded nonchalance, but I noticed his foot tapping out an anxious rhythm on the Persian rug.

Artie paused, his eyes scanning the room before continuing. 'To my dear family, I leave you with this final lesson: in this world, there is only one victor; He who possess a killer instinct and is *not afraid to do what is necessary. I have no doubt that each of you believe yourselves to be deserving. Yet some of you are much more deserving than others and have proven your worth to the continuation of the Weiss legacy. I hope you will take my decisions in good faith and realise I was only trying to do what is* right, *no matter how unfair you may find it.'*

As Artie's words hung in the air, a collective intake of breath filled the room. I felt Miles's hand tighten around mine, his palm clammy with nervous anticipation. We had discussed what we thought the outcome might be and concluded that we didn't want or expect anything. But my God, would it ease some of our burdens if we did. Now that we were here, I could see how much it meant to us both.

'To that end,' Artie continued, his voice taking on a sombre tone, *'I have decided to divide my estate as follows...'*

He paused again, his eyes sweeping across the room, lingering on each face for a moment. The tension was palpable, like a rubber band stretched to its breaking point.

I wanted to scream, *Get on with it then!*

'To my first grandson Miles, his wife and children, a donation of one hundred thousand pounds to Miles's research department at the university, and a further sixty thousand to be split equally for my grandchildren, Callum and Martha, to be used for higher-education purposes only.'

Miles gripped my hand so hard I had a job not to cry out. I pulled away from him, and he looked down at my hand, appalled that he might have hurt me.

'I'm so sorry,' he mouthed.

Artie continued. *'For my second grandson, Tristan, and his wife Miriam, one hundred thousand pounds will be donated directly to Miriam's charitable ventures.'*

'To my nieces, Beebee and Ceecee, who I hope will go on to great things,' Artie's eyes read on, and he cleared his throat uncomfortably, *'and not end up in some seedy nightclub grinding on a pole—'*

I almost choked out a laugh as Mimi let out shocked gasp.

'—I leave the sum of sixty thousand pounds, the entirety of which is to be spent on higher education.'

Tristan just stared ahead, jaw working, his face getting redder and redder. Oh, Tristan was not going to like that at all. It was a miracle he was still in his seat, his body still containing him and not vaporising into red mist.

I saw Clem lean forward, her eyes wide; she might as well have been rubbing her hands together.

'To my son, Fergus, and his wife Clementine, I leave my collection of first edition books and Bluebell Cottage, to live in until their deaths. At which time, the cottage and the surrounding land will pass back to my son George, or his wife, Jeannie, whoever is still living at said time.'

Clem's face fell.

Fergus waited a beat, before his head snapped towards Artie. 'And? What else?'

Artie scanned the paper, before turning it over.

'That's it.'

Fergus shot up like an arrow, 'You've got it wrong, I am the eldest son!' He stormed over to the desk. 'Give me that,' he spat, snatching the will so quickly it gave Artie a paper cut.

Artie glared as Fergus furiously scanned the page.

'Sit. Down. Fergus.' Artie punctuated each word so that

Fergus had no choice but to throw the paper back at him and stomp back to his seat.

Artie sucked on the blood from his finger. 'Now, I trust there won't be any more outbursts?'

We each shook our heads, except for Jeannie, who was grinning from ear to ear like the Cheshire Cat.

'*To my nephew, Quentin, who is currently running the management of Weiss Gold & Co., I leave the entirety of the gold mine and its subsidiary businesses.*'

'He's in prison for murder, so how's that going to work?' Miles said with disdain.

'I shall get on to that shortly, Mr Weiss.' Artie continued, '*And lastly, to my youngest son...*' he paused, raising his eyebrows.

'What?' snarled Fergus, 'come on, out with it!'

'*To my youngest son, George, and his wife, Jeannie, I leave the remainder of my estate, including Weiss Manor, all its contents, and my entire fortune.*'

Aunt Clem let out a strangled cry, her face contorting in shock and fury. Uncle Fergus leapt to his feet again, spittle flying as he shouted incoherently at Artie. Tristan's carefully cultivated nonchalance shattered, replaced by a look of utter disbelief and muttering curses under his breath. Mimi just placed a manicured hand on Tristan's arm, her eyes wide. Toots sat motionless, letting the chaos unfold around her, as if this was just another day.

Amidst the uproar, I glanced at George. He sat there, blinking rapidly, as if trying to process what he'd just heard. Jeannie, on the other hand, was every bit the cat who'd finally got the cream.

I thought Fergus might be on the verge of a heart attack, his face purple with fury as he bellowed, 'This is outrageous! George? That good-for-nothing layabout?'

Artie surveyed each one us coolly.

'If you'll allow me to continue, Mr Weiss?' Artie waited until everyone was sitting in silence once more.

He continued reading. *'Despite my youngest son being completely irresponsible, lazy and prone to his dark moods, somehow, he managed to marry the only person in this family with true work ethic. My daughter-in-law, Jeannie, has proven that she has the Weiss killer instinct – Jeannie gets the job done, as I like to say. And I know, in my stead she is more than capable of keeping the fires of Weiss enterprises burning. Not only that, I know I can trust Jeannie to keep the Weiss name at the forefront of people's minds when it comes to the best in the business, and prevent any embarrassing incidents that may cause harm to our prestigious family name.*

'Jeannie Weiss is hereby the executor of my will. My wife, Thomasina 'Toots' Weiss, will continue to live at Weiss Manor, being cared for by my son and daughter in law, and they will provide her with anything and everything she may need. As for the rest of the family, if they too should prove themselves, Jeannie will bestow unto them whatever she sees fit.

'I hope you all take this with good grace and understand it's nothing personal. I know Jeannie can be trusted to preserve the fortune that I have amassed through sheer grit and determination.

'With best wishes, Eugene Weiss.'

The silence that followed was deafening. It was as if the very air had been sucked out of the room, leaving us all gasping for breath. I didn't dare to look at the others. I just looked down at Miles's hands clutching the arms of his chair; he no longer trusted himself to hold onto me.

'I am also in receipt of an addendum, which was made within the last six months.' Artie flipped over a piece of paper that was stapled to the back and read aloud. '*In light of recent events, income from the goldmine shall be kept in a trust fund for my grandson, Quentin Weiss, until his acquittal. In the event of my death, my daughter-in-law, Jeannie Weiss, will endeavour to do everything possible to see to his release and prevent our good name from further being dragged through the mud.*' Artie flicked through, his eyes scanning methodically. 'I believe that is everything.'

Aunt Clem was the first to break the silence. '*You,*' she directed at Jeannie. 'You're not even blood! Fergus is the eldest son.'

Jeannie's smile only widened. 'Sometimes, Clementine, it's about who has the sharpest teeth.'

Uncle Fergus's massive frame was shaking. He turned to her slowly, and said with lethal quiet, 'What did you do to manipulate my father? Did you poison him against us?'

Jeannie rolled her eyes and swatted the air. 'Oh, please, Fergus, it's nothing clandestine. Eugene was an extremely astute man, he could see what was right in front of him. He wasn't going to do anything out of some misinformed social contract of *fairness.* He built an empire, it was his job to bequeath it to the best person for the job.'

George had sat in silence. He was a man very much accustomed to taking his father's blows and the constant put-downs; a weakling who couldn't even step up to protect his own sons from their grandfather's wrath. It was clear that in

Eugene's opinion, George was less-than. But instead of fighting his way out of that role, George had stepped into those shoes and pulled up a seat by the fire. The first half of his life had been ruled by a domineering bully, and the latter half thoroughly controlled by Jeannie.

Tristan stood up and brushed down his trousers. Striding to the drink cabinet, he poured himself a large scotch. He threw it back in one and let out a bark of laughter that sounded more like a sob. 'Well, looks like dear old Grandad had one last trick up his sleeve. I look forward to proving myself worthy to you, Mother.' His voice dripped with bitterness. 'Come on, Mimi, we've got to get back to the girls.'

The pair left the room without a word, and with much less swagger than they had walked in with. I could see how they would be reeling; their mortgage was huge, Tristan had a penchant for expensive cars and the girls' schooling cost them a fortune. They had been holding out for a massive windfall that hadn't arrived.

Toots had shifted to look at Jeannie. 'You will let me stay here, won't you, Jeannie?'

Jeannie leaned over and put a hand on her arm and said with the smile of an adder, 'Of course, Toots, this is your home.'

'Well, if that's all,' said Miles, standing, 'we'll be off, too. A friend is looking after the children and we said we'd be back before their bedtime.'

'We're going too,' blustered Fergus as he stood up.

Everyone had filed out into the foyer and stood around awkwardly. George couldn't have looked any more uncomfortable. We bade our farewells and thanked Artie Peverill before heading to our cars parked out front.

As we crunched over the gravel, all too eager to get away, we heard Fergus mutter to Clem, '*Killer instinct? We'll show her who's got the sharpest teeth in this family.*' They stormed to their car and flung the doors open, before speeding off in a spray of gravel.

As we drove home in silence, the weight of what had just transpired hung heavy in the air. Miles stared straight ahead, the gears clearly turning in his mind, processing the shock and disappointment of his grandfather's decision.

'Are you okay?' I asked eventually, reaching out to touch his arm.

He flinched slightly, then sighed. 'I just … I can't believe it. All these years, I thought…' He trailed off, shaking his head.

'I know,' I said. 'It's not fair. But we'll be all right, Miles. We have each other, and the kids. That's all that matters.'

He nodded, but I could see the hurt in his eyes. 'It's not about the money,' he said after a moment. 'It's the principle. The way he just … dismissed us. Like we don't even exist. We might as well be invisible, to all of them. All we have ever done is work hard, for ourselves and for the children. And none of them even recognise that, but not only that—' He shook his head bitterly. 'They look down on us for it. He'd rather give his money to a murderer. That's what makes me sick.'

We spent the rest of the three hours' drive home in relative silence. Miles never really got angry – just deathly quiet, which I always found scarier. When we finally pulled into the driveway, our modest suburban home a stark contrast to the opulence we'd left behind, I couldn't help but feel a mix of relief and lingering tension. The lights were on inside, a warm glow spilling out onto the front lawn where Callum had neglected to put his bike away.

Miles killed the engine but made no move to get out of the car. His hands did not leave the wheel. 'You know,' he said quietly, 'I always thought Grandfather respected me. My work, my choices. But now...' He trailed off, his voice thick with emotion. 'I know that he doesn't. And neither does my own mother. I won't ever strive for her approval again.'

I reached over and entwined my fingers with his. 'Your work is important, Miles. What you do matters, regardless of what your grandfather thought, or what your mother thinks.'

He nodded, but I could see the doubt lingering in his eyes. We got out of the car and walked to the front door, the weight of the day's events hanging over us like a cloud.

'You're right,' I said softly, breaking the silence. 'They don't see us, see our attributes or how hard we try or how much we love each other and our kids. But I'm beginning to realise what a blessing it is.'

He turned to look at me.

'Think about it,' I continued. 'Did you see the look in Fergus's eyes? The way Clem was practically frothing at the mouth? They're going to tear each other apart over this.'

He huffed in agreement. 'Yup. And if Grandma Toots thinks my mother will put up with her living with them...' He sighed. 'What's it like, being part of my insane family?'

I looked up at him.

'Would you think I'm crazy if I told you ... I kind of enjoy it?' I grinned.

14

CRACKERS AND CORPSES

'How long?' I asked Miles anxiously.

'How long until what?' he asked. Miles was back in bed, lying under the fresh linen reading his book, as I once again cast an eye over the endless white fields. Further off towards the gates, I noticed someone had built a snowman.

'How long until they come to clear the snow?' I studied the landscape as shafts of sunlight pierced through the clouds. 'It must be soon...'

He turned to reach for his phone.

'Well, forecast says no more fresh snow. I'm sure it won't be long.'

I wrung my hands together. 'It's driving me crazy. Is it not driving you crazy?'

He looked at me over the rim of his reading glasses. 'I can't say I'm thrilled by it, no. But I find the minute you let yourself panic, the worse it gets.'

I didn't want to sound indelicate by asking him if he was

bothered that his grandmother was lying stiff as a board in the pantry. Of course, he must have a torrent of emotions inside, he just didn't show it the in same ways that I did.

We were a fantastic team, we supported each other's careers in any way we could, we would take on extra responsibilities to give the other space when they needed it and we strove to uphold the same values and instil them in our children. I always felt loved and accepted by Miles, but it would be a lie to say I didn't struggle when he shut me out like this. I knew it was a by-product of having an emotionally unavailable mother and a distant father, but I would never give up on trying to infiltrate the dam Miles had built up around his emotions. My only concern was, if I did manage to crack it, what sort of carnage might it unleash?

'Come on,' he said drolly, 'there's nothing better to do than get back into bed, is there? Anyway, we might as well enjoy it; after Christmas, we won't get this time again for God knows how long.'

'Hmm?' I asked, still staring out over the fields.

'With the move. It's going to be mayhem, I'm sure. I know it's impossible with everything that's happened, but try to take it easy. Mrs Harlow just changed the sheets, it's so fresh.' He patted the duvet, putting a dent in the big poofy cloud next to him. 'Let me take that rather fetching but very itchy-looking Christmas jumper off you.' His dark eyes glinted as he flashed me a perfect smile.

'Is there anything you want to talk about?' I offered, 'I'm always here for you to talk to, to cry to... There's no shame in crying.'

'Oh, I know. I always say that crying is the best outlet, you know that. I have no issue with crying. But right now I just feel too overwhelmed to feel … well, *anything*. It's like my nervous system has packed up and hasn't left a note. It's like all I can do is switch into survival-mode and power everything down until we reach Australia.'

I made my way to the bed and reached for him. 'I worry about you and the kids, how what's happened will affect you all...'

'I know, my darling. But if it makes you feel any better, I've already reached out to a grief counsellor in Sydney. They have availability to see all of us, if we want it.'

'You have?' I asked in surprise. Although I don't know why I was surprised; this man was like a self-cleaning oven, a car that drove itself and never needed refilling. It was his defence: being completely self-sufficient after dealing with his family for so long.

'Yep.' He smiled and raised his eyebrows. 'Sooo, are you getting into bed or what?'

I laughed. 'There's no time for relaxing, or for *that*, as tempting as it is. Didn't you get the memo? It's the gingerbread-decorating competition.'

He let the book fall into his lap, raising a brow at me as if I'd gone mad. 'I think it's safe to assume there's not going to be a competition this year.'

I shook my head slowly. 'Your mother has already baked the walls and ceilings.'

'*Oh. My. Christ.*' Miles pinched the bridge of his nose. 'You are joking?'

'Nope – she's got everything set up in the dining room.

Gingerbread houses, icing, gumdrops, the whole works. She said she wasn't going to let a little snow ruin tradition.'

Miles groaned and sat up. 'A little snow? We're practically buried alive out here. Except for Gran, of course.' He paused. 'She's in cold storage with the rest of the pigs in blankets.'

'Miles!' I gasped, half laughing at his gallows humour, 'don't be morbid.'

'What?' he laughed, 'to be honest she's better off than the rest of us. I kind of envy her in a way.'

I walked back to the window, pressing my forehead against the cold glass. The rolling white hills stretched as far as I could see, broken only by the skeletal outlines of trees. It was beautiful, in its way, but also oppressive and claustrophobic. I closed my eyes, picturing Toots's frail body, carefully covered and stored in the pantry. I couldn't shake the feeling that I wanted to run. My brain and body always felt primed, like I could fly from this place at any moment. I kept admonishing myself about our not leaving the house before the snowstorm hit, but we had already packed up our own home ready to be sold and it hadn't seemed right to leave a grieving widow *and* mother. Then we were stuck here … and after that, Toots had expired faster than warm deli meat.

All the while a small voice in my head kept getting louder as the days went on: *Were they accidents?* Do I need to get my family out of here faster than shit off a shovel? It just seemed so preposterous to consider the alternative. I had been part of this family for nearly twenty years and nothing like this had ever happened before. So why now?

'Come on,' I said softly. 'At least the competition will pass the time and give us something else to think about.'

Miles sighed heavily, sweeping the covers back and swinging his legs out of bed. 'Fine, fine. Let's go decorate some bloody gingerbread houses.' He stood up, stretching his arms above his head. 'Though I warn you, I'm just about losing my shit with this family. The gingerbread house may well end up looking like something straight out of a true-crime documentary.'

'That wouldn't be the worst concept we've seen. Perhaps your mother's been bumping people off to knit their hair into all those cashmere jumpers she wears?' I joked, then instantly worried that I'd gone too far, relieved to hear him chuckle as he strode over to the wardrobe and pulled on a T-shirt, black jeans and a grey Fair Isle sweater.

I smiled as he pulled the faintly Christmassy jumper over his head and said, 'Do you like it? Do I at least look the part?'

'Very much so,' I replied. 'You look like you're modelling for the White Company catalogue, while I have *Merry Christmas You Filthy Animals* written across my boobs… Not exactly on brand, am I?'

'But that's the way I like you,' he replied mischievously.

We made our way downstairs, the old floorboards creaking beneath our feet, the sound amplified in the eerie quiet of the snow-muffled house.

The dining room was fully decked out in everything you could possibly want or need for decorating gingerbread houses. Jeannie had truly outdone herself. The long oak table was covered in a red and green tablecloth, dotted with miniature Christmas trees and reindeer figurines. At each place setting was a preassembled gingerbread house, piping bags and dozens upon dozens of neat little dishes containing sprinkles, chocolate chips, and gumdrops. The old gramophone in the corner played Bing Crosby's Christmas hits.

Miles grabbed my arm and pulled me closer. Through clenched teeth he whispered, '*My mother is a mad woman.*'

'I think we already knew that...' I whispered back, suppressing a giggle at Miles's comment, and the absurdity of the situation. We eyed the gingerbread houses and sat in front of the ones we thought looked the best.

'You're here!' Jeannie's voice rang out as she bustled into the room, her arms laden with even more decorations. She wore a Christmas apron tied around her waist that looked like it hadn't seen a speck of flour in its life.

'I thought you two had gotten swallowed up by the bed again. Honestly, I thought the fascination would have worn off by now.'

'Never,' said Miles devilishly.

She eyed us like we were a pair of feral teenagers and tssked. 'Here, I thought we could use some extra sweets, just in case.'

'Yes, that's definitely what the table is lacking,' he said dryly. 'It looks great, you've done more than enough.'

'It really does, Jeannie.' I picked up a piping bag filled with white icing. 'You've thought of everything.'

'It is great, isn't it? It's a shame Toots isn't here to judge the competition. You know she thought of herself as somewhat of a Mary Berry...' Jeannie trailed off looking wistful, before slapping the piping bag out my hand. 'No cheating!' she chided as she placed it back on the table and headed over to the sideboard to pick up the large gong. Carrying it into the hallway, she stood with her feet slightly apart and began belting the bronze disc like the signal for oncoming war. 'It's decorating time!' she yelled into the heart of the house.

Miles pursed his lips. I imagined Toots lying there, the muffled shouts of *'It's decorating time!'* penetrating the closed door of the pantry, and I shuddered a little.

'Come on, get up,' she instructed Miles and me. 'You can't sit there.' She gave me a knowing look that said, *Remember what we talked about? Remember how you needed to keep an eye on Aunt Clem?*

We got up from our seats and stood until everyone else had filed in and we could be told exactly where we were allowed to sit.

Clem was straight in, her wiry hair pushed back by a large black headband. She had been the victor last year, and I could see her jaw was set with grim determination. She walked over to the gingerbread house I'd originally chosen, plonking herself down in the chair and pulling it close to the table with a screech that made me wince. Fergus followed, weaving his way into the room as if he was on a rolling ship at sea. I checked my watch... It wasn't even midday. Early – too early for him to be this far gone.

He plopped down as far away from Clem as he could.

Martha and Callum were next. Martha's cheeks were flushed red, as if the prospect of even decorating was too much pressure ... but then Jeannie did lay it all on pretty thick. Martha had never won, and I knew she was desperate to.

Callum pointed his fingers like a gun towards me, winked and clicked his tongue. I couldn't help but laugh at his cocky demeanour. He seemed buoyed up by what he had done to the twins, and I was desperate to find out what had actually happened.

The twins entered, scowling harder than I'd seen them ever scowl before.

Then, like a light switch had been flicked on, Beebee held her phone outstretched in front of her and held up a peace sign. 'Annual family gingerbread decorating competition,' she said to the camera, poking her tongue out of the side of her mouth.

Ceecee was capturing sweeping shots of the table.

Fergus reached for a gumdrop before Jeannie swatted his hand away.

I remembered Jeannie's warning and made sure to position myself next to Clem. Miles was directed with a jerk of the head from Jeannie to sit next to Fergus and be his babysitter.

Mimi entered last, looking like a trapped rabbit. The twins completely ignored her again. What the hell was going on there? Could what Clem said the other day be true? Was Mimi being unfaithful and the twins were icing her out? If only they knew about what their father got up to… Maybe they did, but as usual their mother was held to a much higher standard.

'While I have you all here,' Jeannie announced. 'Artie Peverill called me to inform me that he has gone through George's will.'

Oh, here we fucking go…

'There were no nasty surprises. It's true to Eugene's wishes on the financial side; there's not much George could change in that respect.'

Of course he couldn't. The man didn't even pick out his own socks.

'But there was one thing.' Jeannie looked a little queasy. 'George has requested no funeral. He—' She put her hand to her mouth, like she couldn't believe she was about to say this. 'He's requested a bag and burn.'

We all looked at each other in confusion.

'What's a bag and burn?' asked Ceecee.

Jeannie breathed like the words were stuck in her throat. 'It's where you don't have a funeral. Your remains are taken straight to a crematorium. No coffin ... no ... no nothing!' Her lip wobbled.

Fergus was frowning. 'That sounds like a jolly fine idea to me. No pomp and circumstance. We just raise a glass to my dear brother and say a few words to those who knew him. Wouldn't mind one myself!'

'Ha,' Clem sneered, 'if you were cremated, the whole building would go up. Petrol would burn with less vigour!'

Callum turned to Fergus and said, 'Have you thought about a sky burial, Uncle Fergus?'

'Is that where you get dropped out of a plane?' Martha asked, wrinkling her nose.

Callum shook his head. 'It's where you get placed on a mountainside and vultures rip your body apart. Very ecofriendly. I'm thinking that's what I'd want.'

'You will not!' I snapped.

Miles looked at Jeannie with concern. 'How do you feel about that, Mother?'

'I've tried to put a stop to it! But ... it was George's last and only wish ... and Artie thinks I should honour it. But it's not the law, I don't have to obey his selfish wishes. We should have a funeral with all of his family and friends there to pay their respects to him. I think he should be buried with Eugene, Tristan and Toots in the family crypt.'

'Tristan's going in the crypt?' Mimi asked, clearly taken aback.

'Yes, of course. If we're opening it up for one, we might as well put the others in there,' Jeannie said so matter-of-factly I was taken aback.

'What about when we die?' asked Beebee.

'Well, we can't *all* fit in there,' Jeannie said.

'So, who's going in?' I asked.

'Well,' Jeannie looked around furtively. 'There's plinths for the main members...'

'Ho no,' said Miles, 'I'm telling you right here and now you won't be putting me in that thing. Scatter my ashes wherever is closest to Liv and the kids.'

'Who's going in then, Jeannie?' asked Clem suspiciously.

'Eugene is in there with his mother and father, and there are five more spaces. For me, George, Toots, Tristan and Miles.'

Fergus's mouth dropped open. 'What about us?' he blustered. 'And Quentin? Quentin was father's favourite, surely he should be in there!'

'Don't you worry, Uncle Fergus, there's always space in the compost heap,' Martha quipped.

Fergus's jowls quivered between barking a laugh and taking grave offence.

'Or, better than that,' Miles continued, 'Quentin can have my space in with the crypt-keeper and her minions.' He looked at his mother. 'You can have Father's spot, seeing as he doesn't want to be in there, either.'

'He *is* going in there,' Jeannie ground out. 'And I'm not a minion.'

Miles raised his brow. 'I called you the crypt-keeper. Is it selfish of Father to want a "bag and burn" as you call it? Or is it selfish to ignore his last wishes and place him next to a man who made his life hell so that you can pretend you're minor aristocracy?'

I tried to remain neutral, but a grimace formed across my lips. This was getting spicy, and I was torn between wanting to flee the scene and reaching for a bag of popcorn.

Jeannie didn't even seem to hear what Miles had just said. 'I've favourited some caskets on the iPad; perhaps you could all take a look at them later and let me know which ones you prefer. Right!' She clapped her hands together as if this whole conversation had never happened. 'Let the gingerbread competition begin!'

It took us all a few moments to put the scrambled pieces of our brains back together. One moment Jeannie was geeing us all up for a gingerbread competition, the next moment she was asking us to pick out caskets. Now we were expected to do a 180 and go straight into baking. I had to wonder whether she had truly lost the plot.

'Why does it feel like we're about to take part in Sweeney Todd's Great British Bake Off?' said Callum under his breath.

I breathed a laugh, feeling like I was trapped on the Waltzer at a Halloween circus and the ride attendants weren't allowing me to get off. I really hoped she wasn't going to deny George his wish. I had no love for the man, but thinking about him lying next to his tyrannical father just didn't sit right with me. Plus, I really *really* hated funerals. So a 'bag and burn' was a win-win all round for me. It could do with a better name, though … the burning came before the bag surely? Or did they put you in a bag and then burn you?

Slowly, everyone began gathering items to begin decorating, the tone shifting to something more sombre than it had been before all the crypt-and-casket talk. As if trying to rectify the situation, Jeannie cranked up the Christmas music. I selected some piping bags and sweets, my willingness to take part in Jeannie's crazed version of reality suddenly deflated. I fumbled to get the icing out, carefully snipping a larger hole, which of course just erupted all over my fingers. I caught Miles staring at the bare house. I caught his eye and gave him a smile and mouthed, *'I love you,'* not knowing what else to say in this moment with everyone around us. He gave me a small but hopeful smile and took a deep breath. I went back to focusing on the roof, trying to create a delicate pattern.

Next to me, Aunt Clem was methodically crushing peppermints under the butt of a knife, gathering them up and letting the sticky pieces fall around the base of her house like red-and-white snow. She flourished her hands like she was creating a piece of high-concept art.

My mind flashed back to Tristan. Blood on snow. I shook my head in an attempt to get rid of the image.

I tried to steady my shaking hands as I piped a wobbly line of icing along the roof's edge. The twins were giggling and whispering to each other, their phones propped up to capture every moment of their decorating process.

Fergus had already managed to sneak a few gumdrops, chewing noisily as he haphazardly stuck candies to his house that kept dropping off. He muttered to himself, his fingers squeezing the piping bag until it exploded and the green icing dolloped onto the tablecloth. 'Damn and blast it all,' he grumbled, reaching for his glass of sherry.

'Remember, everyone,' Jeannie chirped, her voice unnaturally cheery, 'we're judging on creativity, neatness, theming and overall festive spirit!'

I glanced at Miles, who rolled his eyes dramatically before returning to his task. His tongue poked the inside of his cheek as he concentrated on creating a miniature wreath for his gingerbread door.

The gramophone crackled, switching to Bing Crosby's 'White Christmas'. The sound of his smooth baritone filled the room.

Suddenly, Mimi let out a small gasp. 'Oh *shit*,' she hissed. I looked over to see that she had accidentally knocked over her gingerbread house; the sides and roof had shattered all over the table.

The twins sniggered, their phones instantly trained on Mimi's misfortune. 'Epic fail,' Beebee said, zooming in on Mimi's crumbled creation.

Mimi wiped her hands on a napkin and threw it onto the table.

'Oh, just *piss off*, will you!' she snapped, before storming out of the room.

'Charming!' said Clem under her breath as she piped perfect diamonds onto her roof. She punctuated them with glistening blue and white gumdrops.

'Could I borrow some blue ones, Aunt Clem?' I asked.

'Oh no, dear, I don't have enough!'

It hadn't escaped me that she had been popping them into

her mouth. There *would* have been enough for both of us if she didn't keep eating the damn things. Like a dragon with its gold, she hoarded the best decorations and guarded them fiercely. I looked around the table but saw no other blue gumdrops.

'Oh, for heaven's sake,' Jeannie tutted, hurrying over to Fergus. His gingerbread house was listing dangerously, threatening to collapse entirely. 'There's no point now!' she said looking at her stopwatch, 'you don't have enough time to start over,' Fergus listed, just like his house, letting out a low belch.

'Halfway! Thirty minutes left!' Jeannie trilled, crashing the mallet against the gong.

We fell silent, heads down at our workstations. It was a serious competition; we weren't here to make cosy family memories.

Eventually, our half an hour was up, Jeannie banged the gong and we all heaved a sigh of relief. I looked around, noting that the twins' houses weren't even halfway done, as they had started bickering over something and lost focus.

On Jeannie's orders, we carried our houses carefully over to the sideboard to be judged. The twins didn't even bother, they just upped and left their houses on the dining-room table, done with filming their video and not wanting to showcase anyone else's creations. Even Jeannie seemed glad to see them go.

Callum's was first in line. The gingerbread house was kept largely brown, but he'd used green icing, chocolate logs and gingerbread men dressed in green and brown camouflage.

'It's a hunter's lodge,' he said proudly.

'Very nice, Callum,' Jeannie said. 'Very imaginative.'

Miles's was next. It was a higgledy-piggledy mess, but it was a traditional Christmas theme which would undoubtedly earn him points from Jeannie.

She glanced at it for a second. 'Hmm. You can certainly tell you're a scientist,' she said, moving on. Miles rolled his eyes and smiled at me as Jeannie stopped dead in front of Martha's.

'My goodness, Martha, is that Weiss Manor?' Jeannie said, abashed.

'Yes,' Martha replied blushing. She had made columns out of gingerbread offcuts to decorate the front in a Georgian style, and replicated the wreath and the buxus out of icing.

'And who are these four?' asked Jeannie pointing at the figures.

'It's me, Callum, Mum and Dad.'

'I see,' Jeannie said tersely. 'And where's the rest of us?'

'Buried in the back garden?' Callum teased.

Jeannie glared at him. Not the best timing, Cal.

'I didn't have time,' Martha answered. 'But I managed to get Toots in there.' She pointed to the inside.

We all bent down to look into the windows. Sure enough, there was a little gingerbread lady under a napkin.

'Goodness me!' Jeannie's voice rose two octaves. 'Do you think that's funny, Martha?'

Martha looked at her with a deadpan expression. 'No, I do not,' she replied seriously, 'I was trying to make it accurate.'

I gave Martha a squeeze on the shoulder in solidarity, but grimaced to myself. *Oh Martha darling, you're certainly not going to win now.*

Mine sat next to Martha's and was literally and figuratively a world away. I'd crushed up biscuits to make sand around the house, using blue, green and pink icing to pipe tropical flowers and palm trees onto the side of the house. The four gingerbread men wore surf shorts and dresses.

'Very summery, Olivia. What was your inspiration?'

I wanted to tell her the truth, which was that it was obviously inspired by the new life awaiting us the other side of the world, but instead I said, 'Your famous tropical Christmas parties, Jeannie.'

She smiled at that. 'Very nice.'

Callum bumped shoulders with me and mouthed, *'Bullshit'*, and I served him a self-satisfied smile.

Clem's was next. Decorated in blue and white, it was a gingerbread house fit for a snow queen. She had stuck lollipops around the outside, creating a pathway to the house amidst the crushed peppermint snow. Glistening white and blue gumdrops interspersed the intricate latticework on the roof, and piped on the walls were whirling snowflakes.

'Well... I think we know who our winner is ... yet again,' said Jeannie, although she didn't sound too happy about it.

Clem beamed, a glistening sheen of sweat on her brow.

'You've outdone yourself, Clementine,' said Jeannie, rallying. 'Worked up a real sweat, too, by the looks of it! Well deserved. Here—' She handed her a magnum of champagne with a big red bow, and a box of Fortnum & Mason chocolates. 'I wouldn't share this with Fergus if I were you.'

'Thank you.' Clem took them, cradling them like two babies. 'If you don't mind, I'm going to have a lie down. I think I've overexerted myself.'

'I should think you have,' Jeannie said dryly.

Clem headed out, clutching her prizes and walking straight past Fergus, who was dozing in his chair.

'Well,' Jeannie said, clapping her hands together. 'Who's for some hot cocoa with marshmallows?'

As we retreated to the sitting room, Mrs Harlow was coming down the stairs, arms laden with sheets. As Miles hurried over to help her, I couldn't help notice the strange look on her face.

Later that evening, no one wanted a big dinner after consuming too much sweet stuff during the gingerbread competition. Instead, Mimi and the twins opted to graze on the leftovers from lunch and head to their rooms. I rustled up beans on toast for me, Miles and the kids, glad of some time to ourselves.

Miles turned to Callum and Martha, both engrossed in their devices. 'How are you both?' he asked solemnly.

Martha looked up. 'I'm okay.' She shrugged.

'Cal?' Miles ventured. 'How are you doing?'

Callum bit his bottom lip as he concentrated hard on whatever he was doing. 'Yeah, I'm good,' he said absently.

'Please, will you put them down for a second? I want to talk to you.' The kids clocked Miles's sober expression and did as they were told. 'I want you to know something…'

He put his arm around me and gripped me tightly. I had no idea what he was about to say and my stomach did a somersault.

'I hope that your mother and I have raised you in a loving,

harmonious household. We've tried to shield you somewhat from the goings-on in our wider families...' He trailed off, looking to me as if seeking permission to say what he was about to say. I nodded my encouragement. 'I'm sure you've noticed by now that the way the Weisses deal with things is to repress and bury our feelings deep so that we are perceived as strong, resilient overachievers. And your mother's family, well...'

'They like to brawl,' I finished his sentence for him, knowing he wouldn't want to talk badly about my family. 'They love nothing more than a punch-up on a Friday night if someone so much as looks at them the wrong way.'

'They're scrappy,' Miles agreed. 'But Great Grandfather Eugene, he was ... he was sadistic. People who didn't know him would never assume he took glee in crushing people under his boot. And I think it broke Grandpa George. That's why he could never bring himself to stand up for himself or even his children. I have tried so hard to not follow in either of their footsteps—'

'We both have,' I cut in. 'We have tried to bring you up in a healthier way than we were.'

'You've done a great job,' Martha said to both of us.

'Absolutely,' agreed Callum. 'We always feel safe and loved.'

'Yes, but all of this...' Miles said sadly. 'I worry that you use your phones, or your gaming, Callum, or talking to your girlfriend, Martha, to escape. I want you to be able to open up to us. When I saw Tristan lying there ... I felt so desperate. So desperate that the brotherly bond we could have had was well and truly gone forever. I just knelt next to him...' Miles's chin quivered, tears welling in his eyes. The three of us gathered around him and surrounded him in the cage of our arms.

So that's why he had blood on the top of his boots... Thank God.

'You're right, Dad, we do numb ourselves. Let's make a pact,' Martha said, 'that at least once a week we make time for each other; no distractions, just talking.'

Miles and I nodded, smiling. I knew he was thinking the same thing as me ... in a few short years they would be moving on, and our time with them was well and truly running out.

After Callum and Martha headed upstairs, Miles pulled me into George's old office. Checking no one was around to hear, he closed the door softly.

'What's the matter?' I asked, concerned by his expression.

He pulled out a large kitchen knife.

'Mrs Harlow—' he started. 'She was changing the bedding, and she found this under ... under my mother's mattress.'

I frowned, watching the light glint on the knife's edge. 'That's the one that's missing from the block.'

He nodded.

'Under the mattress...' I pondered out loud. 'Do you think she planned to use it? Or is it for protection?'

He shook his head. 'I don't know,' he said simply.

I stared at the knife in Miles's hand, my mind racing. 'We need to put it back,' I whispered urgently. 'If your mother realises it's gone...'

Miles nodded, his face pale. 'You're right. But what if she...' He trailed off, unable to finish the thought.

'We don't know anything for certain,' I said, trying to sound calm. 'Maybe she just feels unsafe with everything that's happened. Let's replace it and keep a close eye on her.'

'But what if she uses it?' he said gravely.

'Then ... well, then we'll know that the recent deaths weren't an accident. We won't let her anywhere near us so that she can use it.'

'That's crazy, Liv. What if she hurts someone?... We should put it back in the block.'

'But if she *is* up to something, she will know that Mrs Harlow was the one who found it. She might do something to Madge! Also, even if we put it back, she can still use it. We can't hide every knife in the house.'

Miles paled at that. If there was one person other than me and the children he couldn't bear to see hurt, it was Mrs Harlow.

'I don't know,' he said, contemplating the options. 'Do you think this means that ... my mother might be a killer?'

My silence spoke volumes. *If* these deaths weren't insane freak accidents, then the only person who was mad enough to be behind them would be Jeannie. We weighed our options, discussing the pros and cons of replacing the knife in the block or putting it back under Jeannie's bed to catch her out in some way. We were no Sherlock and Watson, that's for sure.

In the end, we crept upstairs, our footsteps muffled by the thick carpet. The house was quiet, most of the family having retired to their rooms for the night. As we approached Jeannie's door, I held my breath, straining to hear any sound from within.

Miles slowly turned the doorknob, wincing at the faint creak. We peered inside the dark room. Empty.

'What do we do?' I hissed, suddenly having second thoughts again about putting the knife back. I didn't fancy waking up in the night to a knife-wielding Jeannie.

'I say we put it back. I don't want Madge getting into trouble.'

'Okay … just hurry. I'll watch the corridor.'

Miles slunk into the dark room. I looked up and down the hallway, every creak of the house setting my nerves on edge.

He emerged moments later and gave me a curt nod. We hurried back to our room. As we turned the corner, we practically crashed into Jeannie.

'What on earth are you doing?' she chided. 'You almost gave me a heart attack!'

'We – I, erm…' Miles stammered.

'We've run out of toothpaste. I don't suppose you have any spare?' I asked, heart hammering.

'Yes, I do,' she replied curtly. 'I shall bring it to your room. Was it really a job for the two of you?'

'Olivia gets a bit scared,' Miles said. 'Y'know, it's an old house…'

She eyed me shrewdly. 'Somehow I doubt this one scares easily.'

I had to admit, she was kind of right there.

We headed off to our room. As soon as Jeannie brought us

the toothpaste, we waited until we heard her door click shut, before locking our door and putting a chair under the handle.

That night the wind howled, and rain pelted the windows relentlessly, and neither Miles nor I got a wink of sleep.

15

SILENT NIGHT, SAVAGE TEENS

The next morning, I awoke to Miles shaking my shoulder gently. I hadn't even realised I'd fallen asleep.

'Liv,' he whispered. 'Come look.'

I rubbed my eyes and followed him to the window. The storm had passed, leaving behind a transformed landscape. The endless white fields were now dotted with slushy patches of brown and green where the snow had begun to melt.

'The roads should be clear soon,' Miles said, relief in his voice.

I nodded, feeling a weight lift from my chest. But as I watched a flock of birds swoop across the brightening sky, a nagging worry remained. We might be able to leave soon, but what about everything else? The knife, Toots in the pantry, the tension between the family simmering just beneath the surface…

I showered and pulled on cream trousers and sky-blue polo neck, leaving Miles to get ready. Heading down the sweeping staircase, I was startled by the sound of the gold letterbox clanging. Letter after letter plopped through the front door onto the mat. Mrs Harlow rushed around the corner, a silver tray in hand.

'Oh, thank God,' she muttered under her breath. She saw me and straightened, a stiff smile drawn across her mouth. 'The postman's been.' She pointed down at the scattered envelopes. 'That means we should be able to leave the house today. And—'

I nodded and smiled. She didn't need to finish the sentence. *And we won't have to be under the same roof as a dead body much longer.*

'Would you make a call to the coroner again, please, Madge, and remind them to come as soon as possible?' I didn't like asking Mrs Harlow to do things, it wasn't my place, but I knew she would already have the number and we were all keen to be rid of the shadow that seemed to loom over the house.

Mrs Harlow bent to collect the letters and said, 'Of course, I'll do it now.'

'And, Madge—'

'Yes, dear?'

'There's no need to worry about...' I locked eyes with her. 'About *the thing.*'

She nodded, as unsure as I was whether we in fact did or did not need to worry about Jeannie having a knife under her bed. She bustled off and I headed to the kitchen to find Callum eating a piece of toast at the island.

'Wow, I don't think I've ever seen you up willingly before noon. What's the occasion?'

He chewed on his toast. 'Occasion is, I'm bloody starving. What happened to the hospitality in this place?'

I laughed and came closer to him. 'Tell me, I'm dying to know – what did you did to the twins' TikToks? Something is definitely up with them.'

'A few things.' He shrugged. 'It was a three-pronged attack.'

'Tell me, *pleeaase*, Cal?' I begged.

He leaned in conspiratorially. 'I don't usually like to give my secrets away.' He eyed me. "Cause one day I might need to do it to you. But, in laymen's terms, I used bots, a bit of AI and uploaded a few videos about them. People eat that shit up. They love to turn just like *that*.' He snapped his fingers. 'It's scarily easy to create a smear campaign these days. Especially against fit girls and *especially* nepo babies.'

'Oh *God*, Callum, that's awful! What do you mean, "nepo babies"?'

'A nepo baby. Y'know, nepotism? Mummy and Daddy are boujee, flexin' their drip. Hey, don't hate the player, hate the game. You asked me to do it.'

I grimaced. 'Well, remind me never to get on the wrong side of you.'

Callum smirked. 'Oh, I don't think you need reminding.' He stretched his arms above his head and yawned, just the way Miles did, got up and left, his plate abandoned. 'Catch ya later, Mummy dearest,' he said drily.

I made myself a seeded bagel with cream cheese and headed to the dining room, where the windows were so large I could look outside and survey the potential prospect of freedom.

I was a little crestfallen to find that Fergus was already

seated in there, a bowl of untouched cereal before him, his hand resting on what appeared to be a Bloody Mary.

'Good morning, Fergus,' I said, as cheerily as I could muster. 'How is Clem today?'

'Hmm?' He looked up and noticed me for the first time. 'Oh, I don't know; still in bed. I don't think she's feeling too well.'

Jeannie was hot on my heels. 'Good morning,' she said, eyeing the Bloody Mary. Her mouth twisted. 'Bit of a rough night last night, wasn't it?'

I didn't know if she was referring to the storm or Fergus's drinking.

He grunted noncommittally and took a long sip of his drink. Jeannie and I exchanged a glance of exasperation.

'I've just been on the phone to Stoke Heath Prison,' Jeannie said, frowning, 'to ask about Quentin's release date.'

Fergus turned a shade of grey-green. I swear I'd seen his complexion every colour of the rainbow. 'What did they say?' he asked, bracing himself.

'It's the oddest thing: they said he was released two days ago.' She shook her head, 'I've told them there must be a mistake. I've called his phone, but no answer.'

'Christ, Jeannie. Are you sure you know what you're doing with Quentin? He's my son, but … he's not safe to be around. You're mad to want him near Callum, Martha and the twins.'

'Oh, tish-tosh, Fergus! He made a silly mistake one time. What have the children got to do with anything?'

'Children need to be protected from monsters. I see that now.' He held his head in his hands. 'I see it all now … now that it's all too bloody late! Maybe if I had put an end to Father sooner, Quentin wouldn't have modelled himself on him. Well, I failed at that, too. I've failed at everything.'

I looked from Fergus to Jeannie in alarm. What did *'If I had put an end to father sooner'* mean? Did Fergus kill his father?

Jeannie was surveying him with outright disdain.

'Pull yourself together, Fergus! Eugene believed in Quentin. So what if he got a little hot under the collar, we all make mistakes. I know that whatever my sons did, I'd stand by them, no matter what! Here—' She flung an envelope at him. 'This letter came for you. The postman must not have been able to access the path to the cottage, so left it here.' She watched him, waiting for him to make a move. When he didn't, she sighed with irritation and made to leave. 'You really should check on Clem, she's been in bed an awfully long time. And you should get up and go out and do something with yourself. Make yourself useful for once! Meanwhile, I suppose I'll be the one to track down your son.' She headed out of the door, leaving Fergus silently ignoring her.

I settled into a chair across from him and bit into my bagel. The silence continued between us, punctuated only by the clink of his glass against the table. I had only met Quentin a handful of times before he was incarcerated. From what I recalled, he was not a family man, working all hours at the goldmine, and when he wasn't doing that, he was drinking. Not unlike his father in that last respect. And Miles had told me he had a terrible temper.

'I've had it up to here with that woman,' Fergus snarled suddenly. 'Interfering, downright obnoxious busybody who can't see when she's playing with fire.'

I chewed, watching him. 'I take it you're not happy about

Quentin getting out? But maybe he's changed? Maybe he'll make amends?'

'*Changed?*' Fergus scoffed. 'Men like Quentin do not change. You're lucky, Miles seems to have skipped the violent streak in the family. Perhaps in that respect he's more like George. Do you ever fantasise'—he took a sip of his drink, the celery poking into his cheek—'about the day you'll never have to deal with *her* again?'

I remained silent. But of course I had. Many, many times. I waited for him to say more, but it appeared that he was done.

'So,' I ventured. 'Any plans for when we can finally leave the house?'

Fergus's bloodshot eyes met mine. 'Leave?' he repeated, as if the concept was foreign to him. 'Where's there to go?'

'Well, just for some fresh air. A nice walk down to your cottage, or to the village?'

'Pah! The cottage. It's not my cottage. No.' He got up clumsily. 'No. I don't think I'll go anywhere,' he said, making to leave the room.

'Fergus.' I motioned to his bowl, the letter, his drink.

He ambled back, snatching up the envelope and his drink, leaving me with his bowl and spoon.

A few hours later, the whole family lined up on the front steps of the house to pay our respects to Toots. Well, everyone except Clem, who Fergus said was still soundly asleep.

As I watched the covered stretcher descend the stone steps, I couldn't help but feel a stab of sorrow; Toots had been married in this house, raised her children here, and now she was being carried out for the last time. Sure, she was kind of horrible, and try as I might I couldn't recall a single time she had been *nice* or a pleasure to be around... But still, she was undoubtedly a character.

The men in smart suits were so polite and apologetic, as if it was their fault somehow that we had been with left with Toots's body for days. We watched as they slid her into their van and slammed the doors. We stood unmoving as the dark grey vehicle retreated down the slushy driveway, before an almost imperceptible sound of relief escaped us.

'Goodbye, Mother,' Fergus said solemnly. And I'll be damned if I didn't feel sorry for him, too. He was like some lost, drunken boy who had only ever had two cruel parents who'd never known how to show him an ounce of love. No wonder he was the way he was... No wonder George had been so cut off and remote. And then there was me, an outsider psychoanalysing and sympathising with them, when I knew damn well if the shoe were on the other foot, they probably wouldn't spit on me if I was on fire. And even if they did, they'd be asking for the spit back afterwards.

'Right!' Jeannie said in a high-pitched tone that spelled trouble. 'Time to get ourselves ready.'

'Ready for what?' asked Martha.

'For the tropical Christmas party!'

We all turned to stare at her, jaws practically on the floor.

'Absolutely not, Mother,' Miles said, stepping forward. 'We've gone along with everything else, but we cannot do that.'

Jeannie's head turned towards her son, her eyes glacial. 'Cannot? Or will not?'

'Both,' he replied, jaw set.

'I'm with Miles,' said Fergus. 'It's an absolutely preposterous idea!'

Jeannie turned to face them and squared her shoulders. 'The last time I checked, *I* was the owner of this house. And *I* do what I damn well please in it. As this past week has shown us, we have a finite amount of time on this earth, and I don't plan to spend it moping around, doing nothing with my life like the rest of you!'

Mimi and the twins flinched like they'd been whipped, clearly taking grave offence at her jibe.

'This party has been planned for *months*. People in the community look to me to provide social guidance. I am a leader!' she squawked. 'And as Churchill once said, "if you're going through hell, keep going." I for one intend to do just that!"

I was wondering what *community* she was referring to, because the only community Jeannie bumped shoulders with were rich individuals who possessed something she deemed useful.

'And what's more, I already have spent thousands of pounds on this party! The caterers have the food and have informed me that they are still able to fulfil the delivery now that the roads are accessible. Do you expect me to leave it all to rot?'

'Don't you think people will think it's strange us throwing a party after three of our immediate family members have died?' Miles asked incredulously.

'No, I absolutely do not. I think people look to me to set an example. I've telephoned the usual crowd and told them that the party is back on. Three p.m. sharp. All you lot have to do is wear something summery and drink a bloody Pina Colada!' Her voice was rising as she balled her fists at her side. 'Is that really too much to ask!'

She stormed into the house and slammed the door behind her, leaving us all standing in the freezing cold staring after her.

Grumbling and shaking our heads, one by one we filed inside.

In truth, I was secretly glad the tropical Christmas party was still going ahead, and my grand reveal wouldn't go to waste.

Jeannie's little tirade turned out to be anything but the truth, of course. After a few hours of running around helping to set up the pool room in full Hawaiian regalia and blowing up gigantic floats, we were finally permitted to go to our rooms and change. We all knew when she'd said *"all you have to do is show up and drink a goddamn Pina Colada"* it was an out-and-out lie.

Rummaging through my suitcase, I found and changed into a hot-pink bikini and a floor-length sheer kimono, patterned with grapes and pineapples, that Miles had bought me on our honeymoon. Wrapping my hair into a low chignon, I secured it with a hibiscus flower clip, teased out a few strands and applied some make-up. It felt absurd in more ways than one to be donning such a scanty outfit when patches of snow still clung to the ground outside.

As I applied some lipstick, my mind wandered to the knife under Jeannie's bed, and questions gnawed at me. A soft knock at the door interrupted my thoughts. It was Miles, looking dapper in a Hawaiian shirt and linen trousers.

His eyes went slightly wide when he beheld my outfit, and I hastily tied the strings on the front of my kimono.

'Is it too much?' I asked self-consciously.

He stayed my hand. 'You're never too much,' he said in a low voice, slowly pulling one of the strings undone. 'You look sensational.'

I playfully slapped his hand away as the bow came undone. 'Now, now; people have started to arrive. And I really could do without your mother walking in on us.'

He flashed me a wicked smile and traced his finger down my throat to my boobs, causing my skin to goosebump. 'Well, you'd better believe I'll be seeing you as soon as they are gone.'

'Hmm.' I gave a half grin. 'What about … in the billiards room?'

He groaned in frustration and gave me a tender kiss. 'How the hell am I supposed to wait until then?'

I laughed and kissed him again before turning serious.

'There's something I have to tell you…' My pulse picked up a notch. 'Your mother said that she called the prison to ask about Quentin's release, and they told her he'd been let out two days ago.'

'My God!' Miles's eyes flashed, his pupils dilating. 'What if he turns up here?'

'You think he would do anything?' I asked, heart racing.

'Not immediately. But get a few drinks down him and he'll be up for strangling the next person who breathes in his direction,' Miles groaned. 'Don't worry. I will tell Mother that if he so much as sets foot on the doorstep, then we are gone.'

'Okay…' I said, feeling relieved. Maybe him showing up here was the excuse we needed. 'There was another thing. Fergus said to Jeannie he wished he had seen Eugene off sooner. You don't think he could have killed him, do you?'

Miles took in the information and thought for a moment. 'It could be a turn of phrase, I suppose.' He raked his hand over his face. 'Let's get this circus over with,' he added, his jaw ticking. 'But don't forget, Olivia Weiss…'

'Hmm?'

'You owe me a game of billiards.'

I chuckled and kissed him again softly.

We walked downstairs, the sound of 'Mele Kalikimaka' drifting down the hallway.

As we made our way to the pool room, the décor shifted from traditional Christmas to Hawaiian paradise. In the short time since declaring the party back on, the pool area had been adorned with palm fronds, tiki torches, and a makeshift beach bar. The scent of rum, coconut and pineapple wafted through the air, mingling with the crisp winter breeze that snuck in every time the front door opened to welcome guests.

Each new arrival was welcomed with a colourful lei and the choice of a Mai Tai, Lava Flow or Blue Hawaii cocktail, served in hollowed-out pineapples and coconuts. I spotted Mrs Harlow looking slightly uncomfortable in a floral muumuu, handing out drinks from a tray. Already there were handfuls of Jeannie's 'friends' milling about, chatting and sipping fruity cocktails.

'Miii-lesss!' Jeannie's shrill sing-song voice rang out as she spotted us. She glided over, resplendent in a vibrant turquoise kaftan, her silver hair sprayed to the gods and adorned with parrot feathers. 'Your friend Reuben has come to see you!'

Miles cocked his head and said, 'Who the bleeding hell's Reuben?'

'Really, Miles,' she tutted in a mock-laugh. 'He was one of your classmates at Swanhaven.'

Miles blew out the side of his mouth and shrugged, before leaning over to nab a drink.

'Come on, now, he's come all this way to see you...' Jeannie took his arm and led him away through a cluster of bodies. I watched their retreating backs, feeling a pang of sympathy for him.

I inspected the usually serene space. It had been truly transformed into a riotous tropical oasis; faux vines hugged the arched windows, bamboo panels stretched across every inch of bare wall, and palms were dotted around.

The bar boasted fresh fruit on skewers and faux bird-of-paradise arrangements. Two huge flamingos and a handful of neon lilos floated along the water's surface. It made for a bizarre but pretty juxtaposition of tropical décor against the slushy landscape visible through the windows.

Left to my own devices, I decided to go hunting for the cocktails and canapés.

Making my way through the crowd, I spotted Callum lounging by the pool, his feet dangling in the water. He was wearing board shorts and a plain T-shirt. A young woman I didn't recognise was sitting next to him, giggling at something he'd said.

I grabbed a Lava Flow and made my way over to him.

'Hi, darling!' I said cheerily.

He looked up at me in a horrified warning that said, *What the hell? don't you dare embarrass me.* So I held my hand up, smiled at him, and moved along.

The twins, in matching white bikinis, were reclining on loungers. Somehow, they were perfectly tanned – their caramel skin highlighted by their white-shell bracelets and turquoise anklets – their youthful bodies taut and toned. Martha, meanwhile, sat curled up three beds down in ripped jeans and a Chappell Roan hoody, her head buried in a book. She looked up and eyed the party wearily, then spotted me and scowled, rolling her eyes. Jeannie had forced her here and given her a lecture for not wearing something at least a little summery. Martha had replied that she'd sooner shave her hair off than get an inch of skin out around perverted old men, to which I'd proudly fist-pumped the air behind Jeannie's back.

The twins also surveyed the crowd behind their oval sunglasses, Ceecee saying something to Beebee that elicited a smirk from her characteristically miserable face.

'Hey, Aunt Liv!' Beebee called, beckoning me over. I made my way to them cautiously and plastered on a fake smile that I knew didn't reach my eyes.

'Yes?' I said as I reached them. 'Everything all right?'

Beebee sat up and pulled her sunglasses to the tip of her nose. She leaned in conspiratorially, eyeing my gauzy kimono. 'So, are you on the lookout for men or women? Or both?'

'Sorry?' I asked, confused.

'Your cover-up, the pineapples. Does Uncle Miles just watch or does he join in?'

'I have no idea what you're talking about,' I said, scrunching my face.

'Pineapples is the symbol for swingers.' Ceecee smirked.

I looked down at the pattern. 'It's just a beach cover-up... Miles bought it for me on our honeymoon,' I said perplexed.

'Oh,' said Ceecee. 'Well, we thought you should know that you're basically a walking advertisement for a three-way. Upside-down pineapples mean you're looking for someone to join in or swing with. But hey, maybe that was Uncle Miles's intention...'

They both giggled.

'It's just a kimono. It's really not that deep,' I replied haughtily, feeling my cheeks burn.

'Hey.' Beebee shrugged. 'We don't care what you guys are into.' She put her glasses back on and they leaned back, signalling that they were done talking to me.

I stalked away, hot-faced and raging.

Fergus was at the makeshift bar. Considering how many empty glasses were next to him he was already on his third Blue Hawaii. He lifted a bowl of pudding decorated with fresh fruit and dug a spoon in.

Jeannie spotted him and bustled over, practically slapping the spoon out of his hand. 'I've *told* you a million times Fergus!' she barked. 'That's Haupia tapioca, it has cardamom in it, you fool!'

He hastily put it back on the bar and looked around for

something else to soak up the alcohol. Clem was still nowhere to be seen. I wondered if she was still in bed or if she'd finally emerged, only to take one look at the party and retreat back to the safety of her bedroom.

Mimi caught my eye from across the room and waved. She made her way over to me, navigating the growing crowd of partygoers. A black, tasselled sarong was tied around her hips; she, too, had a toned midriff and expensive-looking tan. Was there a spray-tan booth in the house that I didn't know about?

'Hi, Mimi,' I said, in a way I hoped showed I had compassion for her. She had only just lost her husband, and events had gone so awry it was like it had never happened.

'Oh, yes, you know me. I'm a fighter.'

'Yes, I know....' I trailed off, not quite convinced. 'Have you seen Clem?' I asked, changing the subject. 'Is she feeling any better?'

Mimi shook her head. 'No sign of her. Fergus said she was still in bed. Perhaps it's the flu.' She looked around nervously, before spotting the girls. They were staring at us, and as we locked eyes they sneered and looked away.

Mimi sighed. 'Could you do me a favour, Liv?' I don't remember her ever calling me Liv before.

'Sure,' I replied, 'what do you need?'

'I have been called away on urgent business. The girls ... they won't understand. But could you look after them for me, whilst I'm gone?'

I frowned. There was nothing I could do to look after two adolescents who absolutely despised me. 'Of course I will, but we're all here aren't we? And Jeannie will take care of them.'

Mimi fiddled with a tassel on her sarong. If she didn't have so much botox in her forehead she would definitely be frowning.

'How long will you be gone for?' I asked.

'That's just it. I don't know… I might have to fly to New York.'

'New York? But you will be back in time for Christmas?'

She hesitated. 'Yes – yes, I'm sure I will.'

That was a no, then. 'How can your boss call you away at such short notice to work overseas at Christmas? Shouldn't you be on compassionate leave?'

She dropped the tassel, looking irritated by my questioning. And then I understood.

'I will speak to the girls now,' she said quietly.

I stood watching her with more than a little glee as I sipped the rum, coconut and strawberry slush through a straw. Oh, this little showdown was going to be as delicious as the Lava Flow in my hand. I plucked the yellow umbrella out of the drink and slid it behind my ear with a devilish grin, then watched as Mimi made her way over to the twins, her sarong swaying with each step. As she approached, Beebee and Ceecee sat up, removing their sunglasses to eye their mother suspiciously.

Mimi leaned in close, speaking in hushed tones. I couldn't hear what was being said of course, but their expressions quickly changed from confusion to disbelief, and finally to anger. Beebee's face reddened, while Ceecee's eyes narrowed dangerously.

'You can't be serious!' Beebee's shrill voice cut through the party chatter. 'You're leaving?'

Heads began to turn, and Mimi glanced around nervously before turning back and shushing them.

But Ceecee was having none of it. She stood up abruptly, the sun lounger loudly scraping against the tile. 'This is bullshit!' she spat. 'First Dad dies, and now you're running off to God knows where?'

'You can't do this to us,' Beebee whined, her voice cutting through the party noise. 'It's Christmas!'

Heads turned to watch the scene unfold. Mimi tried to calm her daughters, speaking in hushed tones and reaching out to touch their arms. In unison, they jerked away.

'Don't touch me!' Ceecee spat.

'You're abandoning us, just like you always do.' I saw a tear slide down Beebee's cheek. 'You're a shit mum, do you know that?'

'Look us in the eye and tell us you aren't going to see *him!*'

They stared Mimi down as she gesticulated, saying something inaudible.

So, there was an affair and it seemed like they knew now, too. I still wished I could tell them about their father and what he'd got up to. Mexico was just the tip of the iceberg, if everything we had heard was true.

I didn't hear what Mimi said to them next, but she straightened and walked out.

Making my way over, I downed the rest of my drink and put it on the side.

'Fancy a dip, girls?' I said with a mile.

They stared daggers at me. Shrugging, I released the ties on my kimono, letting it drop to the floor for my grand reveal; that I, too, knew how to do ab crunches.

They stared down at my body before I turned and executed a perfect dive into the pool. When I came up, Martha was shaking her head at me like she was a little disappointed. Then, when she saw their twisted jealous faces, she smirked.

16

DEALS AND DEADLINES

The next morning, the atmosphere in the dining room was icier than outside as we sat eating breakfast. Clem was still in bed, having missed the entirety of the party, which was a real shame because she didn't get to witness Fergus falling backwards off his chair and into the pool.

Mimi and the girls sat in silence as I scraped butter over my toast, pretending to read the paper. Eventually, Mimi got up and said that she was going to finish packing and would be getting the train at noon.

Once she'd left the room, the twins began arguing in hushed tones. While pretending not to listen, I heard Ceecee hiss to Beebee that she was going to leave today, too; as soon as her mother had left, she would head back to uni. Perhaps I should have said something to stop her, or given Mimi the heads up before she left, but the twins were nineteen years old and as far as I was concerned, it was none of my business.

And besides, I understood. We were all itching to escape. All eager to go our separate ways, having being cooped up together for what felt like forever.

We passed the rest of breakfast hinting at our plans for the day, each plotting and making excuses to be where the others were not.

Later, after showering and getting dressed, I grabbed my laptop, a pen and a notepad and headed down into the village to do some admin and ... 'writing'.

I went into my favourite chintzy café, where they still had net curtains and red and white gingham tablecloths. I sat in the window seat and ordered cream tea for one, with extra clotted cream for the scones. Now that I had done my bikini reveal I was going to treat myself to a carb-heavy Christmas until we reached Australia. Heaven.

Opening my laptop, I saw an unread email from the ghost-writer. Butterflies whirled in my stomach as I opened it, and not the good kind.

Ten thousand pounds to write 90,000 words in ten days, and that was his reduced rate because I was a returning customer. I don't know what I had been expecting, but it wasn't that. I pushed the heels of my palms into my eye sockets. How the hell had I managed to get myself into this completely avoidable predicament? Well, I knew how, the real question was *why*, and that question was wholly redundant now anyway.

The fact of the matter was, if I didn't deliver, my publisher could ask for my £20,000 advance back, and we had already spent that and more on our upcoming move to Australia.

Could I ask Jeannie for the money? As a loan? I thought of Clem and Fergus, about to lose their roof from over their heads, and decided that me asking for money to pay a ghost-writer because I had been too pathetic, too bone lazy and caught up in my own shit to do my job would be a big fat no.

I closed my laptop with a sigh, pushing it away. The weight of my predicament settled heavily on my shoulders and the old self-loathing settled like a slick of oil on my insides. I stirred my tea absently, watching the steam curl up from the delicate china cup.

Lost in my thoughts, I stared idly out of the window and saw Fergus hurrying across the street. He was wearing a huge mushroom-coloured trench coat and tweed fedora, looking every bit like he did not want to be seen. So, he did decide to leave the house after all... I wondered what had changed his mind. The need for alcohol was the most likely. He trotted across the road, stopping at the red postbox. He looked both ways before fishing a letter out of the inside of his jacket and depositing it in the box. Then he scurried off down the street and out of sight.

As I spread a generous dollop of clotted cream onto the warm scone, my mind raced through the potential solutions of my predicament, each one seeming more unlikely than the last.

I bit down into the still warm fruit scone with a little shudder of delight, licking my fingers free of the jam and cream. A dark-haired woman bustled straight past the window. Even with her back to me, the flowing black-and-white houndstooth coat instantly told me it was Mimi. She clip-clopped hurriedly in her patent heels, which were completely unsuitable for the slush and ice on the pavements. I watched her with interest as she headed towards the small train station; the roads must still be a nightmare if she was willing to try to get to work – or wherever she was *actually* going – by train.

I stayed in the café, thinking, drinking cup after cup of tea, whiling away the time on my own until the light dimmed and the owner informed me that it was closing time in half an hour. As I was finishing up what could well have been my forty-second cup of tea, the bell above the café door jingled, and I looked up to see a familiar face. It was Miles, his cheeks flushed from the cold. He spotted me and made his way over, a small smile playing on his lips.

'Fancy seeing you here,' he said, sliding into the seat across from me. 'I thought you might like a lift home?'

'How did you know I was here?' I asked in surprise.

Miles shrugged, 'I know you. I know you love this café. And … well, there's only four other places you could be in this tiny village.'

I smiled. I wanted to tell him that I wished we could go home, to our real home … but it was all packed up and ready to be sold; and besides, I didn't think that would be helpful or make any of this any easier.

He glanced at the closed laptop and asked tentatively, 'How was writing?'

'Yes, good,' I said, not meeting his gaze. 'I think I'm getting somewhere.'

And I was getting somewhere. Ten minutes before he walked in, I had agreed to spend ten grand that we didn't have.

'Good,' he said, his eyes lighting up with his brilliant broad smile. He put twice the amount down on the table than the bill had come to, put his arm around me and we headed out towards the car. As we neared the car park, I could have sworn I saw Jeannie's silver BMW turn off the road ahead of us, speeding in the direction of the house.

17

FULL DISCLOSURE

As I traipsed back up the stone steps of Weiss Manor, the frigid winter air struck my cheeks. I remarked to Miles, raising my voice over the freezing wind, that I hoped to God it wouldn't snow again. He merely nodded, looking back towards the stranger's car that was parked on the driveway.

Inside, we followed muffled voices towards the sitting room.

Upon entering, we found Jeannie stood in front of the fire. A tall, smartly dressed man in a suit came over to greet us and a short woman with blonde hair, who didn't rise from her seat, sat perched on the edge of the couch with a notepad.

'What's going on?' asked Miles as the man turned to him to offer his hand.

Jeannie spoke first. 'This is Detective Chief Inspector ... Randolf, was it?'

'Lakeith Randolf,' he said, turning to shake my hand.

'And this is Detective Sergeant Helen Birch.' He gestured at the seated woman.

She nodded curtly, pen poised over paper.

Randolf continued. 'We are here in regards to Tristan Weiss's death. But your housekeeper, Mrs—'

'Harlow,' DS Birch supplied, scanning her notepad.

'Yes, Mrs Harlow also informed us of the unfortunate death of Mr George Weiss, just last week.'

'That's correct,' said Jeannie. 'My husband had a heart condition and unfortunately, we lost him not long before … before Tristan's accident.'

Randolf's eyes searched us, one by one. Waiting.

I pursed my lips together, keeping my mouth firmly closed.

'Has anything else occurred recently? Anything else you'd like to tell us about?'

'Well, yes, actually, Detective,' Miles said. 'My grandmother, she also died a few days ago. She was very elderly, ninety-eight. But yes, it's been rather a difficult time to say the least.'

Randolf raised his eyebrows in a moment of surprise. 'My condolences.' He put his hand in his pocket. 'So, forgive me, but when exactly did your grandmother die?'

'Three days ago,' Miles offered.

'I see. And where did this occur?'

'In the dining room,' I said.

Randolf waited for us to elaborate, but the three of us just stood, staring. He continued. 'And how did your grandmother – sorry, I didn't catch her name?'

'Toots,' said Miles. 'Everyone called her Toots. But her name was Thomasina.'

'I see. May I ask what happened with *Toots*?'

I waited for Miles and Jeannie to say something. They hesitated, so I said, 'We had just finished eating and she had some figgy pudding and then, bam ... like *that*—' I clicked my fingers.

'What do you mean, like *that*?' He mimicked my action.

'She just fell straight forward, into the bowl of figgy pudding. She didn't say anything beforehand, didn't seem in any pain...'

Birch was scribbling away feverishly.

'Should we not call Artie Peverill?' Jeannie said shrilly. 'I really don't think this line of questioning is appropriate—'

'I'm just asking some routine questions, Mrs Weiss. There's no need to worry. It's just ... three deaths in a week, that's a little unusual, no?'

'Life can be a little unusual,' she said tartly. 'That's the nature of the beast.'

Randolf weighed her words before he continued. 'Have there been any ... I don't know, inciting incidents recently? Anything untoward that you've noticed? Arguments, fallings out, disruptions of any kind?'

We all looked at each other for an answer. Of course, the answer was *yes*; power plays, money, alcohol, affairs ... the sheer fact that when it boiled down to it, most of us loathed and detested one another.

'Nope,' I said shaking my head. 'Nothing unusual that I can pinpoint.'

Jeannie was shifting her weight in front of the flames. 'Nothing unusual,' she echoed, her eyes darting to mine for a fraction of a second. 'It's just a very, *very* difficult time at the moment for our family, as you can imagine.'

Miles was cutting his eyes at Jeannie, as if he was going to say something, but thought better of it.

Detective Randolf nodded slowly, his gaze lingering on each of us in turn. The silence in the room was broken only by the crackling of the fire and the scratching of DS Birch's pen. Jeannie's hand fluttered to her throat, her fingers toying with the string of pearls there.

Randolf said finally, 'Do you still have this bowl of figgy pudding?'

'I'm afraid not, Detective. My housekeeper, Mrs Harlow, threw it away.'

'I see,' he paused. 'Well, we'll need to speak with each of you individually.'

Miles cleared his throat. 'Detective, do you believe there to be something suspicious about these deaths?'

Randolf's expression remained neutral, but there was a glint in his eye. 'We're simply gathering information, Mr. Weiss. As I said, three deaths in such a short span of time is unusual.'

Jeannie's shoulders tensed visibly, but she nodded. 'Not everyone is here at the moment. You will have to come back another time. A time when our lawyer, Mr Peverill, is present. I will show you out.'

And that was that. Jeannie led the officers out of the room, both looking back at us, seeming reluctant to leave. We bade them goodbye, and Miles sank into an armchair, running a hand through his hair, his brow furrowed with worry.

The warmth of the fire felt so at odds with the chill that had settled in my bones.

'What do you think they're after?' I whispered, moving closer to him.

Miles shook his head, eyes fixed on the doorway where Jeannie had disappeared with the officers. 'I don't know, but I don't like it. Three deaths… Christ, when they put it like that, it gets harder and harder to live in denial.'

'You don't suspect foul play, do you?' The words felt ridiculous even as I said them, but the detectives' presence had watered a seed of doubt that had already begun to grow.

He considered for a moment. 'Grandmother was ancient, Father had a weak heart, and Tristan…' He trailed off, swallowing hard. 'Tristan's death was a horrible accident. One that when I close my eyes at night, I still can't help but see.'

I rested my hand upon his knee and squeezed. 'I'm sorry, darling,' I offered helplessly.

We walked hand in hand through to the foyer, where Jeannie stood waving off the officers as they headed to their unmarked police car. She told us that they had warned her that they would be back, and that none of us should go too far. Too late for that; Mimi and Ceecee had already managed to elope.

Jeannie was so taut with tension, I thought she might snap at any minute. She gave a final wave and a stiff smile, until she closed the door and practically fell back against it.

'Mimi's flying to New York probably as we speak. And Beebee told me that Ceecee's gone back to university,' she said, her face deathly pale.

'Are you feeling okay?' Miles asked, reaching out an arm to steady her.

She inhaled deeply, closing her eyes, and breathing out again slowly. When she opened her eyes, she managed to school her expression, standing straight again without Miles's aid.

'I've done a very silly thing,' she said softly. 'Very silly indeed. But I panicked. I just panicked and I didn't know what to do.'

'What did you do?' Said Miles, his face changing.

'I-I-I neglected to mention that... Oh God help me... I didn't tell them that ... Aunt Clem is dead, too.'

Miles and I stood there, frozen.

'Aunt Clem – Clem? Our Aunt Clem?' was all I managed to say.

'Yes,' Jeannie said, exasperated. 'There's only one Aunt Clem, Olivia.'

'Oh my Christ!' said Miles. 'How? When?'

Jeannie gave a tiny shake of her head. 'I don't know when. I came back from the village... The house was empty, except for Mrs Harlow, Callum, Martha and Beebee, who were all in their rooms. And – and I went to check on her, I thought she'd been in bed far too long. Fergus has been down at the village all afternoon. He said he was going to get her some supplies from the pharmacy – paracetamol, rehydration salts, that sort of thing. But ... but he still hasn't come back.'

Miles put his head in his hands. 'For Christ's sake, Mother. You lied to the police? Why?'

'What do you mean, why? I'd just that second found her... I hadn't even got my head around it before there was a ring at the doorbell. And they were asking me questions ... asking me like *I* was under suspicion. What was I supposed to say, "Yes, officers, three deaths in a week, and if you've got a spare ten minutes, I'll take you on a house tour to see the full set!"'

Miles stared at her, dumbfounded. 'Yes! Well, obviously not in those words. I suppose you wouldn't want them know the level of your insanity. But by hiding the fact, you've now committed a crime! If you're aiming to make a guilty-as-sin impression, you're definitely going the right way about it.'

'Yes, well, I *am* trying to hide something. We can't let this get out. This is nothing short of a bloody mess!'

'Are you sure?' I cut in. 'Are you absolutely sure she's dead?'

Jeannie gave me a dark look. 'By all means'—she gestured with a grand sweep toward the staircase—'go, go and see for yourselves if you don't think I know what a dead body looks like!'

Miles and I glanced at each other. Then, reluctantly, we headed up the stairs.

The room Clem and Fergus had been staying in lay in the west wing of the house, two doors down from Jeannie's bedroom. We made our way there, each step seeming an eternity. We stood outside the door, both looking at the worn bronze doorknob, neither of us making a move to touch it.

'Ladies first,' said Miles.

'She's your family,' I replied. I took his hand and together we opened the door.

The room was dimly lit, with heavy curtains drawn across the windows. It was freezing cold, the curtains swaying as the sash window beyond was cracked open slightly. Our breath billowed into mist. A musty scent hung in the air, mingled with the faint smell of lavender. As our eyes adjusted to the gloom, we could make out the shape of Aunt Clem lying in the large four-poster bed, her yellow-silver hair spread across the pillow. I could see from here that she was still wearing the hairband she'd worn the day of the gingerbread competition. I realised that it was the last time I'd seen her alive.

Miles squeezed my hand tightly as we approached. I held my breath, half expecting – hoping – to see the rise and fall of Clem's chest. But as we drew closer, the utter stillness became unmistakable. Her face was waxy and pale, her eyes half closed, her mouth slightly open with an inherently displeased expression. There was no denying the absence of life. She was as still as the bedside table next to her.

'Oh, God,' Miles whispered, his voice catching. He reached out a trembling hand to touch Clem's cheek, then quickly withdrew it. 'She's freezing.'

We didn't need to check a pulse. There was no mistaking she was long dead. We stood there, almost unable to prise our eyes away.

Four deaths.

Jeannie had lied to the detective.

And still all I could think was, *God, how I wish I wrote crime novels.*

We were sat around the kitchen island in a numbed silence when we heard an almighty crash outside. Almost as if we were expecting it, almost as if we were anticipating the end of the world as we knew it, and this was just another link in the chain of events.

Rushing out of the kitchen, Miles reached the front door first and flung it open. It was dark outside, slicing rain spitting down and dancing in front of the headlights of a car that illuminated the now broken stone fountain on the driveway.

Jeannie gave a little yelp as Miles flew down the steps towards the car. I knew Jeannie well enough to know the yelp was for the damaged fountain and not for the occupant of the car.

I followed Miles, my slippers slapping against the wet stones. The car door creaked open, and a figure dressed in red stumbled out, silhouetted against the glare of the headlights. I squinted against the dark punctuated by the blazing headlights. There was a big white beard.

'What the hell?!' I exclaimed. 'Is that…?'

As I drew closer, I recognised the pale gold Volvo as Fergus and Clem's car.

'Good God, Uncle Fergus, what happened?' Miles shouted over the patter of rain.

Fergus swayed on his feet, in full Santa Claus regalia.

''Ello,' he hiccoughed. He swayed again and Miles caught him before he faceplanted into the gravel. He leaned dangerously as Miles attempted to get him up to the house.

Jeannie was squinting into the rain and the dark.

'Who on earth is it? What the bleeding hell's going on?'

'It's Fergus,' Miles managed. 'He's absolutely blotto.'

I rushed to help Miles, grabbing Fergus's other arm. My eyes watered at the reek of whisky and peppermint schnapps.

We half carried, half dragged him up the steps, his boots scraping against the stone.

'Careful now,' I muttered as we manoeuvred him through the doorway. Jeannie stood aside, her face skewed with deep irritation.

'What on earth is he doing dressed like that?' Jeannie's voice rose an octave. 'He's dripping all over the floor,' she snapped, before disappearing into the kitchen, likely in search of towels.

We deposited Fergus into the leather wingback next to the fire and he flopped down with a whoosh of air and a groan. With his fake beard askew and his red suit rumpled, he looked like Santa had crash-landed and was deeply regretting his life choices. He was also soaked through, the white trim of his jacket stained an odd pinkish colour.

'Fergus,' Miles said, kneeling beside him. 'Where have you been?'

'I think I broke the fountain,' he slurred, waving a hand.

'Why are you dressed as Santa Claus?' I asked. I don't know why, as there were much more pressing questions, but I really had to know.

He mumbled incoherently about reindeer and chimneys.

Miles looked up at me; the thought had crossed our minds at the same time. We had to deposit Fergus somewhere for the night where he could sober up. And in the morning, we would be tasked with telling him that his wife was dead.

18

INHERITANCE, INTERRUPTED

20th December 2025

Goody goody gum drops – another one bites the dust. I am getting too good at this, one might say I'm developing a taste for it. I knew that old dragon would hoard all the good stuff to win the competition, Clem was predictable like that. A few drops of arsenic onto the blue gumdrops, make sure they were the only ones on the table, and it was only a matter of time before she was hogging them all and gobbling them up like a little greedy guts.

I couldn't sleep. Grabbing my laptop off the side, I crept out of the bedroom and trotted down the landing. We hadn't told any of the kids yet. That horrible task would also have to wait until the morning. I was nearly at the end of the corridor when a voice floated around the corner.

Beebee.

A week away from university and she was now entirely

nocturnal. Perhaps she was always nocturnal, I wouldn't know either way, but what I did know was that nighttime had always been *my* domain. My time to myself away, from the family, and since the twins had taken up their nightly filming routine it had all been ruined. I poked my head around the corner to see her in the middle of making another TikTok. If I came round the corner while she was filming, I knew it wouldn't look good... Perhaps I'd feature in one of her videos, and God knows, I'd do anything to avoid that again.

'Some of you have been asking me where Ceecee is.' She preened herself at the camera. 'The truth is, there's a lot going on behind the scenes that I really wish I could share with you all. But right now, there's more people than just me involved. I really hope you understand and can respect my privacy at this time.'

I dared a glance around the corner. Beebee was sitting cross-legged, leaning against the wall, the blue light from the phone illuminating her face. With an outstretched finger she scrolled, straining her eyes to read the comments as she stopped to read a few out loud.

'Laura-lou asks, "Where is Ceecee, is she okay?" I would love to tell you, Laura-lou, but she isn't answering her phone.' Beebee scrolled some more. 'Faye-darling says, "Where has she gone, though, what if something bad—" Urgh, do you know what, guys? I'm going to come off the live if you're going to keep asking about Ceecee. We had a big argument and she left without even saying goodbye, I dunno what else to tell you.' Beebee sighed in anger and stood up.

My heart lurched. If she went back to her room, she would

catch me lurking in the hallway. Swiftly, I fled back the way I came.

Maybe I could wait in our room and come out again when she'd gone to bed. I heard quick footsteps behind me, the room too far for me to make it back in time. I was sure she'd soon turn the corner and see me, when I saw the line of shadow in the wooden panelling. It was sticking out, not fully closed. This was the secret passage I'd been looking for that led down to the kitchen.

Jackpot.

I hesitated for a split second, then slid my fingers into the gap and pulled. The panel swung open silently, revealing the dark, narrow passage beyond. Without a second thought, I slipped inside and eased the panel shut behind me.

The musty air tickled my nose as I fumbled for my phone, using its dim light to navigate the tight space. Cobwebs clung to my hair and clothes as I inched forward, trying not to bump into the rough stone walls. I could hear Beebee's muffled footsteps receding.

I wound down the spiral staircase, feeling my way, heart hammering against my ribs like I was a naughty schoolgirl. As I reached the exit to the kitchen, a faint glow issued from around the rim of the door.

I hadn't thought this through... What if there was someone already down there? Should I not have been more careful? What if these deaths weren't freak events and I was about to come face to face with a murderer? I felt something crinkly underneath my foot which made me go even faster.

I don't know why, but I didn't feel like it was possible that there was a murderer in the house; it just didn't seem feasible.

But *if* there was … I felt certain they wouldn't get me. I'd put up way too much of a fight for it to be worth their time.

I was at the bottom.

The door to the pantry.

Toots isn't in there anymore, I reminded myself.

I took a deep breath, steeling my nerves. The faint glow from the kitchen was still visible around the edges of the door. Slowly, carefully, I eased it open a crack and peered out, before venturing into the pantry and towards the kitchen door.

Inside, the kitchen was lit by the low drop lights hanging over the island. At first glance, it appeared empty. Then, I saw a figure at the kitchen island, sitting with their back to me.

My heart leaped into my throat. I froze, not daring to breathe.

The figure shifted slightly and I caught a glimpse of silver hair. Jeannie. What on earth was she doing up at this hour?

I dared to peer around further, keeping my body behind the wall.

She sat in front of an open laptop, the keys tapping frantically. Every few moments she would pause, tilt her head as if listening, then resume writing.

I debated slipping back up to my room, but curiosity got the better of me. I watched her.

She moved to the side, and I made to duck back behind the wall. But then I saw it on the screen.

Those unmistakable colours. Black and red.

I knew that page like the back of my hand.

She was on the forum.

My blood turned to ice.

I squinted, trying to make out what she was typing, willing her to move to the side again. The words were too small to read from this distance, but I could see her scrolling, scrolling, scrolling. I wanted to stay, to confront her, but I also didn't want to be caught prowling though secret passages when there was talk of a potential murderer picking off the family.

But I needed to see what she was up to.

Suddenly, Jeannie's head snapped up. I ducked back behind the pantry door, heart pounding.

Had she heard me?

After a tense moment, the tapping resumed. Heart fluttering like a caged bird, I let out a silent breath of relief.

Just then, a floorboard creaked somewhere in the house.

Jeannie's back straightened. She turned in her seat, swivelling to look around the kitchen. I shrank back into the shadows. This was so stupid of me. I needed to get the hell out of here.

She turned back to the laptop. Her fingers flew over the keys as she typed out a new post. I strained to see what she was writing, but the angle was all wrong. Then I heard claws on tile, followed by sniffing. Suddenly Gloria's great big golden head appeared in the crack of the doorway and she nuzzled herself in. She came straight up to me, panting with excitement and wagging her tail. I looked at her, my eyes wide, silently motioning for her to be quiet, my finger to my lips.

Gloria didn't get the memo. She was not cloak-and-daggers like the rest of us.

'Out! Come on!' Jeannie snapped, not tearing away her

attention from the task in front of her, 'No more biscuits, Gloria!'

Gloria snuffed and lolloped back into the kitchen.

Jeannie closed the laptop, picked it up in her arms and followed her out. 'Come on, into bed,' I heard her say as her voice faded away.

I waited for as long as I could, before heading back the way I had come.

Creeping through the darkness, blood rushing in my ears and pounding through my veins, I went quickly back up the stairs.

My foot scraped against something once more. I stooped, my hand grazing over grit and dust before it landed on something small and papery. I picked it up and went as quickly as I could in the pitch dark, back to what I hoped was the safety of our room.

Once inside our bedroom, I had to stop a moment to still my racing heart. Then I crept to the en suite, clicked the door closed behind me and put the loo seat down. Opening my laptop, I went straight to the forum.

SUBJECT: AUTHOR OLIVIA WEISS IS A FRAUD

OpinionatedOgre1

Olivia Weiss doesn't write her own books. See attached, an email forwarded to me by an insider, concrete proof she uses a ghostwriter…

<Attachment-IMG-122025>

BlackP!ll25

This is effing gold!

StaceeBabe

Hahahahahaaaaa we've finally got the bitch!

My blood heated my head and face like magma. The attachment was the email I wrote to the ghostwriter. I must have left my laptop unattended, or perhaps she had paid someone to hack my computer. Was Jeannie the insider or – much, much, worse – has Jeannie been OpinionatedOgre1 this whole time?

I flung my laptop onto the bath mat, turned, and retched into the toilet.

The acrid taste of bile burned my throat as I gasped for air. My mind raced, trying to make sense of what I'd just read. Jeannie, my own mother-in-law. As I wiped my mouth with trembling hands, my mind raced. How could Jeannie betray me like this? And for how long had she been masquerading as OpinionatedOgre1, one of my most vicious critics on the forum? I knew she didn't like me but … betraying me like this? It didn't seem possible, and yet the evidence was right there on the screen.

I splashed cold water on my face, trying to compose myself.

Returning to my laptop, I scrolled through the comments, my anger growing with each gleeful response. These vultures were tearing apart my reputation, my career, everything I'd worked so hard to build. And for what? Clicks? Attention? The satisfaction of bringing someone down?

I closed the browser, unable to stomach any more.

I flushed the toilet, hoping the sound wouldn't wake Miles. I couldn't let her know I was onto her. Not yet. I needed time to think, to plan my next move.

I hastily brushed my teeth and peeled off my clothes to change into pyjamas. As I folded my jeans something fell from my pocket. A packet of Rizlas. The only person in this house that used Rizlas was Callum... Had he been using the secret passage? He must have... When I had opened it, it hadn't been shut properly.

Creeping back into the bedroom, I slid under the covers next to my sleeping husband. His gentle snores filled the room, oblivious to the turmoil churning inside me.

I stared at the ceiling, thoughts bombarding me.

What will Miles's reaction be if I tell him about Jeannie?

Should I even tell him?

What if he already knows?

Was he in on it, too?

Should I confront Callum about the Rizlas?

What if this is all some part of a bigger plan to make sure Miles gets the inheritance and I get nothing, as part of some crazy clause in the prenup?

No, I couldn't think like that. Paranoia would only cloud my judgment. I lay there staring, staring as the same thoughts frenzied faster and faster round and round until I was absolutely sure I'd reached the brink of madness.

The pale sun peeked through the gap in the curtains as I dragged a brush through my hair and pulled on some leggings and an old sweatshirt. To hell with making an effort to please Jeannie's love of aesthetics.

That bitch was going down.

After coffee. A bucketload of coffee.

I wasn't sure what time Miles had got up, but the bed was long cold by the time I prised my eyes open at nine-thirty a.m. I practically staggered downstairs, remembering as I did so yesterday's events. The police officers. Clem, dead in bed. Fergus in a Santa costume crashing into the fountain, Jeannie being my personal online troll, the Rizlas.

Last night, I had been out of my mind, jumping to all kinds of crazy conclusions. But if I told Miles what I'd seen Jeannie doing, he would be truly hurt, betrayed and devastated. More so than me. I knew it would cut him deep and I had absolutely no desire to cause him any harm.

Miles strode into the foyer, a look of consternation on his face. Gloria followed him, tail wagging and mouth upturned in what I'm positive was a smile.

'Fergus is awake,' he said gravely. 'I'm going to talk to him before he has a chance to start drinking again.'

I nodded dumbly and followed him and Gloria towards the dining room, even though he hadn't expressly asked me to.

Jeannie was already in there, arms crossed and lips pressed into a tight line.

Fergus sat at the table, his fine hair flopping over his ashen face, his face puffy and his eyes bloodshot. He looked remarkably like an old basset hound.

'Uncle Fergus...' Miles began gently. 'We have some bad news. Some awful news, I'm afraid.'

He could say that again. News doesn't tend to come much worse than this...

Fergus groaned and put his head in his hands. 'Do we have to do this now? My head is killing me.'

'I'm afraid so,' Miles replied, taking a seat across from him. I hovered near the doorway, not sure if I should stay or go. Jeannie remained standing, her posture rigid.

'Look, I can't even remember what I did,' Fergus said rubbing his forehead. 'There's no point berating me now!'

'It's not about what you did last night. It's Aunt Clem.'

'Oh *God*,' he moaned. 'I don't need her on at me as well. All I ever bloody get is her wittering away in my ear. Nag, nag, nag! All day, every day. You're all on at me. And do you know what—'

'Fergus,' Jeannie warned.

'You can all go and f—'

'Aunt Clem is dead, Uncle Fergus. I'm sorry for your loss.' To my surprise, Miles delivered the blow, got straight up out of his seat and walked out.

Fergus stared after him, glassy-eyed. He looked to me, then to Jeannie, a half-smile quivering across his dry lips.

'Don't be absurd. Clem's asleep upstairs. Did you try shaking her? She's a very deep sleeper.'

'We didn't need to resort to that,' Jeannie said coldly. 'Anyone with eyes can see that she's dead. Go and look yourself, if you don't believe us.'

I shot Jeannie an angry expression. Wow. I always knew

my mother-in-law lacked empathy but seeing it at play like this was harrowing.

'Don't you look at me like that,' she seethed at me. 'I've been dealing with this drunken fool for forty years. She was probably dead when he went to check on her yesterday, but he's always so blind drunk he didn't even notice.' She cut her eyes at him. The house phone began to peal, and after three rings Jeannie turned on her heel and left to answer it.

Fergus stared into time and space, his drink-addled brain fighting to piece together everything it had just learned.

'I'm so sorry, Fergus,' I offered.

His hands began to tremble. 'No. No, no no no no,' he repeated, covering his eyes.

Oh Christ. I was going to have to comfort him, wasn't I? Making my way around the table to him, I hesitated, once, twice, before putting my arm around him and patting him awkwardly. *Where the hell is everyone else?* I thought in desperation. The kids would have been better at this than me.

'I can't believe it,' he said. 'How? How could this have happened?'

'I don't know,' I began. Suddenly, he grabbed my sweatshirt and pulled me towards him.

'You have to help me! I'm done for, everything is well and truly scuppered!'

'How, Fergus? How can we help you?' I said, trying not to recoil at his breath.

His dull eyes were wide as he whispered, 'I've done something very, very silly.'

19

ALL IS NOT CALM, ALL IS NOT BRIGHT

For a moment, I considered whether I could get away with not saying anything to Miles. Not about why I – and now apparently Callum – were sneaking about in the night. Not about catching his mother red-handed, or about what Fergus had confided in me. It dawned on me that things were becoming far too messy, and the last thing I wanted was for anything to delay our move. But then again things needed to be resolved – and quickly – one way or another. That wouldn't happen if I kept everything to myself.

The phone call Jeannie had taken was from a car-hire company. They said that Quentin had rented a car from them four days ago and had failed to deliver it back to them. For some reason, he had given them her contact details; perhaps he'd been planning to drive off with it and leave her liable? Miles seemed particularly anxious about it, so I asked him to come for a walk around the beautiful grounds.

The pathways were still slushy, some of which had now turned to sheer ice, and piles of snow still lay off the beaten track. To my dismay the temperature had continued to plummet, and if there was any rain on the way, it would certainly turn to snow. I threaded my arm through his, and we walked gingerly down the path from the house towards the trees.

'So, how are you?' I asked delicately.

Miles sighed, his breath visible in the cold air. 'I'm … I don't know, to be honest. Everything feels strange lately. Like the ground is shifting beneath my feet.' He glanced at me, his eyes searching. 'How about you?'

I hesitated, weighing my words carefully. The crunch of our footsteps on the icy path filled the silence. 'I've learned some things,' I began slowly. 'But I didn't want to worry you.'

Miles stopped walking, turning to face me fully. His brow furrowed with concern. 'What kind of things?'

I took a deep breath, the frigid air stinging my lungs. 'It's about … Fergus.' I couldn't tell him about Jeannie, not yet. It would raise too many questions, the most pertinent being, *Well, have you hired a ghost writer?* And that would lead to him finding out I had pledged to spend ten grand that we didn't have. I watched his expression carefully as I continued, 'Fergus confided in me this morning something that I think you should know about.'

As I spoke, a gust of wind whipped through the bare branches.

Miles's eyes sharpened. 'Go on…'

'He told me this morning that the letter he posted yesterday in the village … it was to set up life insurance for both him and Clem.'

Miles did a sharp intake of breath. 'Oh … okay, that doesn't sound too good.'

'No, it doesn't. So, is it up to us to tell Jeannie? The police? Or do we wait for them to find out? I just want to get on a plane and for the four of us to get out of here... But I don't know what's best to do.'

Miles's expression was a mix of frustration and worry. 'God, this is a mess. And you're right, we need to get the hell out of here, but not hold things up in the process. I know Uncle Fergus's brain is completely addled, but he's not so far gone that he would kill his wife, then go straight out and apply for life insurance.' He paused. 'Or is he?'

I shrugged, shaking my head. 'It's all circumstantial at this point. But why did he come back wearing a Santa costume? Do you think he was trying to destroy his clothes to hide evidence? Are we being completely stupid in thinking he's too drunk to potentially commit murder?'

We resumed walking, our steps slower now as we both grappled with the implications of what I'd shared. The trees loomed around us, their bare branches casting spindly shadows across the path.

'Did he tell you why he was wearing the costume?' Miles said eventually.

'He just said he'd lost a bet. That the guy in the pub was working as Santa and was as pissed as he was ... and that he can't remember why but the guy liked his deerstalker and his trench coat, and he lost a bet.'

Miles exhaled deeply. 'Let's think this through,' he said after a moment.

I nodded.

'If we tell Mum about Uncle Fergus, it will only make her suspect him of killing Aunt Clem.'

'Well … what if he did? He had the opportunity and the motive. They were desperate for money. What if … what if Fergus is responsible for all five deaths?'

'Five deaths?' He said in confusion.

'Well … think of it chronologically. Toots was convinced someone killed Eugene. So, what if it was Fergus? He assumed at the will reading that the inheritance was going to him. Clem said so herself. And Fergus called your father a "good for nothing layabout" and said that he thought that your mother had manipulated Eugene into leaving them the money. Then, when we were leaving, Fergus said to Clem, "*Killer instinct*? We'll show her who's got the sharpest teeth in this family."'

Miles gave me a suspiciously impressed look. 'Wow, you have a fantastic memory. Have you ever thought about being a detective?'

I smiled. 'Don't judge me but … sometimes I write stuff down to use later. You never know what you might need for a book.' My stomach lurched. If only I had paid more attention.

'So … he kills Grandpa, then what?'

'It seems as though in the last four years their money issues have gotten much worse, that they might have been about to lose the cottage. So then he hears that George and Jeannie are leaving everything to Tristan and Mimi… But that won't take effect until at least either George or Jeannie is gone. He sees George on the ladder and takes the opportunity. Then, he gets rid of Tristan.'

'I just can't see it… But go on.'

'Toots claimed she was on to the murderer. She had to hire

a private investigator. So, at that time he thinks she's on to him…'

'So, he kills his own mother? He's a bastard but … well, I was going to say I can't see him doing that, but I can't say I've ever experienced a moment of love between the family. I wouldn't put it past any of them. So, why would he kill Aunt Clem?'

'I don't know… He needs money quicker? Or just for the sheer revenge of it all? He said she "nag, nag, nags" him all day long. Or maybe she found something out?'

'A solid theory, but all completely circumstantial. We have nothing concrete here. If he's responsible for all those murders, he must be methodical… Why would he throw that all out of the window by being stupid enough to set up life insurance the day he kills his wife?'

I hadn't had a chance to think that far ahead yet. I shrugged. 'Maybe his drinking finally caught up with him and he got sloppy, made a mistake… What if there's two killers?'

'Who on earth would be in cahoots with Uncle Fergus?'

'Quentin. What if their fractured relationship is all one big ruse? None of us suspect Fergus because he's too damn pissed all the time… What if it's been Quentin all along?'

'But he only got out four days ago…'

'Like I said, maybe it's both of them?' I concluded with more than a little uncertainty. It was a big reach, and I hadn't had a chance to think that theory through.

'Let's say, hypothetically, that Uncle Fergus and or Quentin did any of those things. If we tell Mother, she will certainly confront him directly. That could be dangerous if he or they are planning something sinister. And the police... Well, they'd need more than vague suspicions to act on.'

I chewed my lip, considering our options.

'Do you think we are in danger?'

'The odds certainly aren't looking good,' he said. 'All of these deaths, they could be a complete freak accident... As unlikely as that may seem. The police are going to want to speak to us, so we can't leave the country. But we need to be careful. If we keep our eyes and ears open...' He drifted away, a line creasing his forehead.

I reached out and placed a hand on his arm, stilling his movement. 'I'm so sorry, Miles. I didn't want to burden you with this, but I felt you needed to know.'

He covered my hand with his own, his skin cold to the touch. 'No, you were right to tell me. We're in this together.' He paused, looking out at the stark winter landscape.

We resumed our walk, the silence between us heavy with unspoken worries. The trees loomed around us, their bare branches casting spidery shadows across the path.

'What about the move?' I asked tentatively. 'Do you think we should postpone it?'

Miles shook his head firmly. 'No. If anything, this makes me all the more eager to leave. As soon as the police say we are free to leave, we will.'

After we arrived back at the house, I changed into some comfortable clothes and headed to the pool room to check my emails. Or more accurately, to check my emails and worry myself sick about what I was going to do about being outed for hiring a ghostwriter. I scoured the internet for any information about what my publisher might do if they found out... Odds were they would demand I pay my advance back for committing fraud and then we would be £30,000 in the hole.

So caught up in the mess I had created, I walked into the brightly lit room almost in a daze. The smell of chlorine hit me. All signs of the party were gone, and I had no idea whether Jeannie had cleaned in here or if Mrs Harlow had done it, but even the loungers were stacked up and the pool cover was on, as if the place had shut down for the winter.

I wrangled one of the beds off the top of the stack and set it down in my preferred corner. I checked my emails; nothing from my editor or the ghost writer, which was probably a good sign. Next, I went to the forum, willing with every fibre of my being that there would be no new posts.

There were new posts.

BlackP!ll25 was so incensed, so utterly outraged that I could deceive my readers and the world so thoroughly that he had gone mainstream. Not only had he told his gaming buddies to spam my ratings with one-star reviews, he claimed that he had gone to a newspaper and sent them the emails.

Panic rose as I searched.

My average rating had indeed gone down across several of my books. But there was nothing about me that I could find in either the local or the national newspapers.

I felt a mixture of relief and dread. The damage to my ratings was frustrating, but manageable. The real concern was the potential newspaper story. If it broke, my career and reputation could be irreparably damaged.

My mind raced, trying to formulate a plan. Should I come clean to my publisher before the story potentially broke? Or wait and hope it all blew over? Neither option felt good. And then there was grain of sand at the centre of it all – the irritant. The confounding fact that Jeannie had put this out there in the first place. Jeannie's whole raison d'être was to protect the Weiss name, to keep it held in high esteem, both in the circles she mixed with and in the public perception.

The only reason I could think of was that she was trying to undermine me. That in desperation she wanted to put a stop to Miles leaving for Australia; and even better, if she could make him doubt my integrity, perhaps it would sow the seed of mistrust in his mind. If he decided to divorce me, my name being in a public scandal would be more than enough reason to prevent me from getting any money from the divorce settlement...

That had to be her reasoning. That and the fact that she had disliked me from the moment we met. Lost in thought, I didn't hear that someone had entered. A voice startled me out of my spiral.

'Oh, hello, dear,' Mrs Harlow said, surprised to see me. 'I don't suppose you've seen Jeannie anywhere?'

I forced a smile. 'No, I haven't, I'm sorry,' I replied vaguely.

Mrs Harlow frowned at the pool and sniffed.

'Jeannie must have had the pool man come to clean, but I usually let him in.' She looked at me and headed closer. 'Everything all right? You look a bit peaky. You probably shouldn't work in here, the fumes will make you go funny.'

'No, it's okay... I'm fine, honestly.'

'Come on, now,' she said warmly as she sat on the end of the lounger, 'it's me you're talking to. I'm not one of them.'

I glanced at her and saw her kind eyes. She had one of those pleasant, serene faces that reminded me so much of my nanna. My nanna – the only person other than Miles and the kids who'd ever truly cared for me. I smiled back at her.

'Will it stay just between me and you?' As I asked, I knew I shouldn't have even begun to tell her. But I so desperately wanted advice, or just to talk to someone, and she was the only person in the house who was impartial about it all.

'Of course,' she said softly. 'I wouldn't be where I am today without being the best keeper of secrets in the house.'

I took a deep breath, weighing how much to reveal. 'It's just… I've made a mistake. A big one. And I'm afraid it could ruin everything.'

Mrs Harlow's eyes softened with concern. 'Oh dear. What kind of mistake?'

I hesitated, then decided to confide in her. 'I … I hired a ghostwriter for my latest book. And now someone's threatening to expose me.'

Mrs Harlow's eyebrows rose slightly, but her expression remained nonjudgmental. 'I see. And you're worried about the consequences?'

I nodded, feeling a lump in my throat. 'If it gets out, I could lose my publishing contract, my reputation … everything I've worked for.'

She patted my hand gently. 'That does sound serious. But mistakes happen, dear. The question is, what are you going to do about it?'

'Well yes, that is the question indeed,' I said sadly.

'Does Miles know?' she asked.

I swallowed. If there was anyone in the house that commanded Mrs Harlow's loyalty entirely, it was Miles. I shook my head.

'I don't know much about being a writer,' she offered, 'but I do know a thing or two about having a harmonious partnership. I could tell my late husband anything, even the ugliest parts of myself, and he never baulked. The only advice I can offer you is that in my experience, especially with this family, secrets only grow. Maybe you and your family could be the ones to break that cycle.'

She was not wrong. This secret had grown into a monster and sprouted four heads.

'I've always said honesty is the best policy,' she continued. 'But then, Mr Artie Peverill would tell you the exact opposite... And he's been playing the game of secrets far longer than I.' She shrugged.

I wanted to tell Mrs Harlow it was Jeannie who had outed me. But something stopped me. Something told me I still couldn't fully trust her when it came to her longtime employer and the lengths she would go to protect her.

'Thank you, Mrs Harlow,' I said with a smile.

'It's my pleasure. Now any time you need anything, or anyone to talk to, I'm always here...' Her voice trailed off as she spotted something out of the window. She stood up abruptly and said, 'Oh no. What do they want?'

I looked out to see the same unmarked police car from two days ago heading up the driveway.

'This really couldn't come at a worse time,' she said

hurrying to exit the room. I followed her, bracing myself for whatever was to come next.

———————

'Do not speak! Any of you,' Jeannie had hissed at us in the foyer before opening the door. You say, "no comment" until Artie gets here, do you understand?'

'Are they here for Aunt Clem?' Miles asked.

Jeannie's lip wavered. The knock on the door made her jump out of her skin. 'I haven't told them,' she said quietly.

'What?!' Miles boomed.

'Sshhhh,' she hissed. 'I need to minimise the press. I called Artie and he's sending around a man he knows on the force. A very discreet man…'

Miles looked stricken, 'Oh my God, Mother – are you insane?'

The officers at the door were banging loudly now.

'Just keep quiet until I can get on top of all of this,' she commanded. 'Especially you, Fergus! Look at you, you old soak, can't even stand straight.' Jeannie smoothed down her skirt and opened the door.

DCI Randolf and DS Birch stood in the entrance with sombre expressions lining their faces.

'May we come in?' DCI Randolf asked.

'Hello, yes, of course, officers. Mrs Harlow, can you bring us some tea?'

DS Birch's eyes brightened, about to open her mouth to say yes when Randolf cut in, 'No need for tea, thank you.'

We filed into the living room one by one.

'So, officer, we know why you've come,' Fergus drawled. Jeannie's eyes flew open at him in warning.

'You do?' Randolf replied, eyebrows knitted.

'Yes,' Jeannie said quickly. 'You said the other day that you would be returning to question us. But I did tell you over the phone that we require notice to ensure our legal aid is with us.'

'Yes, Mrs Weiss. But I haven't come about that.'

'Oh?' She said, eyebrows raised.

'I have some tragic news regarding Mrs Miriam Weiss.' His deep brown eyes held Jeannie's as he added, 'You might need to sit down, Mrs Weiss.'

'I'm perfectly fine standing up, thank you.' Jeannie jutted her chin out, readying herself for the news.

Randolf took a deep breath. 'A body was found on the train tracks two days ago. After checking CCTV and dental records, we believe it to be Miriam Weiss.'

'Mimi?' I said hoarsely, my legs shaking underneath me. I felt behind me for the couch and sat down. 'Two days ago?'

'Yes. We won't require a formal identification... I don't think that would be advisable at this time. As I said, we have a positive ID on dental records and the CCTV of the incident, which we will share with you in due course. I'm very sorry for your loss.'

'Oh my *God*.' I clamped my hand over my mouth, wanting to retch. Poor Mimi. Poor, stupid, selfish, ridiculous Mimi.

The room fell into a stunned silence. Jeannie's face had gone pale, her usual composure cracking as she slowly sank into a nearby chair. Miles, who had been standing by the fireplace, stepped forward.

'The girls...' he said, his voice tight with emotion.

DCI Randolf nodded grimly, understanding that we would have to tell them that their mother and father were now both dead. 'We later searched the scene and found personal effects that corroborate our identification. Again, I'm so very sorry for your loss.'

I felt numb, my mind reeling as I tried to process this latest tragedy. Mimi, gone. Another death in the family. It seemed impossible, unreal, that Mimi could be dead, too. At this rate, we'd need a group discount on coffins.

Birch cleared her throat softly. 'We'll need to ask some questions. We understand this is a difficult time, but it's important we gather information as soon as possible.'

Suddenly I felt Miles's hand on my shoulder, grounding me. The room seemed to spin as the implications of what DCI Randolf had said sank in.

Jeannie's voice remained steady as she asked, 'How ... how did it happen?'

DCI Randolf's expression was grim. 'Based on the CCTV footage, it appears Mrs Weiss jumped in front of an oncoming train. We're treating it as a suspected suicide at this time. However, the angle is slightly obscured, so we are asking for eyewitnesses to come forward.'

A choked sob escaped Jeannie's throat, her composure finally cracking. Mrs Harlow quickly moved to her side, offering silent support.

'There's just no way,' I began, 'no way that Mimi would end her own life. She has two girls.'

'We're very sorry for your loss,' DS Birch said softly.

I knew what that meant. That people *did* end their lives all the time, regardless of whether they had two children, ten children or no children. But they didn't know Mimi; in fact, I think I knew Mimi better than any of the people in this room. She was egotistical and vainglorious as hell. It seemed to me that the only thing concerning her was how she was going to get back to her love affair, not the fact that her husband had died, or any maternal instinct to be there for her daughters. There was no way she was getting mashed up by a train voluntarily.

But then ... what if she knew something that we didn't. What if she was the killer and could no longer live with herself. What if one of the *girls* was the killer... Maybe then, just maybe.

'Could she have fallen by accident?' Jeannie's voice sounded strangled.

'We are still in the process of analysing the footage. It's unclear at this moment.'

'Could it be murder?' Mrs Harlow said quietly.

'There didn't appear to be anyone near Mrs Weiss at the time of her death,' Randolf concluded.

Mrs Harlow shot me a glance and I felt a chill run through me. The implications were clear – with all the recent deaths in the family, murder couldn't be ruled out so easily.

Miles cleared his throat. 'When exactly did this happen? You said the body was found two days ago?'

DCI Randolf consulted his notes. 'The incident occurred early on Monday evening at Crewe Station, around four-thirty p.m.'

Monday. My mind raced, trying to piece together where everyone had been. I was in the village, writing in the café.

I had been with Miles, hadn't I? Or had I? The days were starting to blur together.

'We'll need to speak with each of you individually,' Birch said gently. 'To establish timelines and gather any information that might be relevant.'

Jeannie nodded stiffly, her face a mask of shock and grief. 'When we've told the girls. We must tell the girls.'

'Before you go, there's something else you should know.' Randolf clasped his hands in front of him. 'A member of our team found a car in a layby not far from here. The car was reported missing when it should have been returned to a rental company four days ago.'

Miles and I looked at each other. Quentin. Quentin is here.

Hot dread ran through me anew.

'Quentin Weiss rented that car,' said Randolf gravely. 'Have any of you heard from him since his release?'

'No,' said Jeannie. 'Not a thing. I've been trying to contact him for days. It just keeps ringing out.'

Randolf gave Birch a look that said they needed to get on with locating him straightaway.

'If you don't mind,' Jeannie said, 'I must speak with my granddaughters immediately.'

Randolf nodded in agreement.

'Do you want me to come with you?' Miles asked Jeannie. She nodded weakly and they left to deliver the news together.

'Shall we head somewhere more private, Mrs Weiss?' Randolf asked. After a moment he repeated, 'Mrs Weiss?' and I realised he was referring to me. There were far too many Mrs Weisses... No. No, there were only two Mrs Weisses left. Two out of five remained. I didn't like the sound of those odds.

20

DECK THE HALLS ... WITH LEGAL FALLOUT

22nd December 2025

I got on the train from the village all the way to Crewe. She didn't even notice me, so self-absorbed and eager she was to get away to her loverboy. It really was testament to her utter narcissism because I was dressed as friggin' SANTA and she STILL didn't notice me. I got on in the carriage behind her, and could see her the whole time laughing away, so happy, even though her husband had not long died and she was leaving her children behind for Christmas. But hey, love makes you do crazy things, I guess.

We had to make a change at Crewe. I didn't fancy going all the way to London so it had to be done then and there. The platform was icy, she stood waiting for the next train, grinning stupidly at her phone, barely paying attention to where she was going. Is there anything worse than that? It's dangerous, if you ask me. Especially when you're tottering about in high heels. It was an accident waiting to happen.

I lay in wait in front of a pillar. As the train came in, her feet

strayed over the yellow line. All it took was a brisk walk past her
and a nudge.

Clip clop clip clop—SPLAT.

I bet she still tried to land on her best side.

I nodded numbly and followed DCI Randolf to the study. We settled into the leather chairs whilst I tried to gather up my scattered thoughts. The reality of Mimi's death was still sinking in, along with the chilling implications.

'Mrs Weiss, can you tell me where you were on Tuesday evening around four-thirty p.m.?' Randolf asked calmly.

I fidgeted, trying to remember. 'I … I was at the village café, writing.'

Randolf nodded, jotting something in his notebook. 'Do you recall what time you returned to the house?'

'It must have been around six or seven p.m.,' I said, struggling to piece together the timeline. 'Miles came to meet me at the café and we went home together… I don't know the exact time, I'm sorry.'

'Can anyone confirm that?'

'The lady who owns the café.' *So far so good*, I reassured myself.

He nodded, jotting something down. 'And when was the last time you saw Miriam Weiss?'

'The last time I saw her was the morning she left to catch her train, so Monday morning. But we didn't speak, she just told the girls she was going to pack and head to catch her train at noon. The last time I spoke to her was at the pool party the day before. She told me she needed to go away for work and asked me whether I would look after the girls.'

'Her daughters? Beebee and Ceecee?'

'Yes, that's correct.'

He frowned at his piece of paper. 'Aren't they are a little old to be looked after?'

'Well, that's what I thought. I did think it was strange.'

'Why did you think it was strange, Mrs Weiss?'

'Well.' I huffed a laugh. 'Like you just said yourself, they are basically adults themselves. I'm sure they don't want or need me to look after them.'

'So, do you have any indication as to why she asked you that?'

'Personally … it seemed like she was going away indefinitely. And with everything that was going on…' I trailed off.

'Going on?'

'The deaths… I don't for one second think that she thought either of them would come to any harm, though, or she wouldn't have left them.'

'Wouldn't she?' he asked, his brown eyes fixed on mine.

'I don't believe that Mimi would ever want anything to happen to the girls.'

'Yet she left them here … despite the spate of unexplained deaths.'

'Yes…'

'Why do you think she did that? Surely her work in insurance isn't so pressing that she can't do it remotely? Or at least, not be away for more than a few days over Christmas?'

'There was a rumour—' I stopped short.

'Please, Mrs Weiss, if you're not transparent with us, you

could make things very difficult for yourself in the long run. I need you to tell me everything that you have seen and heard to help me build a picture of what is going on here.'

'Okay,' I said taking a deep breath, 'there was a rumour that Mimi was having an affair. That she was going to see whoever she was supposed to be seeing. I believe that is why she said she would be gone indefinitely; she was going to spend Christmas with this person.'

'When did you hear of this rumour?'

'The first time I heard it from—'

He waited for my answer.

'F-from Aunt Clem.'

'Aunt Clem?' He turned to Birch. 'Have we spoken to her yet, DS Birch?'

Birch flicked through her notes before shaking her head.

Oh crap. I pursed my lips. Both of the officers watched me, watched every little twitch and tell on my face. *I am not cut out for this*, I thought bitterly.

DCI Randolf leaned back in his chair, his pen tapping thoughtfully against his notepad. 'Aunt Clem,' he repeated. 'And is Aunt Clem staying here, too?'

I shifted uncomfortably, the leather chair creaking beneath me. 'Yes. She's Miles's aunt. Married to Uncle Fergus, who is George's brother. George is – *was* Miles's father.'

I am going to prison for this. God I could kill Jeannie for this, I *had* to tell them.

'I see,' Randolf said, scribbling something down. 'And did Aunt Clem happen to mention how she knew this information?'

I hesitated, my throat suddenly dry. 'She … she didn't say

specifically, no. I only overheard her conversations with Jeannie, and she tried to tell Toots.'

Oh God, oh God. Why was I the first person to be interviewed. I squirmed, growing hot.

'Phew,' I said, fanning myself. 'Is it just me, or is it insanely hot in here?'

'Not particularly,' Randolf said with a bored expression. Birch sat in silence behind him, constantly making notes.

Randolf's eyes narrowed slightly. 'Mrs Weiss, I need you to understand the gravity of this situation—'

'I do,' I said in earnest. A beat passed between us, the air thick and hot. If I didn't tell them now, and one of the others got there first, I would incriminate myself by not coming clean. I had to say something, Jeannie and Artie sodding Peverill be damned. 'Clem – Clem is dead,' I blurted out.

Birch stopped scribbling and they both stared at me.

The silence stretched on for what felt like an eternity. DCI Randolf's expression darkened, his eyes never leaving my face. I could feel beads of sweat forming on my brow.

'Clem passed away in her sleep,' I blurted. 'She's upstairs.'

He looked angry as hell and my breathing quickened. Finally, he spoke, his voice low and controlled. 'Mrs Weiss, are you telling me that there's been another death in this house that you neglected to mention until now?'

I swallowed hard, my mouth feeling like the Sahara. 'I... I'm sorry. It just happened. We found her, um, yesterday, I think it was.'

Randolf exchanged a quick glance with Birch before turning back to me. *'Just happened?* I don't think that counts as *just happened,* do you?'

'Yes, no. It all sounds ridiculous when you put it like that,' I admitted, my voice barely above a whisper. 'But – but Jeannie said she had handled it. That she had called someone. We thought you were here because of that, not because of Mimi.'

'Right.' Randolf's tone was clipped. 'We'll need to examine the body immediately. Sergeant, please call for backup and a forensics team.'

As Birch stepped out to make the call, Randolf leaned forward, his gaze intense. 'Mrs Weiss, do I need to tell you that you have succeeded in implicating yourself by keeping this from us until now? You are going to sit here and tell me everything you know, or I will be forced to file a warrant for your arrest for perverting the course of justice.'

I felt my heart racing, palms sweating as I tried to recall everything I had seen and heard.

Jeannie was pacing, angry at Miles and me that we had spoken to the officers without Artie Peverill present. She had told Beebee about Mimi's death – she said the poor girl was distraught and wouldn't come out of her room. None of us could get hold of Ceecee; her phone was turned off and we had no other way of contacting her. Miles had offered to drive to Cambridge and go to her halls of residence if she didn't pick up in the next two hours.

I sat on the edge of the sofa, my hands clasped tightly in my lap as Jeannie continued her tirade.

'The police are swarming the house, treating it like a crime scene! You should never have spoken to them without Artie,' she muttered for the umpteenth time. 'God knows what you two have said to them.'

'We told them the truth,' Miles said, his voice strained. 'What else were we supposed to do?' He rubbed his eyes, looking exhausted.

Jeannie shot him a withering look. 'The truth? And what exactly is that, Miles? Because from where I'm standing, all of us are looking like suspicious characters in an episode of *Midsomer Murders* right now!'

'We didn't have a choice, Mother. They were asking questions, and we had to answer.'

'You always have a choice,' she snapped. 'You could have insisted on having legal representation present.'

I couldn't take it anymore. 'What does it matter?' I burst out. 'Clem is dead. Mimi is dead. George and Tristan are dead. What difference does it make!'

A heavy silence fell over the room. Jeannie was right, of course. With multiple deaths in such a short space of time, all of us were under scrutiny. The weight of it all suddenly felt crushing. Tears pricked the corners of my eyes and Miles moved to sit beside me, wrapping an arm around my shoulders. 'It's going to be all right,' he murmured, but his voice lacked conviction.

I wanted to scream, '*I just want to go to bloody Australia, Is that too much to ask?*'

Jeannie's pacing slowed, and she sank into an armchair, her anger seeming to deflate. 'I'm just … scared. This is all happening so fast, and I don't know what to do.'

The grandfather clock in the corner chimed, startling us all. Four o'clock. We'd been talking in circles for hours.

'I know it's hard,' Jeannie started again more calmly, 'but we must be careful now. Every word we say could be twisted and used against us.'

Miles stood up abruptly. 'I can't sit here listening to this anymore. I'm going to try Ceecee again.'

As he left the room, I could hear him muttering under his breath, his footsteps heavy on the stairs.

Jeannie sank into an armchair, suddenly looking every bit her age. 'What a mess,' she sighed. 'What an absolute mess. This could've all been dealt with quietly—'

'Quietly?' I gaped at her. 'Jeannie – what the hell are you talking about?' She looked at me, mouth slightly open with shock at my tone. I continued. 'You think that you can control everything and everyone. Did you really think that you could bury the news of several family members dying?'

'*Yes*,' she hissed. 'I did. In case you've forgotten, that was my job for thirty years and I was damn good at it. The *best*. I've buried a number of things with great success.'

'Oh yeah? And how were you going to do it this time ... throw money at it, I suppose?'

She narrowed her eyes at me, assessing me as if she was witnessing the real me for the first time. After a moment she said, 'I don't think I much like your tone, Olivia. You ought to be careful who you get on the wrong side of.'

My stomach juddered as adrenaline coursed through my veins.

'*Wrong* side? Ah. So the psychological warfare of the last eighteen years was just the warm-up? Honestly, Jeannie, I've seen dictators with more emotional range.'

And with that, I stormed out without so much as a glance

back. I stomped up the stairs, my heart pounding in my chest. The nerve of that woman! How dare she act like she could control everything, even now? I reached the landing and paused, trying to catch my breath. The house felt oppressive, suffocating. I needed air.

Making my way to the guest bedroom, I flung off my jumper, expecting to see Miles. Upon finding the room empty, I headed for the balcony, my fingers fumbling with the latch. As I leaned out into the crisp winter air, I heard raised voices from below. Miles was in the driveway, his phone pressed to his ear. He was pacing back and forth, shoes crunching on the gravel.

'Hi, Ceecee, it's Uncle Miles again. Please,' I heard him plead, 'just pick up. Please call me back as soon as you get this. I'm leaving shortly for Cambridge to come and find you. Please, call me or Grandma as soon as you get this...' He hung up and cursed.

'Excuse me, Mr Weiss?' Randolf's smooth voice cut across the driveway. He caught up with Miles and stopped in front of him. 'I would advise against you leaving for Cambridge at this time.'

Miles laughed incredulously. 'What do you mean? You would advise against me going, or I'm not allowed to?'

Randolf considered for a moment. 'I would strongly advise against it. I am not formally placing you under arrest...'

My stomach twisted.

'However, it would be ill-advised to leave on your own when there is a clearly a perpetrator targeting your family, and when you are wanted for further questioning. I can get a warrant, but I don't want to have to do that.'

Miles pursed his lips tightly. 'I need to get to my niece. She has no idea what has happened to her mother. Both of her parents are dead and she's extremely vulnerable.'

'I understand that, Mr Weiss. But instead, I can spare an officer to go to Ceecee's halls of residence.'

'Don't you think the news should come from a family member?' Miles said, outraged.

'Ideally, yes, but these circumstances cannot be helped, I'm afraid. You should all keep trying her in the meantime.'

'Jesus… Okay, fine.' Miles turned away to go back inside the house.

'Mr Weiss?' Randolf called.

'Yes?' Miles said turning.

'We can't seem to open the pool cover, would you happen to know how?'

Miles sighed, looking weary. 'I'll take a look at it,' he said, walking away and leaving Randolf alone.

I watched the DCI for a minute or two. He was looking over the horizon, scanning the grounds. As he turned to look up at the house, I ducked back behind the French doors before he could see me.

21

MULLED WHINE

I t was late. I sat in the living room by the dying embers of the fire with Gloria asleep at my side. The night continued to be my only solitude, and I was finding it increasingly difficult to find sleep. I think I preferred it when we were snowed in. At least then Jeannie had been on her Keep Calm and Carry On kick. At least then we hadn't felt like we were being held under house arrest.

Jeannie had been scowling all day, banging cupboards, and generally making life as awkward as possible. Two officers had remained stationed outside to watch over us, and she was doing everything in her power to make sure they knew they were not welcome, whilst simultaneously letting Miles and I know we were to remain in the doghouse for speaking to them without Peverill.

Two days until Christmas and it couldn't come soon enough.

My editor had emailed me, predictably on her last day before the holidays, chasing me for the manuscript. I held her off, saying I was just making a few final tweaks… She obviously hadn't seen the discussion in the forum, then. Part of me was disappointed that she hadn't seen it. I wanted it all to be over – Christmas, the publishing contract – burn it all to the sodding ground. Raze this shitshow and start from scratch.

Strangely, when I'd last checked the troll site, the post about me using a ghostwriter had been deleted. The other trolls were going crazy asking each other if anyone had seen or heard from OpinionatedOgre1… But it appears she and her profile, and every post she'd ever made, had disappeared off the face of the earth. If only the real OpinionatedOgre1 would vanish… Now that would be a real merry Christmas.

I glanced up as echoing sobs cut through the hiss from the fire. Begrudgingly, I gently moved Gloria's heavy head from my lap and left the warm spot on the sofa. With effort, I managed to open the living-room door without it creaking on its hinges. I waited a moment. The distinctive smell of weed wafted down through the gallery, and a moment later, another choked sob emanated from the landing above.

'I'm just waiting for a few more people to join the live,' Beebee said sniffing, followed by the sound of *shickshick* of the spark wheel on a lighter. A momentary glow from the flame lit Beebee's silhouette on the wall before it was gone again.

'I know – I know, I will get kicked off the live for smoking. But I'm just so fucking *done*.' She paused, presumably to read the comments pouring in. '"You look so pretty when you cry." Aww, thank you so much, Gary1964, but I really don't. Maria Lopez says, "How are you doing honey?" Well, I'm really not good, Maria. *Really really* not good. My parents are dead, and my idiot sister has up and left me with these complete weirdo assholes. Oh, thank you, Dav-o, for the rose!' Beebee let out a squeal. 'Oh my *God,* thank you, Kevin, for the universe! I am going to need all the universes I can get with my parents … *dead.*' She finished the last word with a dramatic quiver in her voice.

I hung back, stranded again. I had almost, *almost* felt sorry for her, until she started practically begging for gifts from what I could only assume were creepy old men. The twins would be absolutely fine as far as financial security went, Jeannie would see to that. A vicious part of me couldn't help but think that maybe the girls would have a chance at growing up a little, dare I say, *nicer,* without their self-absorbed narcissistic parents… Yes, maybe that was a tad too far. Maybe.

Going back into the living room, I peered out of the sash window. The officers were sitting in their car outside. One of them looked up and I ducked back at the last moment. They had explicitly told us to stay in our rooms and lock our doors… I should probably take that advice, I thought shivering. I just couldn't stand much more staring at that ceiling.

I would go back upstairs via the fridge for a late-night snack, maybe sneak a few glugs of wine to help me get some shut-eye, before heading back up by the secret passage.

I had broken sleep. The bedroom was pitch black, some dull noise awoke me and I managed to prise my eyes open to look at the alarm clock. Not yet three a.m. I must have slept then, as the last time I looked it was gone one a.m. When I strained my ears to listen, all was silent, so I let sleep lure me back like the tide.

A bloodcurdling scream cut through the house. Bleary, my head spinning, I forced my eyes open, this time against the blinding sun. I threw back the covers and was on my feet, hurtling through the door. A part of me still felt asleep, and I had no notion of what day, time, month or year it was as I stumbled out of our room and onto the landing.

Another scream. I leaned over the wooden banister and peered down below.

Mrs Harlow stood over a body, her hands shaking and raised to her head.

'Oh my *God*,' I said, barely audibly.

Beebee lay at the base of the staircase. Something about her body looked unnatural. She was all twisted. All wrong.

Mrs Harlow just kept staring down at her, unable to move, to speak. I flew down the stairs and arrived at Beebee's body. I could barely look at her; her hip bone protruding the way it was made me weak at the knees.

Suddenly Beebee jerked and I let out a strangled scream that sounded like a cat being drowned.

She was still again, her eyes staring up at the chandelier above, a dribble of blood running down from her mouth.

'Beebee?' Mrs Harlow knelt down to her. 'Are you okay?'

Beebee didn't respond.

'I don't think she's okay,' I said, shaking my head as I turned away and found a ginormous planter to empty my guts into.

'It's going to be okay, dear...' Mrs Harlow said, as Beebee

twitched again and coughed, spraying Mrs Harlow with her blood.

'*Oh-fuck-shit-christ-almighty-so-help-me-God!*' Mrs Harlow screeched.

I backed further away. The urge to make the sign of the cross with my fingers and chant '*The power of Christ compels you*' at the top of my lungs was strong. But I didn't, of course; that would make me look insane.

I wiped my mouth, my legs feeling like they were going to buckle underneath me. I couldn't look at her broken body, those bones protruding from soft skin made me want to faint, and I had no idea how Mrs Harlow was getting so close to her. I staggered to the front door and clumsily tried to wrench the locks open.

'Wait!' Mrs Harlow hissed. 'Don't go out there!'

'What are you talking about.' My mouth watered and stung as the bile began to rise again. 'We have to tell the police!'

'Let's ask Jeannie first. She'll know what to do.'

'I think Beebee needs an ambulance, Mrs Harlow,' I said with as much conviction as I could, although even I could see it was far too late for that. This girl needed holy water and a priest. I yanked on the doors trying to get out.

'Jeannie's got the keys,' Mrs Harlow said, her voice sounding too flat. She bent low again and tapped Beebee on the forehead. 'There, there, dear. You'll be fine,' she soothed. But it wasn't heart-warming, it was creepy as fuck. I had to get the hell out of here before these freaks broke me like a china doll. With abandon I let out a piercing scream.

Even in such terrible circumstances, it still felt kind of

dramatic to be screaming like a banshee, but I was locked in here and I wanted out. Right. Now.

Jeannie flew down the corridor like a bat out of hell. She took one look at Beebee and joined me in a scream-off.

Banging reverberated on the other side of the door, and the bell rang like a death knell. I pulled and pulled like my puny arms alone would somehow break wood and metal. The next thing I knew Jeannie was beside me with the key, my jailer and my saviour all rolled into one. She twisted the key in the lock and I flung it open allowing the police officers who'd been stationed outside to enter.

'Help her!' I rasped. 'Godammit, someone help her!'

Later that evening, after Beebee had been pronounced dead at the scene and her body taken away, the place was once again crawling with officers and forensics. Before Randolf even had a moment to say boo to a goose, Mrs Harlow was found on her hands and knees scrubbing away the blood at the bottom of the stairs. Randolf practically dragged her away, kicking and protesting, her face still splattered with Beebee's blood from the scrubbing brush and pail. Randolf's usually cool demeanour was lit with wrath as he reprimanded her for tampering with evidence.

I was hauled back into Eugene Weiss's grand office, and DCI Randolf followed me in, contemplating me in a way I didn't like. His jaw was ticking, eyes slightly wider than usual. He was angry beyond belief that another death had happened when the force had been stationed outside to prevent exactly that.

He surveyed me a little longer, until he managed to regain his usual self-control and took a seat. 'Mrs Weiss, would you like to tell me about your movements last night?'

'I … um, yes, absolutely.' I knotted my hands together. I had managed to calm down after my little outburst. It had felt good to lose it for once, but now everyone was looking at me like I was a fragile thing that wasn't quite right in the head; like I might break at any moment. I'd put up with these Weiss fuckers for almost two decades and they thought I was fragile… It was a bloody outrage.

'I was up late … working in the living room, and then I went to bed.'

'And what time was that?'

I thought for a moment. 'Around twelve-thirty a.m., I think.'

'And did you see Beebee at that time?'

'Y-es,' I said reluctantly.

Randolf raised his eyebrows. 'Why don't you tell me exactly what you saw, said and did, even what you smelled, so that I don't have to chase you for the truth?'

I cleared my throat before continuing. *Smelled*, interesting choice of word. They must have found the joint she was smoking, so it wouldn't be wise for me to hide the fact she was smoking weed… But what if that somehow put Callum in the firing line? And there was no way I was going to tell them that a few nights ago I found his Rizla packet in the secret stairwell. I decided then and there not to include anything that I considered a minor detail.

'I was sitting in the living room, with Gloria, Jeannie's dog. I couldn't sleep, because of, well … you know, everything that's been going on.'

'You weren't concerned that being alone late at night might make you a target?'

'Well, I suppose a little. But, I needed space. And well … I just don't think anything will happen to me.'

He stared at me blankly, 'Really. And why is that?'

I huffed a laugh. 'Well, I would see it coming a mile off… I would fight. I've been in this house numerous times, nothing bad has ever happened before.'

'Forgive me, but that seems incredibly naïve of you Mrs Weiss. All the other members of the family have been here numerous times. Yet they are no longer here to tell the tale. Things are happening now, Mrs Weiss, so unless it's you that's committing the murders, or you know the person who *is* committing the murders and feel you have no reason to fear them… I fail to understand your complacency.'

'Yes but—'

'But?'

'Well… I'm not one of them. Me and my family … we are outsiders.'

'Oh? Care to elaborate?'

I smoothed down my jumper and noticed the hem was a little frayed. Idly I began to tease the fibres apart. 'None of them take us seriously. We aren't set to inherit anything, and we won't take part in Jeannie's game where we prove ourselves worthy to become the next landlords of the Weiss estate. That pack of hyenas will destroy each other until only one of them is left standing. They think we're weak, that we uselessly watch them from the sidelines, but they are wrong. We are stronger than any of them could ever be. If you gave them a thousand lifetimes, in every one they would choose wealth, status and power. And in every lifetime my family and I would choose each other.'

'So the four of you aren't one of them. Got it.' He let out a deep sigh. 'But what if this is not about the inheritance? What if this is vengeance?'

'What could we possibly have done?'

'Up until recently there was a member of your family convicted of negligent homicide, which, off the record, looks a lot like a cover-up for manslaughter. Maybe Quentin Weiss blames all of you for his incarceration?'

I gulped. 'Miles and I had nothing to do with all of that... But I suppose he might not see it that way. Do you have any leads?'

'I'm not at liberty to say.'

That means no, then, I thought fearfully.

'So, then what happened?' he asked, urging me to go on.

'I heard crying, so I went to see who it was, and I saw that it was Beebee. She was on the upstairs landing doing a livestream, I don't know whether it was Instagram or TikTok. But she was ... well, in my opinion, she was fake-crying and receiving gifts. So, I went back into the room. I looked out of the window and saw the officers outside.'

He gave a small nod as if to corroborate that he had been told by his officers that I had been seen at that time.

'And then?' he asked.

I took a deep breath. 'And then ... I went to bed.'

'Did you speak to Beebee?'

'No.'

'You must have walked past her to get to your room?'

My mouth twisted firmly shut, not wanting to open. Suddenly I thought that Jeannie was probably right, I needed Artie Peverill.

'Should I wait for my legal counsel before we go any further?'

'You were asked and you declined. Would you like to leave the room, Mrs Weiss? I'm not keeping you here.'

'I er ... no.' I could kick myself. I should have refused to answer his questions, but somehow, I thought that would make me look even more guilty. I wanted them to trust me, to believe me. I didn't want to act like a dick, like Jeannie and the rest of them.

Randolf continued probing, 'What are you worried about, Mrs Weiss? What did you do next?'

'I went to the kitchen. I had some food. And I went to bed via a different route.'

Randolf couldn't hide his look of surprise. 'And what route would that be?'

'There's a passage ... that leads from the pantry to the hallway upstairs, near our room.'

'I see,' he said. 'And do you use this passage often?'

'No, not often. I've used it once before, again when the twins were doing TikToks on the landing.'

'Why did you feel the need to avoid two teenage girls, Mrs Weiss?'

'Because they're bloody awful—' The words were out of my mouth before I could stop them. This was going horribly. 'I'm sorry. I don't know why I said that.'

'Just because you think someone is awful doesn't mean you are a cold-blooded killer. However, sneaking about via secret passages when there's a killer in the house ... that concerns me.'

I looked down in shame.

'So, you took the secret passage?'

I nodded. 'I went to bed. I didn't hear or see anything more until the next morning when I head Mrs Harlow screaming.'

'And Mr Weiss was asleep in bed?'

'Yes.'

'And you didn't hear him get up?'

'No.'

'Was he beside you when you woke up?'

'No.'

'I see.' Randolf pondered for a moment, his finger poised on his lips. After a moment he asked, 'How is your book coming along?'

I blinked. 'Er ... fine, yes.' A rush of adrenaline pounded though my veins. Why was he asking me this?

'You see, we received some evidence back from Miriam Weiss's laptop.' He stared me dead in the eyes. My heart pounded as I waited for him to continue.

'We found that she had been contributing for a number of years to an online forum... one dedicated to discussing your writing.'

My brain glitched as it refused to compute.

'Mimi?' I said dumbly.

'That's correct. You two must have had quite the relationship for her to dislike you so much that she'd spend her free time gossiping about her sister-in-law online with a bunch of strangers.'

A memory flashed of the day in the pool room, before Tristan was shot, when I had been typing out an email to the ghostwriter. But I hadn't actually sent it until later. No … I had looked for the draft, but it wasn't there anymore. She must have emailed it to herself. She must have done it that day in the pool room. But I had seen Jeannie on the site… Perhaps they were both in on it. That would make even more sense, they disliked me enough … maybe one got the other involved.

'Did you know about the website?' Randolf asked.

'Yes,' I replied.

'Did you suspect it to be anyone you knew?'

'*Yes*, I – I thought it was Jeannie. The first time I used the secret passage, I saw that she was on the forum. She doesn't know that I saw her, I haven't said anything to her or … or to my husband.'

'Why?'

'Because I don't want to hurt him. I don't want to drive a further wedge between them when she already thinks it's my fault.'

'What's your fault?'

'Everything. That I took her son away from her. That we don't have enough money. I ruined things by being too working-class, not enough of a go-getter. That it's my fault we are moving to Australia… I never know what she's going to do next. And I fear now that I have told you this, she will find a way to make me pay. That she will make sure we don't get to Australia.'

He looked at me for a moment. 'I see. Mrs Weiss, is there anything else you'd like to tell me?'

'No,' I answered forlornly. I'd already said far too much.

22

SLAY BELLS RING

23rd December 2025

That poor asshole, Beebee. So many avoidable accidents happening these days, when people have their noses buried in their phones, preening into their cameras instead of looking where they are damn well going.

This was the easiest one yet... I didn't even need to get out of bed. I had been watching them, night after night getting stoned or drunk, one night they'd even consumed some sleeping pills they'd found in the cabinet.

I pre-screwed a little hook at the top of the stairs, and once everyone else had gone to bed, I tied a piece of wire around the banister to the hook. I vaguely remember seeing it in a Poirot episode once... The one with the dog. Thankfully, Gloria didn't see me, and even if she had, she would have been as glad as I am to be rid of the nasty little brat.

It was risky I know... But no one even bothered getting out of bed when they heard a noise. Everyone knew those two clowns were up all night, dancing, gyrating and generally whoring themselves out to old men on the internet. And once she was on her own, I knew I had to strike. I did her a favour.

I didn't even see it happen, but I imagine it went something like trip, smack-smack smack-smack—CRACK.

I t was Christmas Eve and no one knew what to do with themselves. We alternated between locking our bedroom doors and sitting at the dining table and staring at each other, sick of the confinement, a fierce determination driving us to want to face each other and say, 'Bring it on.'

We could no longer trust each other, that was a given. But we had to eat, and we all agreed that we would watch as Mrs Harlow prepared our meals – because God knows none of us knew how to cook. Not well, anyway. Madge looked more than offended at the suggestion that we might not trust her after her thirty-five years of service, but we were all under suspicion, so she'd just have to deal with it.

We ate lunch in silence, staring into the middle distance, trying not to catch each other's gaze. Mrs Harlow moved to the drinks cabinet, reached inside and retrieved a bottle of red wine.

'Behold!' she announced. 'Here, see?' She turned the bottle upside down. 'Unopened! I shall now retrieve this corkscrew from my pinafore...' With a flourish, she wielded it in the air. 'I am now going to open the bottle.'

I almost snorted at Mrs Harlow's performance. It was one

I had never seen before and seemed so incongruous with her usual subservient, jolly personality. I loved it.

'Really, Madge?' Jeannie said, going red.

'Shall I open the bottle or is it too risky?' she said, a sarcastic bite to her tone.

Fergus piped up. 'Not for me, thank you, Mrs Harlow.'

Aghast, we slowly turned our heads towards him.

He looked back at us, mouth downturned with a shrug. 'I need to keep my wits about me.' He tapped his knife to his temple.

'Whatever wits you once possessed were eroded a long time ago, Fergus,' Jeannie bit out. 'If I were you, I should enjoy yourself whilst you still can.'

'Mother,' Miles warned.

'Well, he's a bloody buffoon. At least there's one person we can strike off the potential murderer list with immediate effect!'

Fergus looked offended. 'I might like a drink or two, but that doesn't mean I don't know what I'm doing,' he said stoutly.

Callum smirked. 'So, *are* you the murderer, then, Uncle Fergus?'

Martha sat ramrod straight. 'It's not funny!' she burst out. 'You all think this is some kind of joke?' She stood up, scraping her chair and storming out.

'I can assure you, I do *not* find any of this funny,' said Jeannie in a clipped voice. I couldn't help but laugh at the role reversal; this was almost the same conversation the two of them had had about the gingerbread Toots.

'Martha,' I called after her. 'Please, come and finish your food.'

'I'm not hungry!' her receding voice replied as she made her way back to her room.

'Lock your door, then, please!' I called out as her thundering footsteps ascended the stairs.

We sat, eyes darting from one to another, before resuming slurping at our soup. Mrs Harlow grunted as she twisted the corkscrew into the cork. She popped it out and looked around at us, a slightly crazed look in her eye.

'Anyone?' she dared. 'No? Well, more for me, then, I suppose.' And with that she filled her wine glass to the brim, picked it up and took three huge gulps as if she were consuming water and was thoroughly dehydrated.

Jeannie looked at her, bemused. Eventually she tore her eyes away from Mrs Harlow's out-of-character behaviour and said, 'Well, anyway … that detective asked me a very strange question.' She set her spoon down carefully into the bowl. 'He asked me if Beebee had a history of drug use. Can you believe the absolute gall of him?'

I saw Callum imperceptibly tense.

'I can believe it,' said Miles. 'Can't you?'

She looked at him, completely flabbergasted. 'Beebee? *My* Beebee? There's absolutely no way on God's green earth she would touch that *stuff*.'

Miles breathed a sigh like he couldn't be bothered with the battle, but said, 'Most of the kids at Swanhaven were into it when I was there. I can't imagine it would be much different today.'

'You must be joking! I hope you never touched any of it!'

Miles rolled his eyes.

Jeannie huffed. 'Maybe at the kind of school Callum and Martha go to, but not at a prestigious establishment like Swanhaven.'

Callum's cheeks and ears turned pink.

Miles turned a cold stare upon his mother. 'Kids like Beebee and Ceecee can afford to buy whatever class A drugs they want, but you're such a snob that would never occur to you, would it?'

'Class A drugs?' She paled. 'No – there's no way. Absolutely not.'

He threw his hands up. 'Don't believe me, then, I actually *went* to that school, as well as a university not a million miles away in the league tables from theirs, and have first-hand experience of exactly what goes on. But of course, you know best, don't you, Mother. Your Beebee and Ceecee would *never* do such a thing, but my children would?' He threw his napkin onto the table and got up to leave.

She raised her palms up and looked at me as if to say, *What did I do?*

I met her gaze and gave her a hard stare.

'Come on, Callum, let's go,' I said simply.

I was sad to leave Mrs Harlow with Fergus and Jeannie, but she would have to fend for herself. I had my own family to think about. And not just that. An email had flashed up on my phone two hours ago from the ghostwriter.

He had delivered the manuscript with the caveat that there was only *so* much he was able to do in the little time I had given him. *Little time?* What about the £10,000 he was getting paid? Did that not warrant a little more effort?

I pulled on Callum's arm as he was about to leave for his room and whispered, 'I found a packet of these.' I pulled out the Rizlas. 'Are they yours?'

He took the papers from my hand and shoved them into his pocket. 'Yeah, why?'

'Well, I found them in the secret passage. Have you been using it?'

'Yeah... Have you?' He looked at me with incredulity.

'Yes, to avoid Beebee and Ceecee late at night.'

'That's the same reason I did. I got the munchies... Thanks for finding them, anyway.'

I held on to him. 'Please be careful, Callum. The police know about the passage now. I don't want them to think that you might have anything to do with this. Now that Beebee is ... gone ... we won't need to sneak around anymore. Okay?'

'Got it. Thanks, Mum. No matter what the twins have said in the past, or Grandma or any of the others ... I think you're pretty badass.'

'Really?' I lit up.

'Yeah, you're all right.' He nudged me. 'Laters, *mi madre!*'

Callum went back to his room and I trotted away to the pool room, grinning at his compliment. The pool still seemed cold and unwelcoming without the view of the water. I plonked myself down in my corner, opened the attachment and began reading.

The story began with what I had written so far, which considering everything that had been going on, I didn't think was too bad. It just needed a lot of fleshing out. And he hadn't even touched the parts I'd already written. I scowled, reading on.

Chapter four was where he had started. It was okay, but pretty dull stuff. There was nothing quite like reading someone else writing *your* story, putting words into *your* character's mouths that you know damn well they would never say.

Chapter five, six, seven ... boring, boring, boring. Those bastards on the forum could say what they wanted about the quality of my prose, but at least I wasn't boring as hell like most people out there. At least when I wrote, *shit happened.*

I breathed deeply, my anger getting the better of me as I read on, trying to remain impartial. I was halfway through the book and *nothing* had happened, when a man in blue overalls came into the pool room and dropped a canvas bag onto the tiles, the tools inside clattering loudly. He gave me a quick nod in acknowledgment, before bending down to retrieve a crowbar. He began prising open a white box on the far wall, and I tried to ignore his noise as I ploughed through the most boring book in the world.

His wrench was clicking as he pulled out some wires and I tried not to show my irritation. He looked over at the pool, his hand pressed onto something inside the box. It was his turn to huff and sigh as a horrible churning and grinding of metal-on-metal sounded. He swore under his breath.

'How long's it been like this?' His voice echoed across the room.

I shrugged. 'A couple of days, I think.'

'Electric motor's gone. Going to have to order in a new one.'

'Okay,' I said, completely uninterested.

He collected his tools and left again. I read on, sensing that the book was heading in a very disagreeable direction.

When I finally rose from the sun lounger, my entire neck and back had seized up. I shivered at the cold air. Usually, the heat from the pool made this room warm, if a little stuffy. Now it was as bleak and cold as the landscape beyond. I cursed aloud as I saw snow, once again beginning to fall.

Not again. We had to get the hell out of here, and pronto.

An email pinged on my phone and I quickly glanced at the screen. It was an invoice from the ghostwriter for the remaining £7,500, minus the deposit I had already maxed out my overdraft for to pay him. I quickly typed out a response, telling him he had killed off one of my main characters and that was not what we discussed.

It was true, that wasn't what we had agreed upon and I was less than happy. In fact, I was apoplectic. All this time spent doubting myself and my own abilities, and this so-called professional gets paid for producing the dumpster fire I'd just had the displeasure of reading.

I'm not going to pay him, I decided. *Fuck. Him.*

A dog began frantically barking and I almost fell over my own feet trying to get up. I was on edge now; after everything that had occurred, my nerves were completely shot. I scrambled to get out of the room, letting myself outside by a side door. Miles had told me that the police were bringing in cadaver dogs today, and from the sounds of it they had found something. Without thinking, I raced towards the barking, the sound echoing out and reverberating against the manor's stonework.

Down by the gates, I could see the dog handler with his

back to me and a German shepherd scratching at the base of a snowman. My heart seized in my chest. The snowman. The one we'd all seen in the distance and had passed by a dozen times without a second thought. I pushed forward, my breaths quickening.

'What is it?' My voice sounded foreign to my own ears, thin and reedy with panic.

The handler turned, his expression grim beneath the brim of his cap. 'You need to step back,' he warned, 'this is an active crime scene!'

'Miss! You can't be here,' shouted another uniformed officer, jogging towards me with his hand raised.

But I couldn't move. My feet felt rooted to the frozen ground as the dog continued to dig frantically at the base of the snowman, snow flying in all directions. The snowman wore a brown scarf, and his cheerful carrot nose had fallen askew, giving the once innocent creation a macabre, drunken leer. The K9 officer made a clicking sound and the dog stopped digging immediately, sitting perfectly still.

More officers were approaching me now, and I could see Miles jogging over across the lawn, his breath making clouds in the frigid air. My heart pounded in my chest as he approached.

I watched as the snowman's coal eye plonked to the ground; as it did so it took a chunk of snow with it. Underneath, one human eye was revealed, wide and staring. I let out a shriek. The eye looked clouded over, the eyelashes frozen together in clumps.

The rest of the snow began to collapse, the snowman's cheerful façade crumbling away to reveal what lay beneath.

I caught a glimpse of a thoroughly frozen head looking back at us all as if he was just as shocked as we were.

He had changed considerably, but I still recognised him.

Quentin.

I couldn't breathe. The world narrowed to a pinpoint, sounds becoming distant and muffled. Miles was pulling at me to come away. The officers shouting at me, too.

I don't remember being led inside, but I was shaking all over as Miles and I arrived in the kitchen to find the family back out of their rooms again, standing around the island sheepishly.

'Quentin's dead!' I blurted.

'The police just f-found him,' Miles stammered, dithering from the cold and the shock of what we had just seen.

Martha shook her head slowly, 'No … not again. I can't take much more of this. We're all going to die in here!'

'Agreed,' said Callum. '*Please* can we get the hell out of here?'

'Can we?' I asked Miles in desperation.

'I've already asked,' he said, swaying like he was about to collapse. 'Detective Inspector Randolf wants us all close by for questioning. We need to take part in the investigation, or we will only hold up proceedings. If we don't tell them everything we know it could delay us catching the plane to Australia.'

Mrs Harlow was rigid, standing next to a large pot over the stove.

'Quentin? Where was he found?' she asked horrified.

Jeannie stormed into the kitchen, clutching something in her hand. She dropped what looked like a bag of sand into the middle of the island. I swear a plume of it escaped into the air. She glared at us, her eyeballs protruding.

'Here he is!' She gesticulated at the bag.

We all stared at her.

'Mother—' Miles began.

'Just delivered from DHL!'

'Mother!' he repeated forcefully, but she held her hand up to stop him.

'It's George!' She poked the bag like she was going to pop it.

Horrified faces turned to the bag of ashes.

'Artie gave the funeral home permission to send his body for cremation! Can you believe he would do such a thing?'

Mrs Harlow's mouth dropped open slightly. Callum shook his head, which was sunk in his hands.

'A bag and burn! How dare Artie go against my wishes! Well, it's bloody done now, isn't it. We can't put him back in the oven and glue him back together, can we? Just look at this bag!' she wailed. 'I'm going to have to put him in something else … something until I can order a nice silver urn to go into the crypt…'

'Mother, Quentin has just been found!' Miles bellowed.

'Oh yes? And where's he been hiding?'

'In a snowman,' said Martha deadpan.

'Quentin's dead!' I blurted. Apparently, full sentences were failing me. The irony was not lost on me.

Jeannie looked at me, uncomprehending. 'It can't be. He can't be!' she said in disbelief. 'W-where?'

Miles rested his hands on the kitchen island to steady himself. I hooked an arm around his waist in case he really was about to keel over.

'A cadaver dog discovered him buried ... in a snowman,' Miles said grimly.

Jeannie shook, tremors taking over her hands as she got more and more worked up. 'No!' she exclaimed. 'No, no, no, no, *noooooo!*' She grabbed a rolling pin and began hitting the plastic bag containing George's ashes, causing more plumes of dust to escape into the atmosphere. 'It's *your* fault!' she cried as she pounded the bag.

Miles strode over to her and whipped the rolling pin from her raised hand. 'What the hell are you playing at?' he asked incredulously.

'Your father was a weak link. This is all his fault. It's always been up to me to steer this ship, and he should have been there right beside me. Instead, I've been doing everything all these years on my own, and now all my hard work is going to hell in a handbasket! He couldn't even do a simple task like put the lights up without dying on me!' Jeannie breathed erratically. Mrs Harlow approached her tentatively and guided her to a barstool to take a seat.

'What can we do for you, Jeannie?' Mrs Harlow asked softly.

Jeannie was staring at the bag of ashes, panting like a rabid dog.

'I'm going to put the useless bastard's ashes in the crypt,' she said in a low voice. 'Quentin can go in there, too, while we're at it! You can all go in there. We'll pile the bodies up high if we have to!'

'Have you finally gone round the sodding bend?' Miles barked. 'You want someone to help steer this ship? Then I will gladly take the wheel. This bullshit cycle ends here and now, Mother.'

She looked at him, brow furrowed in confusion. After what seemed like an eternity she sagged. 'You're right. Let's do it now,' she said wildly.

'Let's do what now?' Callum asked warily.

'Before we are all snowed in again, let's fulfil your grandfather's wishes and scatter his ashes.'

'But Quentin's only just been found...' Mrs Harlow began, 'don't you think it could wait until things aren't so...' She didn't know how to finish that sentence. It was becoming clear to us all that things were never going to be calm or normal ever again.

'No-no, no one else cares about what *I* want, so we might as well get it over and done with before we're trapped in here again. We'll worry about Quentin and what to do with him when I've been for a walk and had chance to clear my head. We must remain steadfast!'

'Aye, aye, Captain,' said Callum, and I shot him a glare.

We watched aghast as Jeannie headed over to a kitchen cupboard, whipped it open and, standing on her tiptoes, began rooting around for something at the far back. Tupperware and its lids began raining down, crashing loudly to the floor around her feet.

'Let me help...' offered Mrs Harlow.

'No! I have them. Here!' Jeannie pulled out two large, ornate tins and held them out before us. 'Tell me, what do you all think is best, the dark green Harrods ground-coffee tin, or the peacock-blue Fortnum and Mason loose-leaf Assam? Which tin do you think George would prefer?'

We stood staring at her.

'Come on!' she chided. 'We haven't got all day, it's a simple question!'

'Um ... I think Harrods,' I offered.

'Agreed,' said Martha. 'It says "old money" with just a hint of disappointment.'

'Harrods it is!' Jeannie declared, discarding the Fortnum and Mason tin on the side with a clatter. She yanked the lid off the coffee tin, reached for the bag and unceremoniously dropped it inside.

'Right, then. We should go for a walk,' she said decisively.

'But the police...' Mrs Harlow said warily. 'Won't it look bad if we all march out of here for a walk?'

'I am a Weiss!' Jeannie trilled, 'I care not for the opinions of sheep!'

'But the eggnog!' Mrs Harlow lamented. 'It won't be as good reheated. What if it splits?'

Jeannie blew out her cheeks, a nanosecond away from fully blowing her top. She flung open one of the cupboards, flinging drinking bottles and travel mugs over her shoulder in a cacophony of noise. 'Aha!' she announced, pulling out the biggest stainless-steel Thermos I'd ever seen. '*Here—*' She thrust it at Mrs Harlow aggressively. 'Put it in there. It will keep us all warm on the walk and numb the insanity.'

'Whatever you do,' Callum warned, 'don't mix those vessels up. A dose of ashes down the gullet would be hard to come back from.' Martha elbowed him in the gut.

Jeannie left to tell Fergus the awful news: not only was his wife dead, but now his son, too. With dread in our hearts and our minds reeling, we headed to our rooms to collect our coats, hats and walking boots.

I looked at Miles with concern. What if he'd wanted time to prepare something to say about his father? He had told me, Martha and Callum that he wanted to be more open about his feelings, but I could see that the only way he could operate right now was to shut himself down. But there was no time to ask him how he felt about it, as Jeannie began banging the gong like we were in the Blitz and had to get to our air-raid shelter post-haste before being blown to smithereens.

23

IT'S SNOW LIE

18th December 2025

In the early hours of the morning, I was up before the lark and on my way to retrieve the castor-oil plant from the greenhouse, when I spotted a shadowy figure lumbering through the snow around the walls of Weiss Manor. That was extremely odd, because we were completely snowed in; so the fellow must have walked quite a way to get here. The scoundrel was about to jump the fence when he spotted me.

It was that son of a bitch, Quentin, thinking he could swan in here and trade his prison slop for smoked salmon and cream cheese. He stared at me through the railings, and it was like having the devil himself clap eyes on me. Except what Quentin was yet to realise was; he'd always just been playing... I'm the real fuckin' deal baby.

He told me he'd been released and that he'd rented a car but had only made it so far before he'd had to abandon it and walk the rest of the way. He hadn't told any of us he was coming, of course, he wanted it to be a 'Christmas surprise'. I opened the gate and invited him in like the good host I am.

I had zero intention of anyone from the house seeing him, though. Quick as a flash, I grabbed him from behind using the scarf around his neck. I dragged him towards the trees as he fought valiantly; but he obviously hadn't been doing his chin-ups while he was locked away, because he was weaker than a Filet-O-Fish.

After making sure the life was well and truly squeezed out of his nefarious neck, I couldn't very well dig a hole with all this snow. I rolled him about a bit until he gathered up a nice coating of the white stuff, before I sat him up just beneath the treeline. It was still dark enough that I was confident no one from the house would be able to see me. I packed and packed the snow around him, until he no longer needed support to sit up. I fashioned the snow around him and kept packing it in until he resembled a squat little thing. I'd gather the carrot and coal later tonight, I figured, but for now, I tied his scarf around him and patted his cold, snowy head.

He'd deserved something brutal and far bloodier. But if he would insist on turning up unannounced, then he'd have to make do with improv.

W e gathered in the foyer and Fergus was already waiting for us, looking rather lost but surprisingly sober for once.

He looked straight at Miles as he said, 'I can't believe it.' But he didn't sound completely devastated. He sounded more like a man who'd just had a millstone removed from around his neck.

Miles embraced him, and as we headed outside, DCI

Randolf and DS Birch got out of their car when they saw us all filing down the stone steps. Gloria shot off ahead, tail wagging excitedly that she was getting so many people to accompany her, as opposed to her usual drab walk with Jeannie.

'What's going on?' asked Randolf, a deep line creasing his forehead.

'We are going for a walk!' Jeannie said tartly, clutching the Harrods tin in one hand and her walking pole – so firmly her knuckles were white – in the other, her breath misting and floating away in the air. 'Is that a problem, officer? Or are you taking away our human rights now, too?'

He held his hands up in supplication. 'I'm not here to attack you, Mrs Weiss, I'm here to protect you.'

'Pah! Fat lot of help you've been so far! Perhaps you're a murderer, Mr Randolf? Perhaps we should lock ourselves away from you?'

'Please, Mrs Weiss, I can't imagine what you must be going through. But I'm just trying to do my job.'

'Well, do it, then!' she barked.

He took a deep breath. 'I just heard from my colleague, and he said Ceecee never made it to Cambridge. She has not been seen anywhere on campus or in her halls. We can't find any record of her being at the train station.'

Jeannie went stock-still, her lips tightly pressed together. Miles put his hands behind his head, pulling at his hair. *I should really speak to him about that*, I thought. At the rate he was going, he'd be bald by next week.

'Is there anywhere else she could have gone?' Randolf asked. 'We are checking with the local bus and taxi drivers—'

'She would never take the bus,' Jeannie cut him off, flatly.

'I don't think either of the girls have even seen the inside of a bus.' She waved her stick in the air. 'I need to bloody walk. I need to clear my head from all this insanity!'

'Would you mind if DS Birch and I joined you?' Randolf asked. 'We don't think it's wise for you all to go unattended.'

Jeannie's nostrils flared and she stormed ahead down the path, stabbing her walking pole brutally into the frozen earth as she went. The rest of us trailed after her as she steamed ahead like a freight train on a deadline.

I was relieved to have the police with us. I was half expecting to be bludgeoned to death with Jeannie's walking pole. Hell, at this rate I wouldn't be surprised if Gloria turned around and ate me whole. We walked in silence for a while as I tried to put what I had just witnessed with Quentin to one side and raked over where Ceecee could have gone to. She wasn't in the house, we would have seen her by now. The police would have seen her.

We followed the path leading away from the house. It curved around a large pond that was home to a pair of cygnets in the summer months, but was now desolate and frozen over. Gloria sniffed around the edges at the dead rushes.

Jeannie came to an abrupt halt.

'Here we are! The pond. It's as good a place as any, I suppose.'

'As good a place as any for what?' Randolf asked.

Jeannie shook the tin. 'For my husband. Here, hold my pole for me please, Martha?' With her free hand, Jeannie started prising off the lid. 'Does anyone have anything to say?'

'We are really doing this now?' asked Fergus flabbergasted, 'I haven't had time—'

'George wanted a quick cremation with no fuss. So that's what I'm doing. Quick and fuss-free. You were the ones who told me I was being selfish'—Jeannie looked pointedly towards Miles—'so here I am, being totally unselfish!' She upended the tin. Plumes of ash fell, scattering into the air and down on to the frozen lake. In a moment, a cold wind whipped up, changing the course of George's remains and blasting the fine sand into our faces.

'Argh, my eyes!' Martha wailed.

Randolf spluttered and spat. 'Oh, shit. It's in my mouth.'

Miles stared at his mother, then down at the icy lake where his father's remains lay, unable to submerge in the water, just dashed onto the surface where he would eventually melt into the lake, or blow away entirely.

'What on earth has gotten into you, Mother? Why are you so hellbent on being so ruddy disrespectful?'

'Oh, so it's about *you* now?'

'You are insufferable!' Miles yelled. 'Insensitive, selfish, self-obsessed—' He caught himself as he realised the two officers were watching them. But it seemed he couldn't help himself as he continued, 'What I hate more than anything is the fact that you subject my kids to your utter horribleness.' He put his arms around Callum and Martha and led them away.

Jeannie watched them, her chest rising and falling like adrenaline had taken over.

Randolf waited for Birch and said under his breath, 'As soon as we get back, can you put in for a psych eval for Mrs Weiss?'

It took all my willpower not to turn around and beg to read the report once it was done.

We continued walking, the atmosphere buzzing with anger and also a little bit of sadness. This was my least favourite thing about death; even if you didn't have a good relationship with the deceased, it still managed make you so fucking sad. It left a bad taste in my mouth that Jeannie had dashed him onto the ice like that, so full of rage at him just because he hadn't done what she had wanted. But I also knew it went deeper than that; it was a lifetime of disappointment.

Miles walked in line with the children. He was putting their minds at ease, and he somehow even managed to make Martha smile. He was so nurturing, such a natural parent, I envied him sometimes. DCI Randolf caught up with me, whilst DS Birch lagged behind, watching the group from afar.

As we entered the line of trees, Fergus and Mrs Harlow whispered about Quentin, before moving on to what Jeannie had just done... I guessed they were better friends than I had once thought, knowing each other as they had done for over thirty-five years. From the snippets of conversation I caught, she was consoling him about George, Clem and Quentin, and giving him sage advice since she was a recent widow herself. If I was a decent enough judge of character, which I definitely am, I thought that he might soon make a move on Mrs Harlow. Fergus had no idea how to look after himself, and he would need a caretaker. No one was more qualified for that job than Mrs Harlow.

Perhaps he already had made a move. What if... *No*. Preposterous. For a fleeting moment I'd wondered, *What if Mrs Harlow and Uncle Fergus are lovers?*

Fergus didn't even seem that cut up about losing Clem, not in the way I would be if I ever lost Miles. If I put my theory to Miles, I knew he would find it sick and hilarious in equal measure. I watched the two of them with renewed interest.

Our group was well into the woodland now, the trees naked against the chill air, when I plucked up the courage to ask DCI Randolf whether he was married and had children. I knew he didn't wear a ring, but that didn't necessarily mean anything.

'Yes, I am married. But Mrs Randolf and I don't have children.' He gave a small smile. 'Though I might not be married for much longer if I don't spend this Christmas at home.'

'Why wouldn't you be home for Christmas?'

He scanned us all, as if it was self-explanatory.

'Can't you get someone to cover for you?' I asked.

He turned to me and said darkly, 'That depends on what happens in the next few days, Mrs Weiss.'

I squinted up at him. 'Do you really think there will be another death with all these officers around?'

He focused on the path ahead of him and said, 'I just don't think we should assume that after seven deaths and a case of a missing person, this is the end of it.'

I took a moment to glance at each person in turn. Fergus was walking straighter and seemed like he'd had a new lease of life. Each death that had occurred had seemed to lift a considerable weight off his chest. Perhaps the whole drunken-buffoon thing had been an act. He needed money, *badly*, and as soon as possible. The remaining obstacles to his achieving that goal were our family and Jeannie…

I looked at Miles and the kids. There was just no way they

had the ability to be so cold and calculating. Me, on the other hand … now that was a different story. I looked up at DCI Randolf and he was considering me. I wondered if he was thinking the same thing as I was.

'Tell me more about your writing?' he asked.

The last question any author wanted to hear. 'There's not much to tell…' I said, a little more bitterly than I had meant to.

'No? Being a published author sounds great. Especially when compared to dealing with criminals.'

'I suppose so. I just wish the money—' I stopped. I had already done enough to incriminate myself. I didn't need to go any further.

'Yes,' his smile creased around his eyes, 'I've heard it can be a struggle. Who knows. If you and your family get out of this alive, perhaps you could write a true-crime novel.' He laughed like it was a joke. I didn't tell him I'd already been jotting down notes in the app on my phone.

We had walked through the thick of the woods to where the terrain banked steeply up a hill; finally we were beyond the boundary of Weiss Manor. We panted up to the summit, the cold air burning our throats as we clambered up to the stone circle that crowned the top. Gloria made it first, snuffling around the stones searching for a scent. Miles and the kids made it next. They weren't even out of breath as they looked down on us all, watching us as they leaned against the huge stones.

Jeannie came third. She did this walk every day, striding up the slope with her Gandalf-esque walking pole. She was still clutching the empty Harrods tin. No doubt it would be rinsed and used again for blown lightbulbs, clothes pegs or random keys. DCI Randolf and I made it shortly after. Fergus and Mrs Harlow wheezed. DS Birch followed, warily scanning the rest of us like one of us was about to pull out a Tommy gun at any moment.

Mrs Harlow sat heavily on a fallen boulder, grasping her knees as she fought to regain her breath. Fergus was beetroot-red, sweat glistening on his brow.

'Get out – the eggnog – would you – Madge?' he said brokenly. 'I need – a breather!'

She nodded, swinging the huge Thermos up onto her lap and unscrewing the silver cap. 'Oh, drat!' she cried, 'I didn't bring the cups!'

'Just use the lid,' Jeannie snapped, 'I'll go first so I don't have to share any spittle.'

Good *God*. As soon as she said the word *spittle* it put me right off the idea of having any altogether.

Mrs Harlow twisted open the smaller cap inside, looking forlorn at her mistake. She poured the steaming custardy-looking liquid out and Birch gave Randolf a look that said, *'Should we let them drink it?'*

Jeannie caught the look and snatched the lid from Mrs Harlow, taking three dainty sips. She passed it back to her and said, 'See? It's no problem.'

Randolf surveyed her beneath his eyelids before turning to examine the ancient stones. 'So, what are these stones?' he asked.

'It's called Mitchell's Fold,' I said. 'It's a Bronze Age—'

'We're not here for a history lesson,' Jeannie interrupted, turning on Randolf and Birch. 'My granddaughter is missing, and all the while, you two buffoons are up here with us, instead of doing your damn jobs and looking for her!'

'I can assure you, Mrs Weiss, that my team are on the case,' Randolf said calmly.

Jeannie folded her arms across her chest. Mrs Harlow was glugging the eggnog and Fergus's fingers were twitching in desperation for his turn. The kids were inspecting the huge stones as Miles pointed them out. I shot an apologetic look at Randolf for Jeannie's insult.

'Right!' Jeannie ordered. 'Enough of this. We've scattered ashes, seen stones and now we must get back. We need to put our efforts into finding Ceecee if we can't rely on the establishment.'

Fergus eagerly slurped his eggnog, his face still glowing red from the exertion of getting up the hill. The biting wind made my cheeks numb, but I already felt slightly better for being out of the house. Out here, it seemed insane to think that anyone in this group could be picking people off. Each of the unfortunate deaths could be explained away as a very unfortunate set of circumstances. Until Quentin. It was undeniable now that none of them were mere coincidences or accidents. Someone had packed snow around the bugger, and not just that, they'd shaped it into a snowman! For the first time I wondered if I could trust myself. Had it really happened? Was I going insane? Had I dreamt it all? I pinched myself to make sure I was actually here.

We began to descend. I grabbed Miles's hand and pulled him closer to me.

'Did I just imagine it all?' I whispered.

He looked down at me, a question in his eyes.

'Did I imagine what I saw today … with Quentin?'

He studied me, his eyes swimming with sorrow. 'No, darling. I'm afraid it was real.'

'Hang on!' Mrs Harlow called over to us against the wind. 'Fergus needs you to slow down!'

We halted our descent, looking back up towards the pair. Fergus was doubled over, seemingly still winded from the walk.

'Come on, Fergus,' Jeannie called up to him like he was a naughty child. 'It's all downhill from here.'

You can say that again, said the voice in my head.

'I'll stay back with him,' offered Miles. 'You go back.'

I huffed in irritation at the hold up, unsure whether it was wrong to leave them. We watched as Miles trotted back up towards the hill. Fergus went from doubled over, to lurching himself upright. He clutched at his throat and I squinted hard against the biting wind. From here, I was sure his face had turned from its usual beet-red to prune-purple.

'Gosh,' I muttered, 'do you think he's having a heart attack?'

DCI Randolf and DS Birch ran towards him, and the kids and I also started walking back up to see what the matter was.

'Help him!' I heard Mrs Harlow shout.

Not a sound was issuing from Fergus, even though he was thrashing about. I was halfway there when I saw he was bluer than a blue tit. Hands to his throat, he noiselessly looked up towards the heavens, before stumbling back, going down like a sack of meat.

'For the love of Beelzebub, what the fuck's this now?' Callum cursed.

As we reached Fergus, Randolf was radioing for an air ambulance, while Birch dropped to her knees. She hesitated, her head bobbing this way and that as she tried to look in his mouth as Fergus bucked and rolled around like he was on a wild bull. I cursed, panic rising. 'Holy shit, Miles, what can we do? What's wrong with him?'

Jeannie appeared, mouth tighter than a mouse's butt. 'This is what happens when you abuse your body for years and decide to go for a walk. Really, for heaven's sake, Fergus, will you get a hold of yourself?'

Fergus suddenly went completely still, his face and lips turning blue.

Birch leapt into action, craning Fergus's head back slightly and pinching his nose to begin CPR. His mouth was open wide, exposing a gigantic purple tongue that had swelled to three times its normal size. On seeing it, Birch hesitated for a moment, seeming to have second thoughts, but she bent down, putting her mouth on his, despite the giant tongue being right there.

I peered through my hands, unable to tear myself away from the horrific sight of that damn muscle going in Birch's mouth. This woman deserved a pay rise, and then some.

His lips were turning an even darker shade of blue, eyes bloodshot and staring. Martha turned to me and gave me a horrified grimace that was an exact expression of how I felt.

Oh shit. It's happened again.

Mrs Harlow was quivering, a whisper playing on her lips like a broken record. 'No. No. No.'

Miles approached her from behind, putting a warm arm around her shoulders and ushering her to look away. We had all been living in denial... We all had massive targets on our backs and another one was biting the dust before our very eyes.

The Weisses were about to lose their ninth family member, if we counted Eugene. And I did count Eugene... He, too, had died completely unexpectedly when we had all been together. And Toots had seemed pretty adamant someone had murdered him. It was time to wake up and smell the cinnamon rolls... One of us was a cold-blooded murderer.

I looked at Callum's and Martha's faces; each looked as shocked and pale as the other. Then at Mrs Harlow and Miles, the former now crying into Miles's chest as he held her and comforted her. I looked to Jeannie. Jeannie was standing slightly away from us, jaw set, every muscle in her body taut, as if she was a guitar string about to snap.

And what about Ceecee?

Where the *hell* was Ceecee?

24

FROSTBITE AND FINAL DRAFTS

24th December 2025

Is there a person alive who will miss the useless, lecherous old bigot that we all knew as Fergus Weiss? He's most certainly been a permanent fixture on Santa's naughty list, especially after he impersonated him and drove his car under the influence... That day had been a botched attempt. I was all dressed up, disguised as Santa on his way to bump off Madam Mimi. I swung back to the village and saw Fergus heading to the pub. I needed to get rid of the costume, and challenging him to a drinking game I knew he couldn't win was genius. Or so I thought. The pub was dark and he was seven sheets to the wind; to be honest, I was so sure that he would get in his car and end up in a ditch. I just hoped he didn't kill anyone else. Plan A backfired. So plan B it was.

Rule 333 of the 'steering clear of getting murdered handbook,' don't let a room full of people find out that you're allergic to cardamom.

J eannie paced near the fireplace, her eyes darting between Mrs Harlow and the detective. I could see the internal struggle written across her face. She knew something, that much was clear; but loyalty to Mrs Harlow was keeping her silent. For now.

Mrs Harlow was beside herself. We told her repeatedly that it wasn't her fault, that it was an accident. As we consoled her, I saw Jeannie practically bursting, fighting herself not to say something.

We didn't want to drop Mrs Harlow in it in front of DCI Randolf, for what could have been a temporary but extremely dangerous lapse in judgement, but… She *did* know Fergus was allergic to cardamom. We all knew. And even if she had forgotten, it hadn't been that long ago that Jeannie had practically screamed at Fergus in a room full of people not to eat the tapioca pudding because it contained the offending spice.

Somehow, she, or someone else, had put cardamom in the eggnog. Enough to make Fergus's airway constrict. And although the air ambulance had arrived within fifteen minutes, it was already too late.

As I sipped my now cold coffee, my mind raced through the events of the afternoon. Who'd had access to the eggnog? When was it left unattended? And most importantly, who would want Fergus's death badly enough to risk slipping in the cardamom in front of everyone?

As we stood watching Mrs Harlow sob into her handkerchief, I couldn't help but feel a twinge of suspicion.

'And you're certain no one else had access to the eggnog?' DCI Randolf pressed.

Mrs Harlow paused for a moment, then shook her head.

DCI Randolf cleared his throat, his keen eyes scanning the room. 'I need to speak with each of you individually,' he announced, his voice cutting through the tense silence. 'Starting with you, Mrs Harlow.'

As the detective led Madge away, I caught Jeannie's eye. She looked just about ready to break, her lips pressed into a thin line. I knew she was thinking the same thing I was: could we have finally caught the killer?

But what on earth would Mrs Harlow's motive be? That she secretly plain hated us all? Was sick of doing the laundry? She could have just quit, though; murder seemed rather extreme. But then, she'd put up with Jeannie for all these years, the madness was bound to rub off on her at some point.

Miles was on the couch with the kids wrapped in his arms. As the interviews were taking place, DCI Randolf instructed us that a second full-scale sweep of the house was underway. We waited for our turn to be questioned, sitting in silence as our brains whirred with possibilities: the who, what, where and how. We glanced furtively at one another while the fire snapped, crackled and popped merrily in our ears.

The grandfather clock in the corner chimed softly, marking another hour of this interminable night. Eventually, Mrs Harlow emerged from her interview, her eyes red-rimmed and puffy. She shuffled past us without a word, collapsing into an armchair by the window.

DCI Randolf entered and addressed Jeannie. 'Mrs Weiss, you said that a pool-maintenance specialist looked at the mechanism for the pool cover. My officers are still unable to open it.'

Jeannie sat, eyes glazed over, staring into the fire.

Randolf said firmly, 'Mrs Weiss?'

'Hmm?'

'The pool cover, Mother,' Miles said gently. 'What did the maintenance man say?'

'I don't know...' She waved her hand dismissively. 'I didn't even speak to him. George used to deal with all of that...' The corners of her eyes glistened as she continued looking into the flames. I almost wanted to warn her about burning her retinas if she wasn't careful, but I didn't think now was the time or the place.

'I saw him,' I piped up. 'He said that the motor was jammed and that he would order new parts.'

Randolf looked up to the heavens and silently cursed. 'Well, we can't wait for that. We are going to have to cut it open.'

Jeannie's ears pricked up at that. 'You won't damage it, will you? If you do, you will have to pay for it.'

Randolf gave her a long, hard stare that I wished to God I had the balls to pull off.

'Yeah... It doesn't exactly work like that, Mrs Weiss,' he said dryly. I was starting to like him.

He motioned that it was my turn for questioning, and I followed him out. On the way he instructed one of his men to cut open the cover before we headed past the bustling bodies in white overalls through to the study.

As I settled into the leather armchair across from DCI Randolf, I couldn't help but feel a chill run down my spine. The study felt even more oppressive now than the day

Eugene's will was read. The detective's piercing gaze seemed to bore right through me.

'So,' he began, leaning forward slightly, 'tell me about your relationship with Fergus Weiss.'

I sat on my hands, trying to stave off the bitter chill in the room. I wished they'd light a fire in here; this old house was formidably cold in winter when the fires weren't lit. 'Well, he was Miles's uncle. We weren't particularly close, but we were cordial enough at family gatherings.'

Randolf nodded, jotting something down in his notebook. 'And how would you describe his relationship with the rest of the family?'

I hesitated, choosing my words carefully. 'Fergus could be ... a handful at times. He drank a lot. And when he drank he had strong opinions and wasn't afraid to voice them, which often led to tension.'

Randolf's eyebrow arched slightly. 'Strong opinions about what, exactly?'

I shifted uncomfortably in my seat. 'Well, he had some rather outdated views on certain topics. Race, gender, sexuality, that sort of thing. It often led to arguments, especially with the younger family members.'

'I see,' Randolf said, scribbling in his notebook. 'And did anyone in particular clash with him more than others?'

I thought for a moment. I wasn't going to drop my daughter in it. I was about to open my mouth to give some dismissive answer, when a commotion erupted from outside. Shouts and the sound of running footsteps echoed through the halls. Randolf's radio crackled to life.

'Sir. Ten-fifty-four. Ten-fifty-four,' an urgent voice came through the speaker.

Randolf was up and out of his chair, dashing out of the room before he could inform me that the interview was over. I sat for a second to two, before making a snap decision to follow him. He hadn't explicitly told me not to.

I hurried after him, meeting no one on the way who could stop me. My breath echoed as I ran down the corridor to the pool room. When I entered, dozens of officers and workers in forensic suits were gathered around the edges of the pool looking in. One woman in a white overalls was taking pictures of the water, crouching down low to get a better view.

The mammoth pool cover had been wrenched open and peeled back. It must have taken considerable manpower, because that thing was so heavy-duty it operated on motorised machinery. In the middle of the pool, a dark object bobbed. Silently, I took a few steps closer.

Dark hair splayed outwards, drifting in the water. I gasped and Randolf, seeing me, bellowed at me to get the hell out. He yelled at his officers, instructing them that this was a crime scene and should have been cordoned off.

I stumbled backwards, my mind reeling. As I was ushered out of the pool room, I caught snippets of urgent conversation behind me from the forensics team.

'…young female.'

'…been here for days…'

My heart pounded in my chest and bile rose in my throat as I made my way back to the living room, my legs threatening to give way. I barrelled through the door, the family looking up in shock as I entered, their faces a mix of confusion and concern.

'Liv, what's going on?' Miles asked, standing. 'We heard people running.'

I opened my mouth to speak, but no words came out. How could I tell them what I had seen? Before I could gather my thoughts, DCI Randolf burst into the room, his face grim.

'I regret to inform you that we have discovered another body,' he announced.

Jeannie whimpered, her hands shooting to her mouth in terror. 'Ceecee!' she gasped.

He looked over us all. His initial air of sympathy had well and truly evaporated. One of us was a serial killer, and he meant to find out who, before another death occurred.

'Until we can identify the deceased and determine the cause of death, I'm going to have to ask all of you to remain here. I will post one of my officers with you.'

The room fell into a shocked silence, broken only by Jeannie's muffled sobs. Mrs Harlow, who had been sitting quietly in the corner, suddenly stood up, her face ashen.

'I-I n-need some air,' she stammered, making her way towards the door.

DCI Randolf stepped in front of her, blocking her path. 'I'm sorry, Mrs Harlow, but no one is to leave this room until we've secured the scene and taken statements from everyone.'

Mrs Harlow's eyes darted around the room, looking for an escape. I couldn't help but notice how her hands trembled as she wrung them together.

Miles clutched Callum and Martha tightly to him before

clearing his throat. 'Detective, what if this is an outsider? It is not safe here. I want to get my children away from this place.'

Randolf's steely gaze swept across the room. 'I need you all here. I will not leave you alone without an officer present.'

The kids looked at each other, eyes wide. DS Birch stepped into the room, a hard look on her face. She took a seat in the corner and didn't say anything to us. My gut churned as I saw Ceecee floating face down before my eyes. Sure, it was looking with almost near certainty that one of us in this room was a murderer, but the rest of us weren't. And the attitudes of Randolf and Birch were kind of making me angry as hell, because I for one was innocent.

My husband and children were going through enough without being made to feel like pieces of shit, too. I fought hard not to cut my eyes at Birch as she sat straight-backed and stoic, looking at us like we were already inmates in the slammer.

The tension threatened to cut off my airways. There was no damn oxygen in this room; it was sucked up by Jeannie's sobs that had now turned to occasional sniffles. She quickly composed herself, but I noticed that when she took her hands away from her face, her eyes weren't red or puffy from crying... They were as dry as a bone.

I looked at Birch to see if she was seeing what I was seeing, but her attention seemed to be focused solely on me.

I prowled around the sofa as Miles whispered reassurances to the kids. Perhaps Birch found it odd that their own mother wasn't sitting there, consoling them and being the nurturing one... But Miles was always the one who was cool under pressure. I had always been the lioness, ready to tear out anyone's throat who posed a threat to my family.

'Sit down, Mrs Weiss,' Birch warned me.

Mrs Harlow had retreated to her chair, her gaze fixed on some unseen point in the distance. I still couldn't shake the image of the body in the pool. Ceecee. It was her. She'd been missing for days, and now... My mind raced, trying to piece together the events of the past week. Who had seen her last? When? And how did this connect to Fergus's death and all the others before it?

The grandfather clock tick-tick-tocked as we waited and waited, under what was increasingly looking like our jail cell ... or our tomb.

Eventually, we ordered a takeaway which we ate in silence. It would be Christmas tomorrow and the whole thing was of course cancelled given the circumstances. DCI Randolf kept excusing himself as the phone calls from his wife became more frequent. We finished our food and Randolf warned us that once we went to bed, under no circumstances were we to leave our bedrooms tonight.

Everyone had an en suite, so that side of things wouldn't be a problem. An officer brought us up a pitcher of water each with glasses. He even demanded access to the keys from Mrs Harlow and locked everyone in their bedrooms come nine o'clock, with the warning that there would be an officer stationed in the hallway and if any of us left, he would take that as an admission of our guilt.

I was pretty sure that this wasn't allowed, but hey, I wasn't about to argue with the guy. We had nowhere else to go, and they weren't going to let us out of their sight.

I could see in Randolf's eyes that he just desperately wanted to go home to his family, and I couldn't blame him. He also looked utterly defeated at the fact that he appeared completely incapable of doing his job.

I didn't even bother to try and sleep – I knew my traitorous brain well enough by now to know that was a futile effort. The events of the day played on a loop in my mind – Quentin the frosty snowman, Fergus's big blue tongue, Ceecee looking like the girl from *The Ring*. The accusations hanging between our family lay thickly in the air. Miles tossed and turned beside me, his breathing uneven. I knew he was awake, too, likely consumed by the same thoughts.

A floorboard creaked outside our door, and I tensed. Was it just the officer patrolling, or someone else? I strained my ears, listening for any further sounds, but the house had fallen silent once more.

My mind must have plunged into sleep from sheer exhaustion, because at some point I jerked awake to the sound of muffled voices. Glancing at the bedside clock, I saw it was just past three a.m. Through the crack in the curtains, I saw the snow flurrying down outside and heard the wind battering against the windows. I slipped out of bed, careful not to wake Miles, and pressed my ear against the door.

I stayed, straining to hear. I was about to go back to bed when I smelled smoke. With a rising panic in my chest, I looked at the gap underneath the door and saw noxious black plumes wending their way underneath. With a gasp, I banged as loudly as I could on the door. We were trapped, locked inside while someone was trying to burn us in our beds. I shouted and Miles jumped up.

He rushed over to me, as the smoke poured into our room. Together, we pounded our fists against the door. All I could think about was how to get to my children. A terrible fear took hold of me, strangling my voice as we screamed to be let out.

25

ONE MORE FOR THE FIRE

22nd December 2025

A busy day for a double murder. Ceecee had been dead for longer than Beebee, Fergus and even Mimi. She'd been with us the whole time, bobbing along right under our noses.

Silly girl should have just left and gone back to University... Not that I wouldn't have caught up with her along the way. Instead, I found her taking a leisurely morning swim. A pool is not the place you want to be when there's a psychopath lurking in your midst.

I triggered the pool cover, watching it slowly move across the surface. Ceecee was swimming laps, facing away from the advancing material. She reached the edge of the shallow end, diving under and kicking off the wall. She didn't even notice me ... at first. She resumed her front crawl, her hand meeting the edge of the advancing cover. She looked up in shock and, realising what was happening, turned and made her way to the edge. But yours truly was there. I offered her my hand to help her out, and as she reached for it, I quickly withrew it, letting her fall back into the water. It was

quite the struggle to keep her down, but nothing a few good pokes
and a smattering of whacks with a broom handle couldn't solve.

Just goes to show you how little people thought of her – no one
really even tried to look.

We screamed and pounded until our throats were hoarse and stinging from the acrid smoke. Metal on metal scraped, a clunk and the door almost knocked me backwards as it was forced open. I swivelled towards the nightstand, grabbing my laptop and handbag. There was no way I was leaving them behind. For one thing, our passports were in there, and if there was any way we could still make it, even after all these catastrophic events, I wasn't going to miss it waiting for goddamn new passports to arrive.

An officer beckoned us out frantically while plumes of black smoke billowed up and out towards the ceiling, stealing our air as we ducked down low and followed the officer along the hallway. I stopped at the children's doorways, but they were already open and the officer pushed us on from behind, down toward to the stairway.

The hallway beyond the gallery was so shrouded I couldn't see beyond. That must have been where the fire was coming from, but I didn't have time to get my bearings, I just needed air. I just needed my children. We stumbled down the stairs, desperate for clean air in our lungs.

The smoke lessened as we descended, but it still clawed at my throat and stung my eyes. I clutched the banister, my knuckles white, desperately trying not to fall. My heart raced, not just from the exertion, but from the gnawing fear that clawed at my insides. Where were Callum and Martha? Were they outside?

We staggered, spluttering and coughing through the front doors into the crisp night air, gulping it down greedily. My eyes streamed as I wildly scanned the faces of those gathered outside. Flashing lights from fire trucks and ambulances rushed up the driveway towards the house, casting an eerie light over the frightened faces. I pushed through a couple of officers, trying to call out despite my raw and burning throat.

'Mum! Dad!' Callum's voice broke through the siren wails. My legs nearly gave way when I saw that he was dragging Martha behind him. Relief flooded through me as I rushed to embrace them. Miles practically picked us all up in his arms and we stood clinging on to each other. The realisation that we could have lost one another was barely able to sink in amid the intensifying chaos surrounding us as firefighters began issuing forth.

'Oh, my God!' A cracking voice approached us. We untangled ourselves, and Jeannie threw herself into Miles's arms. 'You're safe!' she cried.

'Mother,' he said, examining her for any injuries,. 'Are you okay? What happened?'

Jeannie shook her head, tear-tracks down her soot-powdered cheeks. 'I don't know. I was pulled out of bed by an officer... I would have died, the smoke was so thick I couldn't see a thing. I couldn't breathe! The house,' she wailed, 'my beautiful house!'

Miles looked around, his eyes furtively scanning the people lining the driveway.

'Where's Mrs Harlow, Mother? And Gloria?' he demanded. She shook her head, 'I don't know.'

Miles made to run up back the stone steps, but I grabbed his arm.

'Excuse me, sir, keep clear!' boomed a firefighter. They were ascertaining whether it was safe to enter.

'There's a woman and a dog in there,' Miles yelled over the cacophony. 'On the first floor, third room on the right.' His voice was pleading. The firefighter nodded and relayed the information over radio to his team. It seemed like an eternity was passing us by, when I saw Miles silently slip in behind them and through the dark doorway. I went to cry out for him but it was too late.

The firefighters ran in after him, their protective gear gleaming in the blue lights. We all stood, transfixed, watching the smoke-filled entrance, willing Miles, Gloria and Mrs Harlow to emerge.

Minutes stretched like hours as we waited, the hiss of water from the hoses creating a terrifying symphony. I held Martha close, feeling her tremble against me, while Callum gripped my other hand tightly.

Paramedics led us further away from the house to check us over for signs of smoke inhalation. We kept our eyes glued on the house as firefighters ran back and forth. Eventually, an officer approached us.

'Hi there, I'm Constable Richardson,' she said kindly. 'I will be your liaison until Detective Sergeant Birch and Detective Inspector Randolf get here—'

'There he is!' I cried. Miles was staggering from the house with Gloria in his arms.

'Where is Mrs Harlow?' Callum demanded.

Constable Richardson promised us she would find out and went away again. Miles carried Gloria over to us, her long tail beating against his body. He put her down next to me and we wrapped her in a blanket and smothered her with love.

After ten minutes, Richardson returned. Her eyes betrayed her sadness at the blow she was about to deliver.

Miles let out a strangled cry and stood up, but I caught his hand and held him back from attempting to go back in the house... As if that would achieve anything other than potentially harming him further.

'I'm sorry,' Constable Richardson said. 'The fire originated on the first floor, third room on the right. The firefighters did everything they could.'

I looked around in disbelief to find Jeannie staring at me. Something akin to rage swept across her face, before she looked away.

The world seemed to slow down, the chaos around us fading into a dull roar as the constable's words sank in. Mrs Harlow, the kindly woman who had been a constant presence in Miles's life, was gone. I felt a heaviness settle in my chest, a mixture of grief and desperation.

Miles stared towards the house, as if he might still be able to do something about it. Jeannie stood frozen; her eyes were back on me with an intensity that made me uneasy. I wanted to look away but found myself unable to break her gaze.

'Mum,' Martha whispered, tugging at my arm. 'What's going to happen now?'

I opened my mouth to respond, but no words came out.

How could I explain this to my children when I couldn't even make sense of it myself?

Constable Richardson cleared her throat, breaking the tense silence. 'I can arrange for alternative accommodation. It might be tricky, with it being Christmas – but there are shelters … women's shelters.' She looked at me questioningly.

'We won't be separated,' I said forcefully. 'No … the four of us will be staying together.'

She nodded. 'I will call around, see what I can find.' We watched as Constable Richardson walked away.

'You're going to leave Grandma alone?' whispered Martha.

I looked down at her and stroked the back of her dark hair. 'I think it's safer for us,' I said quietly. 'She will have an officer with her, and so will we.'

'You think she's the killer?' Martha asked, her eyes widening.

'Well, it's not one of us…' I trailed off. It seemed insane. But it was true. It was the only explanation.

I watched Miles comforting Jeannie a few yards away.

Callum leaned into me and said under his breath, 'Once she's in prison, do you think we'll get the money?'

My gaze landed on him; his eyes were fixed on Jeannie.

'Maybe…' I said, my stomach flipping a little. 'But don't say anything to your father.'

Callum scoffed. 'I would never.'

The three of us sat there, watching. Contemplating.

The night wore on, a blur of flashing lights and hushed conversations. Constable Richardson returned, informing us she'd found a nearby Airbnb with availability for the night. As we prepared to leave, I caught Miles's eye. He looked lost, torn between his mother and us.

'Miles,' I called softly. 'We need to go. The kids need to get some rest.'

He nodded, his face a mask of conflicting emotions. 'Mother,' he said turning to Jeannie, 'you should come with us.'

Jeannie's eyes darted between Miles and me, then to the children. 'No,' she said, her voice eerily calm. 'I'll stay here. There's ... so much to sort out.'

I felt a chill run down my spine at her words. Was she planning her next move?

As we climbed into the police car that would take us to the Airbnb, I couldn't shake the feeling that this was far from over. The acrid smell of smoke still clung to our clothes, a grim reminder of the night's events.

The ride to the apartment we were staying in was silent, each of us lost in our own thoughts. Martha had fallen asleep, her head resting on Callum's shoulder. Miles stared out of the window, his face unreadable in the passing streetlights.

At the apartment, we looked around the small living room and trendy kitchenette. We had nothing – no toothbrushes, no pyjamas – and we stank of smoke. Our clothes would most definitely need to go in the bin. One by one, we took showers. I washed my hair three times and scrubbed my skin until it was red raw and then wrapped myself in a clean towel.

As I said goodnight to Callum and Martha, she turned to me and mumbled, 'Are we awful for leaving Grandma alone?'

I put my hand on her cheek, my heart heavy. 'She didn't want to come, sweetheart. Try not to worry, okay? Please try to get some sleep.'

I joined Miles in the other room. He paced the room, before sitting down heavily on the edge of the bed.

'I can't believe this,' he muttered. 'Mrs Harlow.' He looked at me, sorrow lining his eyes. 'She was more like a mother to me than mine ever was.'

I went to him and folded him into my chest. 'I know. I'm so sorry, Miles.' The words felt empty and redundant. There was nothing I could say to ease his pain. Instead, I asked, 'What happened? Did the firefighters tell you anything about how it started?'

He shook his head, his eyes tinged with pink. 'They think it was an ember from the fire in Madge's room. You know how old houses just tend to go up quickly. Perhaps the fireguard wasn't on... Perhaps someone got in...' He held his face in his hands, his shoulders heaving. I so desperately wanted to take his pain away, but I just continued to hold him.

In the cold light of Christmas morning, we were awoken by DCI Randolf practically beating down the front door. I jolted upright in bed, my heart racing as the pounding on the door echoed through the room. Miles was already up, fumbling with the lock. As the door swung open, DCI Randolf burst in, his face grim and determined.

'Mr and Mrs Weiss,' he ground out between his clenched teeth, 'what the hell happened?'

Miles looked at him in desperation. 'Mrs Harlow...'

He skewered Miles in his gaze. 'You were all locked in! How could this have happened?' It was a purely rhetorical question. He was clearly angry with himself for not being there. He slammed the door behind him and pushed past Miles into the room. He paced for a moment before pulling out the chair next to the vanity and sitting down.

He leaned forward, the bags under his eyes telling of the night he'd had.

'Forensics…' He stopped, battling with himself as to whether he should share the information. He sighed deeply and continued. 'Forensics found a kitchen knife…'

Miles's head snapped up towards him.

'Do you know something about the knife, Mr Weiss?'

Miles nodded slowly. 'A week or so ago, after Mrs Harlow had changed the beds, she told us she'd found a kitchen knife under my mother's mattress. We didn't know what to do with it… We didn't want Mrs Harlow to get into trouble. We assumed Mother kept it there for protection…' He stalled, looking to Randolf for answers. 'She didn't use it on Mrs Harlow, did she?'

Randolf shook his head. 'It's too early to say anything about Mrs Harlow's remains. We found the knife lodged between the mechanism used to pull back the pool cover. It wasn't the electrics housed in the box that were the problem…'

'It was the gears.' Miles finished.

'Exactly. Preliminary testing shows three sets of prints, Mrs Harlow's, Jeannie Weiss's and yours. There is another thing… Officers searched the rooms again this morning and found a spare set of room keys in your mother's bedroom.'

'Well, yes, it's no secret that Mrs Harlow and my mother held the keys to the house,' Miles said matter-of-factly.

'Yes ... but Constable Richardson was in possession of Mrs Harlow's set. We were not made aware that they were copies and not the originals. That would have been good to know,' he said through clenched teeth. 'Even if Mrs Weiss did use her keys to get in, how did she do it while my officer was stationed there?'

'And how did Mrs Harlow not wake up?' Asked Miles.

'That I can answer. There were crushed up sleeping pills in Mrs Harlow's water on the bedside table. We found the same pills in Jeannie's bathroom cabinet. But Richardson never left her post, and when she did, she rotated her shift with another officer. The hallway was never left unattended.'

'Could she see the secret passage?' I asked.

'I-I believe so...' he said uncertainly. 'But why would it matter? Everyone was locked in their rooms...'

'I suppose so,' I said thoughtfully. 'Why are you sharing this information with us, Detective Randolf?' I asked.

He raked his fingers through his curly black hair before looking back up at me. 'Because every death in your family could be chalked up to "unfortunate accidents" – except Quentin, of course. That tells me his death wasn't premeditated like the others. He definitely caught the killer by surprise. We need to catch whoever is responsible, and quickly. I've seen things like this before, but never to this extent. If I don't make an arrest, time goes on, and any evidence we've missed gets washed away. We need to move fast.'

'What do you want us to do?' I asked.

'I want you to go for Christmas dinner at Weiss Manor,' he said gravely.

I almost laughed, except it was still a little too soon to be laughing, even for me. But Jeannie was a psychopath and I wasn't going to be setting foot in that house with the kids.

'We will be there,' Randolf said, 'if anything happens. You will all be wearing wires.'

'Is a wire going to help us if she decides to cut us all up with a kitchen knife?' I said, deadpan.

'It won't come to that. She won't do anything so drastic. But if you speak with her, maybe she will slip up. I can't even get near her for questioning without that vampire Artie Peverill threatening me with legal action. Please ... try to elicit a confession. Record your interaction. There might be something that she reveals, something we have missed.'

Miles stared at a stain in the tufted rug. 'Okay, we'll do it,' he said quietly.

I glared at him with my mouth open. 'No, Miles, the kids—'

'We won't let her hurt them. Detective Randolf is right. We can't let her get away with this. And trust me, I know my mother, she can and will get away with anything.'

26

TINSEL, TRAUMA AND
ELEVEN DEAD RELATIVES

24th December 2025

It was the night before Christmas, and all through the house...

I really didn't want to do it. But you know how it is with housekeepers – they see everything – like little pods of cardamom being dropped into the eggnog. If only she hadn't been so observant, she would still be alive.

A carefully placed Christmas stocking, filled to the brim with kindling, a little too close to the flames and poof – up it goes. Mrs Harlow was a good egg. That's why I gave her the sleeping pills, I certainly didn't wish for her to suffer.

The kids thought we were mad, and they were right. This was the worst idea in the history of what not to do around a potential serial killer. But I could see straight through Randolf's motive: the murderer could just as easily be one of the four of us. He wanted to put us in a pressure cooker and see who burst first. Hell, perhaps he was punishing us all for not getting to spend Christmas with his wife.

As Jeannie greeted us at the door, the acrid smell of smoke issued from the open doorway, the odour clinging to every available space and surface. The damage caused by the fire was limited to Mrs Harlow's bedroom and the hallway outside her room. Sadly for us, the kitchen and dining room were untouched. We would be having our Christmas dinner here after all.

Jeannie stood to attention, her eyes wary and glittering as she stepped aside for us to enter. Despite the fire, her silver hair had been blow-dried and she wore red lipstick and a red cashmere sweater with matching skirt that clung to her svelte frame.

'I'm glad you made it,' she said. She turned to Miles, her eyes conveying something I couldn't quite read. 'Let me take your coats.' She smiled. Some of the lipstick had stained her teeth. Pausing in the entryway, she looked around for somewhere to put our coats, and I realised Mrs Harlow usually did such things. Aimlessly, she looked from left to right, waiting for a coat stand to materialise. When one didn't, she threw them in a heap in the corner and dusted her hands off like it was a job well done.

If I wasn't scared before, I was scared now. We made our way through to the dining room, which had been decorated to look like a set-piece straight from a *Downton Abbey* Christmas special. A fire roared in the mantle, the garland surrounding it adorned with sprays of fresh eucalyptus and sprigs of holly from the garden. Tapered candles flickered around the room and the candelabras were wound with real ivy fixed with red bows. Last night's events clearly hadn't put her off making the whole room into a fire hazard.

Jeannie's obsession with keeping up appearances was seemingly undampened by recent events – despite the fact there was no one left to witness this whole bloody charade. The table was set with cream linen and royal blue china, and in a centrepiece red roses were slightly drooping towards the tablecloth, as if they longed to sprout legs and run from the room.

A huge turkey lay with legs akimbo and skin glistening, as if it also wished to take flight. Bowls upon bowls of sprouts, red cabbage, peas, shallots, cranberry sauce and roast potatoes surrounded the bird, enough to feed—

My eyes scanned the table. It had been set for sixteen people.

With a trickling sense of horror I read the names on the place cards.

Eugene

George

Tristan

Toots

Clementine

Mimi

Ceecee

Beebee

Quentin

Fergus

Mrs Harlow

At the end of the table, five cards indicated where the five living members of the family should sit.

It felt like walking into a dinner at Hannibal Lecter's house – waiting to be served brains on toast. But what was more terrifying than knowing Jeannie was crazy? Knowing Randolf was even crazier for asking us to do this.

'I thought about cancelling,' Jeannie said, pouring a generous measure of red wine into her glass. 'But Detective Randolf insisted.' She lifted the decanter to fill Miles's glass to the brim, then moved over to mine, her mouth twisting into a tight smile as she poured. 'Bottoms up,' she said.

A chill coursed through my veins. This was a trap. But then again, that's also what made it so deliciously dangerous. Jeannie had well and truly lost her mind. And we were going to make sure she was locked behind bars.

'Mrs Harlow—' Jeannie took a sharp intake of breath, a sob issuing from her chest before she could stop it. 'Mrs Harlow had already prepared the food. I just had to put it in the oven. One last thing to remember her by.' Her eyes were glassy with emotion as she stared at me, as if all her rage was directed solely towards my existence.

'Sit!' she demanded. The children fumbled to take their seats, their fear making them clumsy. I was not scared of this jumped-up faux aristocrat. I stared straight back at her as I drew the chair back. Miles placed a reassuring hand between my shoulders as he took the chair next to mine.

Jeannie began filling our plates with food whilst we watched her. The silence amplified the sounds of the serving spoons clinking against the china as she served the potatoes, roasted parsnips and turkey until the plates before us were laden. Miles had the honour of pouring the gravy. It would have been a perfect Christmas dinner, if it hadn't felt like the last feast at Dracula's castle.

Jeannie watched our every move as she sat in her chair. Sliding the silver circlet adorned with holly from around the napkin, she whipped the napkin in the air before bringing it down onto her lap. Callum and Martha cast furtive glances towards us, as if they expected something on the table to detonate any second.

Jeannie cleared her throat. 'Let's not let the food go cold,' she said with an air of forced gaiety.

'This is insane,' Miles muttered into my ear.

Jeannie refilled her wine glass. 'Eat!' she insisted once more.

I speared a cube of potato on my fork and raised it to my mouth, wondering whether it would have been safer to eat a live grenade.

'This is nice,' Martha said, the lie sticking in her throat.

'Very,' Callum added.

Jeannie looked wistfully towards Mrs Harlow's empty seat. 'Is the food good? I've never cooked a Christmas meal all by myself before.'

Call me crazy, but the way she said it, I almost felt sorry for her in that moment. I cut a slice of turkey and added potato and roasted shallot. 'It's great. Mrs Harlow would have been proud.'

Miles furrowed his brows at me as if I was traitorous for being nice to her.

'Eugene, George, Tristan, Toots, Aunt Clem, Mimi, Ceecee, Beebee, Quentin, Fergus and Mrs Harlow...' she murmured as she picked at her food. 'The ghost of Christmas present has certainly sent me one big fat F.U.' She looked pointedly in my direction.

Miles swallowed a mouthful. 'Don't be ridiculous.' He gave an awkward laugh that didn't even convince himself. 'Why would the ghost of Christmas present wish to teach you a lesson?'

Jeannie put down her fork and addressed him directly. 'Let's cut to the chase. The detective is using you, Miles,' she said, her voice cold. 'Randolf has you believing it's me. He's sending you on a wild-goose chase.'

'Oh?' I cut across them. 'Who do you think the killer is, then?'

She looked at us all one by one, the reflection of the fire dancing in her eyes, before going back to her food.

'Well, it's certainly not Martha...' she said, chewing thoughtfully. 'She's nowhere near astute enough for that. Got her mind elsewhere ... probably too busy fantasising about muff-diving.'

Callum sprayed a mouthful of water all over his food as Martha's mouth opened in shock, and I readied myself to launch at Jeannie. But Miles gripped my arm, holding me back.

Jeannie cackled under her breath, the firelight catching her wine like a goblet of blood. 'Oh, come on, I'm only saying what everyone else has already thought. I always did love my murder-mystery parties... And now I suppose I've got a real-life one. But I digress... Where was I? Oh yes, muff-diving. I don't believe the killer could be Callum, either,' Jeannie surveyed him with mild disdain and I slapped him on the back as he coughed up his water. 'He's a half-baked, layabout stoner who can't even drag himself out of bed on a good day.'

'Mother,' Miles growled, 'That's enough—'

Jeannie switched her focus towards her son. 'For a time, I thought perhaps it could be you, Miles. I thought you'd finally gone stark raving mad, being married to that nymphomaniac, penniless wife of yours. But then Mrs Harlow died ... and I knew you would *never*, could *never* do that to the only person who mollycoddled you and spoiled you when she thought we weren't looking. I always said to George that her babying you would turn you soft, and it turns out I was right.'

I glared at her. Jeannie was a cold-hearted bitch, but this was a new level of brutality.

Her eyes locked onto mine.

'And so ... when Madge died, I knew it could only be one person.'

'Me?' I said with a little laugh. 'You think I'm the killer? Is that your big revelation?'

'Isn't it obvious?' Jeannie said, raising her glass. 'It can only be you. And now, you've trapped us all in one place so Randolf can swoop in and make his triumphant arrest? It won't work, Olivia.' She took a long drink, her eyes never leaving mine.

'And why's that? Because you're innocent?' Miles asked.

'Yes. And because I'm not the only one with secrets, and the truth will out. The rest of you were so busy looking towards each other, you didn't see what was right in front of you.'

Our old friend the grandfather clock punctuated the silence as if we were sitting on a bomb, waiting to see if it would explode or just fizzle out.

'I don't have any secrets,' Callum said defensively.

Martha shifted uncomfortably. 'Nor me.'

'What about you, Olivia?' Jeannie leaned back in her seat. How was she playing the part of the dastardly villain so well... What was she really up to? My stomach clenched tightly. 'Do you have anything you'd like to share with the group now?' she asked, taking a swig of her wine.

'I don't know what you're talking about.' I shifted uncomfortably as my stomach tensed again.

'Very well, then I will tell them. Your dear mother, despite protesting until she's blue in the face that she's honest and hard-working, has actually been farming off her filthy little pornos to a ghostwriter. And now, she's in the hole to the tune of ten thousand pounds. And that's what we know about. I'm sure it will be much more than that when her publisher finds out she's broken her contract.'

Miles's frown deepened as he turned towards me.

Before he could ask I answered. 'It's true. But I can explain—'

'Save it,' Jeannie hissed. 'You wanted the Weiss inheritance, plain and simple. And today, you came here to finish what you started. You're not here on a reconnaissance mission for Randolf. You're here to make sure you see it through to the end. You're here to make sure that I too have a happy little accident.'

'No—' I gripped my knife and fork so tightly my palms stung. I turned to Miles to explain. 'I was behind with the book, and it just kept getting closer to the deadline, and what with the move, and then coming here, it just got out of control.'

Miles's eyes filled with sadness as he reached his hand out to rub my shoulder.

'It's fine—' he began.

'It's not fine. I'm a fuck-up who spent money we didn't have just to save face… I should have gone straight to my editor and been honest.' My stomach gurgled so loudly that I was almost embarrassed. 'But worse than that, I should have told you. So, in the spirit of transparency … I saw your mother on that forum. I know it was her who was feeding those trolls information about me. I think she's OpinionatedOgre1.'

'Errrrm, excuse my French'—Martha quirked her mouth to the side—'but what in the blue fuck is everyone talking about?' she asked incredulously.

'Ha!' Jeannie's voice rose several octaves. 'You think I would feed some absolute down-and-outs who spend their days rotating online information about our family? No, you stupid girl. You *clearly* haven't been paying attention, have you?'

'What were you doing on there, then?' I snapped as I dug my hand between my waistband and stomach to ease the sharp pain emanating there.

'I was a double agent. Mimi was the mole. She was FantasyWh0re. I merely monitored it so I could feed the information to Artie so he could get it taken down.' She addressed Miles. 'You see how toxic she is? My whole life is dedicated to upholding the Weiss family name, and she thinks I would spread slanderous gossip online to disparage her. She manages to do a brilliant job of that all on her own.'

'Mother.' Miles banged his fist down onto the table causing

the cutlery to bounce. 'You have no right to speak about my wife that way.'

I was about to interject but was rendered speechless as my insides felt like they were caught in a cement mixer.

'You know, there was a moment,' Jeannie said narrowing her eyes at her son, 'when I wondered whether I had underestimated you, Miles. You've developed a temper that I've never really noticed before...'

'Finally, an attribute you could be proud of then? Pray tell, what motive would I have?' Miles's eyes shone with a cruel gleam that I'd never seen before. I looked away, staring down at the food on my plate. A rush of heat invaded my body. Something was not right.

'The money, of course, what other motive is there? I thought perhaps you took Eugene's will-reading the wrong way. I thought maybe you felt like we were asking you to be cut-throat, and then maybe you let things get out of control.'

'So, what, you changed your mind on that simply because Mrs Harlow died?' He was digging for answers, which is exactly what Randolf had told us to do. But I couldn't join in, I could barely hear what they were saying.

'Yes. When Mrs Harlow died. I knew, I just *knew* it was her. That's why'—Jeannie's lips twisted in an ugly grimace—'that's why I had to do this. I had to protect my son and my grandchildren before her bloodlust turned towards you. I did this for *you.*'

All eyes were on her, except mine. Mine were widened in horror as I struggled to get up from the table. I felt a terrible, twisting urgency. Something awful was about to come from one end of my body or the other, perhaps both, and it was imminent.

'Liv?' Miles reached for my arm as I stumbled away from the table. 'Are you okay?'

'Bathroom,' I gasped. My insides roiled, and I stumbled towards the door, knocking over a chair on my way out.

I was not okay. I barely made it across the room and up the stairs before I vomited down my front and keeled over on the landing. Once I was in the hallway, I collapsed against the wall. A cold sweat pricked at my skin. Hot bile rose up into my throat as the pattern on the wallpaper swirled around me. It took every remaining ounce of strength to get to the bathroom and collapse in a heap by the toilet. I was shivering uncontrollably. Was it poison? Panic? Whatever it was, Jeannie had admitting to doing something, I just didn't know *what*.

The door banged open and Miles rushed in, wide-eyed.

'Liv?' He grabbed a towel and wet it in the sink. 'What's going on?'

'I don't know,' I gasped between spasms and throwing up. 'I'm. So. Sorry.'

'Sorry?' He asked in blind confusion.

'The money…' I panted, 'the ghostwri—'

'Stop. Don't. There's no reason to apologise.' He held my hair back as another awful wave took hold of me. He was telling me it was all going to be okay, but I could barely hear him over the pounding in my ears. I panted and dry-retched, clutching my sides as if they'd split open any second.

'Breathe,' Miles said, crouching next to me. 'Just try to breathe.'

I drew a deep breath and concentrated on stopping my insides from coming out.

'I'll kill her,' Miles said, his voice laced with anger. 'Randolf is already there, he's with Mother now, and an ambulance isn't far away.' His hand was rubbing my back but I didn't hear another word he said. The walls were closing in around me. I felt like I was about to pass out.

'Ow! Unhand me, you wretch!' Jeannie's voice pierced through the clamour outside.

'What … has … she…' I tried to get the words out between my laboured breaths, 'done … to … me?'

'I don't know,' Miles muttered through gritted teeth.

'The kids…' I managed.

'They're okay, they're in the study with an officer.'

My field of vision was a pinprick. I felt my body falling, falling through what could have been forever. I was aware of a pain in my stomach – and Miles's shouts, though I couldn't make out what he was saying. The darkness called to me, and I willingly went into it, anything to stop the pain, to make it go away.

It was the end. I was going to die. Jeannie had won.

The room was spinning as the light crept back in. I blinked through a fog, my whole body sluggish and foreign. Someone was talking. Not Miles. Someone else.

'Lucky… lucky she's—'

'Lucky she's not dead?' Miles hissed.

I struggled to focus. The voices were closer now.

'Liv!' Miles's face came into view, pale and desperate.

'What's—' I managed.

'Oh, thank God,' he breathed, clutching my hand. 'Thank God.'

Everything was bright and blurry, but I could make out another figure standing behind him. Tall, with a grim expression.

Randolf.

'Welcome back, Mrs Weiss,' Randolf said, but his voice didn't hold warmth, or sound pleased to see me at all. Miles shot him a murderous look as I tried to sit up, but he gently pushed me back down.

'Don't move,' he said. His eyes were red-rimmed and tired.

'I'm fine,' I whispered, not believing it myself.

'You look like hell,' Randolf said bluntly. 'But you'll live.'

'The kids?'

'They're absolutely fine,' Randolf said more softly. 'DS Birch is bringing them over in an hour.'

'I can't believe Jeannie...' I started to say. It felt like my tongue was wrapped in cotton.

'Yup. She poisoned you,' Randolf said, without any hint of satisfaction.

'Poisoned me with what?' I said.

'Daffodil bulbs.'

'Daffodil bulbs?' I blinked, trying to understand.

'She swapped them for the onions.' Randolf shook his head. 'Something that might appear on the surface to be a stupid mistake. A mistake that could have got you killed.'

I lay back, feeling the weight of it all. So simple and so deadly.

I frowned up at Miles, his brown eyes incredulous. 'I know,' he said bitterly.

'How?' I whispered.

'We found a packet of daffodil bulbs in the kitchen—'

'They were mine,' I gasped at the sudden realisation. 'I bought them at the Christmas-tree farm.'

'Well, they had been opened and several of them had been fried. Your husband says that Mrs Weiss served you all at Christmas dinner?'

'Yes,' I agreed.

'She only put them on your plate. We tried to find the frying pan that they were prepared in, but as everything had been put through the dishwasher, we could find no traces. We found the serving bowl, though. And of course, there's her confession that you caught on your wires.' He straightened and looked out of the window, squinting as if something deeply troubled him.

'Where is she now?' I asked Miles.

'She's in custody,' he replied, brows knitting together. 'She'll be out on bail soon enough, though, I'm sure.'

'What?!' I burst out. I couldn't help myself. My throat burned with the effort and I lowered my tone, rasping, 'She tried to kill me!'

'Yes,' he agreed simply.

I closed my eyes against the nausea that threatened again.

'And now?' I asked, panic rising.

'Well...' He sighed. 'Now she knows she failed, so I guess you'd better watch out.'

'What do you mean?' asked Miles sternly.

Randolf looked him square in the eye and said, 'Rich people, in my experience … they get away with everything.'

I lay back against the pillow and closed my eyes. I felt Miles squeeze my hand. The anger radiated off him in the form of heat.

'She won't,' Miles said, his voice tightening with resolve.

I didn't believe that for one second. Randolf sighed, a long-suffering sound. He left us then, slipping out quietly. Miles stayed by my side, his presence holding me together as I drifted in and out of fitful sleep.

EPILOGUE

MINCE PIES AND MOTIVES

'I hope you understand, Miles, why I did what I did. I only had your well-being in mind ... your future. I had to get that maniac out of your life once and for all. And for Callum and Martha, too. I just couldn't risk anything happening to any of you.' Mother's bottom lip quivered, the crocodile tears in her eyes threatening to spill over.

'So you tried to kill the mother of my children ... for me? To protect us? Or were you protecting your money?'

'I think it's gone way past that now, don't you? This was a matter of life and death, *our* lives, Miles... And now I'm in here.' She said miserably, gesturing to the stark walls and looking down forlornly at her green overalls. Her hair was unkempt, and she wore no make-up, which I had to admit was extremely jarring as I had never ever seen my mother with a bare face or a hair out of place.

She had been in jail for over a week and it might well have been a month. She could never survive in a place like this, let alone going through a trial and going to prison.

'We are leaving soon,' I said brightly, 'for Australia.'

Mother looked at me as if I had just grown three heads. '*What?*' she breathed. 'What the hell are you talking about?'

'Liv, Callum, Martha and I,' I said slowly, to make sure she understood me. 'We are moving to Australia soon. Oh – and we are taking Gloria. I've got her pet passport expedited and her vaccine certificates are all in order. She will absolutely love it there, walks on the beach and playing in the sea... So I really don't want you to worry about her because she's going to be having the time of her life. We all are.'

Now she looked like one of my three heads was wielding a knife between its teeth while one of the others spat in her face. I was tormenting her – perhaps that was wrong of me.

'You're going to leave me here? You're going with *her*? She's a *killer,* Miles!' she shrieked. Of course she had nothing to say about me taking Gloria; she couldn't care less about her. 'We need to formulate a plan together, about how we are going to catch Olivia! And a plan for how we are going to get me the hell out of here!'

I gave her a small smile and rummaged around in my pocket. I bought the crumpled bit of paper out and smoothed it out onto the table.

'I found this. Hidden away in one of your drawers.'

I pushed it closer for her to see and watched as her eyes scanned down the page.

1. Eugene
2. George
3. Tristan

4. Quentin
5. Toots
6. Aunt Clem
7. Mimi
8. Ceecee
9. Beebee
10. Fergus
11. Mrs Harlow
12. Olivia

Her brows furrowed and her mouth opened. 'What the hell is this?' she hissed.

'It's your list... I found it. I shall hand it over to the police, of course. They already have the diary detailing all of the murders and the timeline. Of course, you didn't manage to actually kill Olivia, so the diary doesn't have an entry for Christmas Day because you were carted off straight here. I do hate it when things aren't quite complete, don't you, Mother?'

Her eyes were ablaze with fury and confusion. 'That diary, they brought it out during questioning today... I've never seen it before in my life!'

I looked at her blandly. 'Memory lapse, perhaps?' I shrugged.

'She – she has forged my handwriting! She has set me up! You must believe me, Miles,' she begged. 'I am telling you I didn't do it! And Artie Peverill is ignoring my calls and won't see me!' she wailed.

'Oh yes, Artie. Mr Peverill has a conflict of interest, you see. He works for us now.'

'What conflict?' she snivelled. 'Why are you doing this to me? Why don't you believe me?'

I sighed. She still wasn't getting it. But something told me that somewhere deep down, it might be beginning to dawn on her... Her denial had always been dialled up to a hundred.

'Here's what's going to happen.' I held a finger up to signal for her to wait. I bent down and retrieved my briefcase from the floor, one of Father's old ones with G.W. embossed in gold. I placed it theatrically on the table and flicked open the clasps.

'Here is a confession...' I deposited a document on the table. 'I have tabbed the page you need to sign.'

Mother glared at the stack of paper. 'Why would I sign a confession for something I didn't do?'

'But you did do something...' I flicked the pages between my thumb and forefinger. 'In here are pieces of evidence I've obtained from Artie Peverill. About how you and he and our entire family knew that cousin Quentin killed Omar Akhtar.'

She blinked frantically, her mind trying to catch up. 'That mine worker?' Her voice was getting higher now.

'Yes, *that* mine worker, and he has a name. You all knew Quentin murdered that man, and you *all* covered for him, because Grandfather ordered you to. And you were all too willing to do his dirty work so you could inherit his fortune.'

Mother blinked at me, then the document. She snatched it and flicked through it, her eyes widening as she saw the extent of the evidence I had against her. She dropped it onto the table, her hands shaking. 'Artie – he gave you all this?'

'Not at first. But then I found a key piece of information ...

hidden away in Eugene's office. The missing CCTV footage. Father really should have put a more difficult combination on the safe other than his birthday. But then, he never was very bright, was he? Anyway, I made a copy of the footage and went to speak to Mr Peverill... I think it's safe to say that Artie's life and career are now firmly held in my hands... Just a bit of time and distance away from all of this is all I need to finish him off, too. I don't want any loose ends.'

Unabashed horror flashed across her features.

'Ahh, the penny ... it has finally dropped. You've finally caught up,' I said with a small smile.

'*No,*' was all she could manage. 'No, Miles. No!'

'Yes.' I felt every muscle tense. Finally, after everything I had done, all my meticulous planning – I had fulfilled it.

'You murdered your father... Y-your brother...'

'Yes. And all the others.'

'No! I don't believe you.'

'When are you going to take the wool from your eyes?'

'You're covering for Olivia—'

'Olivia had nothing to do with it,' I snapped.

She was still shaking her head. 'Why? Why did you do it?' Her words were strangled, like she knew why, but the answer was so unsatisfactory she couldn't bear to hear it. 'Not – not all because of that *bloody worker!*'

'Omar Akhtar. Say his name. He had a wife and children. Children who will grow up without their father because Quentin couldn't control his rage.'

'You didn't even do this for the inheritance? You did it all for Omar *fucking* Akhtar and his family?' she spat.

'I did it for him, yes; him and his children and his wife. I did it for those reasons, and many more. The money is a great perk, though, don't get me wrong. And now I can help Omar's family, not that anything will ever mend the destruction Quentin brought down upon them. I also did it for every time one of you put me down. Every time you controlled me and bent my life to your will. Every time Father watched as Grandpa hit me with that belt. Every time you pitted my brother and me against each other and made him into a soulless bastard. For every time one of you put my wife and my children down.'

'I don't – I don't understand this. *She* must have put you up to this!'

I shook my head slowly. 'What sealed the deal was the night of the murder-mystery party, when you announced Quentin was soon to be released. I *knew* he had killed Omar, and I knew Grandfather had covered up for him. That's why I ended the old bastard four years ago. But when you said he was getting out, I couldn't have it. I couldn't have him walking free, wondering who he would turn his rage onto next. I went looking in Grandfather's office for *anything* that might extend his sentence. That's when I saw the witness statements from you, Dad, Grandma, Fergus and Clem. The character references from his young, doting cousins, Beebee and Ceecee. You all knew what he did, and you *vouched* for him to get him a more lenient sentence.'

Mother whimpered.

'What's wrong?' I shrugged. 'I thought this was what you wanted? Aren't I just being the man you made me to be? Have I *still* not proven myself to you?' My tone was laced with sarcasm. I pushed the papers towards her once more. 'It doesn't matter whether you sign it or not, you are going down one way or another. I have planted and tampered with enough of the evidence to make it appear that you committed the murders.

'The antifreeze in the garage used in Eugene's scotch that only has your fingerprints on it. The knife, which Mrs Harlow told the police that she found under your bed, only to reappear inside the mechanism for the pool cover.

'The duplicate key found in your bedroom that was used to unlock Mrs Harlow's room. The fact you tried to kill Olivia with her own daffodil bulbs, which you've already admitted to. The diary found under the floorboards explaining it all in your distinctive handwriting.'

'But – but you wouldn't have killed Madge! You loved Mrs Harlow. I know you did!'

'All right. I'll let you in on a little secret. Madge saw me slip the cardamom into the eggnog. I considered letting her live, but I didn't want her to have to lie or go through the torment of seeing you hauled to prison and not be able to tell the truth. But she still wanted to protect me, after a lifetime of seeing how rotten to the core you all are. It was regrettable. Believe me, I fought with it long and hard. But she didn't suffer – the sleeping pills saw to that. I had placed a highly flammable Christmas stocking too near the fire in her room. I'd filled it with combustibles, and I assume once it heated enough it set alight, dropped to the floor and the rest is history.'

She was vigorously shaking her head. 'They will know it wasn't me. They will see I am innocent.'

'They won't. Don't you see? Even if you can prove that it

was me, you will still go to prison for what you did to cover up Quentin's crime, and for Olivia's attempted murder. There is no way out of this, Mother… Well … except…'

'Except what?' she cried desperately.

'What if there was a way out?'

'Like what?' She said slowly.

'Well, I'm not *totally* heartless.' I took out a second item from the briefcase and placed it in front of her.

'A mince pie?' she said, voice quivering.

'A way out. The evidence is all tied up neatly. I just wanted to see if you could admit to what you had done, to yourself and to me. But I didn't hold out any hope in that regard. There's a cyanide pill in there. Take it … and you won't have to suffer going to prison. You won't live to see the shame brought upon the Weiss name when I give this evidence regarding Omar Akhtar to the police. You won't have to serve a sentence for murders you didn't commit. But you will pay like the others did, for covering up what Quentin did and for aiding his release. And for what you did to my wife.'

She looked from me to the mince pie and back again. 'You horrible boy. You horrid, wicked, bloody heartless boy!' she shouted, and then she screamed. It was a good scream – one I wish I could record and listen to all over again. 'How could you do this to me?' The contempt and disbelief in her tone only strengthened my resolve.

'I'm giving you a choice. You see, I am nothing like Quentin, Eugene, Tristan or any of the others,' I leaned forward, getting close to her face. 'You see now. I'm much, much worse. I am the son you raised me to be – in every way but one. I will do right by *my* family.'

She was silent, staring at me with pure loathing as her face grew redder and redder. Finally, she opened her mouth, 'Let me speak to Artie.'

'No can do, I'm afraid.'

I stood up from my chair. 'This is it, then.' I looked down at her, feeling no sense of satisfaction now that the tears were falling freely down her cheeks. 'Goodbye, Mother.'

I snapped Father's briefcase shut and left her with the documents and the mince pie on the table in front of her.

I turned and walked away, the click of the lock behind me confirming that she was trapped there, with no one left to turn to. I shoved the guards another wad of notes for letting me see her without surveillance. I could do that now... When you're a multimillionaire and the owner of a goldmine, you can do whatever the hell you please.

I walked down the corridor, the sounds of her wailing retreating behind me, and the guards I passed didn't even look me in the eye as I walked out into the early January air and through the gates. A sharp breeze caught me as I stepped down from the steps and walked across to our car.

Gloria sat in the back seat, her nose pressed up against the window. Her whole body started wagging when she saw me.

'Who's a good girl?' I said as I climbed inside. She barked in response. I took a deep breath and checked my watch. I picked up my phone and dialled Olivia to see how she was feeling. 'How did it go?' Her voice came from the other end.

'Better than expected,' I replied, scratching Gloria behind her ear as she wagged her tail furiously.

'Great,' she replied. I could tell she was grinning from ear to ear, even though I couldn't see her face. 'Martha and

Callum are here and the nurse said they're discharging me within the hour.'

'Perfect.' I grinned. 'Now … are you ready to catch that flight?'

ACKNOWLEDGMENTS

I'd like to thank my friend and publisher, Charlotte Ledger, the best pal and publisher in town. Thank you also to the brilliant and hardworking team at HarperCollins and One More Chapter: Chloe Cummings, Grace Edwards, Kara Daniel, Lucy Bennet, Katie Sadler, Jennie Rothwell, Helen Williams and Sofia Salazar Studer. Also, a big thank-you to editors Lydia Mason, Emily Thomas and Tony Russell.

Lastly, thank you to Stuart Bache, fantastic human, husband and cover designer – 10/10, would recommend.

ONE MORE CHAPTER

YOUR NUMBER ONE STOP
FOR PAGETURNING BOOKS

The author and One More Chapter would like to thank everyone who contributed to the publication of this story...

Analytics
Imogen Wolstencroft

Audio
Fionnuala Barrett
Ciara Briggs

Contracts
Laura Amos
Inigo Vyvyan

Design
Lucy Bennett
Fiona Greenway
Liane Payne
Dean Russell

Digital Sales
Laura Daley
Lydia Grainge
Hannah Lismore

eCommerce
Laura Carpenter
Madeline ODonovan
Charlotte Stevens
Christina Storey
Jo Surman
Rachel Ward

Editorial
Kara Daniel
Charlotte Ledger
Lydia Mason
Jennie Rothwell
Tony Russell
Sofia Salazar Studer
Emily Thomas
Helen Williams

Harper360
Emily Gerbner
Ariana Juarez
Jean Marie Kelly
emma sullivan
Sophia Wilhelm

International Sales
Peter Borcsok
Ruth Burrow
Bethan Moore
Colleen Simpson

Inventory
Sarah Callaghan
Kirsty Norman

Marketing & Publicity
Chloe Cummings
Grace Edwards
Katie Sadler

Operations
Melissa Okusanya
Hannah Stamp

Production
Denis Manson
Simon Moore
Francesca Tuzzeo

Rights
Ashton Mucha
Alisah Saghir
Zoe Shine
Aisling Smyth
Lucy Vanderbilt

Trade Marketing
Ben Hurd
Eleanor Slater

The HarperCollins Distribution Team

The HarperCollins Finance & Royalties Team

The HarperCollins Legal Team

The HarperCollins Technology Team

UK Sales
Isabel Coburn
Jay Cochrane
Sabina Lewis
Holly Martin
Harriet Williams
Leah Woods

And every other essential link in the chain from delivery drivers to booksellers to librarians and beyond!